# High Arctic Odyssey

## MYSTERY ON ICE

by Joe Fougere

RoseDog❧Books

PITTSBURGH, PENNSYLVANIA 15238

Editors: Rachel Chartier, L Col F.M. Barnes, RCAF, Mr.and Mrs. Michael and Christine Davies

RoseDog Books
585 Alpha Drive
Suite 103
Pittsburgh, PA 15238
Visit our website at *www.rosedogbookstore.com*

ISBN: 978-1-63867-459-7
eISBN: 978-1-63867-555-6

# Contents

# Contents

## Part 2 Nunavut Burns

# Acknowledgments

I would like to thank the following generous people for their individual contributions towards the production of this novel:

L Col FM Barnes, lifelong friend and great first editor of this novel.

Megan McLean, 16mpm1@queensu.ca, first and extremely capable paid editor of this book.

Mr. and Mrs. Fougere-Davies, for continuous editing and computer skills during production of this High Arctic Odyssey.

Mr. Bruno Tucci of Toronto, ON, for his photography expertise, especially his cover photo of an Aurora.

Robert Service, poet of the North, for his poem: "Cremation of Sam McGee".

Rachel Chartier of St Catharines, ON, for the final editing and preparation of this novel for publication.

# Part 1

## AURORA AND MIR FREEZING

# PROLOGUE

"We will be landing at Thule Air Force Base in fifteen minutes."

Major Shawn Phillips awoke in a hurry when he heard these words over the PA system of the Aurora, on which he was a passenger. He was waking from a really bad dream. It was, in fact, a nightmare. After an enjoyable conversation with Captain Mari Leech, discussing the pros and cons of self-landing versus assisted landings, he drifted off to sleep. Shawn was tired after being up since the early morning. The brief nap invigorated him, and he was ready for the hunt for the missing Aurora.

His dream was about a landing at the Summerside airfield in the early sixties. He had been transferred there after completing his training on search and rescue at the Trenton airfield. Trenton was home to, among other things, the Search and Rescue Centre. His job would be as a SAR helicopter pilot, and head of the Summerside SAR unit with 6 SAR technicians.

He decided to report to Summerside before his official date just to get the lay of the land and to meet some of the airmen, unofficially. These men, such as other pilots, firefighters, and Control Tower personnel, would be his working partners over the next three years or so. As part of his private tour, he visited the Air Traffic Tower.

The day was a bit dreary, with overcast skies. Shawn made his way up the stairs to the control tower look-out. The first hour there was pleasant and educational. However, things started to go awry and he was asked to step aside.

It appeared that an Argus #736 out of Greenwood was planning on making a practice landing at the Summerside runway. The tower was notified by the Radio Officer on the Argus that the aircraft had run into a flock of birds, with several having flown into the props and engine cowling. Within minutes the craft was sputtering and having difficulty staying in the air. The pilot told the tower that Fire and Emergency vehicles needed to be on the runway. Shawn could hear the pilot speaking about various options such as what to do if there was a fire or a need to go around for a second try. He heard the pilot suggest that foam be available to use on the runway, if needed.

The pilot flew around, burning off as much extra fuel as he could while safely manhandling a large airliner that wanted to fly into the ground. With all systems go, the pilot approached from the east. The submarine hunting aircraft got closer to the runway, waddling and wandering throughout its approach. Just five kilometers from touchdown, the engines stopped turning. The pilot was now solely responsible for a considerably heavy glider.

The almost fuel-empty craft didn't make it to the runway. Instead, the landing gear caught the top of the landing lights that lined the landing strip. Shawn could see every movement from his vantage point in the four-story-high tower. The building gave him plain sight of the struggling incoming aircraft, and he thought that he could see the desperation on the face of the pilot. Burned into the memory of Major Phillips was every detail of the crash landing; it was like watching a train wreck movie in slow motion.

The props stopped rotating and the engine ceased sputtering and vibrating, just one mile out from safety. Flames from the props started to trail the plane. Suddenly, the plane's undercarriage hooked the landing lights several hundred feet from the start of the runway. The aircraft tilted to the left until the leading edge of the wing snagged the earth and shrubbery that surrounded the fence on the perimeter. The plane started to flip. It went first to the left, then up righted itself before tilting again to the right. By now the craft had cleared the perimeter's 10-foot fence and had entered the gravel run-up to the start of the landing strip. The wheels collapsed, and the ship started to zig and zag down the runway on its belly. Sparks were raining down everywhere as it slid another kilometer before coming to a grinding halt.

Shawn could still hear screeching sounds to this day. They were genuine in his dream.

The fire and emergency vehicles began to roll. The control tower personnel were yelling instructions to the vehicle operators. In the meantime, the aircraft started to burn. Smoke and flames filled the sky, and Shawn watched in amazement from his vantage point. The vehicles halted, and the firemen and ambulance attendees poured out, carrying hoses and axes and pushing gurneys covered with blankets. Shawn had never felt so helpless; he could do nothing. He would be in the way. He had never experienced anything like this in his entire life.

Firefighters struck at the doors with their tools until they flung them open and rushed in wearing gas masks. Shawn saw two firefighters carrying crew out of the burning plane and handing them to the hospital staff.

The enveloping dream, or nightmare rather, had just played out in his mind during his sleep. This time the sounds and colors were authentic. There was sweat on his brow, and his face was flushed until he realized that nothing was happening to him at this moment. It was all a dream, even if it was a genuine dream! *Just try to relax. Everything is OK*, he silently told himself.

He had learned, days after the crash, that two crew members died in the smoke and flames. The co-pilot was killed in the landing, and a SAR tech died a few days later. The rest of the crew received burns and spent many a day in the hospital. Shawn would see one or two of them occasionally in the Officers Mess trying to enjoy a beer while covered in bandages.

*What are the odds?* thought Shawn, of this dream recurring at the very time that he was on his way to Thule, to set up a mini RCC, to find a possible crash of an airliner. The Rescue Coordination Centre was arranged in order to find a Canadian Forces Aurora aircraft that had been missing for more than twelve hours. It was presumed to have crashed, just like the Argus had done years ago.

Thule bound; he had some time on the flight to think before the Aurora stopped at its destination. His thoughts were about the Argus crew of years ago and the Aurora crew of today. After deplaning, he would make his way to his temporary mini RCC Office. He decided to review his day, up to this moment, just to see how his planning got him to where he was currently at. In his mind, he reviewed the various pros and cons of the Winters SAR mission up to this point. It all started with a phone call, while enjoying an early evening at his home after some Christmas shopping.

# 1    THE WINTERS BRIEFING

26 December 1830 hrs local/Halifax, NOS.

From across the room, Shawn aimed the silver handled gun at the Prime Minister of Canada and shot him dead. It happened just when the PM was launching into another election speech; one of many that were now getting tiresome.  Shawn was in no mood to listen to the Prime Minister rave about his accomplishments, such as the creation of the province of Nunavut. He didn't want to hear any more of what the PM promised to do if he called an early election. Too many high-cost election 'goodies' were part of the PM's gifts during the Christmas holidays. Shawn squeezed the trigger, and the PM was cut off, deader than a door nail, as the TV screen went blank.

Shawn returned the gun-styled remote control to its holster that hung on the side of his Lazy-Boy recliner. The remote was a Christmas present from his daughter, Christine. She knew that he liked to collect kitsch, or things formerly considered to be in bad taste. The small living room had many inanimate objects including a cigarette lighter disguised as a fish and a beer stein camouflaged as a skull. Kitsch was his passion. Kitsch had also become quite collectible. Collectors, like himself, enjoyed objects that masqueraded as other things.

It was a cold night in Cole Harbour, with winds gusting to 30 knots and snow drifting across the roads and fields. It was the type of evening when all Shawn wanted to do was sit at home in front of a roaring fire with a glass of Irish whiskey. He wanted some soft music in the background. Most of the day had been spent running from store to store, shopping at the Boxing Day sales in downtown Halifax, and now he wanted to sit back and watch the flames and reminisce.

He could read a good book or watch the traffic speed by his townhouse at a velocity that was excessive for the snow conditions. He turned on the stereo system, craving some relaxing Bob Dylan music. Instead, the stereo delivered a weather forecaster talking about an ominous low-pressure system covering most of Eastern Canada.

Twenty centimeters of snow had already blanketed the eastern seaboard and another five to ten centimeters were anticipated. After the Halifax forecast, the stereo came to a news announcer describing the havoc created by local drivers, struggling to get home with their Boxing Day goodies, in vehicles still equipped with summer tires. After the weather and local news came reggae music. It was far from relaxing and certainly not of Christmas flavor.

Out of the question was relaxing music on the stereo, so Shawn put it out of its misery and reluctantly returned to the TV remote. When the TV screen beamed to life, a rather bored-looking news anchor in a blue flannel suit was describing and displaying a fuzzy video of a submarine. It was believed to be a Russian sub, reportedly spotted off the coast of Labrador several days ago. The submarine was photographed by a Canadian Forces sub hunter, the Aurora, flying out of the Greenwood base in Nova Scotia.

The same anchorman followed that announcement with a report on some unusual activities by the Russian MIR Space Station. According to him, MIR was exhibiting perplexing signs of returning to earth. The anchor made no further comment about this rare space phenomenon. Instead, he shuffled his papers and waited until a shot of the Prime Minister was superimposed on the screen behind him. He went on to make some condescending remarks about the PM's planned trip to Moscow in late January. The flannel suited anchor was not a fan of the PM. He took pains to point out that it was the PM's third trip to the communist regime since coming to power just four years ago.

The comfort of Shawn's room was broken by the continuous ring of the red Operations phone.

"Major Phillips," Shawn said into the receiver.

On the other end of the line was the Rescue Coordination Centre.

"Distress Air," was stated abruptly, followed by an audible click as the line went dead.

All thoughts of a quiet and comfortable evening at home were shattered as Shawn focused on what he needed to do in response to the call. He switched off the gas fireplace and the TV and raced to the bedroom. He dressed in his air force blue military uniform. Over top of it he tugged on a warm and comfortable air force blue down-filled parka. His pilot wings were clipped on the left front panel. The parka would be a god send in the next sixty-four hours.

Shawn caught a quick glimpse of himself as he passed the bedroom mirror. For forty-eight years old he was still attractive, fighting trim they said, and spry. His brown eyes contained a sparkle that lit up his lightly tanned face. Christmas Day on the slopes around Halifax had brought out the tan, and it contrasted nicely with the dark shading that came from a half-day of new beard growth. Together they gave his face a rugged appearance. His military regulation cut brown hair betrayed his age with a little gray at the temples. Yet he exhibited a younger man's confidence, one filled with ruggedness, strength, and agility. At six- foot -two he seemed to be the 'glamour boy pilot', although that was just the opposite of his personality. Those who knew him would describe him as a stay-at-home individual who preferred spending quality time with a lady friend rather than a night at the local beer hall. He had his collectibles and a seldom seen cat that gave him some form of needed intimacy since his divorce.

When he was flying, he was considered a competent pilot who was always gracious and thankful to the crew that maintained his aircraft. The golden pilot wings were sewn above the left breast of his open tunic. The wings flashed as he pulled the two sides of the parka together and pulled up the zipper. His Air Force wedge was positioned at a right angle on his head with a slight tilt towards the brow. He tugged at his black rubber boots until they covered his black leather shoes.

Shawn grabbed his prepacked flight bag, containing flight suit, underwear, shaving gear, and laptop computer, and left his lakeside home. He felt the cold blast of the wind and snow bite into his exposed face as he walked the short distance to his Ford Bronco. Within minutes of the call, Shawn was driving down Cole Harbour Road in the direction of the Angus L. MacDonald Bridge. Soon he was passing Dalhousie University. It was his Alma Mater, and he had earned Honors in his Environmental Science Degree. It donned on him, during his twenty-minute drive through snowy unplowed roads, that he had no need for the degree during his twenty years in the RCAF.

"Distress Air" was the shortened version of Major Air Disaster. The term was not just a word for anyone involved in search and rescue activities; it was a cry for help. These words signaled the possibility of a large airliner crash with at least ten passengers on board.

The Air Controller called Shawn since he was the head of the Halifax RCC. It was located at the HMC Dockyard at Halifax Harbour. In the case of a Distress Air, the Air Controller would call upon Shawn, as Commander of the RCC, to referee the site. The controller was continually busy answering questions from media, senior officers, squadron leaders, etc. Shawn was called on at any hour if his help was needed, especially with the media.

As Shawn drove towards the Rescue Coordination Centre, he knew that the Air Controller had already taken several actions before declaring a Distress Air.

Once the Centre was notified that an aircraft was overdue, the duty officer at the RCC and the NCO on duty with him would begin to investigate the possible emergency. From a bank of phones on the alert desk, the duty officer determined how many passengers were on board. He wanted to know what radio or rescue equipment was installed on the aircraft, as well as info about a flight plan filed by the pilot from the overdue aircraft. The controller called various airports that were on or near the flight path of the pilot, to learn if he had set down but forgotten to notify the Ministry of Transport Office of his safe arrival; it did happen occasionally.

Shawn left the Dartmouth side of the bridge and turned onto Barrington Street in Halifax. He knew that the Air Controller was now busy finding out what aircraft and crew were available to help with the search. Time was of the essence. The plane had to be quickly found if the passengers and crew on board were to survive the winter weather. Phillips turned into the Dockyard at the North Street entrance.

The gate Commissioner wasn't about to leave the warmth of his kiosk. Instead, he peered through the window, recognized the rank of Major on the shoulder of Shawn's parka and waved him through the gate. Shawn drove down South Street, above the speed limit, and came to a sliding halt at the rear of the red brick building housing the RCC. As he entered the building, a young air force military policeman saluted him and then checked Phillips' pass. The ID badge had been made four years earlier when Shawn first joined the RCC, after twenty years of flying everything from helicopters to sizeable fixed-wing aircraft. That sort of flying activity put gray hair on a head and wrinkles on the brow. While Shawn looked slightly older in person than his face did on the badge, the policeman was satisfied and permitted him to pass.

As he entered the Rescue Coordination Centre, Shawn's attention was drawn to the mass of communications equipment and the barrage of phones, fax machines, and computers. The walls to the left of the entrance were covered by maps of the Halifax Search Region.

The Halifax Search area map showed five million square kilometers including the Maritimes, part of Quebec, part of Baffin Island, and the inhospitable waters of the North Atlantic. The wall to Shawn's immediate right contained organization charts and photos of ships and aircraft. The wall straight ahead held several clocks set at different time zones in Canada, and one clock set at Greenwich Mean Time or Zulu time. In the room's center was a large rectangular table, several times larger than a billiard table, covered by Plexiglas. Under the glass was a large-scale map of Canada. On the Plexiglas was taped a jagged red line representing the flight path of the missing aircraft. The line traveled from the southern part of Nova Scotia, skipped north along the Labrador Sea through the Hudson Strait to Frobisher Bay on Baffin Island. From there it dashed west to Southampton Island then southwest to Yellowknife, on Great Slave Lake, before heading back northeast in a roundabout fashion to Frobisher Bay. Almost as if it didn't know what to do next, the line flew straight north across Baffin Bay to Thule, in Greenland, then made a sharp left turn and headed north where it circled the North Pole. It rushed south, touching on the northern edge of Ellesmere Island, to a small peninsula and settlement known as Alert. The line seemed to hesitate. There was a slight gap in the red tape, but it continued on its route to Thule then dashed southeast to Nova Scotia, and then came to a jagged stop at the home of the bird. Red tape highlighted the area between Thule, Alert, and the North Pole to define the area to be searched.

Immediately, Shawn knew that the missing aircraft was not a civilian airliner but one of their own, a Canadian Forces military aircraft. The only reason an aircraft would fly such a jagged line would be to do a routine patrol of the north. The line ran right through a very highly classified area, shown as Alert. This spot, on Ellesmere Island, was shown on most maps as the Canadian Forces Alert Listening Post and Weather Station, which gave civilians the general impression that it had something to do with the weather. In reality it was a highly classified military listening post dedicated to gathering intelligence and data by eavesdropping on Russian military and government communications. Many Canadian military folks referred to it as their spy station.

Alert was forty-one hundred kilometers from Halifax, eight hundred eighteen kilometers from the Pole, and six hundred and sixty kilometers from Thule. It was billed as the world's most northerly military station, and it was not the sort of place visited by civilian airliners. What the red tape on the Plexiglas covered was mostly Arctic ice.

"Heaven help the crew," Shawn said to no one in particular, "if they are down on the pack ice."

6

# 2    SAR WINTERS

26 December 1930 hrs local/Halifax, N.S.

Aurora aircraft in flight

As he glanced around the Rescue Coordination Centre, Shawn noticed that he was one of the first arrivals. The Air Controller and his NCO were busy on the phones.

"Major Phillips," said the Air Controller, "I'm glad you got here so quickly. The place is a zoo. I could use some help. How are the roads? Will it take long for the others to get here?"

Shawn recognized him as duty officer Lieutenant Mike Reynolds, who was recently posted to the Centre. He had been a navigator at a rescue squadron until a bad airplane accident sidelined him with a shattered leg almost a year ago. The doctor gave him another nine months of desk flying before he could return to the Squadron, the real love of his life.

"The roads are not too bad if you have snow tires and front-end drive in your car. Tell me about the missing bird!"

"It's one of ours. In Greenwood, Nova Scotia, the Squadron got word from the U.S. base in Thule that it was overdue. It's an Aurora reconnaissance plane from 415 Squadron that was on a routine Nor Pat when it disappeared. The last contact by the pilot was with Thule airbase, just after it took off from that airfield. It should have landed back at Thule several hours ago, but there has been no word from the bird. We think it went down somewhere in the twelve hundred kilometer stretch from Alert to the Pole, or possibly in the stretch from Alert to Thule area. Could you possibly call the CO of 415 Squadron, and get some more information on the crew and the plane, while I make further arrangements for the briefing?"

Shawn could hear the weather and teletype machines that lined the partitioned wall. They were pouring out streams of data on highs and lows, aircraft availability, and airport facilities. During the few minutes that he had been at the Centre, some additional RCC staff entered the room and took up their positions monitoring the machines. Through the glass in the partition wall, Shawn could see into the briefing room behind the machines. In the room, all the staff were busy getting ready for the briefing.

Shawn strolled to his office and started to read the priority messages that had piled up on his desk since he left work on Christmas Eve. He was feeling energetic after a small nap early that afternoon. He knew that the next couple of hours could be hectic, based on past operations, and the search might even stretch out to cover a few days. He was used to being occupied. In fact, he had spent ten to twelve hours a day at his job since his divorce. He didn't get to see his daughter these days since she decided to live with her mom. Work had become Shawn's new family.

He had worked with Lt. Mike Reynolds since the young navigator had arrived at the Centre. Shawn had confidence in him, and left him the task of setting up the briefing without further assistance. Instead,

Shawn busied himself with his duties. It was his task to look after the more mundane parts of a search, such as dealing with the press and running interference by headquarters. Most of his duties would come after the search, when he would work with the Director of Flight Safety to determine the cause of the crash and how to prevent a recurrence.

He preferred a more hands-on approach to a search and rescue operation, and liked nothing better than traveling to a remote SAR Centre near the scene of a crash or sinking. He had done so on several occasions, leaving the young duty officers in charge of the Centre. In the past Shawn had conducted some on-site searches as Search Master, especially after he had completed an Air Controller course and a SAR Technician course. But he had not been to a crash scene in the past year. The itch remained to get out and do something more substantial, as nothing beat finding those in trouble and bringing them home to safety.

Shawn was thankful that he would not have to inform the next-of-kin about their missing loved ones; that onerous undertaking fell to the Squadron Commander of 415 Sqn, Lt. Col. "Digger" Holloway. It was time to call the Base to see if the Commander was at his office this late in the evening.

"Colonel Holloway's office."

"If Col. Holloway is in the office, please tell him that Major Phillips of the Rescue Centre would like to talk to him." He heard the NCO tell the CO that Major Phillips was on the phone for him.

"Shawn, I haven't heard from you since we were in Defense College together. Boy, those were good times. I remember what a wild character you were! Well, we better get down to the business at hand. I'm glad you called. My Sergeant and I just got here after Thule called the Squadron about our Aurora. What can you tell me about our missing bird? Did you have any luck in contacting her? Or has anyone told you where she is at?"

"No contact yet, Colonel. I just got here myself due to the slippery roads. We are about to do a briefing on the missing plane and I will let you know the moment we hear something. What can you tell me about the aircraft, the crew, and the mission?"

"It was a CP-140 Aurora, tail number 140739, better known to the Americans as the P-3 Lockheed Orion. We received this plane, and others like her, in the early eighties. Neither she nor any of the other Auroras have had any major maintenance problems. This bird had some radio defects in the past couple of months, especially on her last northern flight, but the technicians repaired the problems before this trip. Still, the bottom line is that there is nothing in the maintenance log to indicate any flying problems that could cause this craft to go missing. Like all Auroras, this one has a crew of ten, consisting of two pilots and a flight engineer upfront, with four navigators and three airborne electronics sensor operators in the aft end. It's equipped with three onboard navigation systems that give the crew an all-weather global capacity. The crew in the back have all the latest in sophisticated electronic detection gear that would enable them to detect submarines. She is carrying only a few offensive weapons in the form of two types of homing torpedoes in the bomb bays.

"Aurora number 739 left Canadian Forces Base Greenwood five days ago on a Northern Patrol mission. I found a crew, many of whom are unmarried, who volunteered to do an early Nor Pat. Most of them have never been to the North Pole or anywhere near it. They eagerly volunteered, especially since the bird was also tasked with dropping goodies off to our servicemen stationed in the North. We were to drop rations, booze, and mail to the residents of our listening site and at the weather station.

"A few of the scientists also wanted to spend their holidays up north so we let them tag along. On this mission, the crew was tasked with not only dropping the rations, but also to watch for Russian submarines since NATO warned us that one or more Russian subs were heading towards Canada. A few days earlier, in the Nor Pat, this Aurora reported that she spotted a sub near Labrador and subsequently lost her. We thought that the sub might have sailed into Canadian waters.

"The scientists on board are from Environment Canada. They wanted to check on iceberg movements and conduct some global warming tests while observing the ozone hole at the Pole. As I understand it, they wanted to measure the hole's size caused by greenhouse gases to see if it has increased in magnitude since their last visit.

"We instructed the aircraft Captain to spend his first night in Frobisher Bay. The second night was to be spent in Yellowknife and the third night back in Frobisher. For the fourth night, the evening before 739 disappeared, the crew was told to layover at the American Base in Thule, Greenland. On the fifth day of the mission, which was this morning, the five-man aircraft servicing crew that was on board for the first four days of the mission, thank God, decided to remain in Thule.

The ten-man aircrew, plus two scientists, would make the last legs of the Northern Patrol, from Thule to Alert, then on to the Pole and back to Thule.

"The aircraft was scheduled to fly home from Thule tomorrow. That's about it, Shawn. One more thing, the guys in the Squadron had a nickname for the old girl. She was the first of the fleet to arrive at the Squadron. It was a gray and misty morning on the day that she arrived. We were all waiting anxiously for the arrival of the first Aurora, and when she flew in, she appeared out of these low rain clouds. There she suddenly was, and one of the guys said she was like a gray ghost with squadron emblems worn off of her primary paint job. The name stuck. The boys lovingly call her the 'Gray Ghost'."

"Colonel, could you fax to me the ten-man crew list and the names of the two scientists? I hope we can locate the aircraft safe and sound on the ground. Just in case the worst has happened I'll need that information."

"Sure, I'll do it right away. The first pilot's name is Captain Frank Winters."

Since SAR operations were named after the pilot, Shawn continued with that in mind.

"We'll start the SAR Winters Briefing in fifteen minutes. Could you please stand by the video conference facilities at Base Operations? We'll be in touch, and we'll let you know if we hear anything from your crew or find your Gray Ghost."

Shawn stole a glance around the room. It held about a dozen officers, several NCOs, and three civilians who appeared to represent the press and TV media. The reporters would be instructed that not all of the briefing information could be published or broadcast at this time. Instead, they would be provided with a news release at the end of the briefing.

Shawn watched as Lt. Reynolds ran through the briefing using information they received by phone, fax, and telex. Only the pilot's name was mentioned since families had not yet been notified that their loved ones were overdue. The Halifax RCC would start the ball rolling by establishing a mini RCC in Thule, as soon as possible, on a spot nearer to the search sector. A Search Master would be named shortly by the Maritime Air Group Commander, Brig. Gen. Shanahan.

Lt. Reynolds, the briefer, said that the search would start with a single aircraft. The first airplane, another Aurora, would be dispatched from 415 Sqn in Greenwood and would proceed directly to Thule, Greenland with the SAR team onboard. Reporters could join the flight if they so desired. None of the reporters took Lt. Reynolds up on his offer. Flying on an aircraft that was identical to a missing aircraft was not their cup of tea.

During the briefing, it became clear that both Cold Lake and Trenton were amid heavy snowstorms forecasted to last for at least another couple of hours and grounding all aircraft. The group agreed that a CC-130 Hercules belonging to 413 Transport and Rescue Sqn in Greenwood, currently at Shear water, Nova Scotia, would return home as soon as weather permitted. Once it arrived back at Greenwood it would load up with rescue equipment and additional rescue specialists, if needed, and fly to Thule. Cold Lake offered to help by stripping a second CC-130 Hercules and loading her up with a dismantled CH-135 Twin Huey helicopter. As in the case of Shear Water, the Cold Lake Hercules would leave as soon as the weather permitted. The helicopter might be needed to pluck survivors off a crash site. RCC Trenton would also have a SAR Herc on standby if needed.

When Reynolds asked the Trenton RCC participants to listen to and watch the briefing, and if they had anything they wanted to add, the Air Controller came on the screen. She mentioned that their teletype at the Canadian Mission Control Centre had received a SARSAT hit originating near Ellef Ringnes Island and the Magnetic North Pole. When the emergency locator transmitter would fall off of an airplane during a crash, the beacon would transmit a signal at 406 MHz to a satellite. SARSAT, the Search and Rescue Satellite System, detected the signal, then analyzed it to rapidly locate the source of the movement. The origin of the signal could be found within a radius of two kilometers, worldwide. The SARSAT would then send a notice, via satellite, to Trenton.

The Air Controller at the Trenton site went on to say that the signal lasted only fifteen minutes before it went silent. At this point the Squadron Commander of the missing plane took over the screen.

"It couldn't be our aircraft," said Lt. Col. Holloway, from the Ops room at Greenwood. "Our CP-140 Aurora was not planned to be near Ellef Ringnes Island."

As Shawn left the briefing room, he couldn't help but notice a news report on the TV that was hanging in the corner of the RCC. The news on the set was about the MIR Space Station. Apparently, the officials at the NORAD Space Detection and Tracking System had just issued a news update stating that the Russian space station was moving out of orbit and headed for earth. It was unknown if this was a planned event by Russian Mission Control or another one of the many problems that MIR had experienced in the past two years.

Reynolds finished the briefing by announcing a bus, now at the door, for anyone going to CFB Greenwood. At the same time, an NCO handed Major Phillips a note from Brig. Gen. Shanahan, asking for an update on the search.

Shawn asked one of the NCOs to fetch his suitcase from his car and deposit it in his office. He then sprang up the stairs to give a quick debriefing to the Commander of MAG.

Shawn's boss, Brigadier General Shanahan, had more responsibilities besides the efficient operation of the RCC. His primary responsibility was to provide anti-submarine warfare protection to the Canadian Navy ships on the east coast. However, he was also tasked to fly sovereignty patrols over the Canadian Arctic. Besides a search update, Major Phillips expected the MAG Commander to ask about resources needed for the search, since the limited resources of spare planes were needed for other tasks.

Shawn needed to inform Shanahan that the RCC might need several non-rescue type planes to help with the search. The SAR aircraft available so far consisted of one Hercules. The Labrador helicopters were grounded, and the Buffalo aircraft were all located on the west coast. The RCC needed the Aurora sub hunters to be used for transport and search spots, and they may have needed other MAG aircraft as the search progressed. While he didn't expect the search plane shortage to be a problem with the Commander, it might not sit too well with the Commander's boss, Vice Admiral "Buzz" Lowery.

Admiral Lowery was the head of the Canadian Navy, who liked to refer to himself as Admiral by dropping Vice from the title. He preferred Admiral since it was a four-star rank, while Vice was only a three-star. As far as he was concerned, it was *his* ships, and their need of protection, that resulted in Shanahan having any aircraft at all.

It was common knowledge throughout Maritime Command Headquarters that there was no love lost between the two senior officers. Shanahan's background was air force while Lowery was a navy man since enrollment. He was considered old school Navy. In the early sixties, the Navy had its own aircraft and aircrew. Buzz Lowery was one of the few that had earned his wings to fly and at the same time could proficiently command a ship. In 1975, when Air Command was formed, aviation was taken away from the Navy and given to Air Command Headquarters. Lowery was given a choice to follow the pilot's career path or continue with the Navy officer's career. He became quite disturbed as he watched pilots that were junior to him become colonels and generals in the air force career path before he even got promoted to the equivalent rank of Navy Commodore. He also watched as some of the junior pilots retired early as generals and went on to higher paying and higher profile jobs in the aircraft industry, while he still toiled in the Navy.

Lowery was not convinced that the Maritime Air Group, under the administrative control of an Air Force headquarters located in Ottawa, could protect his ships better than the Coastguard; a Navy administrator who controlled a group of naval planes from a naval squadron. For this reason, Lowery used every opportunity to let Shanahan know that he and the MAG staff had their offices at his Dockyard only to serve *him* and *his navy*.

Shanahan was out at the moment, so Shawn waited in the Brigadier General's office. As he wandered around the room, he studied the photos of Maritime Air Group planes. There were photos of the old Navy workhorse-the CP-121 Tracker, now retired, another Navy helicopter-the CH-124 Sea King, still flying after twenty-five years, and, of course, the Aurora. There was also a photo of the Argus, which had been retired in the eighties following the Auroras' purchase. The photo triggered a sharp memory of a crashed Argus that Shawn had seen.

Beside the planes were formal photographs of the Queen and the Prime Minister, looking none the worse for wear after being shot by Shawn earlier that day. There was also the standard Chief of Defense Staff photo and a picture of Shanahan's boss, but no photo of Lowery or any of the navy ships. *Perhaps the animosity works both ways,* thought Shawn.

On the desk was a picture of Shanahan and his family. Shawn guessed Shanahan's age at about 49. That was considered young for a one-star general. At his rate of promotion, Shanahan was mostly likely to catch up to and pass Lowery in a few years. That was another contributing factor to the animosity between the Admiral and the General.

Shanahan's family photos showed a proudly dressed man in his Air Force uniform. Shawn noticed that the General's hair was a premature silver compared to his younger and beautiful wife's long blond hair. In one photo, Shanahan was holding her close and smiling. It was a confident smile, and his face showed the experience of twenty-five years of flying almost every plane in the air force inventory. His face also showed the toll on him caused by years of command at the squadron and headquarters. The facial expression in the photo displayed the love for his wife, and at the same time indicated complete competence in his abilities. Shawn put the picture back on Shanahan's desk just as the Brig. General entered his office.

"Sorry I'm late, Shawn. I was with Vice Admiral Lowery. We both came to headquarters when we were notified that one of our aircraft is missing. He wanted me to assure him that he would get the plane that he needs for a joint Canadian/US Naval exercise coming up in the first week of January in the Arctic waters. I guaranteed him that we would provide the sub protection. He also wanted to know more about the submarine, which we think was Russian, spotted near Labrador earlier in the week. Then he told me about a speech that he recently gave in Washington, at a discussion group on Arctic sovereignty, hosted by himself and Admiral Heiserman, Chief of Naval Ops for the U.S. Navy." Shanahan continued with his overly detailed briefing.

"I gather that Admiral Lowery is very proud of his after-dinner speeches. He practically recited the whole address to me. He told the Americans that if Canada is to be serious about protecting its sovereignty in the Arctic, we should have at least six nuclear submarines for Arctic Ocean patrol. We should greatly increase air surveillance, and we should also have two Navy ice-breaking ships, much bigger and stronger than the Navy's previous ships, in the Arctic.

"Both Lowery and Heiserman suggested that a vast network of navigational aids, and an underwater sub detection system, are needed for the Canadian Arctic waters. As Vice Admiral Lowery sees it, his navy ships would act like the coastguard, and they would also escort ships through his arctic waters. To control this third ocean, which the Admiral said would include the Northwest Passage, Beaufort Sea, Arctic Ocean, and the Baffin Bay, he suggested that Canada should set up an Arctic Maritime Command in the Frobisher Bay area, that would be run by a four-star rank. He even mentioned to the group that our newest territory, Nunavut, is vulnerable to a hostile takeover. Of course, he once again suggested that this Arctic navy commander also control its planes. According to Lowery, if Canada is not prepared to implement his suggestions, we will never stop the Russians from sailing into our northern waters and crossing northern Canada without our permission. He was just getting warmed up on his favorite arctic sovereignty topic when his phone rang. I managed to get away from his spiel, I slipped out while he was on the phone. Now, tell me, what have you done so far about the missing Aurora?"

Shawn recounted the SAR Winters Briefing and the plans to establish a mini RCC at Thule. He mentioned the aircraft that were currently involved in the search and those that may be needed later. He concluded by mentioning that Lt. Reynolds was a capable Air Controller, and that the RCC and the search were coasting right along under his guidance.

"We need to find a Search Master to man the Thule RCC," said Shawn.

The MAG Commander strolled to the window and looked out into the wintery night. He seemed to be deep in thought, then slowly turned and spoke.

"I thought that establishing an RCC in Thule was the best route to follow. As for a search master, we have no very proficient men available, and I wondered if you would take on this extra role? How would you like to tackle the task of search master on-site for this operation? Your file shows that you are qualified, and that you even took the SAR Technician course including the training on survival in the Arctic, boat operation, and the use of scuba gear for rescue operations and medical care. You're also a trained parachutist and have led other successful rescue operations. I mention this point only if there is a need for a search master who can jump into a site, should the aircraft be located on the ice. Most of the duties can be done at the RCC. Unless you have any objections, I would like you to fly to Thule as the Search Master. If anyone can find the missing aircraft, I know you can."

"Thank you, Sir, I'll be glad to go to Thule. This search has taken my mind off of boring paperwork. If I didn't find something to do soon, I'd go crazy."

"I saw the bus for Greenwood pull up as I left Admiral Lowery's office, so you best be on your way," said Shanahan. "I'll call Digger Holloway at 415 Squadron and tell him you have my full support. I'll suggest that he tell the families of the crew of our plan to find their loved ones, as well. Can you keep me posted on what is happening so I can keep the Vice Admiral off your back? God knows, you will need a lot of patience and luck to find a thirty-six-meter-long gray bird, appropriately nicknamed the Gray Ghost, by the way, if she is down among all that ice. The last thing you need is a senior officer, like Lowery, trying to make political hay out of this possible disaster."

18

# 3   NATO E3A

26 December 2230 hrs local/Greenwood, NOS.

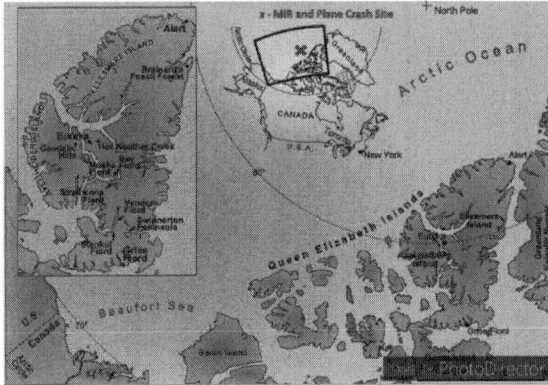

The bus trip to the Greenwood airbase was made exceptionally fast considering the state of the roads. They had been plowed, but they were still snow-covered with icy patches, and periodically, Shawn could feel the bus skid and swerve to the opposite side before returning to its proper right-hand lane. During the trip, Shawn's mind was on the disappearance of the Aurora and its crew. He realized that nearly twenty-four hours had passed since the last contact with the plane. The aircraft could have gone down shortly after its last contact which was just after takeoff from Thule. There was a remote possibility that the aircraft landed at some distant airstrip. As well, was a chance that the pilot couldn't contact the home base for some unknown reason. Shawn was optimistic by nature, so he included this prospect while considering all the options and the work that still had to be done to find the missing plane.

Two scenarios that came to mind were that the aircraft might have radio problems, or that the plane may have landed on the ice with fuel problems. Shawn attempted to visualize what it must be like to be stranded next to a downed plane on the Arctic pack ice. Winds in the red zone on the Plexiglas were forecasted to be around thirty knots. That would push the real temperature at the site to around -30 degrees Celsius. If fully exposed to this fierce cold, any survivor's exposed skin would freeze in less than thirty seconds. Death by hypothermia would likely result in a matter of hours unless the person had some protection from the icy wind blasts. Even if the survivors found some shelter, no one knew how long they could hold out.

In October 1991, a Hercules crash landed in the Canadian Arctic near the Alert Listening Station. The temperature neared -50 Celsius. Thirty-three hours after the crash, the rescue specialists found thirteen people still alive. There had been five deaths in that disaster, yet only one death was attributed to the Arctic chill.

During the bus ride, Shawn estimated that it could take another five hours for his plane to reach the Thule base, and with a quick turnaround the Aurora plane could be used as the first spotter plane in the search area an hour later. The other planes mentioned during the briefing wouldn't be in the search area for at least another seven to eight hours, or more, depending on the weather in Cold Lake and Trenton. The best chance to quickly find the missing plane would depend on how quickly they could get to the search area and commence the search pattern. Once in the area, Shawn hoped to find the missing craft in a matter of hours.

Finding the plane and getting help for its passengers were two different matters. No recovery could be attempted by parachuting from the Aurora since it was not designed for that function. The Aurora would be used strictly as a spotter plane. It would carry a few of the aircraft technicians; those that were fortunate enough to remain at Thule instead of making the last leg of the mission. The Aurora's search flights had to be made from Thule since the runway at the Alert listening station, the closest airport to the search area, was too short for the Aurora.

It was understood by the people involved in the search that the C-130 Hercules could land at the Alert Listening Station and use it as a staging point; assuming that the runway was cleared. The Alert airport wasn't closed due to a snowstorm. The Hercules had to get to Thule, which was a problem at the moment given the fact that storms were raging at their present locations. The SAR technicians that would participate in the hunt and rescue would arrive with the first Herc out of Shear Water via Greenwood. Shawn hoped that he could use some of the American rescue specialists in Thule and find some helicopters in the Thule area. But that was a long shot.

The bus entered the Greenwood airbase and drove to the 415 Squadron building and out onto the ramp. It parked near the plane that was heading for Thule. That plane was an Aurora, tail number 140740; a sister to the missing bird. The Aurora was primed and ready to go.

*Let's hope that it wasn't a mechanical problem that fell the missing Aurora,* thought Shawn. *A mechanical problem infectious to all the other Auroras.*

"Welcome aboard," said a Master Corporal as he directed Shawn to a seat. "We'll be taking off as soon as we get flight clearance from the Tower. As soon as we level out, I'll get you some coffee and a box lunch if you like. Perhaps later you might like to visit the flight deck." Shawn made the necessary pleasantries, and the Master Corporal wandered off to attend to more of his duties.

At 0245 hrs local, with lookouts manning the nose and tail, Search and Rescue flight 342 taxied out from the ramp in front of the 415 Squadron hangar. With a burst of power on the outboard GE-T-56 Turboprops, the Aurora was away smoothly down the taxiway, gently dipping her nose as brakes were applied to keep the speed down. Through the starboard spotters' window, Shawn could see three former anti-submarine warfare planes preserved on blocks for display. Spotlights shone on a Lockheed PTV-7 Neptune, a Canada air Argus, and an Afro Lancaster. His transport to Thule continued towards its takeoff point. The Aurora rolled slightly, crossed the main runway, looped back to its threshold, and with more moans from the brakes, SAR #342 turned into the wind for the final run-up and takeoff check.

Cleared for takeoff, full power against the throttle and brakes released, the craft was away with that magnificent, exhilarating roar from the engines that Shawn missed from his flying days. Speed gathered quickly, the tail was soon up, and corrective rudder action could be clearly felt. A couple of long low bounces on the main wheels and the CP-140 was airborne into the snowy sky. Almost before the wheels were up, the pilot worked hard into a climbing turn, got the feel of the controls, and completed the after-take-off checks. Gradually, the unmistakable tension of the takeoff lifted, and the crew started to busy themselves with changing headsets, loosening harnesses, and general preparations for the long flight ahead, as the pilot set course northward towards Labrador and Greenland.

Twenty minutes after takeoff, a flight engineer brought Shawn his first cup of coffee. He would be kept busy during the trip monitoring the aircraft's systems, conducting pre- and post-flight checks, carrying out simple repairs, and keeping detailed charts. The radar and sonar sets had already been switched on for warm-up and testing. From time to time, Shawn would wander over and gaze at the screens at the TacNav and NavCom stations. On the first occasion he received a brief but explicit direction on their workings from Lt. Boone, one of the Tactical Navigators. Shawn was always amazed at the advancements in anti-submarine technology that had occurred in the past ten years. He finished his box lunch and accepted the pilot's invitation to visit the cockpit.

As Major Phillips entered the cockpit area, he was surprised to find a beautiful young blond-haired woman at the controls in the pilot seat.

"Hello," said the Major, "I'm Shawn Phillips. I am responsible for getting you out of bed and aboard this aircraft at this unholy hour. I'm the Search Master for the SAR Winters mission."

"Hello to you," said the blond. "Welcome aboard. I'm Captain Mari Leech, spelled with an i. I'm the First Officer, and this is my co-pilot, Lt. William Peck. We're from 415 Squadron, and I have heard of you, Shawn Phillips. Your reputation precedes you. Your name is legendary in the SAR business. I've heard about your exploits in finding missing aircraft, and I feel good knowing you're heading up the search for Captain Winters. He is a good friend of mine, along with most of the crew."

"You give me too much credit, Mari, with an i." Shawn knew that she was one of only a few female first officers in the Canadian Forces, and the only one flying Auroras.

Mari briefed Shawn on the routing for the flight and the estimated arrival time at Thule based on a near-maximum speed of 400 knots per hour. After explaining all of the instruments and dials covering the cockpit's interior, Captain Leech invited Shawn to take Lt. Peck's seat and fly the plane. Under the two Aurora pilots' watchful eyes, he was allowed to control the craft for nearly two hours from the right-hand seat. He hadn't previously flown the CP-140, and he was pleasantly surprised to find that it flew much like a jet. It was easy to manage with its light control pressure, particularly compared to the Argus that it replaced. He had flown the Argus for a few hours back in the seventies while on temporary duty in Summerside, PEI. Compared to the Aurora, the Argus was like a lumbering penguin struggling to take off and stay airborne, where the Aurora was like a young bird crammed with energy and eager to take flight. It flew like a dream with very little effort.

"I can't believe how easy it is to fly an Aurora. That's not to take away your skills, Mari, with an i." Both laughed at the remark. "It's just that I'm used to lumbering planes, like the old Yukon that I flew out of Trenton, too many years ago."

"It couldn't have been that long ago. You're still a young man, full of piss and vinegar, with lots of energy and testosterone. I bet you're used to planes with tons of drive, and with fancy young women around you all the time." Mari had decided to start the dating dance. After all, she didn't get to meet young men every day, and Phillips was possibly a bachelor since she saw no ring. She found Shawn cute, and he had a good sense of humor. "I bet your wife, or girlfriend, just hates it when you are away on long search missions."

"Thank you, Mari, with an i," he said with a grin, just to continue the humorous mood. "But I don't have a wife. We divorced a year ago, and there is no girlfriend. To be honest, I do miss female companionship." Shawn decided to join her in the dance. "I haven't spent much time with possible new brides. I miss the intimacy of a woman, and the good times that could be had."

He noticed that Mari was about 5 foot 6, 130 pounds, and full of drive, confidence, energy, and good spirit.

"I notice that you don't have a ring on, so I presume there is no husband, but probably lots of young co-pilots awaiting your attention for a chance at taking you high in the sky?" Shawn didn't mention the double meaning of his words.

"Well, you would be wrong, Shawn, with an n. I prefer older, more mature, and experienced men. Not these young farts that strut about the Officers Mess looking for a young nurse's attention. I was never married, but I came close. I had a boyfriend that I thought would be the one. We met in flight school. He went on to be a First Officer on the Argus while I flew Buffaloes for a while."

"So, what happened, if you don't mind me asking?"

"Well, our love wasn't meant to be. He died in a crash of his Argus while approaching the runway at Base Summerside. He didn't survive."

"I'm so sorry for your loss." Shawn said meaningfully as he had a flashback of the Argus crash that he witnessed while visiting the Control Tower at Summerside. Shawn understood her loss and even felt guilty that he could do nothing to prevent her pain. He would not mention that he was present at the time of the crash. It would only bring back more painful memories for her. Perhaps in another time and another place he would tell her that he was there and saw the terrifying event. He decided to try to lighten the mood.

"I don't know if we will have much time at Thule, but I would like to buy you a drink for lending me your airplane. I need it to depart Thule for the search zone asap, and hopefully we'll spot our missing aircrew or flares or... something." He glanced over to the other pilot and tactfully added, "Lt. Peck, you are invited for a beer. I can only join you once the search is nearly started with spotter planes and helicopters. Mari, I presume that you will be staying at the Officer's quarters in Thule to catch up on your sleep?"

"Not so fast, Mr. Search Master. You can have my plane as soon as we land at Thule, but where it goes, I go. There is sleeping accommodation on the Aurora that is quite comfortable for me. Thank you, Sir."

"OK, Mari. It is a planned get-together, or date, for some time in the future. Now I better get on my laptop and line up more search planes. I can never get enough."

"This may help," said Mari. "I know about a NATO E3A plane that is piloted by a Canadian relative. He is headed this way. It's the AWACS plane flying from the Geilenkirchen Air Base in Germany. The mission for him is to fly to Hanscom Air Base today, and he will be passing over the search area. Perhaps he could spend some time helping with the search before making his way on to Hanscom."

"That would be a tremendous help. The radars on that craft are miraculous. It can spot a jeep driving on the ground from thousands of feet. If my Aurora is down on the ice in the search area, the E3A will spot it. Please see what you can do to make it happen. Now, I need to get back to my laptop."

"That would be fantastic if I can get his superiors to agree. I'll work on it right away." Mari replied excitedly.

Mari and Shawn hit it off right from the start. They discovered that they had much in common besides their love of flying. They talked about flying school, their first solo, playing Crud in the Officers Mess billiard room, and about friends they had in common.

"Did you ever meet a bartender by the name of Hans, who served drinks at the office's mess in Trenton?" Mari asked. She continued without waiting for a response. "I think he's German. I remember how excited he was, watching Crud. Several officers, including myself, chasing a black ball around a billiard table, trying to sink the other balls.

Maybe he just liked to see the bouncing boobs of the women, especially the nurses."

"Hans, yes, of course I remember him. You're right, Mari, he is German. He spent years as a bartender for Canadian Officers at 3 Wing, in the Black Forest in Germany, and later at the mess in Lahr, Germany. He used that experience to immigrate to Canada and become a citizen. He mixed a mean martini."

Shawn discovered that Mari was from the Maritimes, and had attended the University of New Brunswick where she obtained a degree in Forestry. After graduation, she joined the Air Force to see the world. Unlike his divorced wife, Shawn found Mari easy to talk to, especially about their Air Force experiences. Shawn noticed that she frequently smiled, and it made her beautiful face light up. Her eyes sparkled as she related stories about the sights and sounds she experienced on Nor Pats to the North Pole. She was in love with the Arctic, and even described the Aurora Borealis as a symphony of magic shifting lights. She had a pleasant personality, which was evident from her humor and her funny anecdotes about her crew's antics. As they spoke, she handled the Aurora's stick with great skill and agility. Whenever the craft was climbing or turning, she described in explicit detail the various actions that she was doing in the cockpit. She was making the long flight more and more relaxing for Shawn. The time seemed to zip by, and before he knew it the plane was closing in on Greenland's landmass.

As one pilot studying another, Shawn could see that she was very proficient at her job. During the flight, she took complete control of the whole aircraft while issuing confident orders to the navigator, flight engineer, load master, and others. She seemed completely involved with the plane's operation. Shawn had the distinct impression that he could rely on her to give one hundred and ten percent to see the successful completion of his search mission. Her physical features, along with her joyous personality, endeared her to Shawn. He left the cockpit with the desire to see her again, in a less stressful situation. He put it on his mental priority list to see Mari again, ASAP.

Under other circumstances, flying with Mari would have been a more delightful trip. This occasion was anything but fun. Shawn couldn't forget that he was on route to a search area to find twelve men who he hoped were still alive.

During the flight, he spoke on several occasions to the Aurora crew about their roles in the coming search, and about his problem of finding helicopters to participate in the search pattern.

As the Aurora flew north, it passed into perpetual darkness. From the middle of October to the start of March, there was no direct sunlight in the Alert-Thule-Pole search area. The light from the moon and stars, aided by the highly reflective snow, contributed to some natural light in winter. Twilight was prolonged in the Arctic. Complete twenty-four-hour darkness had set in just a week before the aircraft had gone missing. Finding a downed aircraft would be difficult without flares.

Mari's Aurora was approaching Greenland's coast as the Thule tower contacted the plane with landing instructions. The Base was a sprawling Greenland coastal airbase where 5000 Americans operated the largest United States installation in the Arctic. The U.S. Air Force built the airbase on Greenland's Danish Island under a NATO agreement in 1951. It had a 10,000-foot runway, several hangars, a good music radio station, nightly movies, hobby shops, a library, and a well-stocked Post Exchange. It was a reasonably comfortable place considering its location so far north. The only shortage in Thule was women. There were only a few female nurses and entertainers for the hundreds of men who inhabited it.

Landing an aircraft at Thule could be tricky since the airfield was surrounded by high terrain and other obstacles. There was Thule Mountain to consider as well as the four huge radar installations. Each of them was 400 feet wide and 165 feet tall. The runway was lined with white lights that provided little contrast against the white snowbanks also lining the runway.

At that time of the year, the runway tended to be slippery from frost. Snow ridges, made inadvertently by the runway plows, sometimes blocked the landing wheels. While Shawn would have preferred Captain Leech, a seasoned pilot, to make this tricky landing, he was impressed with Lt. Peck's performance. He carried out a smooth asymmetric landing on runway 28. The approach and touchdown were at 11.15 Zulu. The Aurora kissed the runway and rolled until its momentum was dissipated then taxied to a site designated by the tower.

A staff car was waiting for Shawn when he disembarked. The car took him to the Aircraft Operations Building where an airman introduced himself as Captain Reid, the U.S. Forces Liaison Officer for the search. He apologized for the lack of staff to assist the Canadian search team. Most of the personnel at Thule were at home with their families for the Christmas holidays. However, he would provide whatever assistance Shawn needed if it were available at the Thule airbase or Camp Century, located 138 miles east of Thule. He ushered Shawn into a furnished office, complete with a phone, just off the Ops Room. Shawn asked Reid about the availability of U.S. planes to help with the search. Captain Reid confirmed that there were no aircraft at Thule at the moment, nor were there any trained rescue specialists available.

It seemed that Mari's Aurora CP-140 that brought Shawn to Greenland was the only aircraft available for use immediately in the search. When questioned about the availability of a helicopter off the Base, Reid told him about a Bell 212, belonging to a local firm, that was presently unserviceable and unlikely to be repaired for several weeks. It looked like the Shawn would have to rely on Canadian resources, unless he was fortunate enough to obtain the NATO E3A plane for the search. Disheartened, he ventured towards his new office.

Major Phillips finally found some good news. There was a message from the NATO base in Germany confirming that a NATO E3A would be in the Thule area in about one hour. It could conduct several track searches, but only for a two-hour period due to fuel limitations. The message brightened his spirits and built up his hope that the missing Aurora crew would be found safe and well. A second message reported that the storm in Cold Lake had subsided, and a Herc had taken off with a dismantled helicopter on board. It should arrive in about an hour, which was about the same time as the E3A would search the area. He figured that it would take at least six hours to reassemble the chopper at the Thule hangar. If the E3A spotted the missing aircraft, it was feasible, with luck, that at least some of the passengers could be plucked out of the Arctic winds in eight hours.

The only question was, could they survive another eight hours if the craft was down on the pack ice? The final message was another piece of good news from home. It read that the other Hercules from Greenwood, tasked to bring the SAR techs and equipment, was well on its way to Thule with an ETA of two more hours.

Things were shaping up a little, but that could be of small comfort to any survivors that may be out on the ice in minus 30-degree weather, reflected Shawn. It may already be too late for the Aurora crew, but he wasn't about to concede anything at this point.

Mari entered his office to provide Phillips with the status of her Aurora. On the flight to Thule, Shawn had mentioned to her that he wanted her aircraft to be the first to fly to the search area after they arrived at Thule. There was a chance that they could spot a flare or maybe pick up a radio transmission.

"Greetings again, Mr. Search Master. I came to see you," she paused then, with the thought that she may have gone too far. She hastily moved on with the conversation. "To see you, that is, to tell you that my plane has been refueled and we are ready to go. Captain Chris Kendall, who rode in the rear on the trip over here, will pilot my plane while I get some rest in the aft section. We can stay aloft for about 16 hours and that will consume the fuel onboard. Capt. Kendall is in Flight Planning, getting a weather briefing. He has asked me to get your instructions on the search pattern."

Shawn's face brightened when she entered. "OK! Hi again, Mari, with an i, it is always a pleasure to see you, especially with good news. Thanks for letting me know your plane is ready to proceed to the search area. It's difficult to communicate in the Arctic at the best of times, but now there is a new problem. The Met Office just announced that electric storms are popping up occasionally in the search pattern area. They will play havoc with your compass and your radios, especially when you are so close to the Magnetic Pole. If a storm comes up you may have to rely on star fixes, backup radio systems, and radio compass to know where you are at all times and to contact us here in Thule. Once you reach the search area, I want you to slowly use a creeping line ahead search pattern, starting at Station Alert. Fly to the Pole and back, traversing the area in a north-south direction. There are some aircraft technicians from Greenwood, presently at Base Ops, that will act as spotters for you, watching for fires and flares. Heaven knows if they will be able to see much else in the darkness.

"By the way, thanks for the info that you gave to me about your relative's flight plans," Shawn continued. "You may not have to fly this search pattern for the next 16 hours after all. About an hour after you are airborne, a NATO E-3A will be over the search area. The downward looking radar on that craft can spot a flea on a dog's backside."

Mari smiled at the flea reference. Her face lit up, and she was beautiful. Shawn paused for a moment.

"I'll get the pilot of the NATO E3A to fly an east-west track from Thule to Alert. Due to the frigid weather, and its hypothermia effects on survivors, we don't have time to cover the same area twice so we'll eliminate overlapping. Hopefully, between the use of your aircraft and the E3A, we will blanket the search area and find our bird. The E3A is our best chance to find our missing plane.

"It's a good idea to do the briefing on the search pattern now rather than waiting until you are in the air, since there may be some communication problems. We spoke earlier about the difficulty of navigating. As I mentioned, the E3A radar can spot another plane four hundred klicks away. Unfortunately, I can only use the NATO plane for a few hours before I have to let it continue on its mission to Hanscom. The good news is, with its excellent radar, the pilot can cover a four-hundred-kilometer-wide swath at a time. Hopefully, we'll find the craft before your cousin heads to Hanscom. Do you have any survival equipment on board that you can drop if you find our plane?"

"Before we left Greenwood, we loaded two SKADs," Mari replied. SKAD was the acronym for Sea Kit Air-Droppable. "They contain inflatable rafts, which may not be much help on the ice, but they also contain rations and other gear to help victims survive until a SAR tech can reach them. We can drop the SKADS from the bomb bay doors if we spot any survivors."

"Fine! You better get going, Mari. As a call sign, we'll use 'SAR flight 343'. I'll contact your squadron and give them the details. If I'm not here when you return, perhaps I will make a point of finding you. Hopefully, we can have some private time together."

"I would like that. Good luck with your search. I'm looking forward to us getting together and seeing what happens."

Shawn left his office and walked the short distance to Base Operations. In the Ops room, he checked the Arrivals Board for the Herc from Cold Lake; it was scheduled to arrive in the next thirty minutes, followed by the Greenwood Herc one hour later. Capt. Reid was no longer around the office, so he had the switchboard ring the CO at his home. He needed to arrange for hangar space where the maintenance technicians from Cold Lake could reassemble the Huey helicopter. The CO assured Shawn that space would be made to assemble the chopper, to rescue part of the mission, if needed.

Shawn was anxious to learn if any incoming Hercules' spotted the missing bird on their flights to Thule. He used the Ops phone to communicate with the Cold Lake Herc pilot, presently approaching Greenland's shores. The Herc crew watched from their aircraft, looking for flares and listening for SOS calls from the missing plane as they passed over Nunavut. They had not seen or heard anything from the overdue plane during the flight. The Tower Controller broke into the conversation to tell the Herc pilot, once their plane touched down, to proceed in the Follow-Me pickup truck. The truck would lead the aircraft crew to the hangar that the CO authorized for offload. The Herc would be taken to the hangar, the helicopter parts removed, and the Huey parts would be reassembled. Shawn asked the Hercules pilot to report to him as soon as the helicopter was unloaded so that the Herc could be assigned a search area.

Shawn returned to his office to place a call to Halifax. The switchboard operator was able to open a line to the RCC in Halifax, and Shawn updated the Air Controller on the status of the search. The Air Controller promised to contact "Digger" Holloway at 415 Sqn. and Brig. Gen. Shanahan, and let them both know what was happening regarding the missing plane.

While Shawn was on the phone, he saw the 415 Squadron Aurora, with its distinctive Swordfish symbol on the tail, taxi by the window of his office. *At last*, he thought, *one search plane is on its way.*

Returning to Ops, he listened to the conversation about the search and the latest topic of interest which concerned the Russian MIR Space Station, and why it suddenly left orbit and seemed to be headed for earth. There were rumors and speculations about more MIR system problems, but no factual news yet from Moscow or Washington about the latest space spectacle. According to one Ops officer, the NORAD tracking system was now forecasting that it would land in either the Soviet or Canadian Arctic.

"That's all we need," said Shawn to the Ops officer, "a space station landing in the middle of our search area."

The conversation returned to the search when the Ops officer mentioned that the camouflaged Cold Lake Herc was now on the runway and proceeding to its designated hangar to offload the Huey chopper. *Finally*, thought Phillips, *I'll be able to go get the Aurora crew... if we can find them.*

Sir," said an NCO to the Ops officer, "Tower is on the phone. They have the NATO E3A on the radio. Do you or Major Phillips want to talk to the pilot?"

"Have the tower patch the pilot through to us. I want to talk to him on the Ops radio," replied Shawn.

"Thule Ops, this is L. Col. Ashwood of the Canadian Forces, the First Officer on NATO E3A Sentry number 35405, on route over Thule Air Force Base, 35 miles out. Please have the Canadian Search Master give us directions on the search pattern he wishes, and we will be happy to oblige."

"L. Col. Ashwood, this is Major Phillips. I'm in charge of the Winters search. Our missing plane is an Aurora, out of Greenwood. It is missing somewhere in the Thule -Alert Station- Pole triangle. I would like you to fly an east to west pattern from Thule to Alert, then turn around and use the same pattern from west to east. Use your rotodome surveillance radar to see if you can detect the presence of our craft on the land or the ice. You can repeat the flying pattern, edging each time towards the Pole, as often as your fuel and time permits. Be advised that we have another Aurora, tail number 140740, searching south to north pattern from Station Alert to the Pole. There are also magnetic storms in the area."

"Roger, Thule Ops. We are on the way. We will try to contact you through the tower, on this frequency, if we spot anything."

*Well,* thought Shawn, *at least now, most of the search area will be covered.* His next concern was getting the helicopter assembled. If the missing plane could be located in the range of the chopper, they may be able to get the survivors out in the next few hours. As usual, he was optimistic and thought that there would be only survivors rather than casualties.

The Search Master had been researching possible refueling sites for the Huey chopper, which had a range of 250 nautical miles, just in case the downed plane was found beyond its range. It would have to hop and skip its way to the crash site by refueling at a Greenland site before crossing the ocean to Frobisher Bay for further fuel. From Frobisher, it could stop for fuel at several communities, including Grose Fiord, Eureka, and finally, at the Alert Listening Station before heading to wherever the plane was found.

Shawn called the hangar to check on the progress of unloading the helicopter from the Herc. He happily discovered that the Huey was now off the Herc and located in pieces on the hangar floor. The Cold Lake airplane mechanics were scrambling to reassemble the chopper in record time. Meanwhile, the Herc pilot was on his way to see Phillips about a search route. Shawn wanted to have another chopper as a backup if he could find one. After a few phone calls and 30 minutes later, he was able to chase down the owner of the only other helicopter in Northern Greenland, only to find that it would take two weeks to repair the chopper. He could locate a few helicopters in Southern Greenland, but it would take almost two days for them to reach Thule.

Nevertheless, he arranged for two of them to join the search ASAP. During the telephone calls, he took the time to talk with the Cold Lake Herc pilot. The pilot was to prepare his airplane to fly towards Alert and take over the search area vacated by the NATO E3A when it had to return to its flight path towards Hanscom.

After chasing down helicopters, Phillips was delighted to be informed by the tower that the Greenwood Hercules had also arrived, containing the SAR technicians and their equipment. Shawn arranged for the Follow-Me truck to pick him up and take him to the Herc.

The rear cargo hatch door of the Herc was in the down position, so Shawn climbed up and walked into the rear of the plane. The Hercules was considered one of the most versatile transport aircraft in the world at that time. It was used in at least a half dozen tasks in the Canadian Forces including search and rescue, medical evacuation, disaster relief and several other functions. The rear cargo door enabled it to be loaded and unloaded quickly, making it an excellent platform for airdropping equipment and personnel in flight. Its takeoff and landing capability permitted the craft to land and take off in short and austere fields, making it ideal for SAR work. Flying at nearly six hundred kilometers an hour meant that these Hercules' could be in the search zone one hour after takeoff.

Shawn walked further into the hull of the C-130. In the rear of the plane, checking their jumping equipment, were the search and rescue technicians from 413 SAR Sqn. They wore bright orange jumpsuits and red berets, and each had the parachutists' wings emblazoned on the jerseys that they wore over their jumpsuits.

While the SAR team included the ground crew and the pilot, navigator, flight engineer, and others, it was the SAR techs, all 131 of them, who did the actual saving of lives. They rappelled down cliffs, hung on the end of a winch rope, to pluck men from sinking boats. They jumped into treacherous snowstorms to bring medical aid to those wounded in an aircraft crash. There were many stories of heroism in SAR operations, and most centered on the technicians' heroics.

Speaking of heroes, Warrant Officer Rob Mackenzie was too modest to talk about his British Empire Medal for Gallantry, or his Star of Courage for his feats of heroism, which was a big reason why the CO of the SAR Squadron chose him to be the team leader in the risky operation. The team leader would take the first group of parachutists into the crash site once it was found. Rob was with the other technicians in the Herc, checking equipment. Phillips saw him first.

For Rob Mackenzie, it was the greatest job in the world. There wasn't anything else that gave him greater pleasure than rescuing someone from certain death. He was a rugged fifty-year-old who had been in search and rescue operations for the past twenty years. His face was tanned, with piercing eyes, and a bushy salt and pepper style mustache that framed a huge smile, flashing rows of gleaming white teeth. He stood over six feet, and he was in excellent condition at one hundred eighty pounds. When he wasn't flying, he could be found at the Base gym working out or running laps. Rob was originally from New Waterford, Cape Breton. He left home at sixteen to join the air force and become a parachutist. That was all he ever wanted to do, and he had to lie about his age to get accepted into the Air Force. As it turned out, he was the very embodiment of the SAR motto of, 'That others may live', and he had the medals to prove it.

Shawn had worked with Rob Mackenzie during previous SAR missions, including some where Shawn directed the RCC operation and others where he was the search master. Some were successful, but a few passengers and crew of a ship or plane did not survive a crash. In all cases, Phillips, Mackenzie, and the technicians drove to bring everyone out alive. They respected each other's capabilities. Rob appreciated Shawn for his 'never say die' attitude; he would keep the SAR mission running days after other search masters would typically have canceled the mission and called off all search attempts. The Warrant Officer could think of at least two occasions where lives were saved due to either Shawn's perseverance or his stubbornness.

Shawn couldn't fathom having a search team with anyone other than Rob Mackenzie as SAR team leader. The man had a reputation of putting the victim's life above his own, and that fact was reiterated by the rows of medals he wore on his tunic whenever he was on parade. Mackenzie thought it was necessary to take risks in search and rescue work, and the hardest decision he ever made was the decision to give up and go home. In a sense, both of these men were cut from the same cloth.

The Search Master gave rob a friendly bump and welcomed all of the 413 Squadron aircrew and SAR techs to Thule. He briefed them on the search's latest status and assigned them accommodation and space in a hangar for their gear. They agreed to meet at Base Ops in an hour to join in the air search for the missing bird.

While walking from the Greenwood Hercules to the hangar where the Huey was being reassembled, hoping to meet the Cold Lake Herc pilot, Shawn met some ground maintenance support crew from the missing Aurora. They had skipped the last leg of the mission to do some Christmas shopping. The majority of them would soon be on another Aurora, out over the arctic ice, acting as spotters on Mari Leech's aircraft. The rest had stayed in Thule, in case they were needed as spotters on other search planes.

One of the NCOs asked about the rescue effort. Shawn told him about the two search planes in the air, the Aurora and the NATO E3A, the possibility of the Herc joining them, and about the location of the search.

"I guess you will be searching part of Ellesmere Island, near the Eureka weather station?" asked the NCO. "I think that Ellef Ringnes Island was also part of Captain Winters' diversion."

"I hadn't planned on it," said Shawn. "Why?"

"I thought you knew that the pilot was approached by a senior officer from Maritime Command HQ, just before take-off from Greenwood. I happened to overhear some of the conversations. The officer suggested to Captain Winters that he make a small diversion to drop a canister to a friend working at the Eureka weather station. He told our pilot not to say anything about it since it was of a personal nature. I got the impression that the suggestion was more like an order that Captain Winters couldn't turn down. I heard about it again when he mentioned the drop to us, just before departure yesterday. Winters explained that the canister was for a friend whose brother worked at the Weather Station, and it contained some mail and Christmas gifts for him. He didn't seem too happy about it, but joked around and told us that we would miss a fabulous drop, since he would put it right down the chimney of the hut housing the senior officer's friend. I assumed that the senior Maritime Command Officer was some sort of friend of Captain Winters, but the captain didn't like the idea of deviating from his planned flight route. Does the flight plan show that he was going to fly over the Eureka weather station?"

"I don't think so, but I'll double-check the flight plan."

Shawn had no idea that this brief conversation would strongly influence the missing aircraft and crew's search. He continued the discussion in his head as he retraced his steps to the Ops room. As he entered, the E3A pilot was providing a search update from the NATO search plane.

"Thule Ops, this is NATO E3A Sentry. We have completed the leg Thule to Station Alert and are about to make our turn for the next track. So far, we have not spotted any sign of your missing Aurora. We thought you might like to know that one of our radar controllers is picking up some magnetic disturbance over a hundred miles southwest of Alert and well out of the assigned search corridor. Since this is your mission, please advise if you want us to investigate further or to start on our second track."

Shawn figured that checking out the disturbance might waste valuable E3A flying time. The NATO modified Boeing 707 was scheduled to return to its mission in an hour or so. *Should I risk using the valuable flying time to check out the disturbance?* he wondered silently. He could recall previous searches where the missing boat or plane was found hundreds of kilometers off its planned route. But that customarily involved civilian crews. It was highly unusual for a military pilot to be so far off his flight plan. Then again, navigating in the high Arctic could be complicated at the best of times, as he told Captain Leech just an hour before. Before he could make the crucial decision, he would need more information.

"NATO E3A, this is Major Phillips at Thule Ops. Could you be more specific about the magnetic disturbance?"

"Thule Ops, it's quite a large disturbance, large enough that it could be a plane or a ship. It is about 120 miles from Alert and about 50 miles north of Ellesmere Island, close to Ellef Ringnes Island. Anything else you need to know?"

*Ellef Ringnes Island.* The name rang a bell for Shawn. He remembered that the Trenton RCC Air Controller had mentioned that they received a notification by SARSAT of a distress signal in that island's vicinity. It only lasted fifteen to twenty minutes before it was discontinued.

"Is the disturbance anywhere near the Eureka Weather Station on Ellesmere Island?"

"Thule Ops, the disturbance that we are picking up is closer to the Eureka Station than to the Alert station."

Shawn was not a gambler at heart, but his stomach was wrenching, telling him to go with his gut feeling. The short talk that he had with the NCO on the way to Ops was ringing in his ears.

"NATO E3A Sentry, proceed immediately to Ellef Ringnes Island to check the disturbance. I have a hunch, and a reason to believe that it could be our plane. Report as soon as you reach the area."

"Roger, Thule Ops. Be advised that we will not be able to conduct any more track searches by checking out this disturbance."

Shawn had a good feeling that he made the right decision. He knew that E3A time was precious and not to be wasted. He wanted to know just how close the disturbance was to Ellef Ringnes Island. He also wanted to know just who at Eureka was the friend of the senior maritime command officer.

Base Ops provided him with some topographical maps of the island and surrounding area. As he studied the charts, he was joined by the Greenwood Herc pilot, who reported that the plane had been refueled, and the SAR team was now available to enter the search. Shawn decided to hold the Hercules until he heard back from the NATO plane, rather than send the craft on a spotting mission. If the NATO search plane found the missing bird, WO Mackenzie and his SAR technicians would use this bird so they could jump to the site.

The next thirty minutes took forever. Surely the E3A must be near the focal point of the disturbance by now, thought Shawn. The radio transmission from the NATO plane arrived at the same time as his thought.

"Search Master at Thule Ops, we found your bird! It is a plane on the ice, forty-five miles from Ellef Ringnes Island, the nearest landfall. We are over head at this time. We dropped some flares on our last pass and we're pretty sure that it is the Aurora. Unfortunately, we don't see any movement around the downed plane, but from our height and limited visibility it is hard to confirm one way or the other. We will stand by and keep watching for movement."

Shawn was thrilled that the search part of the mission was over, but he was concerned that there wasn't any movement around the site. Surely if anyone were alive, they would wave or signal in some fashion to the overhead plane after it dropped flares. He kept reminding himself that the survivors may have extensive injuries that prevented them from venturing out, or perhaps the wind and the snow kept them from seeing the flares of the overhead plane. He had to remain optimistic.

"NATO E3A, thank you for your help. Did the flares show anything aside from the lack of movement?"

"Thule Ops, the downed airplane appears to be sitting on an ice island that protrudes ten to twenty feet above the rest of the pack ice. We saw some small buildings there that may belong to a geological survey team or oil drilling team, but nothing else. Eureka is about one hundred miles from the downed plane, in case you need a refueling stop for a helicopter."

"Thank you again, Col. Ashwood. I would appreciate it if you could stand by in the area until our other CP-140 can relieve you in about forty minutes."

"Will do, Thule Ops. We can only spare forty minutes of fuel. Now that we are over the site, my radar operator tells me that there seems to be a weaker second disturbance near the main disturbance. It could be something under the ice."

"Once again, thanks for your help. Please proceed on your mission as soon as our bird gets there."

The Search Master immediately opened communications with Aurora #740, now on route back from the Pole and nearing Alert as part of its first search track. Captain Kendall and Captain Mari Leech were ordered to proceed directly to the site near Ellef Ringnes Island, where the missing Aurora was located. They were to relieve the NATO plane and drop survival kits if they saw any movement around the downed aircraft.

The Greenwood Herc pilot was dispatched to Base Ops to round up WO Mackenzie and his crew and escort them aboard the Herc. A check on the weather at the site of the downed bird was also in order. It was time to give the Notice of Crash Location to the home RCC in Halifax. Shawn contacted the RCC Commander. An NCO in Thule relayed a partial NOCL. The notice contained some details about the downed aircraft's location, but was missing the details of the condition of crew on board. Phillips cautioned the commander to give the info only to "Digger" Holloway of 415 Squadron, while he relayed the same information to Brig. Gen. Shanahan of MAG HQ.

Sometime later, the Thule phone operator was able to connect Major Phillips to Shanahan at his home.

"Brigadier General Shanahan, it's Shawn Phillips. I want to update you on the progress of the Winters Search. We have just located the missing Aurora. It is down on an ice island near Ellef Ringnes Island. Unfortunately, the plane that spotted our missing craft site saw no movement near the crash, although there are buildings nearby that the survivors may have gone to for some warmth. We are about to move into the rescue phase of the operation. The Greenwood Herc is now being loaded with SAR technicians and their equipment. They are prepared to jump to the downed plane, weather permitting. We can have the Herc airborne within the next thirty minutes.

"There is nothing more I can do here at Thule except wait for the Huey helicopter to be reassembled, and that will take another four hours. I have a funny feeling about why our Aurora is down on the Arctic ice. My gut feel is based on some information that I casually received, and I would appreciate the opportunity to put my SAR training to better use. I want to jump with the SAR techs from the Herc to the crash site rather than wait for the helicopter to make the trip. If it's okay with you, I'll get Captain Mari Leech, First Officer of another Greenwood Aurora, to take over my office and run the Thule mini RCC. She is a competent and proficient officer, and she will make sure that the Huey chopper is ready to go when I call for it from the site."

The General didn't immediately reply when Shawn stopped talking. Shanahan had paused to think.

"OK, Shawn, I trust your judgment on this one. I know you jumped before, but probably not to a plane stuck on the pack ice. Just make sure you can do it safely. Otherwise, leave it to the real experts that do this sort of thing for a living. There is no doubt that the sooner you get there, the sooner we can find out about the crew and the cause. Perhaps we may not have to ground the fleet of Auroras after all. Get Captain Leech to call the main RCC here in Halifax if she needs advice."

Shawn grabbed his kit bag, and gathered up the various maps of the area where the downed Aurora was sitting. He asked Liaison Officer Reid to provide the same level of assistance to Captain Leech when she took over Shawn's office. After thanking Reid for all of his help, Shawn departed Base Ops and used the Follow-Me truck to get out to the Herc to join Rob Mackenzie and his techs.

# 4    JUMP TO CANADA'S ICE ISLAND

## 27 December 0800 hrs local //Ellef Ringnes Island Area

Having found the missing Aurora, the NATO E3A plane was released to continue its journey towards Hanscom Air Force Base. It was replaced by a second Aurora, #740, flown by first officer Captain Mari Leech. She relieved Capt. Chris Kendall once they learned that the missing Aurora had been found by the AWACS plane from the NATO base in Geilenkirchen, Germany.

While Aurora #740 was circling over the site, the Hercules contained the Search Master, WO Rob Mackenzie and the SAR team with their equipment. The Herc was destined for the Aurora crash location. Shawn would have an hour of transit time to review the area's topographical maps. He spread them out on top of a makeshift table, and he and Rob peered at them.

The radio officer of the Aurora #740 had reported that the downed plane was situated at precisely 78 degrees 30 minutes north latitude and 103 degrees 15 minutes west longitude. That placed the aircraft right between Ellef Ringnes Island and Meighen Island, on the edge of the permanent polar pack ice and not far from the North Magnetic Pole's location.

This spot on the map was labeled as "Canada's Ice Island". A footnote in a booklet that accompanied the map indicated that the ice island broke off from the central ice shelf on the northern coast of Ellesmere Island in 1982. It had moved slowly southeast from Ellesmere to its present position. The map's scale indicated that the ice island was approximately 80 kilometers north of Ellef Ringnes Island and 1,100 kilometers from the geographical North Pole, but practically on top of the Magnetic North Pole as it was currently situated. The booklet's note also mentioned that an ice island was an unusual piece of the landscape. It was not land, not iceberg, and not pack ice. It was a combination of the features of all three; a gigantic slab of freshwater ice, adrift in the Arctic Ocean. Surprisingly, the American booklet contained some interesting information about this ice island. According to it, Canada's Ice Island weighed about a billion tons and measured eight by four kilometers, horizontally. Vertically, it was as tall as a building fourteen stories high, though most of it was underwater. It was so huge and bulky that it dominated the surrounding ice pack. The booklet even stated that the island was afloat, although it was so stable that its motion went unnoticed. It ploughed a path through the ice pack, pushing the smaller pieces of ice aside as if they were fluff.

Warrant Officer Mackenzie spoke to the Major concerning the jump to the site. The pair had refrained from calling it a crash site since there was no indication of a crash. They liked to consider that it was possible that it landed on the ice without fuel. Technically it would not be considered a collision if the craft ran out of power due to human error, unless it was severely damaged in the landing. So far, they had no information on the state of the aircraft nor its inhabitants. Aurora # 740 had been trying for an hour to contact the downed plane, but there had been no response. There was a snowstorm in the area, which reduced their visibility to the point that the aircrew could only see the plane's hulk for a few seconds in the dim moonlight.

The SAR team leader left Phillips pouring over the maps while he attended business with the other SAR techs. He returned thirty minutes later.

"Sir, we'll be over the site in fifteen minutes. The winds are pretty stiff in the area, and there is some snow, but my guys are willing to give it a shot. If you want to jump with us, I'll lay out an orange SAR flight suit, a helmet, your heavy-duty parka, and some other gear for you at the rear of the Herc. I'll help you with your chute and with drop instructions once we get over the area."

"OK, Rob, I'm coming. I have to go use the radio to contact the Aurora circling over the site. I'll let them know that we're nearby and about to parachute in."

"Captain Mari Leech, with an i, this is Major Phillips with rescue flight 344. We will relieve you in the next fifteen minutes. You are free to return flight 343 to Thule. Commander of MAG, Brig. Gen. Shanahan, has directed that you take over the position of RCC Air Controller while I'm at the site of the downed plane. Upon reaching Thule, please make sure that the aircraft technicians finish the Huey helicopters' reassembly in case it is needed. Shanahan suggests that you contact the Halifax RCC if you need assistance."

"All yours, Rescue Three-Four-Four," said Captain Leech. "There is no way any of us would want to jump into that shit in this weather. It takes a lot of balls for what you guys are doing. Have a good flight in your chutes, and for God's sake, be careful. This is Captain Leech out!"

Shawn started to dress in the Hercules' rear, pulling the bright orange coveralls over his flight suit followed by a pair of old mukluks. Rob helped him to pull on his old parka. Shawn carried his white balaclava and lighted helmet to an area near the Herc's door, where Rob helped him with his parachute and checked his rigging for him. The SAR tech front pack included a flashlight, lantern, night vision goggles and spare batteries, while Shawn's also contained his miniature heavy-duty laptop.

Mackenzie spoke to the group that had gathered around him.

"We will be dropping flares that will enable us to see something of the drop site. There is blowing snow and winds of thirty kilometers an hour. The pilot says that he can get as low as two thousand feet, but that's about as close as possible. It looks like a farmer's snow-field down there and we don't know anything about the ice conditions. We are jumping onto an ice island. It is normally flat in the middle, with edges that are covered with tall and jumbled ridges of ice and snow. Try to stay away from the edge of the island. I estimate that we will be hitting the ice at about sixty miles an hour. We'll jump from a thousand feet, so a thirty-second count is appropriate. Flares will be dropped just before we jump. They should give us sufficient light if they're not blown away.

"Once you are down, bundle up your chute and head for the downed plane. At the crash site, we will split up into two groups. Some of you will be sent to gather up the supplies and equipment that will be dropped after we are down. The rest of you will search for survivors. We are stuck on the island until we can get a helicopter to pick up survivors and ourselves.

"That's the situation, guys. Some of you may get hurt in the jump because of the wind, snow, and ice conditions. No one will think any less of you if you decide not to jump. We all have families. If you prefer to stay up here, that is OK. There will be no comments or questions from me. Those of you prepared to go anyway, join me at the door and we'll jump as one. Major Phillips will jump alone and last."

All six SAR techs, and Shawn, stood next to Mackenzie. The Herc load master hooked the static parachute lines to the anchor line cable, and proceeded to open the hatch door while talking on his intercom to the pilot. He gave the thumbs-up, and the SAR group squeezed into the opening. They grabbed one another by the arm and waist and jumped.

Phillips waited thirty seconds, then stepped off the rear door. He dropped into the darkness, seeing nothing until a flare lit up the sky. Shawn was free-falling, so his speed of descent was faster than the others. Below him, he could see one of the techs struggling with his chute; it wasn't opening. Phillips maneuvered his body to bring himself in line with the tech.

He was falling quickly, and within seconds he fell on top of the rolling tech's body. Shawn wrapped one of his chute straps around the tech as they plunged together towards the ice. Shawn's chute filled with air, slowing the descent. They landed as a unit on the ice, and Shawn started to gather up his chute, while limping with a twisted ankle. The tech mumbled a word of thanks and started to move off.

"It's all part of a team effort," replied Shawn.

Back at the Hercules, the load master watched as the techs disappeared into the snowy Arctic heavens. Soon, their helmet lights were nothing more than tiny spots resembling the stars in some faraway galaxy on a clear Arctic night. He pressed the release, which held the SAR survival equipment containing food rations, medical instruments and accessories on its rollers. The equipment slid down the hatchway and out the door into the darkness. The door closed, and quiet and warmth returned to the Hercules fuselage.

Once Shawn landed and did some walking to get used to the pain in his ankle, he looked around to pinpoint the plane's location. Suddenly, a powerful flare lit up the pitch-black night for two minutes, and to his left, he could make out the silhouette of the plane. From his vantage point, the plane seemed to rest on the ice like a vast wounded bird. He knew that he would have a painful walk to the distant shadow of the aircraft.

The Major braced his feet then limped to the remains of his chute, collapsing it so that he wouldn't be dragged any further by the wind filled gutter. He gathered up the chute while checking for bruises and broken bones, finding only the twisted ankle, the odd bruise and no broken bones. He made his way towards the SAR tech who had landed near him. Phillips was relieved to find him in good spirits, with no bruises, after his near-death experience. Together they headed off towards the downed craft.

The Search Master sensed that the plane was out to his right, as they struck the ice. He estimated that they had landed half a kilometer away.

Shawn shuffled over the uneven ice surface, half carrying and half dragging his chute. It might come in handy later. *Who knows? It might be needed later for warmth or dressing a wound,* he thought to himself.

Phillips had a few hundred jumps to his credit since he took up skydiving, but this was the first time he had jumped into utter darkness from an aircraft flying at one hundred fifty knots over an ice island. The fact that he ended up with only a few bruises was a matter of good luck and his good physical condition. He wondered if any of the other jumpers were unlucky enough to land in the jumbled, shattered slabs, boulders, and columns of ice at the edges of the island.

As he made his way to the plane, he could make out, about two hundred meters away, the outlines of several small structures. He thought they were probably left behind by some geological team or some other environmental survey group. He could make out through the blowing snow at least two, maybe three, Quonset huts, and there were also several larger buildings with metal siding. He had read somewhere that geological survey teams typically spent the summer months on the Canadian ice island, just as the Russian scientists spent summers on their ice islands in the Arctic. The American geophysicists spent the summer season on their islands in Antarctica. The Quonset huts, however, were not the target of his march through the snow and ice.

Shawn unexpectedly fell into a trench in the snow. It was cut by the plane as the aircraft slid across the ice cap, obviously on its belly. He hadn't realized that the craft had skidded so far, and that he had landed so near to the absolute path of the downed plane. Phillips continued walking in the drifting snow for another half a kilometer, along the trench, through the blackness that was scarred only by a dim glow coming from the beam of his helmet light and handheld flashlight. He almost bumped into the port side outer engine cowlings, abruptly followed by the port inner engine coverings that were nearly covered by snow and barely visible.

In another few minutes, he had reached the plane. There were no other orange suited men in the neighborhood. Phillips was the first of the jumpers to approach the craft; he must have managed to land closer to the crash site than the SAR techs. The tech he saved was meters behind him as he checked out every gully for survivors.

Waiting for the others to arrive before entering the broken wreck was not an option. Waiting could mean the death of a survivor who may be just hanging on to life. Shawn walked down the outside length of the one hundred twelve-foot plane, around the tail, and up the other side. A simple check of the aircraft indicated that it was reasonably intact except for some damage to the wings and undercarriage area. The doors on the plane were partially covered by the snow piling up against the sides of the aircraft. There were no bodies outside of the plane, and even the area surrounding the aircraft did not indicate that anyone had set foot outside of the fuselage. There were no footprints or clothing or personal stuff to show if anyone made it out of the plane alive.

*It doesn't look right,* thought Shawn, as he climbed up a snowbank and onto the plane's nose. With a well-placed kick, he opened a side window in the cockpit. He dove through headfirst, expecting to land on some of the aircrew; instead, he landed on an empty seat. The whole pilot's compartment was empty of bodies.

A cursory look around the cockpit revealed that the throttles were closed, the undercarriage control was in the down position, and the flaps were at full. The fuel gauge read a one-quarter reserve, and all lamp toggle switches and circuits were in the off position. The crew's chutes were sitting on the overturned seats. The radio was switched to 7MHz. A set of headphones were on the floor, with one earpiece smashed. There was little evidence of impact damage in the cockpit area, but there was evidence of a hasty exit. *But where are the pilot and the co-pilot?*

Phillips continued to look for survivors. He had expected by now to see some of the aircrew in the main fuselage, perhaps one or more of the flight engineers, acoustic sensor operators, scientists, or others. He sent the flashlight beam through the gap made by the door, separating the pilot's compartment from the workstation areas. As he moved through the door he began to pull his parka together, realizing that it was bitterly cold. From end to end, the inside of the fuselage was covered in frost. It was like a giant walk-in freezer. The resupply rations were still in the containers. The blue plastic boxes were small enough to fit through the small hatch leading into the aircraft's belly. There was debris everywhere. Consoles were overturned and gauges were smashed. The floor was covered with equipment that had fallen from overhead shelving. Suddenly, Shawn noticed several blankets piled in a heap, covering something. He moved them aside to find two bodies, obviously dead, given the amount of frost and snow on top of them. A closer examination revealed that the two crew members were killed by flying consoles or pieces of equipment. There were large gashes and bruises to their faces and their bodies. They wore headsets, which made Phillips conclude that they were the TacNav and NavCom operators. They were the only occupants of the crashed plane.

*There is little chance of anyone surviving this bitter cold*, thought Shawn, *unless they wrapped themselves in sleeping bags*. He worked his way down the length of the plane, carefully swinging the light to see into every nook and cranny. He stepped over a radar console ripped from its mooring. The interior was mildly littered with papers, some clothing, box lunches and chutes. But there were no other bodies. And no survivors. There were no other bodies, living or dead, elsewhere in the fuselage or inside or outside of the plane. The rest of the aircrew of the crashed Aurora had disappeared. This was a mystery on the ice for Major Shawn Phillips, Search and Rescue Master.

# 5   MISSING CREW

27 December 1000 hrs local; Canada's Ice Island

Rob Mackenzie and the rest of the SAR techs eventually joined Major Phillips outside of the downed plane. Rob took the opportunity to thank Shawn for saving the life of his fellow tech.

"I saw what you did. The man doesn't want to talk about the incident. His wife said she would leave him if she hears about any dangerous stunts that might involve him."

"Then mum's the word," said Shawn.

Phillips told Mackenzie about the death of the two Aurora crew members. Mackenzie wanted to see the destruction for himself and entered the plane. He, too, was extremely puzzled about the missing aircrew.

Together, Phillips and Mackenzie helped the other techs carry chutes, supplies, and survival gear. They brought them towards the landing area about five hundred meters away, over too rough terrain that caused more bruising and a few twisted ankles. Fortunately, there were no broken bones. Once they assured Shawn that they would be OK, they questioned him about the whereabouts of the aircrew. Like Shawn, they were perplexed that there were no survivors, and only two casualties to be found in the vicinity of the aircraft. The only explanation that anyone could offer was that they must have walked, or were carried, to one of the survey buildings that they passed on their trek to the plane. The missing flight crew must have decided that it would be impossible to survive in the fuselage of the Aurora for any length of time, due to the extreme cold, and opted instead to seek warmth in the nearby buildings. This explanation seemed plausible. They reasoned among themselves that the causalities were left temporarily in the plane while the others made the trek to the shacks and huts some two kilometers away.

Shawn Phillips and the SAR team headed off towards the survey buildings. They were confident now that they would find all of the survivors in one of the buildings since it seemed most logical. The techs reasoned that the building was where they would go if they were in a similar situation. All of them must have survived the crash, and all of them must have made their way to one of the buildings where they would be warmer than in a frigid metal aircraft. They also reasoned that if anyone died in the crash, chances were that they would have been left in the plane where the cold temperature would preserve the body, rather than carry the casualties to the geological buildings.

As they walked, the team got progressively colder. There was no escaping it; it seeped in everywhere. The biting chill poured swiftly through the thickest clothing until every bone ached with it. Three of the six techs that were bruised in the jump, two with swollen ankles and the other with a twisted knee, were helped along by the other three technicians. The three pairs hobbled after the Search Master and team leader, managing to keep up. The slower pace meant that it took them twenty minutes to walk back along the crash trail towards the tin and wooden huts. While they walked, they spread a few feet apart in a horizontal line, using their flashlights, on the lookout for injured or deceased aircrew members. None were found.

Through the blowing snow, they could just see several wooden white huts that were barely covered with tin sidings and flat tar paper covered roofs. The buildings were probably used as living quarters for some of the survey team. In front of them were two larger buildings, similarly clad in tin and tar paper, which turned out to be the cookhouse and the Mess Hall. The Quonset huts, made entirely of metal, were at the end of the line of buildings.

The team approached what looked like the core hut with a gantry over its top. It was the first building they came across. They intended to search each building as they appeared, systematically, not to miss any of the survivors. They broke the lock and entered, their flashlights piercing the darkness. It was soon apparent that the building was vacant, and was probably vacant since it was abandoned at the end of the summer by the survey team. It was dark and dreary and smelled of rotting equipment. It housed ropes and tackle and winches, which were used to lower sampling equipment to the ocean floor. The smell indicated that these ropes were beyond redemption, and would have to be replaced in the spring. The floor contained a trap door used to reach the ice so that the survey crew could carve out chunks of it to expose the sea. The trap door was lifted to expose a drop of twenty feet of cold air to the frozen Arctic water. The twenty-five-year-old ice island's whole history was revealed in ice layers between the surface and the trap door.

The rescuers moved on, as a group, to the six white huts. Each was searched; all were vacant. All contained wooden bunk beds without mattresses and springs, and a table with two chairs. Most of the places had scraps of paper scattered about the floor and some unopened tins of vegetables on bare wooden shelves. The group ventured on to the next set of dwellings.

The larger buildings and Quonset huts remained to be checked. The larger buildings were the most logical place for the survivors to be grouped since they probably contained stoves or heating equipment of some sort. The next building that they approached turned out to be the cookhouse.

The door was unlocked, and they pushed it open and entered gingerly into the darkness. Shawn's flashlight swung around the room, bouncing off the walls before finally finding a resting place on a large cooking stove. No one cried out. The large greasy stove took up most of the room, while reams of wood laid piled in a corner, awaiting their turn to bring warmth and light. The lids were off the stove and stored on the table along with stacks of paper and dried out matches. There were cupboards and shelves around the building to hold the summer supply of food to be cooked, but all were empty at this time. There were no survivors to be found, yet it was the one place that each tech considered as the most logical and suitable facility to bring warmth to an aircrew suffering from shock and frostbite. After a quick look around, the team continued searching the Quonset huts, leaving the other large building to the last.

They entered the Quonset huts, one by one, peeling off and breaking locks and opening other doors. They looked in every corner, every dark space, to make sure that nothing, or no one, was missed. They saw battery chargers, spare generators, gasoline cans, more surveying equipment and some environmental testing machines. They filed out, leaving the doors adrift, and ran to the remaining large building; it too was locked.

They had run out of construction. This had to be where the Canadian aircrew had found refuge. As the team forced open the door, light snow was noticeable on the floor. It had seeped in through cracks between the door and its frame.

All of the techs entered, and all raised their lights towards the ceiling, then the walls, and finally to the floor. Their lights covered the room like a blanket covering a bed. They had found the Mess Hall where the geological crew gathered for meals and social interaction.

In the center of the room was a potbelly stove with chairs gathered around it awaiting their guests' bottoms. You could almost picture the survey crew telling stories as they swirled their coffee in their personally labeled mugs. Shawn's light came to rest on a large Mess Hall table where he observed that some plates and bowls contained scraps of food; evidence that one or more people had been there. Unfortunately, it was impossible to tell if they were there in the past few days or during the summer. The food on the table was frozen solid and unfit for human consumption. A few other tables containing cutlery dotted the hall-like room. Some were missing chairs that had migrated to the stove to absorb some of its life-saving heat.

The SAR techs and WO Mackenzie started a careful search of the Mess Hall, room by room, while Shawn watched in amazement. The building contained only the rescuers. *Where are the survivors?* There were no traces of any aircrew or footprints in the light snow on the floor except those made by the rescue team.

In frustration, they all sat down around the large Mess Hall table, dragging chairs over from the stove area. One tech lit a lantern that he found on a shelf above the wash sink. The light from the lantern gave the room a semblance of warmth.

The situation didn't make sense, and they had to think this one out. There were no living bodies in the plane and none in the survey buildings closest to the wreck. Where could they be? People don't just vanish. Could the flight crew have gone in another direction and found other facilities?

A group decision was made to make the Mess Hall their Ops Centre, and work out of there until they found some answers to their puzzling questions.

The team's first priority was to find the generator and get more lights working. They would put some of the firewood to use by firing up the potbelly stove. After these necessary survival steps, they planned to fan out in a circle and walk in all directions from one to two kilometers to the ice island's edge. But, first things first. Rob Mackenzie dispatched several of his crew to retrieve the rations and medical supplies that were airdropped from the Herc. They were to gather wood, paper, and matches, and bring gasoline for the generator, which they found in a lean-to that was part of the Mess Hall. Within forty-five minutes, the room was becoming fit for habitation; it was now warm and comfortable, and its inhabitants were able to loosen their parkas. Hot coffee was poured, and they consumed some of the rations to give them the energy they would need to continue the rescue mission. There was work to be done so that others could live.

Soon, it was time to return to the Arctic darkness and bone-chilling weather to take up the challenge of finding the aircrew. The mystery continued.

While others were out in the cold darkness, Shawn elected to stay behind and update the Thule RCC and the Herc crew, by radio, on the status of the search. Before the SAR crew departed, Shawn had one of the technicians set up the radio that was airdropped to them along with the other rescue equipment. It had survived the plunge to the ice and appeared to be in good working order. He used the VHF radio to contact the Hercules flying overhead.

"Rescue Flight Three Four Four, this is Major Phillips, Search Master for SAR Winters. You are released from the search to return to Thule. I would appreciate it if you could please send a message to Thule Ops and Maritime Command Headquarters for the MAG Commander and the Rescue Coordination Centre." Shawn took a breath and continued with the message to be relayed to various departments.

"Huey helicopter not needed at this time, but it should be ready for pickup of the SAR techs on short notice. The downed aircraft, better known as the Gray Ghost among squadron personnel, has been found and searched. The plane crashed on landing and is destroyed. There are two casualties still inside the aircraft. The remainder of the aircrew is presently missing. No survivors have been located. To emphasize, after a thorough search of the wreckage and some nearby buildings, we found two casualties and no, repeat, no survivors and no other bodies. We will continue looking for the missing crew. End of message. Phillips."

"Search Master, this is the First Officer from the Canadian Forces Hercules. Your message will be sent. We will return to Thule for refueling. A radio message received from the mini RCC in Thule has advised that the Cold Lake Herc is now heading out here to replace us as your cover. If you need any assistance, please contact Rescue Flight Three Four Six. I'm sure the pilot of that Herc will oblige."

Almost an hour after they left, the first SAR tech returned; he had seen no survivors, no bodies, and no place where the crew of the downed Aurora might have taken cover. The story was the same for each of the other techs.

Rob Mackenzie was the last to return. He had walked two and a half kilometers to the edge of the ice island, yet saw nothing but pack ice surrounding it. He reported finding a canvas tent covered with holes, belonging to the survey crew, about a kilometer west of the camp, but the tent was vacant and contained only ice melting equipment and instruments.

The situation was puzzling for Shawn and the others. It was well-known that the Air Force Standard Operating Procedure for survival required crew members to stay close to the downed plane. For some reason, in this case, the flight crew seemed to ignore the SOP. The rescue specialists had walked almost two kilometers in every direction radiating from the plane without finding any survivors or bodies. *Could they have missed them?* Shawn wondered. It was almost as if the ice had opened up and swallowed them.

The team had a brief conference and agreed that they would rest for the next couple of hours before covering the island once again. As a last resort, they would walk the island's circumference along its edge and look out to the surrounding pack ice to see if the missing crew may have ventured out onto the ice for some unknown reason.

After a four-hour rest the team did another search of the island, including another quick check of all the buildings, with negative results. They shuffled around the edge of the island, looking for any evidence that the crew had climbed down from the raised plateau and walked out onto the ice. Nothing was found. One of the techs did point out that part of the pack ice near the edge appeared to have been cleared and refrozen, since there was an area about one hundred and fifty feet in diameter that had chunks of ice surrounding a relatively flat ice surface. This area stood out as different from the rest of the sea ice which was cluttered with many large slabs of broken ice and pressure ridges. At the time, these ice features appeared insignificant. Major Phillips broke the silence that followed the observations of the SAR tech.

"I have to agree that particular ice surface is different." He pointed out towards the cluttered refrozen ice. "For once, my Dalhousie University environmental studies comes in handy. I know for sure that the area is either a frozen polynya, which is a hole in the ice, or alternatively, a submarine has recently busted through the ice at that site. It could have later submerged and the water refrozen. We need to check out that area a little more carefully to see just what happened at that spot."

They didn't find any footprints or dragging marks in the snow leading from the edge of the island. The team drew the obvious conclusion that the aircrew had not passed that way. Phillips, Mackenzie, and the techs used the waning light from their flashlights to find their way back to the survey camp.

Arriving at their make shift Ops building, they gave a lot of thought to their next move. As a group, they decided that before they quit, they would conduct a further search of the surrounding pack ice. The ice was their only hope of finding any evidence that the crew did exist after the plane struck the island. None of the eight team members could fathom why any of the aircrew would venture out onto the pack ice when there were splendid buildings that could be used to protect them until help arrived. Still, they all agreed with the plan to search the pack ice since it was the only place that had not yet been searched. It was the only hope that they had left. The team tried to catch some rest, but sleep wouldn't come. It was a mystery to every one of them what had happened to the crew of the plane, many of whom were their personal friends.

# 6    SEA DEVIL AWAY

20 December 0900 hrs local\New London, Connecticut

Six days before the search began for the Aurora, Bill Hayes sat behind a small desk in his cramped stateroom aboard a nuclear submarine, the U.S.S. Sea Devil.

Hayes opened the black leather briefcase containing the sealed orders handed to him at the Pentagon by the Director of Submarine Warfare, Rear Admiral B.E. Gunston. Hayes had been called to Washington on short notice just after he and the nuclear submarine crew had returned home from a sixty-day sea voyage. The Rear Admiral insisted on him personally flying to Washington to pick up the orders rather than forwarding them by the normal naval mail route.

While handing over the orders, the Rear Admiral seemed perplexed that he didn't know the content of the charges. He mentioned that they came directly from the Chief of Naval Operations, Admiral Reiner Heiserman, and were for the 'Eyes Only' of the Commanding Officer of the Sea Devil.

"It's not every day that a submarine commander gets direct orders from a four-star Admiral without the input of his boss."

Hayes and his crew were relaxing after returning from a NATO exercise in the North Atlantic. They were looking forward to spending the Christmas and New Year holidays with their families and friends. Sailing on short notice was a new situation to Commander Hayes.

He had no wife or children who would be disappointed in him returning to the sea so soon after a previous long voyage. He had no immediate family at all. The Navy, with the Sea Devil, was his home. The Sea Devil was his activity centre, where even his spare time was consumed. He had enjoyed the last fifteen years aboard various ships, and he resisted all attempts by his career manager to take a posting to a shore billet. Born on the east coast to poor parents, he endured many a day alone as his mother worked cleaning the homes of others, and his father sailed on many coastal freighters. While he loved both of his parents, it was his father that he idolized. He couldn't wait to follow in his footsteps, spending his life at sea. He was fascinated by the idea of living the life of a sailor. As a child, he spent all of his spare time at the seaside or at the dock aboard the liner on which his father was serving. The standard joke in the family was that he had seawater running through his veins instead of blood. Thirty years had passed since early childhood, yet he still longed for the open ocean waters.

For Hayes, there was once a woman who was the love of his life. Unfortunately, that love was torn away from him by a drunk driver. Hayes never dated again.

He was a tall and good-looking man with brown eyes and short black hair. He wore a full beard, as did his father, when he was working the ships. Onboard his boat, Hayes wore navy trousers and a turtle neck sweater with epaulettes containing his rank. He was at home in his cramped cabin, and loved to listen to classical music while updating his log or reading navy literature, including orders and regulations.

His friends would describe his personality as cheerful and full of life. Hayes kept healthy with an exercise routine that he did aboard ship, and he could be seen jogging along the Thames River whenever his ship was in the docks. As a leader, his men adored him because he stood up for their rights, and he protected both them and their families by using his rank and connections. His men would often introduce their wives to him, stating he was their captain, with a particular pride. Hayes was very proud to be the skipper of the world-class nuclear submarine, and he would do anything for his crew. They were his pride and joy; they were his family. He never regretted the time that the Navy took him away from the city or his relatives. The Navy had never given him cause to doubt his decision to spend the rest of his life at sea, nor was he ever in doubt that the submariner's life was the best decision he ever made.

"What do we have here?" he wondered, as he opened the envelope from Admiral Gunston. It looked like a new set of orders. Hayes read them out loud.

"These orders for the Sea Devil are in three parts. The first part can be read now, at home base, and the second part is to be read when the sub arrives at its destination. The third part is to be read later."

These orders sounded mysterious to Hayes. According to the first order, the captain and crew were to leave within 64 hours, with the utmost secrecy, for a point described as 80.0 degrees latitude and 100.0 degrees longitude.

Hayes was so curious to know where they were going, a destination that required so much secrecy, that he immediately used the intercom to call an aide to obtain half a dozen charts of different parts of the globe. Calling for maps for other parts of the inhabited world, he managed to maintain the secrecy of the actual destination.

The only map that mattered revealed that the point described in the orders was in the midst of the pack ice just off Ellef Ringnes Island, in Canada. The chart had a footnote to the effect that Canada claimed the waters surrounding the Queen Elizabeth Islands as Canadian territorial seas. Hayes was aware that the U.S. and Russians considered that area as international waters. He could see that one of the reasons for the secrecy might be to keep the Canadian government in the dark about a nuclear submarine in so-called Canadian waters. Apparently, the Chief of Naval Operations was operating on the principle that 'what you don't know won't hurt you'.

What Hayes had to do immediately was to get his sub ready for its journey without disclosing the exact destination to the crew. He knew from experience that if one crew member knew the mission's location, there was a high probability that the destination would leak out to others within hours. He decided to only disclose a little info to his Executive Officer, or XO, as the position was labeled in the U.S. Navy. For his other officers, Hayes used a few white lies. He told them that the ship was headed for a point near the U.S. airbase at Thule, Greenland. It wasn't far from the truth. Thule was also in Arctic waters, so by telling the officers that they were headed for the U.S. base, he could get them to load the supplies and equipment that they would need for Arctic operations without them knowing where they were actually going. His plan was to sail almost to Thule, then alter course as the sub neared Devon Island on the Canadian side of Baffin Bay. Only then would Hayes head into Canadian Arctic waters at Perry Channel. He had given the new mission considerable thought.

The next twenty-four hours were hectic as Hayes and his officers ordered and received, on a top priority basis, Arctic clothing, food and medical supplies, spare parts, ski-doos, torpedoes, camouflage material, and hundreds of smaller items. The Commander had to occasionally use the Rear Admiral's name to get the necessary equipment installed on an ASAP basis, especially since it required many hours of civilian overtime work. Still, it was essential equipment, and supplies and name dropping would enable the craft to get what it needed to navigate under the Arctic ice floes with a higher degree of safety.

The engineers installed inverted tachometers and two high-strength divers lights, mounted in such a fashion that Hayes would be able to see the underside of the ice. They were synchronized to work together with a closed-circuit TV and contained a lens mounted topside that faced upward. The television transmitter was placed on the main deck, ten feet in front of the sail. It was wired so that it could be controlled from the sub's control room. With Hayes' instruction, the dockyard ordered and installed a top-of-the-line inertial navigation system and two additional compasses. Since the orders indicated that the mission was to be completed at all costs, and to be on the safe side, Hayes ordered additional automatic weapons for his crew to augment the ship's Tomahawk missiles.

For the classified operation, the XO, Lt. Commander Jack Murphy ordered, through non-Navy sources, the latest charts and publications covering the entire area from the North Pole to New London, including Greenland and the Canadian waters. He even drove a hundred miles to the source to pick up the documents personally.

It was not unusual for nuclear subs to venture under the geographic Pole. There had been a number of submarines that had mapped the ocean floor under the ice since the Nautilus crossed the Pole in August 1958. The Skate surfaced at the Pole in March 1959. Getting maps of the ocean floor was not a major problem, but obtaining information on ice conditions, specifically just how deep some of the enormous blocks of ice protruded beneath the surface, proved more difficult. Fortunately, Hayes was able to locate a squadron that had some U.S. Navy planes that were involved in a joint U.S.-Canada Photo Reconnaissance Exercise in Alaska and North West Territories during the summer months. After a few phone calls to the Squadron Commander, whose aircraft had recently flown over the Canadian Arctic, Hayes was authorized to use film taken by squadron aircraft as it flew over the Canadian ice pack. The XO was dispatched to fetch the film.

On reviewing the film, Hayes and Murphy looked for massive pressure ridges or icebergs stuck in the pack ice. They reasoned that a considerable ice projection above the surface of the pack ice would have corresponding bubbles underneath it. The underwater protrusions would be a potential problem if the ship encountered them while submerged. If the Sea Devil came upon any monstrous piece of ice projecting thirty feet or more under the surface, the navigator would have to steer carefully, taking the submarine either around it or under it, with exceptional care, so as not to strike it with the sub's sail.

The film revealed several ice ridges that they estimated as twelve feet thick and fifteen feet high. The locations of these large rafted ice projections were dutifully noted along with drift conditions. The squadron film also showed several polynyas as well as some leads where the sub could surface if need be. Some of these polynyas remained unfrozen year after year. There was one large polynya within a couple of miles of their destination. Of course, this particular one could be frozen over by three or more feet of ice, if it still existed. The Sea Devil could burst through recently formed ice if the polynya was still there. However, with the ice constantly shifting, there was no guarantee that it would exist on the day the Sea Devil arrived.

Once the crew was assembled, the Executive Officer put them to work storing all the supplies. Next, he assigned them the duty of removing all identifying signs and markings that indicated the ship belonged to the U.S. Navy. Even the name, Sea Devil, was removed from the hull.

The Chief of Naval Operations, Admiral Heiserman, made an unexpected visit to the ship, a day before the scheduled departure date. Captain Hayes took the opportunity to brief the Admiral on the preparations that he made for the mission.

The Admiral was generally pleased with the submarine's readiness, but he had come early to make some additions to the preparations already made by the captain.

"I've taken the liberty of adding a new crew member to your ship. He is Battery Commander Marsh, and he is a very proficient Surface-to-Air Missile Operator. I can personally vouch for his expertise since he sailed with me on several trips along the Vietnam Delta. We have also requisitioned the latest portable SAM launcher from the Navy's inventory. Together, Marsh and the launcher will give you the extra protection that you may well need on this voyage. It's most likely that you won't need the SAM, but this mission is so important that I insist you have these missiles on board."

"I thank you for your good intentions, Admiral, but decent bunking onboard is at a premium. Several of my men are capable of using missile and rocket launchers, so I would prefer to use my own crew."

"Nonsense. I insist. He was with me for years, so I know that he is used to bedding down almost anywhere. Besides, your men have other primary duties that may require their presence during any submarine emergencies. I'll just brief Marsh on his duties and tell him that he is to take whatever space you can assign to him, and he is to stay out of the way of your crew unless he is needed."

Heiserman sauntered over to the man he referred to as Battery Commander Marsh.

Hayes watched as the two men spoke, although Admiral Heiserman seemed to do most of the talking. At times, they appeared to be whispering and looking at him and the Sea Devil with bewildering faces. They laughed occasionally and shook hands. It was strange, to Hayes, to see a four-star Admiral shaking the hand of an enlisted man. He was unable to hear their conversation, and it would have saved him a lot of future grief and heartache if only he had the foresight to listen to what the Admiral said to the new member of the Sea Devil.

"Remember," Heiserman said to Marsh, "I don't want this sub, or myself, connected in any way to this operation. Do you understand? I'm counting on you."

Heiserman returned to Commander Hayes, wishing him a successful mission, then departed.

The next day arrived quickly, and it was time to get underway. The Sea Devil slipped quietly away from the dock and headed down the Thames River into Long Island Sound. Hayes had done all he could do in the short time he had to prepare for the voyage. To the best of his knowledge, no one knew of their destination except himself, his XO, and the Admiral who issued the strange orders.

Mid-January would have been a better sailing date as far as Commander Hayes was concerned. Then, his crew could spend shore time and the Holiday season with their loved ones. However, Admiral Heiserman had insisted that the journey be done immediately, otherwise it would be too late. After leaving Long Island Sound, the Sea Devil sprinted into Brock Island Sound, then headed north while still cruising on the surface. Shortly thereafter, Hayes prepared SSN 664, and the 142 enlisted men and 14 officers on board, for a journey into forbidden waters.

"Clear the bridge! Clear the bridge!" ordered the officer-of the-deck over the speaker system. All onboard could hear the two blasts of the diving klaxon. Hayes saw that the dials in the control room showed all hatches were closed, and that all radio masks and periscopes were protracted. An engineer pushed down on the proper switches, and the

Sea Devil's ballast tanks began to fill with seawater. The diving planes on the sail were adjusted, and the 292-foot craft slipped quietly beneath the waves.

To reassure the crew that there was nothing unusual or unsafe about the voyage's initial departure, Captain Hayes addressed the team over the P.A. system.

"All hands! This is Captain Hayes. You will find this to be an interesting cruise. We are to proceed, under sealed orders, to a geographical position near the U.S. Air Force Base at Thule, Greenland. Only as we approach Thule will our final destination become known. We are under orders to maintain secrecy during the trip. As a result, we will not be breaking radio silence until we are on station. In the next five days, we will be cruising at thirty knots while submerged. We will pass the city of Halifax, Nova Scotia, head for Cape Breton Island, and pass through the Cabot Strait and Strait of Belle Island, between the northwestern tip of Newfoundland and Labrador. We will head north along the coast of Labrador towards southern Greenland. We will do everything necessary to avoid detection by our own aircraft and Canadian ASW aircraft. That is all. I will speak to you again as we reach the edge of the drifting pack ice."

During the next five days, the crew stood four-hour watches as well as repaired and cleaned equipment. Off-hours were spent in their bunks, the crew recreation area, or in the galley where they filled themselves with excellent food and beverages. They watched movies and videos, played their stereos, and engaged in different kinds of games.

Several crew members availed themselves of the exercise machines and weightlifting equipment. The officers used their free time to keep up with their reading while some studied for exams.

Commander Hayes kept mostly to himself. When he was not on the bridge, he was in his stateroom focusing on his final destination and concentrating on the problems that he might encounter during the mission. He gave considerable thought to the Chief of Naval Operations and his quirks.

Hayes wondered just who this Admiral was. The Chief of Naval Operations, Admiral Reiner Heiserman, was not completely unknown to Commander Hayes. They had met once before at a cocktail party in Washington, while the Sea Devil was in the dry dock for a few weeks. Hayes was attending a refresher course on Anti-Submarine Warfare. He couldn't recall much of their short conversation during the cocktail party, but he could recall, vividly, the lecture given by the Admiral at the school the next day. Heiserman was talking about SOSUS, the Sound Surveillance System. It was the U.S. Navy's underwater detection system. Heiserman had explained that each sub had its own distinctive sound or signature, and that it could quickly become recognizable.

To Heiserman, there was no doubt that he considered the so-called Northwest Passage as international waters and strongly condemned Canada for claiming these waters as their own. He went on to say that he was in favor of any action necessary, even military, to show Canada that these waters, and the whole of the Arctic, were vulnerable to a Russian takeover, threatening the security of the U.S.

Heiserman wanted hydrophones planted on the floor of the Arctic, come hell or high water. It was obvious to Hayes that the Admiral was not impressed with Canadian efforts to keep Russian submarines out of the Canadian north. The Canadians had no nuclear subs of their own, to operate under the ice, to find Soviet subs.

The Admiral was quite passionate about the need to detect Russian subs by their sounds. A submarine's noise originated from propeller turbulence, and Soviet-built propellers had been noisier than Western-built propellers.

The Russians had found ways to decrease the sound of their subs. They insulated the propulsion unit from the hull with resilient mountings. They had enveloped the outside of the relief with an anechoic coating, which reduced the amount of energy reflected by an active searching sonar. They rounded out the hull's shape to minimize turbulence, and they built the hull using titanium to reduce the magnetic effect of the hull and avoid triggering mines. The titanium also minimized the possibility of detection by airborne Magnetic Anomaly Detection equipment. MAD equipment was carried by NATO planes, including those of the U.S. and Canada's Aurora aircraft. With those types of improvements, the Russian SSNs had become substantially more elusive.

Hayes remembered that Heiserman ended his lecture by swearing that he would find a way, any way, to put super sensitive hydrophones in the so-called Canadian Arctic, with or without the help of the Canadian Government.

As he laid on his bunk, Hayes stopped wondering. He remembered the rage and the power that was in Admiral Heiserman's voice when he spoke about the need to protect Canada's north from Russian subs. It was not that the Admiral had any love for Canada, but mainly as a means of protecting the U.S. from missiles that these subs may lob at his country.

Hayes warned himself about the temper and rage of the Admiral. The man's ideas made him the type of man that one didn't want to cross, because he would hunt down and take revenge upon whomever did.

Throughout the Navy, it was rumored that Heiserman was an ambitious man who stepped on subordinates to achieve his goals. It was considered unwise to get in his way, either physically or verbally, during one of his tirades. His six-foot-three stature gave him the advantage of fighting to obtain the men and equipment he wanted for a particular mission. His height and loud voice often gave him verbal superiority in any debate. Hayes figured that Heiserman's biggest disappointment was that he could not bully his way with the Canadian government. Still, he did influence some senior Canadian naval officers who were putty in his hands.

There appeared to be only one other goal that Heiserman pursued with greater zeal; he spared no effort to procure sufficient backing and funds to enter the presidential race. As he saw it, by becoming President, he would not only put his stamp on the U.S. Government and U.S. military policy, it would give him the personal comfort and respect that he craved.

Hayes was half awake and half in dreamland. He foresaw in his dream, Admiral Heiserman destroying the Sea Devil. He awoke abruptly when Lt. Cmdr. Murphy knocked on the cabin door, wishing to discuss additional security procedures. All thoughts and dreams about the destruction of the Sea Devil vanished. Hayes' short nap gave him the second wind that would see him through another eight hours on the bridge.

# 7    UNDER THE ICE

Dec 24, 1200 hrs local, Off Ellef Ringnes Island

The trip north, to this point, was uneventful for the Sea Devil except for one occasion when the sub was on the surface, along the Labrador coast, and Hayes wanted to check navigation and receive radio messages.

While operating the ship's bridge, on the sail, a spotter saw a Canadian Aurora, a sub- detecting aircraft, flying towards them. The alarm was raised, and Hayes ordered the Submarine to make an emergency dive and alter course. There was no action taken by the sub hunter, which continued to its destination. Hayes waited twenty minutes before bringing the sub near the surface to check, by periscope, the darkened sky for evidence of the aircraft. There was no sight of the plane on radar or through the scope; apparently, it had returned to its original flight path. After another twenty minutes, the sub returned to her original course. Had the sub hunter reacted differently, the future of the Sea devil might have been more glorious.

A few days of sailing passed without any memorable events. On the fourth day out of port, the navigator presented Captain Hayes with the Sea Devil position on their map. The sub was still in Baffin Bay, a thousand kilometers from the entrance to Perry Channel. Hayes decided to stay with the plan to sail north along the Davis Strait and Baffin Bay, hugging Greenland's coast, thus maintaining the impression that the Sea Devil was headed for Thule through international waters.

The ship sailed into the perpetual darkness zone on that day, and later that same day, the sonar operator reported the edge of the drifting pack ice off the coast of Greenland, approximately fifty nautical miles from the Arctic Circle.

The sea ice caused a bit of concern for Hayes. He guided the ship to periscope depth and ushered the sub closer to the edge of the ice, moving at dead slow speed. The newly installed spotlights shone brightly, like a lighthouse beacon, onto the ice surface. For a considerable period, the Captain inspected the long rugged line of ice in front of him. Several sailors desired a look at pack ice, so the second periscope was raised for them. Hayes could see that the ice was not stable. It consisted of a mass of jagged chunks that had broken off the Greenland ice cap and floated until piled up. Some of them were twenty feet high. Many of the pieces were of massive size, several tons in weight, and dozens of feet across.

After checking the ice conditions from head-on, Hayes commanded the sub to run parallel to the irregular edge for a mile or two, to see if long leads were heading north. If he could find such a lead, the sub could sail near the surface, perhaps, for another hour or two, thereby delaying the impending dive under the ice.

Slight movements in the ice were visible through the scope. The larger blocks seemed to wallow gently in the water. Once in a while, a part of the underbelly side of the chunk was seen. It was darker than the greenish tinge near the top of the piece. Periodically, a spray of seawater squirted between the ice, coating the sides of it and practically freezing to the mass. Little, if any, ran down the side. Some of the beacon light reflected off the ice clumps while throwing ominous shadows on others. Hayes turned up the magnification of the periscope, and it made the scene even more eerie and unsettling.

The lumps of ice were solid, but the surrounding ice was so loose that neither people nor polar bears could stand on it. As the Sea Devil ran along the edge, Hayes could find no leads, and the pack ice seemed to become more solidified. After he and the XO had inspected the ice sufficiently, the decision was made that there was no point in delaying the inevitable dive. The navigator confirmed the geographical position of his ship for the captain. Using both hands, Hayes gently shoved the handle controlling the hoist of the hydraulic periscope and watched as the silver metal tube slid quietly into its housing.

"Take her down to a hundred feet," Hayes said to the Diving Officer. The sub proceeded under the ice. It was the first time the Sea Devil and any of its crew had submerged under any pack ice. Reaching for the handset and the speaker switch of the PA system, Hayes gave his team some assurance.

"Listen up men! This is the captain. We are now under the floating ice. Our ship has no danger. Our tachometers show that the ice is jagged and broken and protruding under the surface only to six feet. As a result, we have over 55 feet from the top of the sail to the ice, and we have 65 feet under our keel. We are now relatively safe from detection unless there is another sub under the ice with us. Should anything happen to our reactor, we can easily surface through the pack. If worse comes to worst, we can use our torpedoes to blow a hole through the ice. We should be off the coast of Thule in twenty-four hours. Out!"

Hayes preferred not to deceive his men about their final location, but he was a firm believer in the 'need to know' principle of security. If one didn't need to know some classified information, it shouldn't be told to them.

As the Sea Devil drove ever northward, her sonar operator watched conscientiously as the sonar probed ahead. Hayes listened for any mushy return echo that would spell danger, even though the sub was proceeding cautiously. The sub was not like a car that could almost stop on a dime. She would continue to glide forward, even when the propulsion was cut to a dead stop. That could mean disaster, mostly if the sonar operator missed a return echo. The only evasive action the captain may have, if there were not plenty of warning of danger ahead, was to turn onto another bearing or dive deeper using an emergency dive. The Sea Devil's sonar operators were among the best-trained seamen in the U.S. Navy, and Hayes felt comfortable enough in their competence that he left the control room and retired to his cabin to do some thinking and perhaps have a needed nap.

Several hours later, the ship's telephone rang in Hayes' cabin. It was the Executive Officer.

"It's time for the course change as we discussed, Captain."

"OK. I'm on my way." He was laying down and thinking about how to make the course change when he must have drifted off to sleep. He again had the dream about Heiserman and something dangerous happening to the Sea devil.

"Make your course due east to Jones Sound," Hayes instructed the officer who had control, "then follow the route plotted on this map, through the Queen Elizabeth Islands to Ellef Ringnes Island. Increase speed by ten knots until we reach the Sound."

Once again, he addressed his men on the ship's general communication system.

"Men! As per our sealed orders, we have made a course change that will take us into Canadian territorial waters. We are to proceed discreetly to a point just north of Ellef Ringnes Island, where we will open our mission orders. Regretfully, it may be several more days before we will be near our Air Force Base at Thule. Hopefully, at that time, we can arrange for you to visit the base and the PX for a little post-Christmas shopping. Out."

The chatter among the crew rose a decibel or two at the news that they could be at an Air Force base in several days. The discussion among them centered on what they would do at Thule and what they would buy at the canteen. No one gave any thought to the fact that they were entering the waters of a foreign country without permission.

The waters of Jones Sound were not as deep as those of Baffin Bay, off Greenland's southeast side. Hayes wished that he had access to the many depth soundings that he was sure were made by Canadian research teams over the last ten years; they would have made his task a hell of a lot easier. As it was, the submarine had to slither her way north between Devon Island and the southwest tip of Ellesmere Island, then pass Graham and Cornwall Islands in Norwegian Bay, continuing under the multi-year ice at Amund Ringnes Island, onward north to Ellef Ringnes Island, and finally, a dogleg towards their predetermined destination. The Sea Devil was now in the neighborhood of the North Magnetic Pole.

Occasionally, the navigator had to avoid large hummocks that protruded many feet below the surface, blocking the ship's way. Thankfully, the fathometers and sonar worked exceptionally well, so he knew in advance of these blockages. Whenever they encountered such a protrusion, the captain ordered that it be approached at a crawl speed. Using their measuring devices, high beam lights, and closed-circuit TV, Hayes, the XO, and the navigator looked for ways around the ice mass if the ship couldn't pass under it safely. It was a slow and tedious journey that took the boat twice the planned time to reach its destination. Eventually, the Sea Devil arrived at longitude 100.0 and latitude 80.0 as dictated by the Chief of Naval Operations.

Once the ship was on station under the ice, the Captain needed to surface to let Washington know that he was ready to carry out the submarine's mission. The upward beamed thermometer indicated that the ice above the ship was a solid cover. The polynya on the film no longer existed as open water; it had long since been frozen over or covered by the drifting ice.

Hayes ordered the Sea Devil's speed cut to minimum creeping speed and brought the ship up gently so that the top of the scope, when raised, would be around twenty-five feet from the underside of the ice floe. He reached for the handles and slowly brought the periscope up from its well until it was level with his eyes while simultaneously increasing the magnification.

Looking through the lens, what he saw resembled what a fish in a fishbowl would see by looking upward. The overhead ice seemed like a glass ceiling with an uneven surface. The beams from the lights, mounted on the sail, reflected off the ice's underside and the surrounding seawater, making him feel small and insignificant. The scope was rotated slowly through three hundred and sixty degrees, revealing nothing in the seawater, not even fish. The submarine was at her required position yet there was nothing underwater to tell the captain why the ship was there. The sub would have to surface. Perhaps at that time they would see something that might explain to Hayes why the U.S. nuclear sub was hundreds of miles into Canadian waters.

The thermometer found another polynya near the one on the film. It was covered by four feet of ice, which should be no problem for the Sea Devil to break through. The shipyard manager had assured everyone that the changes made to the sub would allow the ship to surface through six feet of ice. Circling the polynya while diving deeper to seventy feet and directly below the thinnest part of the polynya, Hayes trimmed the sub and gave the order to bring her up.

"Stand by the radio and have the bridge party properly dressed to clear the ice," Hayes said to the Executive Officer. Then to the Diving Officer, "Bring her up so that only the sail is above the ice. Keep her on an even keel as you bring her up. Watch for any changes in the water's specific gravity. There will be freshwater trapped directly under the ice that will affect the buoyancy. Bring her up at a steady rate."

Hayes heard the sound of air blowing into the tanks and the gushing of water. The sub started to rise. He had to house the scope so that it would not buckle as the top of the sail hit the ice under the surface. The bow planes were next to be rigged in. He was reaching for the microphone to notify the crew that they were about to surface through the ice, wanting to spare them from any surprises, when the sub hit the ice with a jolt.

There was a loud crunching sound, and the deck seemed to drop away from Hayes' feet for an instant. As he regained his balance, he could hear more creaking of stressed metal along with the rattling of vast blocks of ice against the sail. The scraping sound of ice on steel stopped for a moment as the sail broke through. The sub continued to rise.

"Blow the ballast!" yelled Hayes, just as the sub made contact with the ice above it.

Within moments, the Sea Devil had cracked the sheet of ice, and the sail was resting above the surface of the pack. Hayes raised the search periscope very slowly, hoping that there wasn't a ton of ice sitting on top of the hole where the scope rose from the sail. Luckily, it went up without a problem.

There was twenty-four hours of darkness in that part of the Arctic at that time of the year, but he dared not turn on any searchlights to see if there were dangers present. Hayes did a quick 360-degree check for signs of, or lights from, anything on the surface or above it. A slower examination using a night vision scope only showed that neither man nor beast had ventured out in the cold.

"Do an electronic sweep," ordered the Captain. The electronics officer raised the antenna mast, and watched the frequency scanner closely.

"Nothing in the immediate vicinity, Captain."

"OK! Let's go topside to see why we are here."

There was some ice on the hatch, but nothing that would prevent it from opening. Hayes gave the order to clear it, and the bridge party started to squeeze their way up the ladder and through the portal. The bits of ice on the bridge were quickly tossed over the side using shovels and hands. Within minutes, the bridge party leader reported that the bridge was clear of obstructions, and the XO directed them to make their way back to the warmth of the crew's mess.

Hayes was still under orders that the sub was not to be detected. Before exiting the sub to the sail, his first command was that a lookout be posted, and that the lookout was to be changed every twenty minutes.

The Captain and the XO climbed to the bridge and viewed the surrounding pack ice with their night glasses. There was nothing to see except mounds of broken ice in all directions. The wind howled and ripped at their parkas, but the cold night didn't give them any reason why they and their crew had made the trip to be on station near the Magnetic Pole on Christmas Day.

Captain Hayes returned to his cabin and opened the safe containing the second set of mission orders. They were also from Admiral Heiserman and included explicit instructions on the next steps in their operation. The orders read:

*TOP SECRET-OPERATION POLAR GLORY*
*To: Commanding Officer-Sea Devil-Captain B. Hayes*
*From: Chief of Naval Operations-Admiral R. Heiserman*
*Subject: Rendezvous with MIR*

*On 28 December at approximately 0100 hrs (plus or minus 2 hours) Arctic Time, the Russian Space station* MIR *is expected to return to earth within a fifty-mile radius of a point located 80.0 degrees' latitude and 100.0 degrees' longitude. You are to recover the black box, computer, and several other listed items from MIR with the utmost speed and secrecy and proceed to a submerged point off the capital city of Nunavut-Iqaluit, in Frobisher Bay. Under no circumstance are you to take any action that may cause you to be detected by any foreign country. Should you be seen, you are to take whatever action is necessary to prevent the knowledge of U.S. involvement in this rendezvous from being disseminated. The mission objective is only to be shared with limited officers aboard the Sea Devil. Confirm by a message that you are in position and that orders are understood and destroyed.*
*Admiral L. Heiserman*

Captain Hayes read the orders a second time, folded the paper, sealed it in an envelope and deposited it back in the safe for the time being. At least he finally knew why he was there.

*How does Heiserman know that MIR will land at this location?* The question bothered Hayes. The possibility of sabotage touched his mind and was gone in a flash. It was replaced with the thought that it couldn't happen. *But could it?* He didn't understand how the Admiral knew of the space station's landing so much in advance of its return from space, and why it was landing there and not in some area in Russia. He was convinced that there had to be a logical explanation. Perhaps the United States had some agreement with Russia. He wondered what was on the videos and recordings that made it so important that he should risk his crew's lives to recover them. Remaining undetected could be tricky, especially when news hit the TV stations that the spacecraft was going to land in the frozen Canadian wastelands. Until that time, the Sea Devil should be relatively safe. However, once the news was out to the Canadians and the Russians, their danger increased tenfold.

What he should do until the spacecraft arrived was the next logical question. He could order the ship to dive and remain in a holding pattern around the polynya for the next twenty-four hours, then hope that they could find the polynya again around the space station's ETA.

Alternatively, he could stay where he was with just the sail protruding above the ice. The latter option allowed him to be open for any messages beamed his way and to track the space station as it descended. Knowing where it landed would speed up the recovery of the recorders, film, and computers, assuming that the craft didn't destroy itself or sink into the depths of the Arctic waters. This latter option allowed the ship to depart the area quickly if foreigners came looking for MIR. After considering and evaluating the alternatives, Hayes opted to stay on the surface and keep a constant electronic watch.

The Captain of the Sea Devil dictated a message to be sent directly to Admiral Heiserman, advising him of the ship's arrival. Hayes needed only to sit and wait for MIR. He surely didn't think, last Christmas, that he would be spending this Christmas Day standing on the bridge of a submarine at the magnetic north pole, under a frigid sky, with the Aurora Borealis as his Christmas lights.

Since it was Christmas Day, he suggested to the XO that he stand down the crew, except those posted to lookout duty. The crew were given drinks and allowed to erect a makeshift Christmas tree, sing Christmas songs, and exchange gifts if they so wished. They were allowed to venture onto the bridge and view the expanse of the ice under the moonlight. The crew was used to the hardships of duty while in a sub, so spending Christmas Day at the top of the world, under darkness, and with winds pushing the temperature to -35 degrees, was not so out of the ordinary for them. This Christmas would be one that the crew would remember, thought Hayes. How right he was!

# 8 MISSILE ATTACK

25 December, 0200hrs local, Thule, Greenland,

An hour before the Distress Air event developed in Halifax, Captain Frank Winters was sitting in the first officer seat of his Aurora, in Thule, Greenland. He had the same exhilarating feeling that he had every time he strapped himself into the pilot's seat on an Aurora. He once described it to his wife of twenty years as the greatest thrill of his life, but it was the beginning of the end for him as a submarine hunter.

The plane had just taken off from Thule Airbase with a ten-man crew and two scientists onboard. Frank was sitting at the controls of Aurora #739, on flight Alfa Foxtrot 739, on the fifth day of a six-day unscheduled Northern Patrol. He was enjoying the power of the bird as it roared from the tarmac and grabbed for the open skies. The engines' power gently rocked him in his seat as the craft reached the apex of its climb and leveled out at ten thousand feet. He was in a festive mood, after all, it was the Christmas holidays and today would be a routine operation. With luck, they should be back at Thule in time for a delightful Christmas supper at the Officer's Club.

The official flight plan called for one leg from Thule to Alert to drop off some Christmas supplies and packages for the spy station's inhabitants. Then on to the magnetic North Pole where the scientists would conduct some experiments on global warming for a few hours, followed by a flight over the Pole to view the ozone hole. Then finally, the last leg of the trip that would bring them back to Thule. Not on the official flight plan, but noted in his flying log, was a short trip over the Eureka Weather Station to drop off a canister given to him by Vice-Admiral Lowery. The note in the record read: "25 December, make an unofficial and unrecorded detour to Eureka Station, as requested by Vice Admiral Lowery, to drop off a canister."

The Aurora crew on this flight consisted only of essential aircrew members since the support crew, consisting of aircraft technicians who would typically travel on the craft as it flew from location to location, had requested that they remain behind in Thule for this particular flight. Since this part of the Nor Pat was relatively routine, the support crew and aircraft technicians wanted to stay at Thule to ride out their post-Christmas Eve party hangovers. They wanted to partake in a little pre–Boxing Day sales by spending their hard-earned dollars buying goodies at the PX at low American prices. The PX was scheduled to start its sales on Christmas Day. After all, there wasn't much else to do at the Thule Airbase besides drink and shop.

On their trip to the North, first-timers couldn't wait to fly over the geographical North Pole so that they could tell their family and friends that they had been to the top of the world. There was less excitement among most Nor Pat crew members to see the North Magnetic Pole, shown on the flight maps as located in the Queen Elizabeth Islands. Perhaps the lack of excitement was due to the nature and movement of the Magnetic Pole, which hid its exact location. When discussing the it, scientists, including those on board, would only refer to its average site.

The Pole could not be defined as a point on a map. Instead, it was an elusive target, in constant motion as it traveled a daily jagged elliptical path in a clockwise direction over a wide area. The only thing that a crew member would see in the Magnetic Pole area was a compass needle turning lazily and unpredictably in all directions because of the lack of horizontal magnetic pull. Frank readily agreed to the ground crew request to stay behind since he could easily understand the PX's attraction, and the Mess', comparing the joy filled places to the bleakness of a snow-covered and ice-encrusted revolving spot on the Arctic Ocean.

Frank Winters had another reason for exuberance; the next day was his forty-ninth birthday, which meant that he had less than a year until he reached the compulsory retirement age for the rank of Captain. When he returned to Greenwood, the first thing he planned to do was to submit his retirement papers. As much as Frank loved flying Auroras, he had decided that it was time to call it a day. Just a week prior, Frank had a discussion with his career manager in Ottawa, who promised him that any request for extension of his service career beyond the age of forty-nine would be favorably received and likely approved.

The manager even said that there was an excellent chance that Frank would be promoted to Major during the extra year, should he ask for an extension. An extension and promotion meant that he could stay in the service until he was fifty-five. But the career manager was unable to guarantee him that he would be transferred from Greenwood to Trenton, where he could fly the Forces' Boeing 707s. Ever since he was a little boy, he wanted to play with the 'big boy toys'. That would be the ultimate in his career.

Unfortunately, the Air Force had enough Boeing 707 pilots for the next few years, so his choices consisted of staying at Greenwood and flying Auroras for several more years or be posted to Defense Headquarters in Ottawa. The latter suggestion was something that Frank would avoid like the plague. He had already flown the Aurora for four years, and he wanted to move on to bigger aircraft that would enhance his chances of joining Air Canada after his retirement. He and his wife had quietly considered that this would most likely be his final year with the Forces. Frank planned to submit his retirement papers the following week and be out as a civilian in a few months with a full pension.

During the past couple of months, Frank had used some contacts to feel out the possibility of flying the 'big boys' with Air Canada, out of Toronto. His contacts assured him that his four years of flying Auroras were already sufficient to guarantee employment. They indicated that within a few months he could be employed flying 707 cargo runs from Toronto to the west coast. This was fine by him since he had little tolerance for passengers' shenanigans.

Employment with Air Canada depended upon, among other things, his remaining healthy. Frank managed to jog a mile a day whenever he wasn't flying and considered himself fit and agile. He had full use of all of his faculties and extremities, so passing the Air Canada physical was not foreseen as a problem.

One of the reasons for Frank considering leaving the Forces was the monotony of the flights to the North, and the fact that the Nor Pat took him away from his lovely wife and their two teenage kids. It was time for him to settle down in one place, where his kids would have an attachment to a 'home' town and perhaps, in time, attend a nearby university. His father had already agreed that he would sever part of his grape farm in the Niagara Peninsula and build a home. The Niagara region would be ideal since Frank would be near his aging parents. He could also commute to Pearson Airport, in Toronto, for his Air Canada flights. There was even the nearby Brock University that the kids could attend without facing pricey residence fees. A nice thing about Air Canada work was that cargo flights were one-day affairs. Frank would be able to spend the nights at home with his wife and kids.

While he regretted being away from his family on the holiday, he knew that this would be the last time it would happen. He was looking forward to the new year, and all the happiness that he was sure it would bring him. With these happy thoughts in mind, Frank settled in for the eight-hour flight.

There were also some troublesome thoughts. He was a conscientious pilot, and he resented that a Senior Officer by the name of Vice Admiral Lowery, from Maritime Command, had placed him in a situation where he was to make a deviation in his route, but to keep this favor on the QT. The Admiral was asking him to fly a flight path that was not filed with the Transport Department. He had approached Frank near his aircraft wearing full uniform with Admiral rank.

"I need you to do a little favor for me, and in return, I will do something for you that you." Lowery mentioned how this favor would help the pilot's request be approved for an extension in his retirement age. Frank didn't like the fact that the deviation to the Eureka Station was not on the posted flight plan. On the other hand, what harm could it do? Would it advance his chances on retirement and promotion? If only he knew the answers to his own questions.

"What is it you want me to do?"

"I have a relative who works at the Eureka Weather Station, and I want to surprise him with a Christmas present. I have a small canister that I would like you to drop to him from the towrope bay door. It will mean a slight deviation from your route. Since this is a personal matter, that could cause me career problems, I don't want you to record this deviation or my name. Anywhere. Understood?"

Frank reluctantly agreed to the Officer's request. His afterthoughts made him realize that the request was more like a blackmail order. One that he could not refuse if he wanted a career extension. The Senior Officer had purposefully, it seemed, dropped by the flight line at the last minute, just before the engines were started. The Vice Admiral had given him no written instructions, and Frank had no time to get the approval of his squadron commander, L. Col. Holloway. He did have time to mention to one of his ground crew to check the canister drop door on the aircraft. He said he was doing a favor to help out a fellow officer by dropping a canister at Eureka.

Fortunately, the drop site was near the North Magnetic Pole, which allowed the scientists to conduct experiments. This would also provide an immediate explanation for the detour, should the squadron commander ask about the trip to Eureka. Frank had decided that he would attend to the drop as his first order of business. Once the canister was dropped, the plane would return to its planned flight path and continue its primary mission to Alert, to drop supplies that would bring goodwill and cheer to the folks that inhabited the Canadian Forces' most northerly post.

Frank's aircrew and the ground support crew had their own Christmas party the night before at the Rec Centre at Thule Air Base. While many of them missed having Christmas dinner with their own families and friends, they were professional enough to realize that the sacrifice was worthwhile. It brought some happiness to people who rotated in and out of Alert, the listening post, for six months of the year. Those at Alert went long periods without any personal contact with their wives and children.

The mood of joy and goodwill carried over from last night's party to today's flight, with many of the crew jesting with the Flight Engineer about his performance as Santa Claus. Like Frank, they were looking forward to the completion of today's mission and the return to the festive atmosphere at Thule.

After an hour of flying, Captain Winters passed control of the aircraft to the First Officer and went aft to have a chat with one of the Environment Canada scientists.

"Doctor Webster, how are you doing? We will be over the Eureka Weather Station very soon, and then we head for Alert and the Pole to conduct your experiments. Unfortunately, with the clouds and darkness we'll not be able to see much of these two stations, but you are welcome to join me up front in the cockpit."

"Thank you, Captain. I've seen both locations many times from the air and the ground, so I'll pass on your invitation."

"Perhaps you can tell me something about the weather and listening stations. It must be interesting to work there."

"Well, I know more about Eureka, where I spent six months, than I know about Alert. As you know, Alert has other military functions that don't allow civilians to be posted there. Besides its military role as a listening post, Alert is also the home of Environment Canada's High Arctic Weather Stations, better known as HAWS, along with Eureka Station and even Ellesmere Island, Isachsen, Resolute Bay, and Mould Bay. Few Canadians know about Alert, or that it was built on the most northerly point of land in North America, 817 kilometers from the Pole on the very edge of Ellesmere Island, on the Lincoln Sea."

Webster continued to extend his knowledge.

"While I was at Eureka, we had monthly contact with Aurora pilots who passed overhead. As for Station Alert, we never spoke about the military function, but we all knew that it eavesdropped on the radio traffic that occurs in Russia. I suspect that you know more about the activity at Alert than I do. As I recall, Eureka is 100 miles from the drifting North Magnetic Pole. It's located on the western side and near the middle of Ellesmere Island, on Eureka Sound, near Nansen Sound and Greely Fiord.

"At the weather station, there's a permanent staff of nine. They use seven or eight buildings, some built-in 1947, to observe the weather as well as to provide a platform for a host of scientific activities. Studies of global warming, white wolves, ozone measurements, radioactive sampling, monitoring of air chemistry, Arctic haze experiments and Arctic communications are all carried out there. The nine Eureka residents don't get too lonely. They get visitors during the summer months when tourists visit the site.

"As a pilot, you know that only small planes or helicopters can land at the site during this time of the year. There is no possibility of landing a large plane, the size of this Aurora, on the five-thousand-foot snow-covered gravel runway. Although, I have heard that occasionally, the C130 Hercules have landed during this dark season.

"If you ever get the chance to visit Eureka, you will find it has some comfortable facilities, a few barracks for sleeping and some rooms with large screen TVs and billiard tables. That's about all that I can tell you, unless you have specific questions?"

"Do you know any of the staff at Eureka?"

"I know the Chief Officer of the Station, Brian Lowery. He and I once worked together at Maritime Command in Halifax."

"That's interesting. What did he do at Maritime Command?"

"I believe he was a weatherman in the Navy. Like most of the Forces' weathermen, they all had an Army Captain's equivalent rank until the seventies. As you know, they've all been replaced with NCOs and civilian weather forecasters, which was cheaper for the Defense Department. Quite a few of the ex-force's weathermen joined Environment Canada when they retired."

"How did he end up as the Chief Officer in Eureka?"

"Most of the officers that elected to join Environment Canada started at the bottom of the seniority pole and wouldn't be given the command of a weather station for at least ten years after joining the department. Since Brian made command in much less time, he would have needed many pulls from some senior officials to get the job as. He probably had an acquaintance with some significance, who yanked some strings to get him the Eureka job. It surprised me that he got the appointment. Come to think about it, his brother, Admiral Buzz Lowery, is the Chief of Navy operations."

"Why the surprise?" asked Winters. The pilot had put two and two together, and he now knew who the senior officer was. The one who indicated that he could end Frank's future career plans.

"Because he was sick with cancer two years ago. As far as I know, it is still in remission. Now that you mentioned it, there are, I believe, many other weather stations in the North that are also manned by ex-navy pilots. Together they would constitute a large mob. Just kidding."

"Well, thanks, Doctor Webster, for the brief history of the weather station. You have been a great help."

"Please, Captain Winters, before you return to the cockpit, could you tell me what is happening to the MIR Space Station? Doctor Oxford and I are interested in the experiments conducted onboard the spacecraft, and we heard several days ago about its erratic behavior. We have been so busy the last few days that we have not been able to follow the news."

"I haven't been paying too much attention to news about MIR, but I recently spoke with NORAD HQ and they are predicting that the Russian Space Station will fall towards the earth, possibly in the Canadian Arctic. Again, thanks for your help, Doctor Webster. Since you have seen the weather stations before from the air, perhaps I can entice you to join me up front as we near the geographical North Pole. You might find it interesting to be at the Pole and pass through all the world's time zones within minutes, and to see in person that at the Pole there is no more north direction. At the same time, south lies in every order."

Returning to the cockpit, Capt. Winters was more and more curious to know the contents of the canister that was to be dropped at Eureka. Just what was in it, that was so important to the sender, that Lowery would practically force the pilot of a sub hunter to detour from a planned flight path, and to keep the detour a secret?

The flight from Thule to Eureka, on the tip of Grenville Island, took approximately two hours. During the flight, Captain Winters and the co-pilot spoke about the territory over which their aircraft was traveling. Most of the flight was over the new Canadian province of Nunavut, created officially only recently. The territory was about two million square kilometers. It spanned three time zones yet had a population of only twenty-five thousand, of whom eighty-five percent were Inuit and most were under the age of twenty years.

Frank, like almost everyone else in the Forces, was aware that the only protection that this huge landmass had against intruders was a small part of the Canadian Rangers; a 3500-strong branch of the Armed Forces spread across the whole of Canada's North. The Arctic Rangers of Nunavut were part of this force, and they numbered in the hundreds. It was easy to identify a Ranger in uniform since they all wore a red baseball cap and a red sweatshirt with the Ranger crest. Against the vast arsenal of weapons that an invader could launch against them, each Ranger was issued with a 303 Lee Enfield rifle, left over from World War Two. For the most part, the Rangers were Inuits who lived as hunters, trappers, anglers, loggers and outfitters. Rather than station well equipped regiments in the North, the Defense Department would rather boast about the work that the Arctic Rangers did, reciting the story about the Rangers finding parts of a Russian satellite that fell in the eastern Arctic in the early eighties.

Capt. Winters considered it unlikely that any foreign power would bother raiding such a barren and desolate part of the North since, for the most part, the Nunavut land was rocky tundra with stunted vegetation located above the tree line and was snow-covered during the nine months of winter. Besides, the whole territory was extremely cold during most of the year. Frank glanced at the plane's instrument panel at the thought of the temperature; it indicated that the outside temperature was -30 degrees Celsius.

The pilot stole a look out the aircraft's window to see if he recognized any of the few visual topographical features. He grabbed a map that was in the briefcase near his seat, but it was of no help to him. All the plans contained both the English names of places along the route and the new names in Inuktitut, the Inuit language. He would have to stick with the old English names since he could never pronounce names such as Iqaluit, the capital city on Frobisher Bay. He knew approximately where they were, relative to the ground, but it took the help of the navigator to pinpoint their location. The navigator placed his index finger on the map at the words 'Grise Fiord', while pointing out the cockpit window and holding a thumb down to indicate that the community was passing underneath. Frank again peered out the window, but he could not locate Grise Fiord. It was the most northern community of Nunavut, with a population of 130 souls. He couldn't see any lights where the community should have been.

"How much longer before we reach Eureka?" Frank asked.

"About twenty-five minutes."

"We better contact the weather station, and let them know about the little package that we are dropping on them. They will need some time to get into a position to spot the flare and pick up the canister."

"OK, I'll find their radio frequency and give them a heads up about our approach."

Just then, their conversation was interrupted by an intercom transmission coming from one of the airborne electronics sensor operators in the rear of the aircraft.

"Captain, I think you should come and take a look at my radar console!" Frank could detect some concern in the operator's voice, and he and the navigator darted to the back of the plane. The radar operator was hunched over the radar set, his face washed by a sickly green light from the scope. The blip on the area indicated a large object was stationary on the ice surface ahead of the aircraft.

"What is it?"

"Unless this machine is spooked by all these magnetic storms, it looks like there is a huge metal object on the ice surface, about a hundred miles from our position, and it is not moving!"

Winters was aware of magnetic storms that had caused havoc with their radios and some of the airborne electronic sensors during the past couple of days. Fortunately, the storms hadn't affected the navigating system, which seemed to be functioning normally. Frank considered the possibility that the radar console was still being affected by the storms, but quickly dismissed the thought.

"Do our maps or charts show any big metal thing that could be in that location permanently, like a sunken ship, a drilling platform, or crashed plane?"

"No, Sir. I already checked. There are no known wrecks of any type in that area."

"The briefings that we had at the Squadron, before we left Greenwood, didn't mention any ships that would be passing through the Northwest Passage at this time of year. Did you hear of any of our subs being in the area?"

"No, Sir. At the briefings that I attended at home, and at Thule, there was no mention of any of our ships being in the area. Could it be a large burg stuck in the multi-year ice pack?"

"They wouldn't show up on the screen," said the console operator.

"Then we better check it out." Frank returned to the cockpit and directed the co-pilot.

"Our radar operator has spotted a disturbance ahead. We'll bypass Eureka at this time and alter course to approach the disturbance from a northerly direction. It may be something belonging to another department like an RCMP ship, but it may also be an intruder such as a Russian sub. We will fly a wide half-circle and come at it from the North. If it is an intruder, they wouldn't expect us to approach from the direction of the North Pole."

Frank reached for the intercom mic and spoke to his crew.

"This is Captain Winters. We are changing course towards Ellef Ringnes Island to check out a blip on our radar screen. All operators, focus your attention in that direction and keep me informed, especially if it starts to move. Expect contact in thirty minutes. Maintain normal drill for tracking subs at sea."

Frank could hear movement in the rear of the plane as the rest of the crew took up their positions at their consoles and made preparations for a possible contact with an enemy ship.

"What do you think it is?" asked the co-pilot.

"Could be anything from a civilian ship stuck in the ice to a Russian sub, but I'm not taking any chances."

"Shouldn't we contact Thule, or home base, and let them know that we have a mysterious contact?"

The question brought back to mind the request from the senior officer to keep confidential that the Aurora was in the Eureka area. Yet the Standard Operating Procedures required that Frank report all mysterious contact. He decided to compromise; he would mention the disturbances to Thule in a general manner while maintaining secrecy. The compromise would satisfy the officer's request while meeting the criteria of the SOPs. He had already decided that he would disobey the officer's request should the contact prove to be some civilian ship in need of help or if there was an intruder.

"OK, get Thule Ops on the radio, and I'll talk to them. It will probably turn out to be nothing of consequence, and we may get a lot of people nervous at Thule or Base Ops, but SOPs require that we report the possible contact. Hopefully, these magnetic disturbances will allow our radio call to get through to Thule."

The First Officer went through the procedure for contacting Thule. He tried several frequencies without success.

"No go, Captain."

"Alright. Keep trying. Let's check out the contact. I'm sure we'll have plenty of time to let the base know what is happening if it turns out to be something serious."

Frank took control of the aircraft and altered its course to make a forty mile half circle. The Aurora was now bearing down on the target from the North, heading south towards the rendezvous point. During the wide turn, the airborne electronic sensor operators continued to maintain the object on their screens. Since there was no movement or change in the blip on the screen, it seemed apparent that the thing, whatever it was, had not detected the presence of the Aurora. The plane was approaching the spot of the disturbance at 200 knots cruising speed. The sensor operators kept up a continuing dialogue with the captain.

"I'm willing to bet my next month's pay that it's the conning tower of a sub under the ice," said an operator that Frank considered to be one of the best in his trade.

"OK, we'll go on that assumption. Can you tell the nationality of the sub?"

"We can't use the sonobuoys on account of the ice unless we can find a polynya or lead near the target, and without the reading of the sonobuoy, I can't pick up the sound of the sub's motors, so I can't tell its nationality."

"Flight Engineer, prepare some flares to be dropped as we pass over the area. Perhaps we can identify the sub from its sail, if we can see it. We may even spook it into leaving our waters."

"Roger, Captain."

"I'm betting that it's an intruder sub," Frank confided in his first officer. "Try calling it on different frequencies to see what their reason is for being here in our neck of the woods."

"Submarine, this is a Canadian Forces Aurora aircraft on sovereignty patrol. Identify yourself and advise why you are in Canadian waters." The co-pilot waited.

"No answer, Captain, but I'll keep trying."

"OK. Tell them that we have authority to use force to protect our sovereignty." Frank continued, "Flight Engineer, drop the flares. Prepare a sonobuoy and a torpedo. I doubt if we can drop either one, but you never know, we might get lucky and find a lead near the sub."

"Captain, I can now definitely confirm that it is a sub that is shown on my console, but I still can't identify it. The sub has a rubber coating that prevents me from getting a good read," said the sonar operator. "We really need to drop a sonobuoy to get a better reading of its exact location and identity."

"Still no answer, Captain," the First Officer shouted into the headset microphone. "The flares lit up the skies, but I can't see anything yet. Can you get any closer?"

As Frank maneuvered the Aurora to circle the area surrounding the sub, he reduced the plane's altitude on each pass. As the flares began to fade, neither he nor the first officer could make out any details of the sub, although it seemed to be on the surface and wasn't diving. The sub was operating in blackout conditions.

"I'll make a pass directly across its sail at one thousand feet. See if you can determine what nationality it is. This would be a good time to have guns mounted on this bird so we could strike the bow of that tin can."

He brought the Aurora into a dive, ten miles from the sub, and flew straight at it at a thousand feet. The plane passed over the sail and everyone on board the aircraft strained their eyes to catch a glimpse in the rapidly fading light from the flares. There were no signs on the sail to indicate its origin, nor did there appear to be any life on board. Shortly after passing over the sub, the aircraft flew over a large, almost flat surface of ice, several square kilometers in size, containing over a half dozen small buildings. The plateau-like ice stood out from the other ice surfaces since it was almost twenty feet higher. Frank climbed the plane back to two thousand feet.

"Still no response to our call for identification, Captain. I'm picking up the sound of running engines but they aren't going anywhere. Maybe they're stuck in the ice. On the last pass, I did catch a glimpse of a lead about one mile from the sub."

Frank spoke into the intercom connected to the co-pilot and flight engineers.

"We are not having much success in establishing its identity. I'll make another run. Flight Engineers, prepare a sonobuoy for dropping. I'll open the bomb bay doors. See if you can drop a sonobuoy in the lead near the sub and keep the torpedo primed, just in case."

Again, Frank eased the Aurora's controls to bring it around for another run towards the sub, this time from five hundred feet with bomb bay doors open. Suddenly, there was a streak of light approaching the aircraft. Small flames seemed to come from the rear of the projectile. It approached so rapidly that it was impossible for the vast Aurora to veer away.

"Missile launched on our track! Two Miles!"

"Son of a bitch!" said Frank, as he tried in vain to turn the aircraft away from the approaching missile. "Prepare to launch the torpedo as soon as we are over the lead. I may not be able to save this bird, but those bastards are not getting away with shooting at my plane!"

The crew hustled to change from dropping a sonobuoy to unleashing a deadly fish. As the aircraft approached the open water and the sub, Frank reached for the intercom button.

"Let her go," he ordered.

The plane climbed into the dark skies, running and turning away from the missile. All aboard heard the torpedo hit the open water and start its run to the sub. The Aurora had no defense against the missile except to outmaneuver it, since the ESM package was inoperative.

Capt. Winters kept the plane turning and climbing, hoping to shake the rocket at a higher altitude. But this missile was seeking heat, and it rushed onwards towards the Aurora. The plane's fate was sealed. It had no outside defense and no foil to be released to fool the missile.

"Captain, we are picking up some engine sounds. The sub is diving, and our fish is following her. Our computer is trying to identify the sounds. An initial analysis indicates that it's an American sub, but the computer needs more data before it can be confirmed."

Suddenly the streak of light caught up with the aircraft. Everyone on board heard the explosion and felt the shuttering in the plane simultaneously. The craft bounced in the air, and the engines began to wail as they struggled to hold the craft in the dark sky. It was only a matter of time before they would fail at their daunting task.

"We've been hit by the missile. We are losing altitude. They're obviously not friendly. Hang on, let's see if we can get this bird under control. I just wish I could get a better shot at that bastard sub. I would put the second torpedo down its periscope and up its ass." Frank said to his co-pilot.

Unknown to Frank was that a missile had sheared off the outer tip of the right wing, and the shrapnel from the blast tore a hole in the forward fuselage. Flames were biting at the part of the wing that had been amputated. The cabin instantly depressurized, and the captain had to instigate an emergency descent from five thousand feet to a lower altitude. He heard the flying equipment and supplies hitting the inside of the main cabin.

Captain Winters desperately wanted to find a suitable spot to land his stricken aircraft among the packed sea ice which lay beneath the diving plane. His attention was moved to the speedometer. It was reading 170 mph and falling. All the while the Aurora was being shaken violently by the turbulent winds. Winters selected wheels down, hoping that he could spot a level landing plateau somewhere in the area highlighted by the flicking of the landing lights. The alarm sounded so that crew could strap themselves in.

The race to the ground lasted only seconds. Frank was able to spot icy plateaus that he had seen earlier; they appeared to be smoother in the fast-fading flare light and in the glare of the moonlight. The plane's landing lights were not much use because of the snow. What he saw was a plateau that was surrounded by broken ice. It was approximately twenty feet taller than the pack ice. Wrenching the plane around, he managed to line up the craft to approach this large plateau; he was desperately trying to conserve height. In the moonlight, he could see the small huts. The plane was losing height quickly. She was now much closer to the ice than she was just a few seconds ago.

"Try and get some power up to see if we can land on that plateau," Frank told the co-pilot.

The First Officer managed to increase the engines' revolutions on the wounded plane. The plateau loomed out of the darkness, now nearly a mile away, but the craft was rapidly descending just below the lip of the flat surface.

"Help me get her up a bit more!" yelled Frank, as he tugged at the controls. Suddenly, they heard scraping sounds as the wheels just cleared the lip at the top of the plateau. The craft was now up and over and onto the table. The wheels tore at the ice chunks that littered the flat surface.

"The torpedo has struck something-" broadcast the radio operator, just before he was slung out of his seat and flying down the extent of the plane's interior. The other console operators were trying to duck chairs and poles that camouflaged themselves as missiles.

The captain cut the remaining engine power, and the aircraft almost immediately belly flopped onto the heavy snow and ice, much like a stone skipping across open water and running out of energy. The nose of the craft nudged, rose, smacked down harder and rose again. There were jarring vibrations and grinding tearing screams of metal being tortured and twisted out of shape. The plane started to cut a straight swath, 150 feet wide, through the snow sculptured waves and mounds of ice. Instantaneously, the aircraft started to shed some of the lighter pieces of metal from its torpedo bay doors and from the flaps at the back of the airfoils. At the same time, the nose wheel made contact with the ice surface. A fraction of a second later, the engines on the port side started to dig semicircular furrows into the ice with the edges of its metal casings, since the plane had keeled slightly to the left. Once the fuel tanks ruptured, flames spilled over the leading edge of the port wing; the inboard engine was also on fire. A blaring alarm suddenly went off, signaling the blaze.

The props of two engines on the starboard side dug into the ice as the weight of the aircraft was shifted to the opposite side. The remainder of the damaged wing buckled. As the front undercarriage touched the ice, the aircraft's nose scraped temporarily then rose again. The door of the forward wheel well ripped off and went flying through the air, landing fifty feet away. That was when the landing gear collapsed. More pieces of the craft were flung through the air, snow, and ice, as the craft collapsed onto itself. It continued to slide along the ice, gouging an eighteen-inch-deep depression, the width of the fuselage, in the snow crust.

Sixty feet later, a twenty-foot section of the right-wing, including the outboard flap, was torn off. The front undercarriage was completely torn from its mounts and left in the wake of the aircraft, now some hundred feet from its impact point. The engines had completely stopped rotating, jammed with chunks of ice that were picked up and thrown by the sliding plane. Amazingly, the fuselage was still completely intact while the aircraft continued to shutter and jerk, jolting along the surface. Flames started to erupt from the starboard wing, but were almost immediately extinguished by the flying snow. The fractured wings continued to cut through snowbanks like a hot knife through butter. All at once, the skidding craft hit a wall of ice with its nose.

Captain Winters had the foresight to secure his waist and shoulder harness before impact. He was flung from his seat into the ceiling of the cockpit. The harness was defective and loose enough for his head to hit the cockpit ceiling. He crumbled like a rag doll to the floor, unconscious.

The First Officer was not completely buckled in, and the impact of hitting the wall of ice resulted in him being projected out of his seat into the windscreen's metal frame. In a moment, both of his legs and one arm were broken. The momentum in his body had not yet dissipated; he bounced off the frame like a broken rag doll and landed, wedged between his seat and the wall partition.

The hit into the wall of ice, by the sliding chunk of metal formerly known as the Aurora Nor Pat Flight, slowed the aircraft considerably. But it still continued to slide forward. It crossed a fifteen-foot trench in the plateau, coming heavily to the other side. The starboard outer aileron came loose, as did a section of the keel beam followed by the inboard high-speed aileron from the right airfoil. The impact on the other side of the trench resulted in the plane giving up the balance of its nose. Landing gear was dragged along the crash path. It had been three seconds since impact, and other sections of the damaged body continued to be wrenched off.

During the slide, in the next two and half seconds the aircraft discarded a twenty-five-foot portion of the port wing, and the flames that had existed on the wing were now wholly extinguished. Fuel continued to spray out of the large holes ripped in the tanks, drenching the ice behind the sliding craft. Mercifully, the aircraft, flight Alfa Foxtrot 739, came to an abrupt halt when it struck with tremendous force a twenty-foot-high ridge of ice. It was almost a quarter-mile from where it had touched down, poised over a small gully in the ice surface of the plateau. The central fuselage's underside was held aloft by the remnants of both wings and the tail section.

# 9    AURORA CRASH

25 Dec 1300 hrs local, On Canada's Ice Island, Nunavut

Captain Winters' plane had crashed. He was hurt, but alive. He awoke from unconsciousness and wondered how long he was out. It was anyone's guess. He struggled to get to his feet and reached down, closing the main controls and disconnecting the circuit -breakers. Looking out the broken but still intact windshield, he could see no fire. There was little likelihood that the plane would explode, at least not in the next few minutes. While reaching under his seat to retrieve a flashlight and some flares, he could see that the Emergency Locator Beacon had not fallen off during the slide. Instead, it was wrenched from its perch and thrown out the side window of the plane.

Frank swung the flashlight beam to the face of the First Officer, who was slumped in his seat. The officer appeared to be unconscious but not bleeding. With a bit of careful tugging and pushing, Frank was able to open the flight deck's overhead escape hatch. He found the strength to maneuver the First Officer out onto the nose.

"I'll be back in a moment with bandages and with braces for your legs. Just hold on."

He then noticed his own blood on his face. It seemed to be only a flesh wound, and he had no broken bones, as far as he could tell.

The captain focused his attention on the remainder of the plane's crew. He turned and opened the door into the aircraft's main fuselage. Moving cautiously, he reached the console of the radio operator. The operator must have hit his head on the radio; he was face down on the table fronting the radio display. The radio set was shattered, and glass and dials were scattered around the table and on the operator. The operator moaned and opened his eyes. He seemed to be alright except for a bump on the head.

When Frank reached over to touch his arm, to help him make his way out of the plane, the operator shook his head and indicated that he could make his way out through the flight deck escape hatch. The captain moved further into the main cabin area. He noticed that some members of the crew had also fetched flashlights. The beams of light flashed in every direction as they checked on their circumstances and their fellow crew members.

Captain Winters saw that something large had clobbered Lieutenant Miles, the senior navigator, on the back, leaving him crumpled and head down on floor of the plane. A large suitcase, belonging to one of the scientists, had broken loose from its storage area and struck the navigator. Its contents of experiment equipment covered the floor around the navigator's body. The lieutenant struggled to get to his feet, and Frank held out a hand to assist him in getting out onto a portion of the wing through the emergency window.

A member of the crew called for Frank's attention and help. Together, they found two crew members lifeless on the debris scattered floor. Looking closely, Frank could tell that both were deceased. They had lengthy gashes on their faces and ugly blue bruises over most of their bodies. These injuries presumably came from glass, equipment, and missile like objects flying inside the craft during the crash. Frank recognized them as the TacNav, Lt. Archie McNeil and the NavCom, Lt. Rolling Roach.

Frank directed that they be wrapped in blankets and placed in the sleeping area of the plane.

"Later, we will find a proper place to put them until we get rescued."

Other crew members glanced through the aircraft's portholes on either side of the fuselage, looking for flames. One of the navigators had partly unlocked the rear left emergency window, bringing in a smell of fuel that hung in the air. They could see behind the plane, a trail of fire that lit up the sky about fifty feet down the crash path, feeding on the fuel that had splashed out of the wings. It was moving towards them.

One of the scientists was making an effort to open an emergency exit over the other wing area, but the exit was covered with cases from the resupply stores meant for Station Alert. He was in a frenzy as he tore away at the obstacles blocking the hatch, preventing him from opening the door. Struggling to remove the last of the boxes, he grabbed the lever and gave a sharp twist, which caused the hatch to open just a fraction. He put his full weight behind it, extending the opening. This was a new and easier exit, and he stepped out onto the remainder of the wing.

Captain Winters was starting to feel the onset of shock, yet he persisted in looking after his crew's safety. He made his way down the center of the fuselage, dodging boxes and consoles torn from their mountings. Buried under some debris, he found one of the electronic sensor operators. By clearing it away, the operator was able to stand up. Frank plodded to the left emergency hatch where he helped the other scientist, who was dragging a lacerated knee, proceed out through the new exit. The Flight Engineer approached the hatch holding up two of the sensor operators, one under each arm; they too escaped through the hatch, with the Engineer remaining near the outside of the escape door.

"That's the last of the living crew," said the Flight Engineer. He reached inside and helped his captain out of the buckled aircraft and onto the wing. Together they jumped off the wing and onto a fifteen-foot mound of snow.

In the freezing cold weather, decisions had to be made speedily. People's lives could be lost in moments unless everyone was organized to help one another. Frank didn't hesitate to take control. He directed a crew to fetch a makeshift stretcher and bring the co-pilot from the front of the cockpit. Another crew was dispatched to retrieve Miles, who was now astride the fuselage, and a third man was sent to gather up all the parkas and blankets that were strewn about the plane. The captain did a quick count of those that he could see in the light from the moon and the burning fuel's flames. His own self-preservation was denied until he was sure that everyone was accounted for and had protection from the blasting winds and blowing snow. After all of the crew were covered with parkas and blankets, there were other urgent matters that required Frank Winters' attention.

"Keep an eye on everyone to see that shock symptoms don't creep in," he told one of the navigators. "Keep everyone together and calm them down while I check on the fire situation further down the crash path. We need to extinguish it before it reaches the plane. I'll be back in five minutes. If I am not back by then, send someone else down the path to spread snow over the spilled fuel."

Climbing down the snow mound and onto the ice surface, he started to walk around the downed Aurora. His legs and arms were bruised from the crash, and he was sure that a part of one leg was not getting a full supply of blood since he could feel the numbness in it. His fur-lined boots were in the aircraft when they left Thule, but they could be anywhere now. While the black leather shoes were more comfortable to wear while flying, they were not designed for walking on snow and ice. He slipped and fell on several occasions, causing more bruising, before he learned to walk carefully and slowly. The frigid cold was starting to cause numbing in his toes and in his instep.

With his flashlight, he was able to see that the front of the aircraft was intact. The fuselage itself looked complete. The doors were shut and only the escape hatches were open. The metalwork seemed to be trustworthy and undamaged. However, the tail and prod containing the avionics package were a little twisted and slightly out of line. One thing was sure, this Aurora would never fly again. At the front of the plane, he switched on the emergency locator beacon. It was sitting in the snow and ice, leaning on the nose of the aircraft. The ELB was their lifeline. Its cry of help would be heard by satellites and passed to the nearest Canadian Rescue Unit.

Captain Winters knew that the sub, with its missile launcher, was still in the area, but he had to take a chance and light a flare since his crew needed help as soon as possible. He lit a green flare on the off-chance that some civilian aircraft might spot it. The burst exploded with light. It blanketed the Arctic sky at first, then concentrated in only one area.

In the glare of the morning, the light betrayed the real damage of the captain's beloved plane as well as the harshness of the real estate where it landed. Unfortunately, it also showed on their faces just how frail the crew was in this godforsaken ice mass.

Together, Frank and the scientist walked down the crash path towards the advancing fire. About thirty feet from the wreck and another twenty feet from the burning fuel they stopped and used their boots to shovel snow over the path of spilled kerosene. They watched, in fascination, as the flames slowly reached the spot where they stood, then fizzled out.

Frank and the scientist made their way back to the plane. They zippered up their parkas and drew tightly the strings of their hoods. White plumes of breath hung in the cold air before their faces. For the first time, Frank began to feel the enormous weight of their survival problem and the penetrating nature of the cold.

"Jesus Christ, it must be -30 degrees," he said to no one in particular as he looked up at the moonlit sky. "Hard to believe that 10 minutes ago, we were up there at ten thousand feet without too many worries."

*What do we do now?* was the question on Frank's mind.

# 10 MIR SPACE STATION

26 Ember 2330 hrs local, MAG HQ, Halifax, Nova Scotia

The Commander of Maritime Air Group, Brig. Gen. Dave Shanahan, had arrived at his office just after the RCC had given him the information about the missing aircraft. Major Phillips was his RCC Commander and also the best Search Master in the Canadian Forces. He needed Phillips at this RCC to aid lessor qualified search officers. The General had tremendous respect for Shawn Phillips. In appointing him as SM for the Winters search, Shanahan had complete faith that the Major would not rest until the aircrew and passengers were safe. In the past, Major Phillips was also able to provide leads as to what caused an aircraft to crash. The sooner that this information became available to MAG, the less likelihood of having to ground the fleet of Auroras.

In the past, the General spent days bunked up in his office suite. His beautiful wife understood that it was all part of being in the military, especially being in command.

Shanahan was half listening to the radio as he did his work. He only half heard the radio announcer's spiel when he mentioned something about MIR possibly landing at the North Pole. The MAG Commander turned his attention to the radio's content.

"MIR Crew Leaves Space Station Empty", "MIR's Main Computer Shut Down", and "MIR Dead" were just a few of the headlines printed in newspapers several months ago. On this day, news came from the radio broadcast.

"Something new is happening to the Russian Space Station. The station is moving out of orbit... but more about this in a moment." The announcer promised to bring the listeners up to date on the MIR space station's current activities.

The voice on the small radio, on one corner of the General's desk, started speaking again.

"In August, the occasion of the headlines was the departure of the Russian-French three-man crew, just before the end of the last MIR mission, that would leave the troubled craft to fly unmanned before it was scheduled to plunge to earth next year. The two Russians and one

Frenchman on that mission had just installed and tested a vital back-up navigation system designed to keep the space station from crashing down to earth, a fear expressed by many of the former astronauts that lived on the craft. The same astronauts are quoted as saying that there are many space experts who have doubted the safety of leaving MIR abandoned and cruising in orbit. They say that the crewless craft could plummet to earth, despite the new navigation system that was designed to keep it in orbit. Are their fears about to become a reality?" The announcer paused for effect, then plunged on with his documentary.

"The Russian Space Agency was planning to send a funeral team to the station, early in the new year, to shut it down completely and remove all essential components including computers and recording devices. It would then be driven out of orbit to plunge into the Pacific Ocean. Have the Russians changed their minds, and are they now crashing it to earth?"

The radio announcer continued his newscast documentary as Shanahan walked around his office, lost in thought, trying to comprehend the words in the message he received from Shawn Phillips, and the unbelievable story that the crew of the Aurora was missing from the scene of the downed aircraft. He vaguely remembered the announcer continuing his dialogue.

"Today, the American Space Agency has announced that MIR is descending towards the earth. It was anticipated that MIR would slowly descend, approximately four miles, in the months following an evacuation. However, the rate of descent is much greater than anticipated. At the current rate of downward movement, it could strike earth within the next 48 hours. So far, there has been no comment from Moscow." Once again, he paused for effect in hope that the listeners were riveted to their radios.

"The MIR Station weighs 140 tons, and it would have a devastating impact on our planet if it doesn't completely burn up in the atmosphere on re-entry." There was a crashing sound that the announcer felt was necessary to establish a shock effect.

"The MIR space station has run up some impressive statistics since it was first launched 13 and a half years ago. There have been over 77,000 orbits, each of which lasts approximately sixty minutes. At least 154,000 sunrises and sunsets have been seen by MIR. It has traveled an estimated 2,070,000,000 miles. It travels at 17,500 miles per hour at 350 to 400 kilometers above the earth. 71 different spacecraft of eight types have docked with MIR since its birth, and there have been over a hundred visitors to MIR from 9 different nations. There have been almost 17,000 scientific experiments conducted. It has passed over every country in the world and photographed every square inch of territory. But it has also had some problems during the same time frame."

Shanahan lowered the volume of the radio while he used the phone. He needed to talk to the Commander of Maritime Command about Major Phillips's findings and his plan of action.

"This is the Commander of MAG. I would like to talk to Vice Admiral Lowery. Is he available?"

"General Shanahan, this is Captain Martin, an aide to Admiral Lowery. I'm sorry, but he is away for a few days."

"Being the Christmas and New Year holiday period, I was sure that he would be in the area with his family."

"He has made another of his sudden trips to the North. He is visiting Iqaluit, in Nunavut, for a few days."

"I didn't know that there were regular scheduled commercial flights to the capital of Nunavut, especially during the holidays."

"A U.S. Navy plane belonging to Admiral Heiserman has picked him up at Shearwater."

"OK. Let me know when he returns." As he replaced the phone, he found it interesting that Admiral Lowery had sufficient drag in the Pentagon to get a U.S. military plane, belonging to the U.S. Chief of Naval Operations, to fly him to the Arctic's east coast. He wondered just what it was that made the Admiral leave Halifax in such a hurry.

General Shanahan returned to the radio and increased the volume. The announcer was still describing MIR and the problems that it had in the past.

"As I mentioned earlier, MIR has had its problems. For example, there was the fire in February of '97. The fire destroyed two oxygen generators, and the crew had to wear oxygen masks while trying to fix one of the generators. At that time, the station needed an emergency supply of spare parts. In July of '97, an unmanned supply ship that was being docked by the crew on the MIR crashed into the Spektr lab. The accident's damage included forty percent loss of power-generating capacity and most of the lab research. Then, there was the July '97 incident, when one of the tired crewmen accidentally pulled a cable and it switched off MIR's on-board computer, heating, lights, and navigation systems, which sent MIR into a spin. Accidents such as these, along with severe financial problems, led the Russians to conclude that MIR should be shut down before it falls. The funding situation is so grave that the Russian government agreed to film a Pepsi commercial aboard MIR for a million dollars," he continued.

"Reliable sources indicate that Moscow is prepared to sell some selected data obtained during the past decade to the U.S., to help them with their planned International Space Station, for one hundred million dollars." The announcer went on, using a more scholarly voice.

"Just what comprises this huge piece of space junk that is heading our way? It consists of six pieces, or modules. The forty-three-foot MIR core module serves as the principal space station control element. It contains the main computers, communication equipment, recording devices, kitchen, and hygiene facilities, and it's also the primary living quarters. The operations area of the MIR core is the control area for the entire complex. From here, the crew members can monitor and command all core systems, the science equipment, the recording devices, and the video and photography equipment, as well as the piloting station. It has five docking doors that can be used to enter or exit the module. This central module serves as the principal propellant storage unit, and its jet rockets assist in controlling the station's altitude.

"The MIR modules, and its equipment, mean that 130 to 140 metric tons of out-of-control space junk will be falling on the earth, perhaps on some heavily populated area, shortly. We all recall the last piece of radioactive Soviet space junk that fell in the Canadian Arctic wilds.

"As of this moment, neither the Pentagon in Washington nor Ottawa Defense Headquarters have indicated if an effort will be made to shoot MIR down if it heads for North America."

The announcer was about to wind up his documentary when Shanahan decided that he had heard enough about MIR. Little did he know that the fortunes of this craft would affect his life, and the life of his country, in the coming days.

In the meantime, his main concern was the lives of his ten crew members and the two scientists. They were in serious jeopardy somewhere near the North Magnetic Pole, rather than some hypothetical situation involving the spacecraft. The MIR descent was probably some gimmick thought up by the Russians to get the Americans to pour more money into their black hole of a space program rather than build the new International Space Station. In all likelihood, the Russians would probably fire the MIR rockets to get it back in its orbit within the next few days. He shut off the radio and longed for more information from Phillips on the whereabouts of his Aurora crew.

# 11   AURORA CRASH SITE

December 1200 hrs local, Canada's Ice Island, Nunavut

Back at the crash site, Major Shawn Phillips, the Search Master, decided to continue searching for survivors. The cause of the crash required a meticulous approach. No stone was to be left unturned to get the answers. But first things first. He had to communicate again with Brig. Gen. Shanahan, but it was more important first to obtain additional information regarding the crash and the survivors.

Now that the lights were working in the make shift Command/Ops Centre, and there was warmth seeping into all corners of the building, there was work to be done. Warrant Officer Mackenzie and Major Phillips held a strategy session on what to do next.

"This one's got me stumped! Any ideas?" asked Shawn.

"We checked every square inch of the island and found nothing but the wrecked aircraft. It's extremely unlikely that the aircrew would have ventured out onto the ice cap, especially since there were probably some injuries or fatalities as a result of the impact," stated Mackenzie, contributing his initial thoughts to the briefing.

"There has been no significant amount of snow since the crash," Shawn added, "otherwise, the plane and surrounding area would be covered. We should see footprints or indications of activity by the crew. If they were picked up by someone in a helicopter, or by several dog sled teams, or by a train of ski-doos, you would think that we would have seen or heard something about rescue attempts. Someone would have tried to contact us by now, or there would be some evidence left at our plane.

"As I see it, we only have one choice. We have to go back to the plane and examine it thoroughly to see if there is any evidence in its vicinity. Maybe if we investigate in greater detail we can determine the cause of the crash, and that may shed some light on this mystery. I'm not, nor are you, an aircraft accident investigator, but together, we may be able to spot something unusual that can lead us to our missing crew."

"Sounds like a reasonable plan," Mackenzie said. "We can take some of the men with us to help out, while the rest stay here. Maybe someone, or something, will show up, and whoever stays behind can monitor the radio."

"Just keep one or two men here to monitor the radio, and have the remainder scour the island one more time. They can concentrate on finding the emergency beacon. At the Winters Briefing in Halifax, the RCC from Edmonton mentioned that they had received a brief signal through SARSAT from this area. It may have come from our plane. Apparently, it only lasted fifteen minutes before it stopped. Have your men look closely near the plane and along the debris trail, but check elsewhere as well. I would like to know if the Emergency Locator Transmitter failed or if it was turned off," replied Shawn, concluding the briefing.

Phillips, Mackenzie, and the rescue specialists departed for the plane, their flashlights and electrical lanterns replenished with new batteries. During the entire journey they flashed their lights in all directions looking for the ELT and anything else that could help them find the aircrew. The use of night vision glasses along with the flashlights allowed them to find, inspect, and examine every piece of aircraft debris along the thirty-minute trek to the downed bird. As they walked toward the plane, they walked along a gully made by the aircraft as it slid from its initial impact with the ice surface. The gully contained pieces of aircraft debris and crew luggage, but no casualties. There were no cries for assistance. There was nothing but the moaning of the blistering polar wind.

As they came within sight of the wreck, the full extent of the damage was evident. The craft was flat on its belly, straddling an ice gully, with its landing gear completely missing, as were parts of the wings' flaps and sections. There was a large rip in the cockpit, a hole in the forward fuselage, and the windshield was cracked, but intact. The fuselage itself appeared to be mainly complete, but the tail assembly hung at a twisted angle. The emergency beacon was located near the nose of the plane. It seemed to be turned off.

There was evidence of a fire, especially around the remaining section of the right wing, but it was evident that the flames had not engulfed the entire aircraft. So far, they could not see anything that may have caused the plane to crash; most of the damage had likely occurred during impact.

It was possible that the accident could have occurred due to pilot error, or a problem with the aircraft or its instruments. Phillips recalled reading about the failure of key Aurora cockpit instruments. An alert notice posted in the 435 Squadron canteen mentioned a flight director indicator, a baseball-sized device that told a pilot whether the plane was banking, climbing, or descending. The hand on it became frozen without warning, leading to catastrophic crashes. The device had become jammed on other Aurora aircraft several times in the past three years, and in most cases, it did not alert the pilot that it had become frozen. The rogue readings could cause the four-engine aircraft to inadvertently crash. The pilots were advised to fly higher than 250 meters in poor visibility, so as to give them a chance to recover from misleading readings. This may or may not have been the cause of this accident, and it could easily be determined by examining the aircraft's black box.

There was little likelihood that this aircraft would be removed from the ice until the spring, when there was more daylight. The Gray Ghost would fly no more. The plane's parts would eventually be accumulated and carried out by helicopter to be later be reassembled in a hangar in Trenton. While the actual cause of the accident could take months to determine, Shawn was intent on doing whatever he could to find some cause, if possible. The sooner that the accident source was determined, the better, since learning the cause could prevent similar accidents. In turn, there may be no need to ground the Aurora fleet. Major Phillips decided to investigate the crash to the best of his ability during the little available time until a helicopter came to get himself and his rescue team home from the crash site. There was a chance that he and Rob Mackenzie would spot some cause of the aircraft's obvious defect; one that would have resulted in the crash.

It was evident that the exterior of the aircraft provided no clue to the cause of the crash or to the whereabouts of the crew. Only one wing was viable since the other was buried in snow. Major Phillips and WO Mackenzie entered the interior of the plane through the same egress that they had used previously.

The first thing Shawn noticed when he entered the cockpit area was that the main controls had been shut down, and the circuit breakers had been disconnected. This was an indication that someone, mainly the pilot or co-pilot, survived the crash and was capable of taking action to prevent a fire or explosion. Phillips walked through the cockpit door, followed by Mackenzie, into the main cabin. Their lights flashed over the frost-covered walls. There was blood on pieces of equipment and parts of the interior of the plane.

*Could these pieces have caused the deaths of two crew members?* wondered Shawn. Their bodies were still on the bed, like part of the structure.

Phillips and Mackenzie moved about the aircraft, gingerly stepping over fallen radar scopes and resupply packages. There were no messages posted on any of the consoles or on the craft's doors. There was no evidence left by the crew of their plan to be found. No effort was made to provide a would-be rescuer with a trail to their whereabouts.

Shawn remembered that one of the aircraft technicians at Thule had mentioned a canister that was destined for Eureka. Shawn moved some of the packages and canisters, looking for the one that was headed to that destination. It would have caused this plane to divert off its posted flight plan. A diversion that may have ultimately led to the craft's destruction.

Most packages and luggage were stored in the belly of the aircraft. Shawn reached down and pulled up the door that covered the short stairway into the underbelly of the craft. They both descended the stairs and flashed their lights around the first storage area that they came upon, the one used for torpedoes. The torpedo bay doors had been ripped off during the aircraft's slide to its final resting spot. The cold arctic wind could be felt much more readily in this part of the plane. Shawn noticed that there was one torpedo ready for launch, but the second one was missing. *Did it fall out of the bay doors during the skidding? Was it launched against someone, and why?* He wished that he could answer these questions.

On the rack in the next storage area was a canister equipped with strobe lights and chemical glow patches. It was the durable plastic reusable canister that would have been dropped with a mini parachute, through the torpedo doors, at the Eureka Weather Station. Shawn opened the locked lid of the canister and removed a small package that he placed in a secure pocket of his parka to be scrutinized later.

Mackenzie and the Search Master carefully made their way to the aircraft's emergency power source, located just below the cockpit area. All of the plane's in-flight electrical systems converged in this area. It fed power to everything from the black box to the plane's radar, navigation, and communication systems. Phillips stepped around a bulkhead wall that was supposed to protect the black boxes from tumbling cargo and any other loose items in the electronics bay. He immediately noticed that the Cockpit Voice Recorder and the Flight Data Recorder were missing.

The CVR taped all the cockpit noises, including pilots' voices, engine noise, and radio conversations. The FDR recorded all essential information such as altitude, airspeed, and flap position. These so-called black boxes, which were actually painted orange, were solid-state recorders encased in a crash and fire-resistant titanium box. They were designed to record the many movements of the plane, including the twist and turn gyrations, control inputs, and the condition of many aircraft systems at any moment during a flight.

While it was possible that the black boxes may have been ejected through one of the many torn holes in the floor of the aircraft, the trailing wires gave the distinct appearance that they had been ripped out of their mountings. When operational, the boxes gave off a pinging noise for a lengthy period of time after a crash, but no such sound had been heard by himself, nor by his men, when they had walked the length of the crash trail. It was extremely unusual that both recorders were missing. *If both recorders didn't get ejected out of the aircraft as it slid to its deathbed, then who removed them and why?* More questions for Shawn to ponder.

Shortly after completing the preliminary investigation, and upon leaving the cold dark husk of the aircraft, Rob Mackenzie and Shawn Phillips met up with several SAR techs on their way back to the warmth of the Mess Hall. The techs reported that they were unable to find the emergency beacon that they were looking for, although they had seen several pieces of aircraft debris. Shawn was hoping to find the torpedo and the black boxes so that they could be delivered to Ottawa, to the Safety Board, for analysis. Unfortunately, the techs had not seen either of these items. They mentioned that they found a lengthy piece of a wing that was some distance from the crash site and not on the crash path or in the debris field. The fact that this section of the wing was a considerable distance from the crash route intrigued Shawn. *It must have come off the plane before it crashed, but why?*

Major Phillips insisted that they all retrace their steps to see if they could relocate the wing's remnant. It took twenty minutes of searching in the minus 30-degree Celsius weather before they stumbled upon the wing fragment. Shawn circled the wing's length and bent to examine parts of it, especially a burnt area of the wing where it joined the fuselage.

The glow from his flashlight spilled over the full length of the wing, revealing that it was a twenty-foot section of the left wing, and it had considerable damage done to it. What caused the burn was on his mind.

There was one occasion, in the past, where Shawn had seen similar damage to metal. He recalled a visit to the Canadian Army base in Sorest, Germany, to watch mock tank battles. During one such mock attack, a missile destroyed an unserviceable tank. He was taken to see the tank damage after it was hit. It now seemed to him that there was a great deal of similarity between the torn and burnt metal of the wing and the torn metal on the tank in Germany.

His experience convinced him that the damaged area of the wing was caused by a missile hit. *But from where, why, and from what?* There was no doubt in his mind that the aircraft crashed because of this twenty-foot wing section. It greatly affected the airworthiness of the plane; it would not stay airborne for long if missing this large a section of the wing. Birds with only one wing didn't fly. That was Shawn's experience.

Shawn called Mackenzie over for a side conference. He theorized that the craft had been shot down by a missile, and that it most likely came from a submarine, although another airplane or raiding party could have also fired the fatal shot. Mackenzie needed a closer look at the damaged wing. He examined it in detail and reached the same conclusion as Shawn.

They decided that they should proceed immediately and directly to the Mess Hall and voice their suspicions to MAG Commander, Brig. Gen. Shanahan. They were concerned that whatever brought down the plane may still be in the area. Both were worried about the safety of the airmen as well as the SAR techs. They lengthened their stride to quickly reach the safety of the Mess Hall. The crew needed to be forewarned. The survey buildings offered a little security based on the premise that 'out of sight, out of mind' was true. But then again, if the intruder didn't see survivors near the plane, they might be looking for them.

When they reached the Mess Hall, Shawn noticed how much frost had coated the door hinges, and it was built up half an inch thick on the windows. It even crept up from the floor on the inside walls. Luckily, the area near the stove was snug. The hall provided some safety from whatever force blew the wing off the plane. Shawn and Rob agreed that posting a sentry outside would be murder in the -30-degree temperature. It was also doubtful that any enemy would be out in the extreme cold, even if they knew about the team's presence.

The techs that had remained behind in the cabin reported that there had been no incoming radio calls during the time that Phillips and the other specialists had been investigating the aircraft. Shawn decided to contact Shanahan from his laptop computer, sending a signal via a polar-orbiting satellite. It would relay the message directly to Shanahan in his Halifax office. The message could be encoded, and this form of communication was more secure than a radio call.

"The totality of the ice island was searched again today without finding the missing crew. The emergency beacon has been turned off, and the black boxes are missing, along with one torpedo. The boxes may have been deliberately and hastily removed. My initial investigation of the plane and the debris field indicates that the plane was downed by a missile that tore off a large section of a wing. The one torpedo that was missing was perhaps fired on an intruder, or it fell off during the impact slide, but has not been found. We found some blood in and around the aircraft. It is most likely that the crew survived the crash. Advise if any unusual military activity is spotted in the area by North Warning System at the automated radar sites.
Signed, Major Phillips."

Shawn sent the email and sat back, relaxed, and awaited a reply. He hoped that Shanahan was monitoring his computer for incoming messages. One of the techs passed him a hot coffee.

Within an hour he received a reply from MAG.

"Use extreme caution. No aircraft activity was noted by NWS. Our Alert base has neither seen nor heard any communication from foreign militaries, nor has NORAD detected any intrusion over any Russian aircraft's polar route. However, Russian subs were spotted in waters off the east coast of Ellesmere Island last week, by the Americans. I suggest that you investigate the possibility that a sub may have surfaced in the area. Could you determine why the aircraft was well off its planned flight path? All info that you learn is to be classified as Top Secret. For your info, yesterday the Commander of Maritime Command forewarned and forecasted, to Canadians, the possibility of aggression, in the near future, by foreign agents in our Arctic zone. Keep me personally posted. Report again in six hours. MAG."

Looking around the room, Shawn could see that all of his troops were exhausted from the flight, the jump onto the ice island, and the constant search of the ice and buildings. He suggested that all of the men get some well-needed rest before they would have to make the trek once again to the crash site. He had Mackenzie set up the radio and open a channel to the mini RCC in Thule.

"Capt. Leech, this is Major Phillips. I need you to dispatch your Aurora #740 to our location and search for a submarine or any military units capable of launching missiles. Exercise extreme caution in this area. If found, do not engage. Please have the Aurora pilot contact me when he or she reaches our area. There may still be a need for helicopters. Please continue to arrange for them to be made available on short notice. That is all."

"Roger, Major Phillips," replied Mari.

Shawn hoped that this brief short-burst transmission would go undetected by any enemy listening in. He wished that he was sitting at a table at the USAF Officers Mess having a rum and coke with Mari, instead of dealing with a missing crew of an Aurora and the fact that his team could be in mortal danger.

After a moment of reflection, he retired from the main part of the Mess Hall to a private room, where he reached into his parka. Inside a large pocket was the package he had removed from the canister while he was on the crashed plane. The label on the box was addressed to B. Lowery, Chief of Eureka Weather station. He stared at the package for some time, trying to decide if it had anything to do with the downed aircraft. The fact was, Capt. Winters had made a detour to the Weather Station area after talking to a senior officer from Maritime Command.

Shawn recalled that this bit of information had been passed to him by Aurora's maintenance technician, who had remained behind in Thule. If the aircraft had not been in the Eureka area, it most likely would not have been shot down. There may be some obvious answer why this package was addressed to someone named Lowery, given the fact that there was an Admiral Lowery at MAG. He decided that he needed to know what was in the package. He opened the box carefully so that it could easily be resealed later and sent to Mr. Lowery, with apologies. Inside the package, he found $50,000 in U.S. notes, a well-oiled .44 magnum handgun, and a message.

"Have your troops prepared for the last days of December. Heiserman will contact you. Think global warming. Buzz."

There was only one 'Buzz' senior officer at Maritime Command Headquarters. Shawn knew for certain that it was Vice Admiral Lowery, the Commander of Maritime Naval HQ. It was he who sent the package. The question was, why the note and the gun? And, just who were the troops, and what was their mission?

Phillips was certain that Shanahan would want to know about the contents of the package and the note. This information would be passed along with any other info that the search team gathered.

# 12   HARDWARE TO NUNAVUT

24 December 1700 hrs local, Halifax, Nova Scotia

After work, Brig. Gen. Shanahan walked down Barrington Street, in Halifax, to catch a bus to his home. It was Friday, and it had been a long tedious week. On most Fridays, he would have gone to the Officers Mess for some TGIF refreshments and snacks for a few hours until his wife got home from her law practice. But today, all he wanted to do was to catch a bus home and relax with his dog. While waiting for the bus, he picked up a copy of the evening edition of the Halifax Herald. The headline of the paper caught his eye. It read: "Commander's Gift to Ottawa".

There was a photo of Vice Admiral Lowery in front of two helicopters and fifty men dressed in army fatigues. The second photo was of a ship with about fifty sailors standing on the deck. The story mentioned that Admiral Lowery had held a press conference very early in the day at the Iqaluit Airport, better known by most Canadians as Frobisher Bay Airport. The paper mentioned that Lowery was dismayed at the lack of concern by the current Canadian government over the protection of Canada's sovereignty, especially in the Canadian Arctic. Lowery reportedly said that each year the Northwest Passage, an inland waterway, was claimed by Canada as a territorial waterway. However, several nations, including Russia and the U.S., treated the waterway as international waters.

The press article mentioned that the Admiral referred to treaties when asked by reporters about NATO's use of the Passage. Apparently, U.S. warships using the seaway were covered by bilateral defense agreements, and NATO treaties allowed free passage to NATO ships. Icebreakers came under another agreement.

Lowery spoke about the legendary polar route, between the Atlantic and the Pacific Oceans, undergoing profound and wrenching changes. Not only were oil drilling platforms sprouting up like dandelions. There were mining operations, gas explorations, strategic military operations, tourism, shipping, and other industries. They were all invading the Arctic. They were ruining the environment to the detriment of the native population and its culture.

He said that there was even evidence that some landings from foreign ships had been made on Canadian soil.

"There may even be 'aliens' living in our cities and towns, especially those in the North, that were deposited on our Arctic shores by these marine crafts completely ignoring and making a mockery of our immigration procedures. Some of these 'landees' are spies out to take over our Northern lands."

The newspaper indicated that newsmen pressed the Admiral to name countries. Admiral Lowery mentioned Russia on several occasions but didn't respond when asked if the United States also used the Passage. He did mention that the SS Manhattan sailed through the Northwest Passage in 1969 without permission while the ship flew the U.S. flag. The paper read that Lowery sarcastically said that the government's response to such incursions was to revive the Canadian Rangers and issue each of them with a red baseball cap and an old rifle. To underscore the threat that he foresaw, he mentioned that the nuclear submarine, USS Sea Dragon, made the first submerged transit of the Passage in the sixties. There had been hundreds of similar passages under the ice since that period.

The Halifax Herald continued on to report that Lowery had criticized the PM for visiting Moscow on several occasions. He felt that Prime Minister Le Chance should be making a greater effort to protect the entranceways to our North, rather than holding further talks with Russian representatives. According to the paper, Lowery mockingly said that it would not surprise him if the PM were in Moscow at the same time that Russian troops were landing in Canada's unprotected north country. The newspaper quoted the words of Lowery.

"The solution to the lack of protection of our North is that Canada needs to run a string of sounding devices along the floor of the Arctic. The devices should also have connecting mines that could be activated at will by Naval authorities when there is an unauthorized entry."

Also, according to the Herald, Lowery elaborated on the need for the Arctic to have a fleet of ships and airplanes along with the crews to man them. They would be deployed to any spot in the Arctic when a situation required them. Lowery stated that he had made such recommendations, on several occasions, to Canadian Forces Headquarters senior staff. He had personally spoken with several politicians, including the PM and the Defense Minister, yet nothing was being done about the problem.

When questioned, Lowery mentioned that the Americans were concerned with what was happening in the Arctic, especially since it could affect their security. It was entirely feasible, according to Lowery, for an enemy of the U.S. to enter the Arctic and fire off missiles that could hit any city in Canada and in the U.S.

The newspaper reporter quizzed the Admiral about discussions with U.S. Naval authorities. Lowery responded by stating that he had held talks with some Pentagon senior Navy officials about the Canadians' progress in defending their seas. As a product of these talks, there was a joint U.S. and Canadian Naval Exercise off the Arctic Eastern Coast in the first week of January to demonstrate the mutual concern over the sovereignty issue.

The Herald continued with the front-page news, received from the international press corps that had attended the briefing. Lowery had told the press about the valuable resources that existed in Nunavut. For example, there were vast mineral resources such as gold and diamonds, and there were huge deposits of oil. He spoke about hardworking Northerners, especially the Inuit who had occupied the land for hundreds of years, and how they were not benefiting from these resources. Lowery talked about the immediate need to protect these people and these resources while Ottawa played footsies with the Russians.

Shanahan sat on a bench near the bus stop and continued the article.

The paper reported that Lowery could wait no longer for the government to get off its backside and do something for these people, as well as protect the fragile Arctic environment. He and his friends were making a fantastic gift to Canada and Nunavut. He had managed to recruit several hundred former naval personnel, who had volunteered to live in and become residents of the Arctic as part of the Nunavut Reserve Forces. Private donations would pay them, and not one red cent would come from Ottawa. These soldiers and sailors would be well-armed with rockets and missiles to defend the territory. More recruits were on the way, and they would eventually be in every coastal outpost in the Arctic. In the meantime, the first fifty of these recruits were on display for the press briefing.

The Herald indicated that one of their reporters asked about the facilities that they would use. According to Admiral Lowery, the recruits were being housed at the Frobisher Airport, in the six hangars initially designed by the Canadian Forces for the Forward Operating Location Detachment in the early nineties. They also had use of an operations unit, a living area with washing facilities, and a Mess Hall. The hangars were located near the runway since the men would also operate airplanes and helicopters donated solely to the Arctic defense.

The donated aircraft and helicopters would include eight AH- 64A Apache helicopters, two of which were now on display. These helicopters had been used in Panama in 1989 and subsequently in the 1991 Gulf War. These aircraft had now been donated to the Nunavut Forces, said Lowery. The two helicopters on display were armed with missiles and rockets, and they had a turret under the forward fuselage housing a 30 mm gun with tons of ammo.

Fuel caches were established to allow the planes to fly anywhere in Nunavut. The fuel caches would be located throughout the territory, according to the reporter who spoke to Lowery, and that the eight helicopters would soon be located in the major communities of Nunavut, including Alert, Grise Fiord, Resolute Bay, Cambridge Bay, Rankin Inlet, Pond Inlet, Eureka, and of course, Iqaluit. Since Frobisher Bay airport would be the main operating base for these helicopters, there would be at least two of them there at all times.

The Halifax paper wrote that Lowery said that he and his followers would be using the Logistic Support Site built for the North Warning System, especially its radar tower and satellite communications. The followers would be located there for the foreseeable future.

Besides the men and the helicopters, Lowery also spoke about the fast attack and patrol ships that were being donated to Nunavut. He provided the reporters with photos of a B7 Hovercraft at the Frobisher Bay harbor that was designed to operate over land, water, and ice. The photos showed that the craft was armed with depth charges, torpedoes, and missiles. Sonobuoys were also visible.

The Herald remarked that Lowery took care to point out that ships such as these would be situated on the Arctic coasts throughout Nunavut, on the floating sea ice, or they would be tied up at wharves, such as the new wharf in Frobisher Bay, whenever conditions allowed. The sailors and soldiers would be circulated between the ships and their onshore homes on a rotational basis. Lowery said that the forty-five hundred residents of Frobisher Bay would seldom see these defenders, yet their presence would add to the area's economic welfare.

When asked by the press if the Premier had agreed to this defense force, Lowery responded that he was sure that the local RCMP detachment was incapable of handling any raiding party that may come ashore from a foreign vessel. He explained that the plans for this force were in the works long before the most recent election for Premier. Furthermore, that he had the full support of Willie Nageak, who also ran in the recent election for the Premier position.

Shanahan didn't know what to make of this news event. What he did know was that he needed that drink now, so he hailed a cab to take him to the Officers Mess.

At the Mess, he spoke with a few other general officers who were all under the opinion that Lowery would be history by Monday morning. They felt that Lowery went too far, especially in his criticism of the PM. Shanahan wasn't too sure. The move might be popular with Canadians being that it was defending Canadian lands, something that the current government was neglecting. At the same time, the so-called gift was a saving of tax dollars.

The other Generals agreed that the PM was always one who read the public mood before making decisions. Shanahan expected the PM to invite Lowery for a visit to his Sussex Drive home, in Ottawa, and order him to bring his force under the Canadian government's control. It would be interesting to see what Lowery would do.

Would there be a showdown over his ploy, or would he end up being promoted to a four-star Admiral to run this new force? Would the PM dictate Lowery's force to join the regular force? Would Lowery quit and end up running his own private navy?

Shanahan thought that perhaps his nemesis would no longer be in charge of Maritime Command. Perhaps, Lowery would be out with a 'volunteer retirement' golden handshake. Perhaps, he would end up as a four-star Commander of an Arctic Naval Force.

*What would the PM do?* he wondered. *The next couple of days could be interesting,* he thought.

Shanahan had no idea how interesting they would turn out to be.

# 13    THE NEW FLORIDA

7 December, 1000 hrs local, Frobisher Bay, Nunavut

The day following his news briefing, the one covered by the Halifax Herald, Admiral 'Buzz' Lowery made an appointment with the Premier of Nunavut, Sean Alaka. He was driven in a limousine to the Parnell building. It was being used as a legislative building while a new Legislative Assembly building was being constructed next door. He slowly walked up the stairs and entered the brightly lit doorway. A commissioner at the entrance announced his arrival to the Premier's secretary. Lowery entered the Premier's office and shook his hand as the Premier invited him to sit and asked the secretary to bring coffee.

"Good day, Premier Alaka. I would like to talk to you about the need to provide additional military protection to your province."

Lowery couldn't help but notice that the Premier was a dozen years younger than himself, and that he looked more like a Southerner than a native Inuit. Lowery had been told that the Premier was a graduate of Osgood Hall Law School, in Toronto, and that he had a thriving criminal law practice before deciding to return to his home in Frobisher Bay to work on the creation of the new territory of Nunavut.

Nunavut was a separate territory, apart from the Northwest Territories. It was previously controlled by government in Yellowknife. Alaka had used every opportunity during his battle for independence to argue that the people of Nunavut were different from the Dene that ran the government in Yellowknife.

Alaka argued that the Dene were not providing good service to his Inuit people. It was only natural that his people would elect him as the Premier of the brand-new province.

"Good day, Admiral Lowery. Tell me why you think we need more protection than that presently provided by the Government of Canada."

"I don't know if you heard my news conference yesterday. I mentioned that this great land holds millions of dollars in natural resources, but it could be readily taken from you by any large-scale raiding party that has the intention. The Government of Canada provides you with a few hundred untrained and under equipped Arctic Rangers and flies over Nunavut every few weeks on their Nor Pat patrols. That so-called protection would not stop a properly equipped force from taking over your government and stripping this province of all its wealth. Just look at the fact that there are foreign ships, including Russian submarines, passing by your doorsteps practically every day without the approval of Canada. One of these days, one or more of those subs are going to stop and set up their headquarters, and there will be nothing that the Canadian government can do about it once they are rooted into the environment.

"Or, there could be a huge oil spill, as one example, that would ruin the beaches, coasts, and animal life for a hundred years. The ship that causes the damage won't even slow down to see the devastation. This land could use a system of underwater cables and mines that could be used to detect ships and keep away those that are dangerous, such as tankers full of bulk oil. This province needs its own tri-service force equipped with armed ships, planes, and personnel carriers."

The Premier listened intently until Lowery finished his arguments.

"We intend to press the government for additional forces for this area because of some of the reasons that you mentioned. We feel that Canada's Armed Forces brings economic activity to an area, and we are one of the few provinces that are not benefiting from the presence of a Canadian Forces base. What would you like from my cabinet?" Alaka queried.

"In my news conference, I mentioned that my friends and I are donating a large number of assets to Nunavut, including men, planes, ships, and armaments. We feel that these assets should be used exclusively for Nunavut's protection and not mingled with those of the Canadian Forces, where they could be moved elsewhere. We feel that you and your cabinet should recognize the Nunavut Forces as your exclusive military, and I gladly offer my services to you as its Commanding Officer."

"My Cabinet and I thank you for your offer. Last night, we discussed your news briefing at our caucus meeting. We feel that we are no different from the rest of Canada, and we don't see the need for an exclusive force. The Cabinet has confidence that the Canadian government will do the right thing, and that they will accept your assets and then provide them exclusively to us as part of the Canadian Forces. We will rely on them to provide the necessary funds to operate the assets and to name the commander of these forces."

"Premier, I believe that you are making a mistake, and I hope that it doesn't come back to haunt you."

"Be that as it may, we still have a hundred percent confidence in the Prime Minister. Now, if you will excuse me, I have another meeting."

Lowery left, filled with frustration, and returned to his suite at the Navigator Inn. He told his aide to bring him Willie Nageak.

The aide drove around Frobisher city checking on the whereabouts of one Willie Nageak.

Willie had run for the position of Premier as a long shot candidate. Most other qualified candidates knew that they couldn't beat Sean Alaka, so they didn't waste their time and money. Willie decided to let his name stand, but made no substantial effort to beat Alaka. In fact, he didn't even show up for any of the election debates held throughout the new province. When the election was over, he had received less than one percent of the votes. He now spent most of his time in the billiard room of the Royal Canadian Legion in Frobisher, where he was an associate member.

Lowery's aide didn't have any problem finding Willie in his customary seat, sitting with his friends at the bar. For the price of a beer, he agreed to accompany the Aide to Lowery's suite.

"How would you like to be Premier of Nunavut?" asked Admiral Lowery to an astonished Mr. Nageak.

"That would be nice, as long as I don't end up in jail," Willie replied in jest.

"Maybe it will be Premier Alaka," said Lowery. Nageak didn't know if he was serious or not.

"I can arrange it for you to be the next premier of this province, if you want to be. You see, I am not very happy with the current premier and his cabinet. He is making irrational decisions, plus, he sold out the people of Nunavut, and now he is just a puppet of Ottawa. He is letting huge corporations come into your land, stripping it of its wealth. Furthermore, he is not prepared to fight Ottawa to have military protection of your people and your heritage. It looks like he is willing to let the Russians, or any other foreign governments, sail your waterways and march unopposed onto your land. He can't see that this beautiful land is a prize worth taking, by any large force that wants it. My military experience tells me that Nunavut could easily fall to any organized force, believe me. I seriously want to know if you want to be premier."

Willie Nageak thought about it for a moment.

"Yeah, why not? What would I have to do? Who do I have to kill?" he said with a grin.

"I'll make you premier on one condition! You must name me as your Defense Chief of Nunavut Forces and as your Finance Minister. If you are prepared to do that, then you only need to await my call. I have a feeling that Alaka and his Cabinet will not be around for much longer. In the meantime, you can go back to playing pool at the Legion, but keep your mouth shut. Tell no one about this conversation."

Willie Nageak could live with that arrangement. Rising from his comfortable chair, he accepted fifty bucks from Lowery to buy himself some beer and left the building.

Admiral Lowery's frustration was starting to settle, but he felt a need to talk to his kid brother. He lifted the receiver of the phone, and asked the hotel receptionist to try to contact his brother, Brian Lowery, at the Eureka Weather station.

He sat back in the hotel's lazy boy chair with a whiskey and soda while waiting for the call to go through. Plans were fermenting in his mind, but first he wanted to discuss them with Brian.

Later, he would discuss the subject with Admiral Heiserman of the U.S. Navy. Lowery knew that there was little likelihood that the PM would agree to let him stay on in Frobisher as a four-star Admiral and run his new force.

It was Lowery's opinion that Ottawa had no foresight, and the Chief of Defense Staff was a pussycat when it came to dealing with the Prime Minister. The PM didn't tolerate anyone who made his government look ineffective. In his mind, Lowery could already foresee a showdown with the PM, the CDS, and possibly the Defense Minister, over who was going to control all of the military assets that he was fortunate enough to accumulate. One thing was for certain, he would not be pushed around. When the time came, Admiral Lowery would do what was best for Admiral Lowery.

The phone rang and the receptionist let him know that the call could go ahead.

"Hello little brother, how is life treating you?"

"Just fine, Buzz, how are you doing? I heard your news briefing. Hell, that is quite a force that you've got for yourself."

"You bet it is. I spoke to the Premier today, and that asshole won't let me run it. He wants to turn all of my equipment and men over to Ottawa to run it. Can you believe that idiot?" Lowery said with exasperation.

"Are you going to let him do that? You went through all the effort to get these people and all that equipment, and now the politicians just want to push you aside. Christ, I never saw you back down from any politician." Brian was surprised that his older brother was having any kind of problem.

"I don't think I'll let them push me around, but I want to hear the offers from the Chief of Defense Staff first. You know that I want to stay here in Nunavut to be near you, so I'll ask the Chief to let me run the new force from here. If he created a new four-star position and named me to fill it, that would also be the answer."

"What will you do if he doesn't agree?"

"I'm not sure yet. I think that with all these forces, I could easily take over Nunavut if I wanted to. What do you think?"

"Hell, that would be great! And that's what I would do if I were you. We need a strong leader in charge of this province. It's rapidly going downhill with this new government. The Cabinet is too weak in the knees for me, and I think that you would make a great premier."

"Thanks. I would probably let someone else have the premier chair, but I would still run the province. There may have to be some bloodshed here in Frobisher and maybe elsewhere in the province. The blood would belong to those that would oppose my agenda. Could you live with that?"

"I'm with you one hundred percent. Just tell me what you want me to do. You know that my followers and I can easily handle it. Hundreds of your old Navy buddies are here in Nunavut, and you know that they would willingly fight for you. How would you handle opposition from Ottawa?"

"I think that I have a way around that. You know how the Quebec government wants out of Canada. Ottawa has agreed that they can have a referendum to see if the people want to opt out of Canada. Well, as I see it, with Nunavut being its own province, we could also have a referendum. Ottawa would not dare to interfere with us expressing our democratic rights after allowing Quebec to have two referendums. A new government of Nunavut could declare, as its first act, that it is independent and will have a referendum, after the fact, to confirm that's what the people want. What do you think of that logic?"

"That might work, Buzz. You wouldn't have any problem, with your golden tongue, convincing the residents to go for independence. Hell, as a fallback position you could easily flood the province with your old navy buddies and guarantee yourself a 'yes' vote. But you may have to buy yourself some mercenaries to hold the fort until the vote is taken."

"I thought about that. I want to talk to Admiral Heiserman to see if the U.S. Forces would protect a republic struggling to be born, and to see if he can get some more funds to help keep our friends loyal. By the way, I did send you more money but it got lost in a plane crash."

"I could use replacement funds if you can get them to me. If you did become premier, what would be in it for you? I know that you would likely get the fourth star from the Canadian Forces in the next two years if you stayed with them, so why risk the future promotion?"

"I really would like to get that fourth star, but it's not likely to happen. You and I know what it's like to grow up in a small town like Cape Breton, where the only livelihood comes from the sea. We both swore that we wouldn't spend all of our lives fishing like our father did. That's why we both joined the Navy with you as weatherman and me as a cadet. You were happy to spend twenty years, then retire as a Lieutenant, but I always wanted to return to Glace Bay as a four-star Admiral, just to show the guys that we grew up with and who are still fishing. You also know you can be anything you want to be if you're willing to move away from that God forsaken place and reach for the brass ring. That's why it would be nice to have the highest rank." Lowery took a sip of his drink and continued.

"But, the Canadian Forces presently has only one four-star position, and that is the Chief of Defense position. It will be vacant in the next two years, but it's generally rotated among the different forces, and it is the Army's turn to have the next four-star rank. Since I am in the Navy, I would have to wait another four years. I couldn't wait that long, so I'll take my chances here in Nunavut." Lowery was on a roll with his plans.

"I didn't mention it earlier, but I have an arrangement with Admiral Heiserman. You may not know it, but he wants to be president of the United States. It will take a lot of money for him to achieve that goal. His plan is to steal all the data aboard the Russian spacecraft, MIR, and sell it to the highest bidder, most likely the Chinese. There has to be millions and millions of dollars of data aboard that craft. You do realize that the spacecraft has passed over every country in the world during its lifetime. It's photographed every military installation on the planet during the years. That is powerful data, little brother. The problem is, how does he get his hands on it? He thinks that he has found a way to bring the craft down at some deserted spot and then strip it. He thinks that a place like the vast quantities of vacant land in the territory of Nunavut would be an idealistic place for a spacecraft to land. The pack ice surrounding Nunavut would serve his purpose. Or, even the ice surrounding the Pole would be ideal. It sounds like an impossibility, but he has his dream. If the craft lands outside our control territory, then we would need to find a way to get the MIR data to Nunavut.

"He needs to make sure that he is not spotted stealing the data. He thinks that someone like me could prevent observers from recording his recovery of it. He also thinks that he could achieve his objective if I were commanding the territory where the craft would land. He is willing to give me tons of military equipment, an arsenal, men, and money, to become the ruler of Nunavut. As premier, or leader of Nunavut, I would prevent anyone, or any nation, from trying to steal back his mother lode of data.

"You asked what's in it for me. As you know, I would like to be a four star to finish my career at the top. I always try to be successful. I always want to be at the top, regardless of whatever I attempt. I could be a four-star in Nunavut, and as a bonus I could pick up a huge amount of land that would set me up for life. This Nunavut land will appreciate in value due to global warming. What do you think of this plan? Am I crazy?" Lowery finally breathed, after revealing his plans to his brother.

"Of course not, Buzz, you know that I support you in whatever you want. If you are in favor of this plan, then I will do whatever you need to achieve it. I say go for it. Yours and Heiserman's plans are a secret with me!"

"I sent you some literature on global warming. One piece had evidence and says that the polar ice cap is melting extremely fast. As I see it, unless the ozone hole is closed soon, this frozen land of ours could become beachfront in the future. If we accumulate land now, we could have as much land as a new Florida. We would be rich. We would be set for life.'"

"Buzz, I have read all the papers you sent me. I don't know how long it would take for this area to become a new Florida, but one thing is for certain, that it will happen, since the countries of the world are not cooperating on cutting down the emissions of harmful gases. It would seem like a good idea to buy up as much as possible of the land, before someone else has the same bright idea."

"Well, little brother, I've got to go now, but I wasn't talking about *buying* the land, if you know what I mean. I have ways and means of getting as much land as I want. Anyway, I'll let you know how things work out."

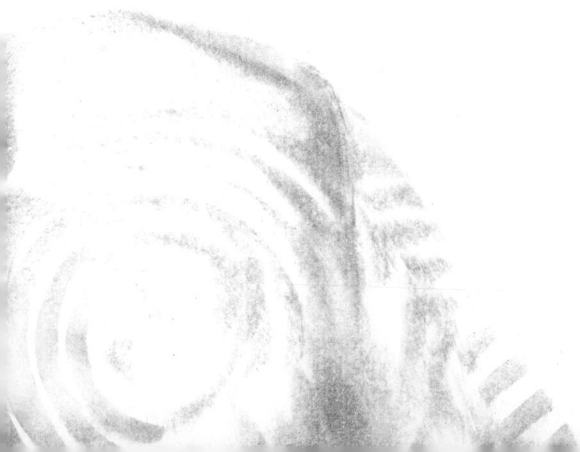

# 14   THE DESCENT

26 Dec 1800 hrs local, Korolyov, Moscow

At about the same time as the search was being organized in Halifax, Vasily Vinogradov had just returned to work on the evening shift. He had several days of vacation in the Russian countryside. His wife, Katerina, had been nagging him for months to take time off from his job as Propulsion Engineer at the Russian Mission Control Center at Korolyov, a Moscow suburb. She wanted him to spend some time with her at their dacha. He had to admit that his work on the MIR project had consumed all of his time in the past several months, especially since the space station had been having so many problems. The nearly fourteen-year-old station, that was originally designed for five years, was nearing the end of its useful life span. He and other engineers were discussing plans on how to bring it to a conclusion, but there were several people in the space agency, and in the Russian government, that wanted to keep MIR alive.

Like most of the ground controllers, Vasily had to moonlight as an interrupter if he was to maintain his dacha. Working two jobs was stressful, and the situation placed strains on his weakened marriage. But the holidays in the country had made him more relaxed; he and his wife had spent most of their time together working in their garden and visiting the local sites. The time away from his project had resulted in a stronger marriage, and they were once again blissfully happy. He couldn't recall the last time that they had so much sex. It was probably before they were married and only dating. That was fifteen years ago. At the time he was a young university student in Moscow, full of wonderful ideas, and she was the daughter of a Soviet diplomat. The past week was so wonderful that he promised his wife and himself that they would take more time at their retreat in the coming months. More time for more sex. That was the plan.

When Vasily entered the Control Centre for his first evening shift, some of his gloom and doom attitude had returned. The dreariness seemed to fill the mausoleum-like room. The Centre, also known as

TsUP, was a dark, chilly and drafty place. It had spacious corridors, and the linoleum covered floors often cracked when you walked on them.

Carrying his thick woolen sweater, Vasily walked through the huge break area leading to his desk. A sweater was a necessity if you were to survive the nine-hour shift. It was noticeable that the Centre was practically vacant. Generally, the vast room, containing over fifty consoles, wall maps and video displays of the world, along with reams of data on the front wall, was usually bursting with activity, especially during a launch. About fifty people worked, as a team, in Mission Control. Each team worked nine-hour shifts. On most occasions, the room also contained many of the engineering staff who supported the mission, should there be a peculiar problem. Today there was little more than a handful of staff in the Centre.

The Centre had four parallel rows of consoles for the staff, as their workstations, but most of the room workers were standing around talking. A few were reading newspapers and some were sitting in front of their consoles but not staring at their screens. There was no one on the surrounding mezzanine that was often crowded with space tourists. It was obvious that the Centre was not in an operational state at the moment. Only the MIR space station was of interest at this time, and MIR was dormant. The last cosmonaut had departed the station several weeks ago.

Vasily noticed no flight controllers present in Mission Control, which was unusual since they were present in quantity when there was a crew in orbit. They had to talk directly to the crew members and guide them in their mission. When present, the flight controllers directed the entire day for the crew, and even woke them up in the morning with music. Those that were in the Control Centre this evening were specialists who received information from the spacecraft's computers. A few were reviewing older data to assist them with their next main project-the International Space Station, a joint Moscow and USA project that also had the backing of thirteen other nations.

He pulled out his swivel chair, sat down at his console, and turned on the old computer. It was necessary to take extra care to avoid the electrical shocks that often accompanied such a maneuver. He cleared away some papers that had been worked on by the previous shift. The screen in front of him came to life, filling itself with a jumble of numbers before settling on a graphic map of the world, containing a blip. Vasily glanced at the world's main wall video map and noted that MIR was passing over Mexico. His computer screen gave him the exact same location every few minutes and would update itself, just as the video map on the front wall brought MIR's latest location to the attention of the whole room.

As the screen on his terminal brightened, he noticed that the Latitude changed from 12.0 degrees to 21.0 degrees Latitude and from -82.2 degrees to -74.9 degrees Longitude. But it was the altitude that caught his attention. MIR was flying at 343.7 altimeters but it changed to 300.0 kilometers as the screen updated itself. He knew that the altitude changed plus or minus a kilometer from minute to minute, but not as much as forty-three kilometers.

The normal altitude of MIR had ranged from 325 to 400 kms, as it circled the earth every hour. Occasionally, MIR tended to drop orbits, slowly and over a two-week period, by a few kilometers. This pattern would be followed by a slight jet burn, activated by the flight controller, that would boost it back to its original orbit.

Vasily anxiously waited for the next readout. When it appeared on his screen, it read 275 kilometers. The space station was descending. Was this planned? Did the engineers finally reach an agreement on how to bring down the craft while he was away? Or was this another system problem with MIR? Previous issues had recently made the spacecraft spin out of control until the craft was manually stabilized by the crew onboard MIR at the time. In July, a rate sensor cable was inadvertently disconnected, causing a loss of power to MIR's altitude control computer, causing the craft to lose its orientation to the sun. It took the use of MIR's thruster jets to restore its control.

These problems led to a widespread belief that MIR was old, stuffy, accident-prone, and often packed with rubbish.

The next reading showed the MIR location as 250 kilometers above the earth. The rate of descent was slowing but the space station was still losing altitude. To be on the safe side, Vasily decided that the ground controllers had to be warned.

He pushed the alarm button, and immediately the conversation in the room came to a halt. Several engineers rushed to their consoles while the senior Trajectory Officer hastily made his way to Vasily's station.

"What is wrong?" asked the officer.

"MIR is losing altitude. Was this planned? I just returned from holidays, so I am not aware of any planned descent."

"Let me see. There has been no decision yet to end MIR."

The screen changed again and the altitude read 240 kilometers. The Trajectory Officer sped to his console; the descent had to be stopped. The space station had to be stabilized, and perhaps later returned to its original orbit. Only then could they take the time to determine the cause of the rapid fall. The engineers worked feverishly to bring the space station under control. Flight controllers were called, and they dashed to Mission Control to take charge. On arrival, they ordered that a signal be sent to MIR's computer to perform a ten-second firing of one of the two large engines on one of the modules used for making significant orbital changes. The descent stopped, and the control room cheered when it occurred. To get the space station back to its original altitude, the Flight Controller called for the same engine to be fired for a burn of one minute and forty seconds, in the first of several maneuvers that he expected to make over the next few days, that would eventually raise MIR to its regular circular orbit which averaged around 343 kilometers altitude. The scientists and engineers initiated the command that would set the process in motion.

Nothing happened, because the engine didn't ignite. A second attempt was made but with the same failure. The Flight Controller tried several other maneuvers, but the craft remained at 240 kilometers above the earth's surface. Since MIR was stabilized, the engineers made a group decision to temporarily suspend efforts to raise its altitude and instead concentrate on the cause of its descent.

The flight controllers met with other officials of the Russian Mission Control Centre to review procedures and to discuss options. Vasily was asked to attend by the Flight Director, Mikhail Goncharov, who had overall responsibility. Goncharov briefly reviewed where MIR was, where it could go, and where it had been.

He was emphatic that the Mission Control Center was to work twenty-four hours per day, if necessary, to make sure that the craft did not descend any further. He reminded all workers present, that the plans called for another Soyuz mission in the new year, to retrieve the computers, recorders and cameras, and anything else that was useful for the ISS mission. Goncharov stressed that it was very important that the computers be fetched, since they contained more than thirteen years of raw data consisting of experiments, conversations, overflights, pictures of space phenomena, and much more.

He reminded everyone that after the next mission, the plans called for the use of five crewless Progress Cargo ships, docked to MIR, one at a time, to lower it to just over 75 miles, before it would plunge into the Pacific.

The actual descent would occur by using a signal to the cargo ship that would start the burn of its rocket engine. The cargo ships would then be used to control the fall of the craft over eighteen months. Otherwise, MIR would fall out of orbit towards earth within two years on its own. The conservation volume in the room grew, as some engineers argued that some huge chunks would hit populated areas. In contrast, other engineers said it was impossible to bring MIR to earth without it burning up in the atmosphere. One thing that all the engineers agreed on that day at Mission Control was that no one had sent a signal to MIR to start its descent.

"It had to be a system failure," said one engineer.

"OK, let us do a hundred percent check of all systems," said the Flight Director.

"That would take weeks."

"Do it!"

Later in the day, the MIR descent started again, and the action caught Mission Control entirely off guard. More surprisingly, the station began to separate from itself. Kvant 1 and Kvant 2 modules were the first to leave the unit and go their separate ways into the black void of space. A short time later, the Kristall and Priroda modules separated and floated free. Spektr was the last to let go. That left just the MIR core module, which descended to 200 kilometers above the earth before it once again stabilized. All six units were floating on their own, since the hatches were all closed off by the last departing MIR crew. These separated modules were lighter than the MIR core and would most likely burn up on re-entry to the atmosphere. The MIR core was in the lowest earth orbit, and there was considerable doubt if it would suffer a similar fate.

The Control Centre was in a panic. There was no doubt that the end was near for MIR. It was happening before their eyes, and before they had a chance to remove precious cargo. Every effort that tried to boost the stripped craft back to its former orbit had failed. Engineers were blaming one another for the latest setback in the life of the crippled, and seemingly jinxed, spacecraft. Most were now resigned to its demise. It was just a matter of time before an announcement would be made to tell the world that the craft was returning to earth, and that it could fall on a populated area.

Of course, the Russian government would do whatever it could to prevent such a tragedy from happening. There was talk about blasting the craft from the sky if it didn't burn up, but it was unrealistic given the possibility that it could land anywhere on the earth's surface. When questioned about its impact point, the engineers recalled that the U.S. Space Station, Skylab, impacted the earth's surface in July, 1979. The debris dispersal area stretched from the Southeastern Indian Ocean across a sparsely populated section of Western Australia.

What the Russians were concerned about was the data that was aboard the craft. This data, especially regarding the world's military installations, was worth billions of rubles. The data could be parceled out, for a price, to the friends of Russia.

Vasily continued to monitor the data coming from the MIR core module. As he looked at the reams of data, he saw one piece of information that caused him some confusion. It seems that the craft had received a command just before its latest descent, and that command didn't come from Korolyov Ground Control. He scanned the rest of the data that his console had received and printed out before he returned to duty. Sure enough, the data showed that a similar rogue command had been received before the initial descent. That was interesting.

He checked the data that streamed out of his printer just after the craft had stabilized from its descent. It contained two commands; one that was from his Flight Controller and a second, unusually coded command, that was received by MIR just before it stabilized. He reached for the latest stream of paper, and quickly spotted the command that stabilized MIR just moments ago. This latest order had not been sent from this building, thought Vasily. The engineers had been cheering their stabilizing of the craft on its first major fall, when in fact, it wasn't their doing. It was purely coincidental that their command reached the space station at the same time that a rogue order put the brakes on MIR's descent.

He gathered up the stack of papers and proceeded to the Chief Flight Controller's desk, where he dropped the pile of data. He pointed out the commands, and the difference between those sent from the Mission Centre and those that the module had received elsewhere.

"I suggest we contact military Headquarters. It is my belief that MIR's descent is not caused by more system problems, but rather from some mysterious commands, not from our consoles," said Vasily.

"You are suggesting sabotage by someone? Can you identify the source of the commands?"

"Not at the moment. I can't tell yet, the source of these strangely coded commands. Perhaps, someone in the Centre had some part in it."

"Vasily, we need to keep your findings quiet for the time being. Could it be the Americans? They are jealous of MIR's achievements, and it will take them years before the ISS will be up and running and producing quality experiments like our craft."

"Like the Americans are always saying, 'Anything is possible'. The U.S. Space Agency was allowed to send commands whenever one of their cosmonauts flew on MIR. But their orders were always routed to this Centre to be reformatted to the codes that we established. These commands don't contain our codes."

"I'll call the General that's responsible for security at the Space Agency and brief him on your findings. It is up to him to make preparations to recover MIR, should it be commanded to continue its descent to earth, and should it survive the plunge through the atmosphere."

Vasily returned to his work station and spent the next few hours attempting to locate the source of the mysterious commands to MIR. His work was interrupted by an uproar in Mission Control, indicating that MIR was descending once again. He hastily read his computer screen and immediately punched in a formula that would input several equations and plot the expected crash point of MIR. The screen displayed the startling results. Unless the MIR core stabilized, its remains were destined for an impact in the Canadian Arctic, near the Magnetic North Pole.

# 15   SEA DEVIL TRAPPED

25December 1200 local Ellef Ringnes Island Ice fields, Nunavut

"Aircraft sighted, aft!" yelled the surprised lookout. One minute he was listening to Christmas music in his ear phones and cleaning the frost from his night glasses. The next moment, he was staring at an aircraft approaching him at 200 knots per hour, at a thousand-foot altitude.

Commander Hayes, Captain of the Sea Devil, reacted instinctively to save his ship and the crew of one hundred fifty-six men.

"Clear the bridge and dive!" The words left his mouth within a second of hearing the lookout's shrill call. Action was immediate. All the men on the bridge scrambled down the ladder, slamming it closed and locking the watertight hatch door. All the while, the klaxon horn was sounding.

"Hatch secure!" came the frantic call of the Officer of the Bridge, the last man down the ladder. Jack Murphy, the Executive Officer, yelled to the Diving Officer as soon as his feet hit the lower deck.

"Take her straight down to 300 feet."

The DO's left hand flew to the controls for the hydraulic pumps. His right hand reached to the switch for the air intake valve to provide ventilation to the below decks. It had to be closed when diving. He pressed the button to the central air valve and opened the main ballast tank vents. He watched the primary air blow valve control, as the open main ballast tanks started to take on a thousand tons of water. The ship should be sinking beneath the ice, but it was not moving. It was wedged in between it.

"Captain, we seem to be stuck."

"Try it again, open the ballast vents some more."

More water was added to the ballast, but the ship did not become submerged. She seemed to be wedged between two colossal pack ice sheets, one on each side, while chunks of the ice inched up the sides of the vessel. Apparently, the lookout was too busy watching for aircraft, and had paid no attention to the slowly shifting, creeping ice masses.

"The prevailing winds during the past couple of hours must have caused the ice to drift close and crush against the hull. It's produced a suction effect on the ship," said Hayes. "Try rocking her. Shift ballast from one tank to another, side to side and fore and aft, to rock her free." Hayes was calm although his heart was racing. The enemy aircraft was approaching the stricken sub.

The maneuver had some success. Hayes could feel the Sea Devil struggling to break free of the deadly grip of the ice. But she was still not submerging.

"We're sitting ducks unless we do something," said Hayes to Murphy.

"We hear the aircraft radioing to us to identify ourselves, we could answer," stated the communication operator.

"We are under orders not to be seen or heard by anyone that would identify us as an American ship."

"The aircraft co-pilot is still trying to identify us, and he is now threatening force."

"We'll go back up to the bridge," Hayes spoke to his XO again. "Bring along our portable missile launcher, and one of our crew to operate it. We may have to fire a warning shot to keep the plane at a distance until we can break free." He turned to the diving officer before heading out.

"Keep her rocking, she's breaking free, I can feel it. Let me know the moment that she struggles loose, so we can clear the deck."

Hayes and Murphy climbed the stairs and stepped out onto the bridge of the sail. The aircraft had released flares to light up the night sky, highlighting the black Sea Devil's outline against the white background of the Arctic ice. Thankfully, the bursts of light were fading fast. Chances were that the aircraft still hadn't identified his ship as American. Using his night binoculars, Hayes could see the plane in the distance as it turned to make another run. It descended to a lower altitude to make its pass, and he could see that the bomb bay doors were now open.

"It's a Canadian Air Force Aurora," said Murphy. "It's an ASW plane. It has no missiles, only homing torpedoes and sonobuoys." His sentences came in short bursts as he recalled some facts from his briefing notes on Canadian warplanes.

"The Aurora has torpedoes, but a torpedo wouldn't be of much use when we are surrounded by ice."

"Captain, look about two miles out. Directly in the Aurora's path is an open lead. It must have opened up in the last couple of hours, by the same winds that crushed the ice against our sides. If he drops a homing torpedo in it, the fish might find us. It would be a long shot, but it is possible."

Footsteps were pounding on the stairs. The officers heard the feet hit the sail bridge, and turned in time to see Battery Commander Marsh firing off the surface-to-air missile. It was headed in the direction of the plane.

Marsh would argue, later, that he had overheard the captain ask for a missile operator and launcher, and he was available as the Sea Devil crew were all busy trying to free the ice-bound sub. He had used his rank to replace the man chosen by the Executive Officer and decided that he would handle it himself. He had rushed up the stairs of the sail, to the bridge, just in time to see the Aurora open its bomb bay doors.

"Christ, man, you shouldn't have done that!" screamed Hayes. "The pilot was likely only going to drop a sonobuoy so he could identify us. He would have to be extremely lucky, or extremely good, to hit that lead with a sonobuoy or a torpedo. Now we have to get out of here! If the missile misses, he will call for reinforcements, and they won't look too favorably upon us. How in hell did you get up here, and why in hell's name did you fire that goddamn rocket?"

"Sorry, Sir," said Marsh. "Your men were busy, so I came. I'm sorry, I just panicked!"

"There's no time to talk about it now," said Hayes. "We've got to get the hell out of here!" The three men scrambled down the ladder, and again, slammed the hatch shut. Murphy called the officer who was in charge of detentions, and had him take Marsh to the brig holding area. He briefly explained to lockup personnel that a SAM was launched without the captain's authority.

"Torpedo in the water, starboard side!" shrieked one of the sonar men.

"Missile impact!" yelled another.

"How in the hell did the aircraft bombing technician manage to get that torpedo in that small area of water?" asked Hayes. Whether it was skill or luck, it made no difference. That fish was on its way and looking for a target. "What is the bearing and range of the torpedo?"

"Heading straight for the Sea Devil at three thousand yards."

"We are trapped!" exclaimed the Diving Operator. "Do we have time to free ourselves, or should we shut everything down and hope the fish won't find us?"

"Keep her rocking and fire off a noisemaker. Keep me informed on the range."

The Diving Officer kept adding water to the ballast tanks, rocking the ship, and blowing out the water. She was breaking free.

"One thousand yards," announced the sonar operator.

Suddenly, the ship came free and dropped straight down, with the careful balance of the diving planes. Once below the surface of the ice, the bow began to incline. The depth gauges showed that the sub was a hundred feet below the surface, eighty feet below the ice, and going deeper.

"Fire another noisemaker. Right twenty degrees rudder," Hayes ordered. He appeared calm on the exterior while his nerves steadily frayed. "Set course two-zero."

The Sea Devil continued to dive while turning. She was now at two hundred fifty feet.

"Torpedo now at one thousand five hundred yards and heading for the noisemaker. It is pinging away, but not at us."

Without warning, a large underwater explosion rocked the submarine back and forth for several minutes. Some of the crew fell against the instrument panels, while those strapped into their seats, or holding on to rails, had to reach for handholds to steady themselves.

"The fish most likely hit the submerged part of an iceberg that we passed," said Murphy.

"Damage and Injury Report?" Hayes queried.

"A few minor leaks, easily repairable, and one sailor with a sprained wrist."

"What about the plane?"

"It's going to crash."

# 16   RESCUED

25 December 1330 hrs local, Canada Ice Island, Nunavut

There was a disturbing noise on the headphones of officers aboard the Sea Devil. Only a sliding, crumbling plane could cause such a horrendous noise. Hayes heard the grinding, twisting vibrations of the aircraft crash. The sound was the hulk of an aircraft giving up its life as a flying machine. The death spiral lasted just several seconds before the sounds ceased mercifully. He handed the earphones back to the radio operator. *Just how many precious souls were aboard, and how many hearts have stopped*? thought Commander Hayes.

*We have to do something*, he contemplated. If there were survivors, they wouldn't last very long in the sub-zero temperature, in addition to the freezing drifting snow and ice. While the crew was under orders from Admiral Heiserman not to be identified as Americans, they still had to do something since the surviving airmen could not be left out in the Arctic weather to die. There had to be something that they could do. Hayes was not the kind of sailor who could let defenseless men die simply because some officer had ordered him to do so.

"Navigator, find that open lead where the torpedo hit the water."

"It is one hundred fifty degrees to the starboard and at a distance of two miles."

Hayes ordered the coarse adjustment, and within ten minutes, they were beneath the open water.

"Skipper, open water is directly overhead."

"Take her up slowly. Let's make sure that we are directly under open water. I don't want part of the sail to hit. I know of at least one Skipper that bent his periscope and tore off an antenna when the sub inadvertently hit some ice. Bring her to periscope depth." The Sea Devil rose willingly.

"Up scope," ordered Hayes, as the ship neared the surface.

The search periscope slid noiselessly from its well and rose upward. Hayes held it firmly as it broke the surface of the water. He quickly walked the scope in a full circle, with the lens reflected upward to catch any aircraft that might still be in the vicinity. There was none. He made another quick circle to check the surface. There were no ships or machines or anything else on or near the pack ice. A slower rotation caught a glimpse of a fire that could be seen on a much higher chunk of ice, several hundred yards away from his ship.

"Hear anything, sonar?" asked Hayes.

"All clear, skipper."

"I see no surface activity and no aircraft. I do see a fire in the distance, but it is starting to fade. Bring her up to the surface, and we'll check from the sail," Hayes instructed Murphy.

The Sea Devil popped to the surface like a cork at the bottom of a bottle. There was no crushing of ice nor the squealing of chunks of ice sliding off the hull. The ship was in its element. They found that the ice's lead was large enough for the submarine's 292-foot length to fit snugly.

The hatch was opened, and Hayes and the bridge crew scampered up with their night glasses in hand; all of them used their glasses to check the skies and the surface for aircraft and ships. All was clear. The XO fired a flare that lit up the sky and briefly pinpointed the downed plane's location. They concentrated their glasses on the sparkling flames, and they watched as the last of the flare light died.

"Did you see the flickering fire?" Hayes asked Murphy.

"The aircraft appears to be on some sort of plateau, much higher than the surrounding ice."

"I think there may be survivors. We need to do something. It would be murder to leave those poor devils out on the ice at this temperature. Any ideas, Jack?"

"I could pick about thirty men and gather up some medical supplies, blankets, and warm clothing, and then try to reach them. Our away crew could be there in a half-hour to forty-five minutes. Think about what you want us to do with any survivors, Captain." Murphy was also concerned about the temperature's effect on any surviving airmen.

"That sounds like a viable plan, but I want you to lead the group. Any idea of how we will keep the Canadians in the dark about our nationality?"

"We could wear our white Arctic Clothing, without badges or ranks, and wear our balaclavas."

"What about communication with the Sea Devil and with each other?"

"Any communication with the ship will have to be done well out of the listening range of the Canadians. I'll brief the men that they are to be silent. When we need to communicate, we could use a foreign language. The Reactor Control Officer and I both speak Russian, and we can use it when necessary."

"That might work. I can't think of a better plan. OK, give it a try. Keep the balaclavas on while you are in their presence. Take your rifles, too. They know that our missile brought them down, and they probably have weapons of their own on the aircraft. If you come under fire, immediately abandon the rescue and leave them to be found by their countrymen. I can't risk losing any of my crew."

"What do you want me to do with the survivors, if there are any? Shall I just provide them with blankets, medical supplies and radio, and leave them?"

"We have to stay in the area, at least for the next forty-eight hours, awaiting our mission objective. We could do as you say and make them warm and comfortable and tend to their injuries, and then leave them with some communication device to contact their base. The problem is that they may get help from some rescue team before our mission is accomplished. The airmen, or their rescuers, may interfere with our mission, and I can't risk that possibility. There are probably no more than fifteen of them, the size of a regular Aurora crew," stated Hayes, pondering the best course of action. He had a better idea.

"I've given it some thought, and I think it's best that we bring them back here, where we can keep an eye on them. We can hold them in the forward storage area and tend to their injuries. If they can't be found, they can't tell anyone about our objective or who we are. We will need to remove all remaining identifying markings from the Sea Devil.

"I'm not sure what we'll do with them later. I doubt that we can drop them off at the nearest community, but we could drop them at remote landfall with tents and a radio transmitter. However, they may be able to recognize the outline of our ship and transmit that information before we can continue, or finish, our mission objective. I'll have to contact Admiral Heisman to arrange for a pickup at sea, under cover of complete darkness, by some unidentifiable small boat, after we have accomplished our goal. It will then be his problem to deal with the survivors. That's the only plan that I have momentarily, so bring back anyone alive, but keep them blindfolded. Also, keep me informed by radio."

"OK, Skipper."

Commander Hayes watched as Murphy and the party of men set out for the plateau and the crashed aircraft. The lights of the ski-doos bobbed and wove in the black sky, as the men zigzagged to avoid the ice ridges that protruded up, reaching nine meters high in some spots. The machines had to slow occasionally to prevent clipping the jagged ice boulders. There were times when it looked like they were driving through a maze. Murphy was the lead driver who blazed the trail and whose responsibility it was to avoid crevasses that could easily swallow up the vehicles and their passengers.

Hayes tightened the strings of his parka hood. The gusting winds were almost as cold as the winds and gusts of snow and shrews of ice that his men would face as they drew further and further away from the comfort and warmth of the sub's heaters. Hayes imagined how painful it must be for a badly wounded airman who could be paralyzed by an injury. Plane crashes generally resulted in victims who were lacerated by flying metal. Plane crashes were also about bodies attached to their seats, that land hundreds of yards from the final impact point. It was possible that these airmen could be suffering from hypothermic shock. All he could do was to pray for these helpless men. There was guilt in his heart. The aircraft's downing could have been prevented had he only watched who entered the bridge.

Soon, the lights of the ski-doos could no longer be seen. Hayes descended the stairs by the sail and headed to the radio operator.

"I'll be in my cabin. Let me know immediately when Murphy calls."

Murphy and his party reached the foot of the ice cliff just below the lip of the ice island plateau. It had taken an hour of detailed travel over the pack ice and high-pressure ridges. The path had required some heavy manhandling of the snowmobiles and sleds. They were rocked and buffeted by every bump on the route by swaths of drifting snow. The jerking and swaying of the sleds, towed behind the ski-doos, only added to the riders' discomfort. They had to detour around the spot where the Sea Devil originally surfaced. The oval hole surrounding the sub had already frozen over with a thin sheet of ice. When they reached the plateau, they saw that it was impossible to reach the top of the ice island with the machines. The ski-doos were left below with two guards, while the group gingerly climbed the twenty-foot cliff of ice to the plateau's top. Each of the them carried warm clothing and medical supplies in their backpacks.

Upon reaching the top, they clamped on their skis and fanned out until they found the initial impact point of the aircraft. They found it easier to walk, using their snow shoes, along the path of the sliding aircraft trail than on the shale ice. They moved slowly forward in the valley made by the plane and watched for victims of the accident in and around the crash path. They trekked silently along in a single file, and only the XO used his flashlight. Each of the sub men sheltered and cradled their guns in their arms. The white protective Arctic clothing made them appear like ghosts in the blowing snow.

The team passed several pieces of metal that had been torn off the plane, both large chunks of metal and smaller parts of the aircraft's underbelly. Each piece was briefly examined before moving on, and they spent extra moments looking around the area where the undercarriage was found. No black boxes were found, and no victims were seen. They proceeded up the trail. As they approached the bulk of the crashed plane, their pace slowed considerably.

Lt. Cmdr. Murphy faced the group, pointed to his mouth, and wagged his gloved hand in front of it to remind them that they were not to speak. They cautiously approached the wrecked craft. Murphy pointed to half the group and indicated with his hand that they were to circle the plane from the right, while he and the group's balance would circle from the left. They crept silently around the plane until they met one another on the other side. The Reactor Control Officer, the left circling group leader, spoke in Russian to Murphy, stating that they had seen no one. Murphy flashed his light onto the open side door of the aircraft and motioned that he was to be followed.

He and the RCO entered the plane slowly, aware that any of the survivors could gun them down instantly if they thought that they came from the sub that fired a missile at them. The two officers crept along, searching the cockpit area and the full length of the plane. No one was on board. *What gives?* thought Murphy. *Where is the aircrew?* He was mystified.

Commander Murphy was very proud of his crest and emblem collection. He managed to obtain a small ornament, or emblem, from the ship, base, or squadron that he was visiting, everywhere he went during his military career. He had already accumulated over two hundred items in his collection of crests, ranging from the ships of Argentina to naval bases in the United Kingdom. He had a knack for removing crests or identifying knickknacks from almost any surface without damaging it. Later, when he returned to his billet, he would transfer his latest trophy to his collection wall. Seeing no survivors in the wreck, he took a moment to look around the downed Aurora aircraft to see if there were any treasures in view. He saw the 415 Greenwood Squadron crest on a small coffee mug. He instinctively pilfered the mug and stored it in a small bag containing maps of the Arctic Islands.

He saw no aircrew moving in the plane, but he did see the two causalities of the crash. They were covered with blankets and light snow that had drifted into the a/c through tears in the metal body. He reasoned that someone from the aircrew would eventually return to collect the bodies. He, too, decided to leave them since Captain Hayes was only concerned about living crew who could identify the ship. He exited the plane through the hatchway.

Outside the plane, Murphy shone his light on the snow near the door. There were many footprints and other evidence that someone, or something, was dragged off in a northerly direction.

"It appears that some crew members have survived the crash, which will make the Captain happy," remarked Murphy. "We'll have to follow the trail to see where they went. Did you notice the LET beacon near the nose of the plane? Send someone to shut it off. We don't want any mysterious searcher to spot us. Also, get the Chief Electrician, I believe he's part of your group. Get him to go to the cockpit and find the black boxes. If they are still installed, rip them out and we'll take them back with us. One of the aircrews may have made a recording of our propeller and it could identify our sub as a U.S. Navy boat."

Within ten minutes, Murphy noticed that drifting snow was quickly covering their footprints and those of the aircrew. One of his men notified him that all three items were now on the way back to the snowmobiles to be safely stored in saddle packs.

The party set out again, following the fast-fading tracks of the survivors. They led away from the aircraft and the edge of the ice, towards the ice island's center. Murphy guessed that the tracks were made less than an hour ago. It would take a similar amount of time for his men to overtake them. The question was, what do they do when they reach them? The Captain wanted the survivors to be brought back to the sub. Alive. Would they have to use their rifles to force them? Or could they be persuaded to come along peacefully? He hoped for the latter.

Murphy stopped and raised his night goggles to his eyes. In the moonlight, he could see a gathering of people at a distance of three hundred yards. They were stopped, and it appeared that some of the injured airmen were being examined. The night goggles revealed one survivor walking ahead of the others. The Executive Officer spoke quietly to the RCO.

"It appears they are seeking a place that might give them some sort of protection from the elements, at least until a rescue party arrives. They look to be heading for a particular place, maybe one they saw while approaching our sub. The golden rule among these flyboys is never to leave the scene of an accident or crash. They would only leave the plane if they knew of a location that would lengthen their lives.

"Our best chance is to surround them now. You take half of the group and go left, as we did on the plane, and my group will go right. Split up your men in 5-foot intervals around your semi-circle. I'll give you ten minutes to get in place. In exactly ten minutes, we'll advance the circle towards the Canadians. Remember, no English. Go."

The RCO positioned his men as Murphy instructed him. When ten minutes had expired, he raised his rifle. His men followed suit, and they all advanced towards the survivors of the crash as one moving hoard.

The appearance of these twenty-eight men dressed as ghosts, coming out of the blowing snow with their rifles at the ready position, caught the Canadians off guard. They were startled and in no position to take any action or to reach for any weapons.

"Tell them in broken English that we are here to help them and provide medical aid," Murphy said, in Russian, to the RCO. "Explain to all of them that it was an accident, that the missile was fired by a nervous seaman. Tell them to throw down any guns or weapons that they have on them, and we'll give them medical help immediately."

The RCO delivered the message in heavily accented broken English to some surprised looks on the Canadians' faces. There was one officer, of Captain rank, who was injured and lying on a makeshift stretcher. It had been made from one of the fold-out beds from the plane. The man's arms and legs were strapped to the bed with bandages.

"We better do as he says," said the disabled man, who was the co-pilot, in a voice that was quivering with pain. "We are outnumbered and outgunned. We need medical help now, or some of our crew may not make it to see the arrival of our rescuers."

The flight engineer threw down his gun onto the ice and the others followed, dropping their weapons. The XO gave the white-clad submarine crew the OK signal, and they approached each of the survivors cautiously. They did a quick body check for more weapons before loosening up their backpacks and extracting the supplies. They spoke not a word, even though the Canadians asked questions. Murphy waved the Reactor Control Officer to one side and talked to him in English.

"That's a great accent! Get your communications specialists to come over here so I can update the Skipper. We will treat the wounded as best we can and provide them with warm clothing and blankets. Again, in your accent, I want you to tell them that we are going to take them to a sub that will bring them to the nearest Canadian port. Ask them to come along peacefully, but point out that our Captain wants our ship and crew to remain nameless. We want no publicity. In a nice way, tell them that we will unfortunately have to blindfold them to avoid the media later. Tell them they are in no danger. Also, let them know that the sub will take them to safety. Tell them that the trip back to the ship will take an hour, and that it requires a bit of walking, but we have some transportation waiting at the edge of the plateau."

The RCO acknowledged, and spoke in broken English to the Aurora aircrew, relaying all of the information provided by Murphy. Shortly thereafter, a communications link was established between the Sea Devil and the XO.

"Sea Devil, this is the Executive Officer. Connect me with the captain."

Commander Hayes took the transmission in his stateroom and asked for a report on the situation.

"Eleven aircrew and two men in civilian clothes are now under our control, and their injuries are being treated. Our ETA at the Sea Devil will be one hour and fifteen minutes from now. Aircraft instruments have been seized and will accompany us. Over."

"Officer, is everyone OK?"

"Confirmed, skipper."

"Wipe out every trace of your presence in the area. Signal when you are near the submarine, and I'll meet you on the ice pack. Out."

The XO picked out two of his men and gave them instructions out of the listening range of the aircrew.

"I want you to hang behind with your flashlights. Use your skis to flatten out all our footprints in this area, along our route, and around the plane. Close all exits on the plane. Don't leave any traces that indicate that we were onboard. The blowing snow should wipe out any prints that you miss."

Murphy gave the forward sign, and everyone started the trek back towards the plane and the snowmobiles. Some of his men carried the stretchers while others helped the walking wounded. The Canadians provided no resistance. Murphy, and mainly the RCO, had obviously convinced them that they would be home with their families within days.

At the edge of the island, the Canadians walked together. They passed a few hundred yards wide of the wounded plane and trudged along until they made it to the edge of the plateau. The aircrew was carefully lowered down the twenty-foot slope and placed on the sleds or snowmobiles, depending on their condition. The convoy once again made its passage to the sub by skirting ice ridges and open leads. A short distance from their destination, Murphy held up his hand with the stop signal. A small flare was lit to let the sub know that they were nearby. The blindfolds were put in place, and everyone waited.

Commander Hayes arrived within ten minutes, wearing Arctic gear complete with balaclava and goggles. He was briefed by Murphy well out of earshot of the foreigners.

"You did a good job, Jack. Now comes the tricky part. We need to get the aircrew onboard without them knowing that we are Americans. There are no markings on the Sea Devil to indicate a U.S. Navy boat since they were removed before we left port. The sub itself won't reveal our identity. All of the sailors on board have been briefed to remain silent for the next thirty minutes. Bring the survivors on board one at a time, and we'll put them in the enlisted men's mess. With any luck, we can be out of this godforsaken place in the next two days since our mission objective will be landing in this area in less than twelve hours. I'll head back and clear the path from the hatch to the mess area. After they're safely in mess, I'll send the ship's doctor to them along with a couple of guards for the door."

Murphy and the RCO split up the responsibility for getting the survivors stored in the mess room. The RCO directed outside operations, helping the aircrew up the side of the hull and down the hatchway, while the Executive Officer fetched each of the arrivals and detailed one of his white-clad crewmen to bring them to the mess. The exercise took twenty minutes. The gear and machines were all brought aboard, and the hatch secured. Hayes gave the order to submerge and to proceed two nautical miles from the open lead, and to circle under the ice to await the arrival of MIR in the dark Arctic skies.

The space station, as if on cue, once again left its orbit and commenced its journey to earth to fulfill its destiny with the Sea Devil.

# 17    TREK FOR SURVIVAL
### 25 December 1400 hrs local, Canada's Ice Island, Nunavut

Captain Winters gathered his crew around him in the lee of the plane, while the injured co-pilot rested at the nose.    He addressed the survivors.

"I will lay it on the line to you as I see our situation. I would ask for your opinions and suggestions after I'm finished. We are stuck on an ice island, and we didn't get a chance to send off a May Day call before the crash. We were unable to let anyone know about the sub. No one knows we are here until we are overdue for our ETA, at Thule, in three hours from now. It will be almost twenty-four hours before any of our rescue planes will be looking for us, since it will take Thule several hours to figure out that we are missing. With the time difference between Thule and our home base at Greenwood, it will likely take them six to eight hours just to find enough planes to fly here to start a search. In the meantime, we need to find some protection from this cold weather.

"We are approximately 700 kilometers from the nearest military site at Alert, and a bit closer to the Eureka weather station... maybe three hundred kilometers. Any over-land, or I should say over-ice, rescue attempt, from Alert or Eureka, would take several days since they have no planes, just snowmobiles. You all know that our aircraft was hit by a missile from an unknown sub that may still be in the vicinity. It is quite possible that the sub could send a force to help us, but their reasons for doing so would be suspect. I can't think of one reason why they would shoot us out of the sky, then make an offer to help us, so we better be prepared to guard against the possibility that they may come after us with hostile intentions."

Captain Winters paused to tighten the strings on his parka hood and pull the zipper up to the neckline.

"We are fortunate that most of us survived the crash, although we have lost two precious crew members, and some of you have serious injuries. The question is, what should we do now? We have two options. First, we can stay with the plane as we've been taught in survival school. There are some pros and cons to that option. There is some food on the plane, but the plane offers no protection from the frigid cold. There is no heat, and it will soon be like a freezer. It is also too dangerous to light a fire in the aircraft or near the craft because there is a lot of spilled fuel, and a fire could quickly get out of control. Without heat or protection from the wind chill, we won't survive very long, so we have to conserve our body heat. The cold air burns up your energy, and it will deplete at a tremendous rate. There is some extra clothing on the plane, but it is now minus 30 degrees with the wind chill, and I expect it to get colder because our last forecast mentioned colder Arctic air descending in this area. The extra clothing will retain some body heat but it won't be adequate until we find some kind of shelter.

"Our second option is to trek to some buildings that the co-pilot and I saw before the crash. Several huts are in the area, and were probably used by some geological surveying crew or oil rig crew during the summer daylight months. Most likely, they would have some sort of heating system and probably even a generator. There may even be a VHF radio transmitter. These huts are about two kilometers away. I know that we can reach them even if we don't have any snow boots or skis, but trekking there won't be easy. The buildings will give us some protection if the submarine crew shows up. We might be able to hold them off with some guns that are in the aircraft. What do you think?" Winters studied the group, awaiting their input on the situation.

"I like the second option," declared the Flight Engineer, speaking first. "I think heading for the buildings would be our best bet. We could pack up all the clothing and food that we have and bring it to the huts. Once we get there, we can make a fire or get some stove working at one of the buildings, something that we can't do here."

"We've got to do something for the co-pilot," said the second navigator. "His injuries are not life-threatening but if frostbite gets to his legs it easily could become life-threatening. There are probably proper beds in one of the buildings that we could use to make him comfortable. I vote for the buildings."

"If we left the aircraft, I'm sure that a rescue crew would easily find us at the survey buildings, especially if we left a marker," said a sensor operator. "We could bring along the flares to use if we hear any search craft in the area."

"Could someone go to the buildings and check them out and come back here and tell us what they found?" asked one of the scientists.

"If we are going to go to the buildings, we have to go now, before that sub crew gets here. We can't take the chance that they show up here while we await the return of our scout to the building," said the other scientist.

Captain Winters judged everyone to be in agreement. The buildings offered a better chance of survival than staying with the aircraft, and it was now appropriate to get on with the transit.

"OK, then it is settled. We'll gather what we can from the plane and then head for the surveying site towards our northeast. Anyone that wants to go on board the plane can do so, to retrieve personal items, but make it quick. Remember, we can't carry our luggage. I suggest that you bring along all weapons that you can find, such as guns and knives, or anything else that can be used to defend yourself. Flight Engineer, take someone with you, reenter the plane, and open the main door to the cabin."

Frank Winters designated two others to gather all of the food and clothing that they could find from the baggage area.

Within a matter of minutes, the cabin door was forced open. The Flight Engineer had to use an ax to bust open the door that had jammed in the crash. Frank entered the cold dead aircraft. The porthole windows were covered with ice, and frost was accumulating on the inside walls of the plane. Using his flashlight, he found the medical kit, the petty cash funds, and the pistol that were stored in the plane's safe. He took the aircraft log with him as he exited the wounded bird.

Some of the clothing was distributed among the crew, to be put on immediately, while the remainder was stashed in knapsacks. The food was placed in the care of one of the navigators, should it need to be rationed in the event that the crew was not rescued for several days.

Finally, they were ready to be on their way. All of the survivors raised their hoods and drew the zippers on their parkas, hoping to minimize exposure of their skin to the biting cold. They said farewells to their deceased crew members, who were their friends, in case they were not recovered later.

Without snowshoes or skis, walking was difficult. Crew members slipped and fell when they stepped on ice patches, yet they made progress. The co- pilot's makeshift stretcher was initially dragged, but it caused so much discomfort to his injuries that his navigator friend picked up the end that was being hauled along the ice and carried it.

Frank looked back occasionally, but couldn't see the plane any longer, nor could he see the buildings that he thought were just ahead. This would be the wrong occasion to have made a mistake and trekked away from the huts instead of towards them. He hoped that his judgment was not wrong and that they were to the northeast of the plane. Snow started to blow, and he was worried that they might have even passed the buildings. By his estimation, they had been on route for nearly forty minutes and covered nearly two kilometers, and yet they still had not reached the buildings. According to his calculations they should have reached them by now. Worried, he spoke to the group, after holding up his gloved hand to get them to stop.

"I don't understand. The buildings should be just ahead, just over the next ice ridge." Frank struggled with the cold as he spoke. "I sure hope that I didn't make a mistake and head the wrong way. You guys take a rest while I'll scout ahead for the buildings, and I'll make sure that no one from the submarine is using them." He walked off alone with the pistol in his hand.

Captain Winters was right. He walked a few hundred yards in the blowing snow and practically bumped into the first of the buildings. There appeared to be six smaller huts, two larger buildings, and a few Quonset huts. Time was an important consideration, so there were not enough hours to search all of the buildings. He headed for the largest one, broke the lock on the door with his pistol, and entered what turned out to be the cookhouse building. He flashed his light around the room and saw no one, nor was there any indication that anyone was at the entire site in the past few months. Satisfied that his crew could find warmth and security here, he headed back with the good news.

As he approached the area where his injured crew were resting, he heard someone speaking. The words sounded strange. It could have been the wind, but the words didn't sound like English words. Captain Winters walked cautiously towards the pressure ridge, where he left the crew, then crept ahead quietly.

As he glanced over the brim of the ridge, he saw a large number of men wearing white Arctic clothing and carrying rifles. They had surrounded his men, but at the same instant, they were helping the crew with their medical needs and providing them with more warm clothing and blankets. They were most likely from the submarine, but the number of men made it impossible for him to do anything.

Remaining hidden, he could only watch as the entire group, including his crew, left the area. They were heading in the direction of the downed plane. He reasoned that they were most likely going to the sub, and there was no point in following them since they might spot him and start shooting. Winters remained silently where he was. He also had to take into consideration the possibility that he could get lost in the blowing snow. He was unable to use his flashlight without being spotted. Frank decided that his best plan was to return to the buildings and hope that he could locate a radio transmitter to let his base know about the sub, the downing of the aircraft, and where his men were taken.

The trek back to the buildings was time-consuming without any light, but he eventually reached the cookhouse that he previously entered. He turned on his flashlight and saw a huge stove containing space for frying eggs or meats. There was also a table containing boards and cutting knives, and a cupboard with a few cans of lard and some dried-up vegetables. Off to the right, there was a smaller room that appeared to be an office. Opening the door and entering, he saw that the room contained a desk covered with scattered papers, a dresser, a small couch, and a chair. In the middle of the desk was a radio transmitter.

No one would expect the radio to be in the cookhouse, but the surveying boss wanted some privacy from the workers who would occupy the recreation and eating facilities. The transmitter was dismantled, its parts laid out neatly on the desk. Attached to one piece was a note, it was made out to the radio operator's replacement.

"Do not move. New tubes will be delivered with the first resupply in the spring."

Having survived an air crash and the long trek with his crew, only to see them snatched from him, Captain Winters' forty-eight-year-old body needed a rest. It ached from the impact, and the cold was biting at the marrow of his bones. For the past couple of hours, he had worked tirelessly to keep his crew alive. He was exhausted and nearly numb from the cold. But it was not the tiredness that wore him down. It was the thought that there was nothing more that he could do now for the crew. While his body was resting, his mind was still working. At least he could think, and he needed to consider why the submarine would fire on his plane and why armed men would take away his crew. Frank's mind raced over recent world events. He watched newscasts several times a day, read at least two newspapers, and used the Internet in the evenings to get the lowdown on what was happening around the world. He knew the content of all of the recent news stories, but none of them seem to fit with the need to bring down his plane with a guided missile.

On the UHF radio, on the flight to Eureka, he had heard the news about the problems that the Russians were having with the MIR Space Station and its fall from orbit. At Operations, he had been briefed about Russian subs that had been seen at the entrance way to the Northwest Passage. Could the two be connected? He wasn't even sure if it was a Russian sub that had attacked the Aurora since one of his electronic sensor operators thought that he detected the engine signature of an American sub. In the back of his mind, intuition told him that the descending space station had brought about this unpleasant situation. His eyes were starting to glaze over, and he was too tired to reason out the connection between the two events.

Captain Winters looked around the office. He pulled open the double doors at the bottom of the dresser and saw six blankets and a pillow. Maybe there were women on the survey team. It would seem that the geological survey team's boss used the office for more than just communicating with his head office.

Frank spread two of the blankets and pillows on the small couch, laid himself down, and pulled the others over him. The extreme cold was affecting his blood circulation, especially in his feet and fingers. He tucked his knees up, shoved the aircraft log under his bum, and reached under the blankets to tighten up the parka zipper. He lowered his head onto the pillow and went into a heavy sleep; one that lasted nearly forty-eight hours and almost took his life. The fatigue, combined with the cold weather, sent Frank into a hypothermia induced coma.

# 18   RACE FOR SPACE STATION

26 December 1830 hrs local, Siberian Military District HQ,
Novosibirsk, Russia

"Sir, there is a call from the Commander of Special Service Troops," said the aide to his General, the Commander in Chief of Siberian Military District.

The General turned away from his tenth story window overlooking the center of the city of Novosibirsk with its 1.4 million people. His eyes could see the tops of hundreds of buildings, but it was the residents of the town, walking the street below his view with their multi-colored multi-layered clothing, that commanded his attention. It was nearly January and frigid, yet the center square was filled with people bustling about with their daily activities of buying food and other items from the market square vendors at the end of the street. Many of them came to see the New Year Tree that glowed with its red and blue lights, while the children climbed about a cabin of ice. He would swear that the aroma of nabobs could almost be smelled in his top-floor office. He reluctantly left his lookout and moved over to his soft leather swivel chair, where he sat down and pushed a button on the secure telephone.

"Yes," the General responded.

"Thank you, Colonel-General Nikolaev, for taking my call. I am General Sergeyev, Commander of the President's Special Service Troops. You probably know that my 10,000 special service troops are responsible for anti-terrorist specialist training and sabotage and diversion operations. You are probably not aware that I also have authority regarding our space program. This is especially the case when sabotage is suspected. You may have seen the President's directive allowing my Alfa and Zemit units to draw on a reserve of 70,000 intelligence and security personnel from the Spetsgruppa Commando Forces, many of whom are stationed in your military district.

"You are, of course, in complete command of all military forces within the Siberian Military District. Your troops are deployed in Omsk, Novosibirsk, Tomsk, and as far north as the Taimyr Peninsula. Your strengths are in several other centers and in the Republics of Tuva, Khakass, and Alnitak. My military documents show that you have military ships and subs at Nordvik, near the new Siberian Islands, close to the North Pole. I have called to ask for your help in an urgent espionage matter regarding our space program, that recently occurred in your domain. Let me give you a little background.

"The Russian people do not know yet that there is a problem with our space station. Earlier today, it started to descend on its own accord. It seemed that MIR was headed towards earth. I reiterate that this was not a planned descent and all initial indications were that there was not another system problem that was causing the drop. Mission Control managed to stabilize the fall at one point, but it has started to move closer to the earth's surface again. While it was stabilized, one of our brighter propulsion engineers noticed that the fall was preceded by a mysterious command that didn't come from Mission Control. We have not yet identified the source of this command, but we expect to identify it in the next few hours. In the meantime, the space station is still descending, and Mission Control now suspects sabotage. Someone or something is causing the station to react to rogue commands.

"Our President has warned that the space station's contents must not fall into foreign hands, and I have been given authority by him to take whatever action is necessary to make sure that it doesn't happen. The latest projection of the path of MIR, if it continues to descend, is that it will crash near the North Magnetic Pole, if it doesn't burn up in the atmosphere. If it does burn up, we will have to take retribution measures against the organization or nation that caused it to happen. Our main concern is that the supplier of the rogue commands may have devised a way to bring the craft through the atmosphere without it burning up. If this should happen, it is conceivable that the persons responsible may be after the station's valuable contents.

"We need to be prepared to mobilize our troops on a moment's notice, to reach the impact site before the saboteur's forces. Your military troops seem to be in the best position to be deployed to the Pole before any other forces. You also have Tactical Air Forces that you can use for this mission as well as your hunter-killer subs. Under Presidential authority, I task your helicopters, airborne forces, and subs to be on standby to go to the Magnetic Pole on a moment's notice, should MIR reach earth without burning up. I need not have to emphasize that we must win this space station race at all costs. Of course, all of this information is Top Secret and can only be shared with your most trusted advisers. The President will be sending you a message, confirming that I have the authority to ask for such assistance, and I will follow up on our conversation with the details in a message of my own."

"I will do what I can to help you, General Sergeyev, with the resources that I have. But as you know, our budget funds are tight, and my troops have not been paid for several months. Will your command fund these special operations?"

"That can be arranged, Colonel General. I'll mention it to the President."

"Very well. At my daily briefing, it was mentioned that the weather in the Polar Regions is deteriorating and it may take a day or so to clear. Do you want us to capture and secure the remains of MIR, should it survive the atmosphere and impact, or do you wish for us to destroy it as it enters the earth's atmosphere?"

"That is an excellent question. There is material on board that our scientific community would like to retrieve, so we would prefer that you fetch this material for us as our priority. If the enemy reaches the crash site first and is attempting to retrieve its contents, then you are authorized to eradicate them and bring back the remains of the space station."

"The North Magnetic Pole is presently located amid the ice pack claimed by the Canadian government as their territory. Shall I contact the Canadian military or the Canadian government?"

"I wouldn't worry about that aspect of this mission. Canadian sovereignty over that part of the Northwest Passage is widely disputed. The President is expecting another visit, shortly, from the Canadian Prime Minister. And our illustrious leader has indicated that he will deal, after the fact, with the Canadian authorities. In the meantime, we will proceed with our task, without asking permission to use their claimed airspace, waterways, or ice mass."

"What if we reach the scene and the Canadian military have MIR?"

"If they are guarding MIR, that is one thing, but if they are removing any of its contents, then that is a different scenario. As I said before, MIR must not fall into foreign hands. For all we know, it may have been the Canadians that caused MIR to descend. You are authorized to take whatever action is necessary to return with the MIR items. You must prevent them from getting into foreign hands."

"You will let me know when MIR is on its final descent and what items you want us to retrieve?"

"Time is of the essence. Mission Control will contact you as soon as they are definite that the space station will land in an area near your district. At that instant, they will tell you what they want and where it is located in the space station."

"In that case, I'll start immediately. I'll dispatch a sub to an area under the North Pole's ice. The nearest sub is at Arkhangelsk, less than 320 kilometers south of the Arctic Circle.

"It could take a few days of sailing, depending on ice conditions. My armed paratroopers, helicopters, and planes will be on standby within a few hours to airlift our troops to the area. It may be twenty-four hours or more before the weather is clear enough. Jets with missiles can be scrambled on short notice and report to us on activities in the predicted impact zone."

"Helicopters containing troops need to be on the ready to parachute to the predicted site should activities indicate that it is necessary. Would this be a problem?" asked Sergeyev.

"Depending on where the space station impacts, there could be a problem reaching it. There is a lot of piled up ice at the moment. Some of my helicopters don't have the range to fly over the North Pole from their current operating bases. I could move them to the closest land military base. I will also establish some refueling caches on one of the Russian ice islands."

"I will leave the details to you and your staff to work out. I want some of our Zemit commandos to join your paratroopers as soon as you identify the staging area. I will start the repositioning of troops. I can fly them out of Leninsk airfield, near the Baikonur Cosmodrome, to the location of your aircraft."

"OK, it is agreed. I will await your signal and reply to it as soon as it is received."

Nikolaev hung up the phone and told his aide to call his senior staff officers to a meeting in his office in one hour.

The Col. General returned to his lookout and was soon deep in thought. He was due to retire in six months, and he didn't need an international incident to mar his career at this point. What would happen to his job and pension if there was a military showdown with his troops and those of Canada? There was always the possibility that the Americans could enter the fray, on the side of Canada. Perhaps the messages from General Sergeyev and the President would cover his ass. He would have to wait and read the content of the messages from the Commander of Special Service Troops and the President. In the meantime, he continued to enjoy his view of the waterfront with its heavy ship and barge traffic, while watching the people of Novosibirsk as they enjoyed the cool evening air.

### 27 December 1700 hrs local, Korolyov, Moscow

At Mission Control, in Moscow, the MIR core had once again stopped its descent at 150 kilometers. It seemed to have established a pattern of falling and stopping. Whenever the craft was in a rotation that carried it across the Canadian North Magnetic Pole, it would go into a descend mode. At the moment, it was still on track to land in the Canadian Arctic. If the pattern continued, the spacecraft could be slowed to the point that its last stopped altitude position would allow it to fall its remaining distance to the earth's surface without burning up on reentry.

Vasily Vinogradov continued his review of the software programs for the space station. The task involved finding all of the rogue commands and tracing them back to their source. He was still not sure if a programmer was involved, and he could not ask for their help without divulging the fact that someone, perhaps in the space program, was sending unauthorized messages to the MIR computer. Asking questions could cause someone to alert the sender, resulting in a situation where the saboteur would never be caught, and Mission Control would never know why it was done. There were thousands of pages of program text and instructions that he had to review.

By using the previously found unauthorized commands examples and by setting them up as a model, he was able to establish a string of similar executed commands. They were all traced. And not to an outside source that sent them to the spacecraft, but within the spacecraft itself. They came from an onboard computer. The commands that came from within the MIR core indicated that the various commands had been fed to the computer from a terminal onboard MIR at some time in the past. Vasily also determined that the origin of the orders occurred just before the last Soyuz departure from the station.

Vasily spoke to the Chief Flight Controller, who was working with him to solve the source of the mysterious commands.

"You can see here that all of the commands executed to date came from a terminal in MIR."

"Have you found any more recent rogue commands? Can you stop them from being executed?"

"They are probably deeply hidden, like a virus, within one of our onboard computers. It seems that the commands are executed when a specific event occurs, such as a date, a location, or by the amount of time that has lapsed at a certain altitude.

"Unlike a virus, we can't build a command scanner that will dig out and kill them. Our programmers can make updates that scan for new viruses every month but finding commands that are sitting amid millions of other commands will take us more time than we have."

"So we can't stop them from executing? What about shutting down the computer?"

"I tried that. I have identified the infected computer, and it is acting on instructions that are already in its system. It will not accept any commands from us."

"You mentioned that the first executed command was fed to the computer just before the Soyuz leaving MIR after final closure... who was on that last mission?"

"Two of our cosmonauts, Dmitri Korolev and Alexander Markov, along with a French guest cosmonaut by the name of Jean-Paul Savard."

"I believe that they are all still at our training facility. I'll get our security staff to have a little talk with them to see if they notice any unusual activities. You keep working on finding the destructive commands. Maybe we can anticipate the next descent."

# 19    SURVIVOR FOUND

24 December 1400 hrs local, Canada Ice Island, Nunavut

Major Phillips took inventory. He had some of the answers that Brig. Gen. Shanahan wanted, but not all of them. He knew that the Aurora had deviated from its planned route. The detour was on the request, or rather the command, of a senior Maritime Command Headquarters officer, who wanted the craft to fly over Eureka. He was fairly certain that the senior officer was Admiral Lowery. It could be surmised that while on route to Eureka, something, possibly a sub, enticed Captain Winters to fly further off course to where it eventually crashed. It was unknown why this latter change wasn't reported to the home base. But there were still some other unanswered questions that would have him wait before communicating with the MAG Commander.

Shawn, Mackenzie, and several of the SAR techs set out to circle the ice island once again to see if there was any evidence that a submarine was in the area and could still be sitting on the surface nearby. As they strolled towards the cookhouse, the building's door suddenly blew open. It could fill with snow in less than an hour, and the building might be needed later to house any arriving rescue personnel. Closing the door, Shawn noticed that the lock, which was probably put on the door by departing environmentalists, was no longer firmly hanging on the locking mechanism.

Previously, the rescue specialists had carefully suspended the locks on the locking flange of the buildings after they had been searched. The cookhouse lock was now dangling from the flange. Why was it not securely locked? Did one of his techs forget to properly engage the lock on its hook? Mackenzie previously mentioned that the cookhouse had not yet been thoroughly searched.

"Why is this door open?" asked Mackenzie.

"That's a good question. We better check this one," replied Phillips.

They entered the cookhouse. It was freezing inside, and snow had already settled on the floor in less than three minutes. Frost covered the windows.

Their flashlights covered the room, stopping momentarily on the stove and cooking utensils. In their minds, they were expecting to find several survivors. Upon seeing nothing of the sort, they were once again ready to leave when Mackenzie's light fell on a door partly covered by a curtain. It was a door to a lean-to.

Phillips mentioned to Mackenzie that he wanted this lean-to opened and the room checked.

The Search Master and the leading SAR tech walked over and pulled open the door of what appeared to be a small office. Stepping inside, their lights found a broken desk and an office chair with wobbly wheels. The glare of the lights continued to dance over old luggage, lawn chairs, and a broken file cabinet that was empty. The lights eventually fell on a large couch. It was piled with old blankets and used clothing. The wind from outside invaded the lean-to, causing the pile to fall to the floor. On the couch lay a body wrapped in a parka and covered in more blankets.

Shawn moved quickly about the room to reach the person on the couch. He and Rob reached down and gently straightened out the body. Mackenzie could detect a faint pulse, but it was apparent that the person was suffering from a severe case of hypothermia. He called for two of the other SAR techs waiting outside the door. They covered the person with some of their excess clothing as the other tech ran back to the Mess Hall for more blankets and something to use as a stretcher. Within minutes the tech had returned carrying blankets, and together they wrapped the missing crew member. Shawn removed the gun from the frozen mitten hand and picked up the logbook that the person had tucked underneath him. The almost lifeless body was hurriedly carried back to the warmth of the Mess Hall to be given better medical attention.

Major Phillips could recognize the almost frozen features of Captain Winters, pilot of the Aurora. Winters was like a mummy. None of his facial features moved. His eyes were frozen shut. *Could this man be saved?* The question flashed through the minds of the Search Master and the techs.

The Search and Rescue Technicians were not only a crack unit of search and rescue specialists, they were also trained paramedics. They had spent months taking medical training to deal with all types of injuries that they may encounter during rescue missions. They were instructed to comfort and care for the sick and the injured, including those suffering from fire burns and hypothermia.

Captain Winters was barely alive. He tried to open his eyes, and he could scarcely see the Canadian flags on the parkas of those tending to him. He tried to speak, but his voice was thick and slow, and his frozen jaw refused to budge. He reached out, at least in his mind, but his arm refused to rise to greet the angel in the orange parka. The lead SAR tech and Mackenzie agreed that the pilot was in the final stages of severe hypothermia, dehydration, and frostbite, and he was perched on the thin edge between stupor and death.

When one tech removed the mittens from Captain Winters' hands, he revealed frozen stumps that were black and swollen. Removing the shoes displayed toes in similar condition. The captain's feet were covered by swollen waxy-looking flesh. There was no doubt that his feet were frozen solid. Blood was barely circulating through his lower limbs. Winters drifted in and out of consciousness while the technicians tried to increase the circulation in his limbs. Each time they moved his arms or legs, the pilot groaned in agony. The techs used their paramedic skills to bring Captain Winters from the edge of hypothermic death to the land of the living.

There was no way that Captain Winters would be in a position to answer any of the Search Master's questions, so the best bet was to leave the techs to get on with their life-saving skills. Phillips ordered the rest of the team to continue to search for other survivors.

Phillips took Mackenzie and a few other techs to continue their search of the pack ice surrounding the island. They split up, and Rob's crew went in a clockwise position while Shawn's group went counterclockwise, meeting somewhere near the middle of the island.

They walked on the top of the plateau so they could see the maximum distance out onto the surrounding ice. Since the top was twenty feet higher, their lanterns and lights shone a considerable distance out onto the ice. After an hour of struggling along the circumference of the island, Shawn's group had not seen any markings or evidence on the ice pack or on the cliff edge to indicate that some sub or other means of transportation had been in the vicinity and had carried away the crew of the Aurora. The techs were shivering from the Arctic winds, and Shawn was cold, but he was not ready to give up, not at least until he met up with Mackenzie and his group.

After another fifteen minutes of trudging through snowdrifts, the lights of Mackenzie's group slowly approached the Phillips team. As they grew nearer, both groups continued to shine their lights out on the ice pack.

Simultaneously, both sets of lights landed on a circular pile of ice chunks with a flat center. It was two hundred feet away from the edge of the plateau. Together they climbed down the cliff and cautiously walked out onto the surface, where they found a newly frozen section of ice. There was no doubt that this area was different from the surrounding ice. It was approximately 150 feet in length and 25 feet wide. There were ice chunks around the circumference. They could tell that the flat ice was thinner than the ice outside the wall of ice chunks. All in the group were confident that a sub had surfaced at this very spot. Not only had the sail been above the ice but also most of the hull. The ice had broken as the sub surfaced, and chunks of ice had fallen to the sides around the hull's complete length. When it submerged, there was open water that quickly froze over.

The sub had been at this very spot and now could lie dormant just below the same ice that they stood upon. They quickly left the area and made their way back to the Mess Hall building.

The lead rescue specialists reported that Captain Winters was resting comfortably and would survive the hypothermia, but his condition required that he be sent to a hospital as soon as possible since he would most likely lose some fingers and toes. His legs, which had frozen, needed immediate treatment or they would have to be amputated. The morphine that they had given to Winters would wear off in an hour. On that occasion, they might be able to speak to him.

Shawn asked that Mackenzie again establish contact with the mini RCC at Thule. Within minutes, the connection was established.

"Thule RCC, this is Major Phillips for Capt. Mari Leech."

"Go ahead, Major Phillips, this is Leech."

"I need a helicopter ASAP at this site. No further info can be provided. Advise."

"I will dispatch one within the hour. ETA is three hours."

"Be advised that danger previously advised confirmed and still exists. Out."

"Understood. Out."

Shawn hoped that the sub had not picked up the transmission since it seemed likely that the sub crew didn't know that one of the air crew had survived. It was important that the information about the survival of Capt. Winters be kept secret, at least for the time being.

Phillips was reasonably sure that Captain Leech would signal Aurora #740 that a sub did exist and that it was most likely still in the area and dangerous. The Aurora could take the necessary precautions to guard itself and to protect any friendly helicopters as they arrived at the crash site. At the moment, only the chopper requested by Phillips was friendly and invited to proceed to the island.

An hour after Frank Winters had been found, he awoke and screamed in pain. He could barely talk, but he struggled desperately to speak to the person in charge of the rescue operation. The tech gave him more morphine and told Shawn that they could talk for about fifteen minutes before the medicine took effect.

Shawn introduced himself and assured Frank that he was being looked after and should be on the way to a hospital within a few hours. Frank spoke slowly. He was in considerable pain. With great difficulty, he recanted all that he knew about spotting the sub, the missile, the crash landing, the casualties, the crew's trek towards the survey buildings, and the capture of the crew by the sub's crew. He barely mentioned his own escape to the survey building. Shawn listened to the entire tale and refrained from asking questions until Frank concluded his story. He needed answers that he could give to Shanahan. The pilot ended his account of his adventure, and Shawn took the opportunity to ask some quick questions before the pilot fell into another deep sleep.

"How many of the ten crew and two scientists survived the crash?"

"My two most competent console operators were struck by flying pieces of wood and metal during the crash."

"Any serious injuries that could result in a casualty?"

Again, Winters spoke with considerable pain.

"The co-pilot has some broken leg bones, but I think he will survive. I... I saw the sub crew give medical help to the others who had cuts and bruises."

"Why would the sub crew take your crew, and where?"

"I don't know why, but they walked towards the edge of the ice plateau. I suppose that the sub was there and they were taken onboard."

"How come they didn't get you?"

"I left my gang as they needed rest, and I wanted to find the survey buildings. I went on ahead. I was gone about forty-five minutes when I returned. I was about a kilometer from the crew when I saw that they were surrounded by about thirty men with rifles. They didn't see me, and I managed to elude them. I'm only happy that my crew had the good sense not to mention to the armed men that I was on my way back to them."

"Why would a Russian sub fire on your plane?"

"I'm not sure. I'm not even sure that it was a Russian sub." Winters stopped. Shawn waited intently, hoping that the pilot had not fallen into unconsciousness, but Winters spoke again.

"One of my crew thought that it was an American sub. Perhaps the black box tapes could tell you more. I did hear some voices that didn't sound like English." He stopped again. There seemed to be something vital that he was struggling to remember. Finally, he said, "I think there may be a connection between the sub and the MIR space station, but I'm not sure."

"The emergency locator beacon and black box are both missing. Without the beacon, it took us longer to find your plane. Did you try to radio us about the sub and its location?"

Winters was getting tired, and his words came slower.

"The First Officer tried, but there was a magnetic disturbance that blocked the transmission."

"Did you not hear our plane looking for you, and our team searching for your crew?"

"We didn't hear any planes," replied Winters, after about a minute. "I think that the crew had been taken away by the sub before your plane got overhead. After the people from the sub took the crew, I didn't hear your plane because I came to one of the buildings to rest. I guess I just blacked out from the fatigue and cold."

"Could you tell me what you were doing in this area when your flight plan was for Station Alert and the Pole?"

The answer to this question seemed to sap the last of Winters' strength.

"I was asked, on the QT, by a senior officer to drop a personal package to Eureka. I decided to do it, and we detected the sub before we were able to drop the box."

Captain Winters' words were slurring, and it was apparent that while his pain was decreasing, the medicine was taking him out again. He described the situation at Greenwood with Admiral Lowery.

"This is important to me," Shawn stated, trying for one more question. "I need to know the name of the senior officer."

Captain Winters took some time to answer the question. Even in his dazed state, he was debating with himself if he should get the senior officer in trouble for making a deviation in Frank's flight path for personal reasons. Finally, he knew that it might be necessary for his crew's safety that he put the answer into words, regardless of the pain.

"I want you to promise that you will do everything possible to find my crew and return them safely."

"I will personally stay on this ice island until we find your officers and crewmen," declared Shawn.

"It was Vice Admiral 'Buzz' Lowery. The canister was for his brother at Eureka." Captain Frank Winters' head dropped to one side as he slid into a painless sleep.

Major Shawn Phillips had important information for Brig. Gen. Shanahan. He needed to get this new info to him immediately. He sent his encrypted email message to Shanahan shortly after Captain Winters was overcome by the morphine. The message read:

"Captain Winters was found alive but suffering from severe hypothermia. A helicopter is on route to take him to Thule. A missile from a sub brought down our plane, but the sub is no longer on the pack ice surface. All other crew and passengers survived the plane crash, except two operators. A large group of shore sailors captured all remaining crew and passengers. They were taken aboard the sub which may still be in area. Destination unknown, as is the ID of the sub. It could be Russian, American, or other. Our survivor believes that it is possible that the sub was in the area waiting for the fall of the MIR space station. In reply to your question regarding the location of the aircraft, the Aurora was in the Eureka area on the request of Vice Admiral Lowery. I strongly recommend that my men stay in this area a little longer to find our missing crew. Phillips."

Major Phillips assisted WO Mackenzie and the other techs in preparing for the helicopter's arrival and the evacuation of Captain Winters. Two of the SAR techs who suffered injuries in the jump would travel with Winters to provide medical assistance. Several flares were set up in the snow to help the pilot find a safe landing site.

Within an hour, a reply was received from Shanahan.

"The Aurora's captain is not to be released to anyone except the officer in charge of the mini RCC at Thule. He is to be placed in a guarded medical facility under the supervision of Canadians. I will arrive in Thule aboard the next Aurora within twelve hours to take charge.

Permission granted for you and your men to remain on-site. Keep me personally informed on all aspects of the search. Exercise extreme caution. Shanahan."

A tech was monitoring the radio and awaiting a transmission from the sub-hunting Aurora flying overhead. He was also awaiting transmission from a helicopter coming to pick up Captain Winters. The First Officer of the Aurora was the first to contact him.

"Calling Major Phillips at the crash site."

"This is Phillips. Keep transmissions to a minimum. A submarine was in the area, and it brought down one Aurora already. Please exercise extreme caution. Question, have your crew detected any submarines or military activity in the immediate area? Over."

"Negative. All clear. We will remain in the area and on alert for the next couple of hours. Over."

"Be advised that there is a Thule rescue helicopter on route to this location in the next two hours. Please provide protection until it has a hasty departure back to Thule. Out."

"Will Do. Out."

All was quiet for the next one and a half hours. The radio broke the silence.

"Major Phillips, this is Aurora. No foreign military activity has been detected. The helicopter that you are expecting will arrive at your location in fifteen minutes. The pilot requests that you provide some flares or lights at the location you want him to land. Out."

"Flares are being lit. Out."

Mackenzie directed his men to wrap up Captain Winters in several blankets and place him on a stretcher. They covered his face to conceal his identity, then scrambled to assemble a hamper of medical supplies that they would need on board to keep the survivor sedated for the trip to Thule. They had been forewarned that they were not to mention Winters' existence while at Thule. The person on the stretcher was to be identified as a SAR tech injured in the jump to the crash site. Rob then sent the other tech out in the snow to light the flares.

The helicopter came upon the survey buildings from the southwest. The pilot was in contact with the Aurora overhead and knew that the turnaround time on the site would be short. The chopper descended quickly to the area surrounded by flares and hovered momentarily before dropping the final ten feet to the ice surface. The craft finally settled on its springs while the rotor blades blew the snow in whirls about the craft. A person in a parka slid open a side door, stepped out, hunched down below the rotating blades, and ran towards the Phillips group. At the same time, two techs gathered up the stretcher and strode out to the helicopter. They handed the stretcher to the crewmen inside the helicopter then scrambled to get aboard.

The person in the parka approached Phillips.

"It's me, Mari. What's happening?"

"Mari, it's very nice to see you again. I just wish it was in warmer and more luxurious surroundings. That was Frank Winters, pilot of the missing Aurora, who was just put aboard the chopper. He's suffering from severe hypothermia. Shanahan doesn't want anyone to know that he survived the crash. You will have to make some arrangements before you land in Thule. He is to be escorted to a Canadian guarded area and medically treated without the Americans at Thule knowing about him. If anyone asks, tell them that one of my SAR techs got injured."

"Are you OK?" she then hastily added, "and the rest of your crew? What's with all the secrecy?"

"It's because two of our airmen have been killed, one is seriously injured, and Captain Winters is in an induced coma. All survived a missile attack by an unknown sub. It could have been American, so I don't want the Americans at a Thule to know that one of Aurora's crew is alive to bear witness to what happened to the remaining crew. They were captured and taken aboard an unidentified sub. The submariners don't know that they missed one of the crew. If they did, they might attack again to preserve their identity, even though we don't know its nationality."

"Where are the sub and aircrew now?"

"I don't know. The sub could still be in the vicinity but just under the ice. That is why you must get out of here fast. My techs brought the bodies of the two crewmen that were on the plane so they can be taken with you now to Thule for examination."

"What about you?" asked Mari, who instantaneously realized that she should have asked what would happen to everyone still on the island.

"Shanahan said that I could stay here with the rest of my men to see if we can locate more of the crew. By the way, he will be with you in Thule in the next ten hours. You better get going before the sub realizes what you are doing here. Here, take this with you." He handed her the aircraft log.

Mari didn't know whether to salute Major Phillips or kiss him, or just tell him to be careful. In the end, she tied up her parka hood and ran for the helicopter. The door slid open to let her in. It lifted off quickly and was lost in a moment in the snow.

Shawn and Rob walked back together to the lit building. The remainder of the techs followed. Inside, the radio came to life.

"Major Phillips, this is Aurora. The helicopter is safely on its way to Thule. We will stay in the area for a few hours then depart for Thule for refueling. Out."

"Copied. Out."

Shawn was touched that Mari cared enough to make the trip herself to the crash site. She could have sent someone else, but she was a conscientious officer. Perhaps she also cared a bit about his welfare and wanted to see him again, just as he longed to be near her. That thought made him warmer inside the Arctic hut, even as the cold winds just outside his cabin door were minus 30 degrees Celsius.

# 20 FIERY FINISH

27 December 2000 hrs local, Korolev, Moscow

Vasily was fairly certain that he could predict the next fall of the MIR space station. The virus commands seemed to activate whenever MIR was on its polar track, and it was due to pass over the North Pole on its next orbit of the Earth. Unless the destructive commands could be deactivated within the hour, it was most likely that MIR would make its final plunge straight to the ground, or in this case, directly to the polar ice. Unlike some of the engineers, he was also reasonably confident that MIR would fall to Earth nearly intact, even though it was asymmetric. Its shape would normally cause the solar arrays to bend and buckle quickly, but some strategic burns of the core's booster rockets would slow it down to the point that it would not burn up as it reached the Earth's lower atmosphere. He predicted that somewhere in the mass of commands in MIR's computer memory, there were commands that would cause the rockets to fire. He had less than an hour to find them.

His fellow engineers were predicting just the opposite. Most were still under the impression that the MIR de-orbit was due to a system problem. They were forecasting that it would come streaking from the heavens at a shallow angle at 17,500 mph, heated, braked, and buffeted by an increasingly thick atmosphere. Many of the more bombastic engineers were sure that MIR's impact point could not be forecasted. They even went so far as telling the Chief Flight Controller that the craft's complex configuration would make it difficult to predict its landing track. However, they predicted that 90 percent of the 140-ton MIR would be vaporized in the heat of reentry into the atmosphere. They forecasted that the balance would most likely land in the Pacific.

The Chief Flight Controller had a dilemma. Should he now alert the troops and helicopters in the Siberian Military District to take off for the Magnetic Pole? That would possibly cause political problems, if not a war with Canada and NATO. Or should he play the safe bet and concur with most engineers? The decision could wait until it fell, hopefully, in the ocean. His fallback back position was that he could always deny that a propulsion engineer had forewarned him verbally of the slow descent of MIR. The same engineer had forecasted that its impact area would be the Magnetic North Pole. He made the safe decision and did nothing, thus losing valuable time in the recovery operation.

The Chief Flight Controller had been briefed by the Commander in charge of the Special Service Troops. In turn, the CFC informed the President of Russia via the Security Chief in Moscow. The briefing concerned the conversations that the special forces held with the three crew members on the last Soyuz mission to shut down and depart MIR.

The briefing mentioned that the two Russian cosmonauts had not noticed anything unusual during the entire mission they completed with the French Cosmonaut. The mission had gone according to the operations manuals. When the mission was over, they closed down the central computer to allow its resources to be conserved for the final clean-up and de-orbit crew's docking, later in the year. They secured all the hatches between MIR's modules as per the standard operating procedure. Before they made the final exit to the Soyuz ship, ending thirteen years of human-crewed space missions in the station, they posed next to the airlock hatch while souvenir photos were taken.

Just after the final picture was taken and before the hatch was sealed, the French Cosmonaut, Jean-Paul Savard, returned through the airlock to obtain a quick last photo of the interior of the MIR core for his scrapbook. He was alone in the middle for five minutes before he floated weightlessly to the exit. The Soyuz space flight home to the Baikonur Cosmodrome was routine, according to the briefing.

The Flight Controller mentioned the findings of the security briefing to Vasily Vinogradov.

Vasily suggested that it would take less than five minutes to turn on a terminal in the MIR core, insert a disc, and download commands to the computer. He recommended that the French Cosmonaut not be allowed to depart Russia until an investigation was completed on the suspected sabotage.

Vasily watched nervously as MIR commenced its next journey around the Earth. Just as he predicted, a rogue command turned on the computer control of the rocket engines normally used to adjust MIR's orientation and altitude. The rockets fired upwards, pushing the craft downwards toward planet Earth. The firings were intermittent and slowed the crash to such an extent that there was no vaporization. The craft tumbled erratically out of its low orbit. Mission Control Centre engineers signaled that it was a repeat performance of MIR's problem in July. The streaming data to their terminals and screens indicated that MIR's main computer had failed, leaving the station with no altitude control and limited power. Vasily tried several commands and maneuvers to rectify MIR's descent, but his solutions were beyond his input and that of all the other terminals there.

Anyone watching the skies over the North Pole that night would have seen some blazing fiery streaks as MIR passed through the high stratosphere. They would not have seen any disintegration. They would have also heard a shaking sonic boom along with its footprint or trail. Of course, if they were in the area, they would have heard and felt the impact of the craft as it bounced along the sea ice before coming to a halt. The blip faded from Vasily's computer screen as the craft struck the ice. The altitude and latitude of the craft were no longer displayed on the giant wall map at the front of Mission Control.

The Mission Control Centre suddenly went quiet. There were puzzled looks on the faces of everyone, especially the engineers. How did this happen? What should we do now? Only Vasily and the Chief Flight Controller had any answers.

The Chief Flight Controller had gambled and lost valuable time. MIR had indeed crashed in the Canadian Arctic just as predicted by his propulsion engineer. He recovered his wits within minutes, picked up the secure phone, and contacted Colonel-General Nikolaev. He relayed to the head of the Siberian Military District the location of the MIR wreckage. The Chief Flight Controller apologized for not reaching the General earlier about the descent. He lied and said that the final descent was not predictable, nor could its landing point be determined in advance with any accuracy. He explained that the final plunge had taken less than twenty minutes, and there was no time to alert the jets with the missiles. He wished that there was a lot more time so that the jets would have blown the craft out of its death plunge. It was best that the General's resources be deployed at this time to guard any parts of MIR that survived the crash. Choppers could now deploy the General's troops to recover the essential pieces of MIR. He would fax to the General the location of MIR and a description of the prized items that needed to be fetched and preserved.

The Chief followed up this call with one to General Sergeyev and told him the same lies. He confirmed to the Commander of Special Service Troops that the Siberian Military District Headquarters in Novosibirsk had been advised that the remains of MIR were now scattered over the sea ice near the Magnetic North Pole. He neglected to mention that there was a reasonable possibility that the majority of the craft was intact and that it survived the plunge to Earth. He did suggest to the Commander that the French Cosmonaut be investigated further for possible sabotage. The General agreed and indicated to the Flight Controller that he would contact the President. They would release a statement to the world that MIR had accidentally fallen out of orbit, and they would take full responsibility to clean up the debris.

The statement would not mention the suspected sabotage, nor would it mention that Russian troops were now on the way to guard the wreckage. The General would advise the President to call the Canadian PM and let him know that some recovery personnel were on the way to the fallen space station. The President would suggest to the Canadian PM that he may want to pass the information on to the U.S. President. He would advise the PM that the recovery crew would be in and out of the area within a few days. The call would emphasize that such a recovery was necessary to obtain millions of dollars of equipment needed for the International Space Station. The recovery of these items would save millions for all the nations in the ISS program. The call would not mention that Russia really wanted to recover the 13 years of data accumulated by MIR, including experimental and observation data, worth billions. Russia did not want to share it with the world unless it was purchased.

Gen. Sergeyev placed a call to the Commander of his Alfa Commando Unit, led by Colonel Viktor Padalka.

"General Sergeyev, you said that I was to come urgently."

"I'll make this short and sweet. You are to take your unit immediately to the airbase at Dickson in the Taimyr Peninsula. Once there, they fly to the Magnetic North Pole to be prepared to parachute if necessary to the ice. They need to be ready to spend up to a month on the polar ice cap. You will be required to recover individual items from the downed MIR space station and sink the remainder into the sea. You may encounter some resistance from Canadian or American forces, but these items from MIR must, I repeat, must return to the motherland at all costs. It is our priority. If, for some reason that is impossible, then and only then are you authorized to destroy the remains of MIR.

"I want you there within twenty-four hours. You are to make connections to obtain the necessary transport. At Dickson, you will be met by men from the Spetsgruppa Commando Forces currently under the command of the Siberian Military District HQ. You are to place these men under your command and take with you as many of them as you need to bring back these treasured items. I am putting you in charge of this recovery operation, not some officer from Siberian Command. You will have to deal with anyone who resists you from returning our special top-secret equipment. This operation has the full support of the President of Russia. Understood?"

"Yes, General."

"The District HQ has agreed to have several KA-32 Helix helicopters at your disposal upon your arrival. You are probably familiar with them. They are a twin-rotor helicopter used for attack, assault, and troop transport, but they are used for anti-submarine warfare at Dickson, so the HQ Commander tells me. They have a speed of 168 mph and a range of 248 nautical miles. It is armed with machine guns, At-6 missiles, 57 mm rockets, and 30 mm gun pods. Use them to protect our MIR and your men if you need to and call district HQ if you have questions.

"There is also one of our subs on route to the crash location. You can call upon it for help, if needed. If you need further assistance, there is also a division of airborne troops on standby. If you can't retrieve all the classified MIR equipment for any reason, you are authorized to dynamite it. Any questions?"

"General, I will need a list of the special items that you want to be retrieved from MIR."

"The list is being faxed to you at this moment. Now get going on your way. I have to send off several messages to Novosibirsk HQ and Dickson airbase. Keep me informed, use the personal codes that you used on your last mission."

At Novosibirsk, Siberian Military District HQ, Col. Gen. Nikolai told his aide to call, once again, all of his staff officers. They arrived one by one and took up their seats around the conference table.

The General opened the meeting by drawing a string that opened curtains revealing a huge wall map showing all of Siberia, the waters surrounding the North Pole, the Pole itself, and the Canadian portion on the Arctic Circle. The map also showed the location of the Dickson airbase in the Taimyr Peninsula. It also highlighted the Arkhangelsk submarine base, a refueling cache on Somnolent Island, and a large X marking the impact point of MIR.

The General stated that this would be their operations room for the next few days. He outlined the process as discussed in messages between himself and General Sergeyev. He articulated the arrangements made to obtain helicopters containing Alpha Commando Troops of the Special Service. They would amalgamate with some of their own soldiers, and together they would arrive at the crash point, where the commandos would set up camp. They would guard the remains of MIR until all classified material on board the craft was removed. The material would either be transported by helicopter or in one of their subs that would surface near the space station, and the equipment would be loaded on board. The helicopters would be in the air and on route to the site by break of dawn tomorrow.

One of the staff officers asked if there would be any problems retrieving the equipment since it wasn't on Russian Territory. The General replied that the President would deal with the political fallout with Canada and the United States.

"The U.S. may feel threatened by our troops so close to their country, just as they felt threatened by our missiles in Cuba. If there is a conflict, our commandos will handle it, or they will blow up the remains of MIR and head back home."

Since there were no further questions, he closed off the meeting by reminding the staff officers that they would be on duty in the operations room on a rotational basis. They needed to be prepared to take necessary action should any foreign government interfere with the operation. The meeting ended with an explanation.

"By the time you wake up tomorrow, the Special Service Troops, along with some of our pilots and soldiers, will be on route to some foreign territory. I hope that they all return safely with the items that our space program wants for the International Space Station. I only hope that this does not lead to an international incident that gets blown out of proportion and leads to a more serious conflict. God help us all."

# 21 FLYING ARCTIC ROVER
28 December 0700 hrs local, Canada Ice Island, Nunavut

Major Shawn Phillips turned on his laptop computer, and the "you have mail" message appeared on the screen. The message was from Brig. Gen. Shanahan, who was now situated at the mini RCC at the Thule Air Base. The email read:

"NORAD advises that the unmanned MIR Space Station is now descending towards the North Magnetic Pole. It may pass over or impact near your site. MAG headquarters would like to know details, e.g., is it intact? Elaborate and confirm possible connections between it and sub. Shanahan."

Shawn and Rob urgently grabbed their parkas and night vision goggles and went out into the frigid night air.

"See anything?" asked Shawn.

"Over there, to your right, in the direction of the North Star. There's a light in the sky."

"Yes, I got it now."

They, along with the SAR techs, watched as the streaking light came towards them. Indeed, they all stared at the starlit sky since it was not every night that they witnessed a 140-ton space station flying towards the Earth.

It was ending its thirteen-year existence. Their first impression was that it wasn't moving as fast as they thought it would. There was a streaking trail of fire behind MIR but it was not a fireball, as the radio broadcast had led listeners to believe. In Shawn's opinion, on its speed and its small fire trail, there was more than a fifty percent chance that it would not burn up before it reached the ice. For some reason, some words of Robert W. Service's poem, The Cremation of Sam McGee, came to mind.

> "There are strange things done in the midnight sun
> By the men who moil for gold;
> The Arctic trails have their secret tails
> That would make your blood run cold;
> The Northern Lights have seen queer sights,
> But the queerest they ever did see
> Was the night on the marge of Lake Lebarge
> I cremated Sam McGee."

This was one of the queerest and strangest sights that Shawn had seen in his lifetime.

They could make out the spinning movements of the MIR craft as it hurled towards them. The sound of its movement through the dense air was increasing. It was a piercing sound like the one made by a wolf nearing the end of its life. The space station and its fiery tail were going to pass right over the ice island and the shivering airmen. The MIR was so close that it was magical; they felt that they could almost reach up and touch this fantastic piece of scientific achievement. It flew by them as if it was landing in slow motion. As it passed, it was heading towards the far end of the island, away from the end containing the ruins of another incredible air machine. The streaking light was fading as it descended towards the horizon of the ice plateau, then it was gone, only to be replaced by a terrific sonic booming noise as the craft impacted the ice. The sound was followed by a vibration that they could feel in their boots. A second but less noisy boom followed the vibration, then all was quiet. The group saw no fireball either before or after the impact.

Shawn, Mackenzie, and the four technicians stared for several moments at the horizon, where the craft disappeared. They turned to the warm shack that they now considered home. Shawn went to the computer and typed a reply to MAG.

"MIR has just landed, approximately four km off our current position. It did not burn up on reentry, but probably suffered severe damage from the impact with the ice. It is Captain Winters' firm belief, based on his intuition, that there is a connection between the mysterious sub and the fall of MIR. It is almost as if the sub knew that MIR would land in this area and is waiting for it. The sub is probably Russian, but doesn't necessarily have to be, especially if MIR descent was arranged in advance by someone other than the Russians. It could be someone or an organization from many nations. Phillips."

The reply was instantaneous, indicating that Shanahan was sitting at the computer terminal in the RCC office at Thule.

"Winters is probably right. It is most likely that there is a connection between the sub and the space station. If so, the sub commander will probably try to reach the remains of MIR. Is it possible that you could arrange for your group to observe the MIR remnants to see if the submariners approach it? Unfortunately, the Aurora #740 that was your protection is now back in Thule for fuel. It will be back to your site within an hour with Capt. Mari Leech at the controls. The Aurora will spot any subs that are still in your vicinity. In the meantime, you will have to undertake visual observation if possible. Shanahan."

The possibility of visual observation was discussed among the group. Phillips drafted his reply.

"Never say die. Every attempt will be made to get to the site of the impact. Maybe one of the buildings might have a snowmobile left behind for the next bunch of scientists. A check will be conducted of all buildings here to see if we can find some means of transportation and weapons. Advise Vice Admiral Lowery in Halifax of the situation to see if the CO of Eureka, his brother, has a means of getting to MIR? Advise."

Again, the reply from Shanahan was rapid. It was similar to a chat line on the Internet.

"Take extreme caution should you venture out onto the ice cap to observe MIR... Lowery is no longer in Halifax but in Frobisher Bay. He is apparently making a gift of men and ships to Nunavut to protect their assets. In return for the gift, he has offered to be CO of such forces... PM has yet to speak about Lowery's gift to the Nunavut Inuit nation."

Phillips fired off a quick response.

"Captain Winters was tasked by Vice Admiral Lowery to drop a package to his brother at Eureka. The canister containing Lowery's package was found in the plane wreck. When I opened it, the package contained $50,000 in cash, a gun and a note which read 'Be prepared for the first week of January. Heiserman will contact you. Think about global warming. Buzz.' End of note. Interesting, what does this all mean?"

"Deliver the package to me and tell no one else at this time. FYI, the Alert listening station has advised NDHQ that there is significant radio traffic between Moscow and an airbase near the North Pole's Russian side. The NORAD bunker also reports that their satellites have spotted aircraft and helicopters accumulating at the same base. Earlier, a submarine was also seen heading for its headquarters in Siberia. It could be obtaining supplies for a trip under the polar ice cap. Shanahan."

"The SAR teams need to know if any Russian aircraft are seen heading our way. Also, advise the condition of our patient. Phillips."

"At the moment our patient is slowly recovering. Amputation of several toes and two fingers had to be done. Identity still a secret...The patient credits the work of your team with saving his legs and arms. Good work. Out." This latter news made the SAR techs, who were reading over the shoulder of their Search Master, smile with joy.

The near recovery of Captain Winters called for a mild celebration of hot coffee that the team made from a tin of old coffee found in the cupboards in the Mess Hall.

The geological survey crew was obviously expecting to return in the spring since the cupboard was also stocked with some cans of beans and tins of Spam. These foods were frozen, but the techs managed to get them opened and warmed up so that they were edible. After the brief celebration, they gathered around the stove and discussed their options. Phillips addressed the group first.

"We will have to search each of the survey buildings again to see what we can use for weapons and transport. Maybe we can find some skis or snowshoes or something that we can use to get out on the pack ice to MIR. We could also use some markers and rope to identify our trail so we can find our way back to this place."

"Since we could be here a few days, we may as well make an inventory of what else is in the buildings that we may need, such as weapons, food, clothing, heating materials, and similar stuff," noted Mackenzie.

"Is there anything else that we could use from the plane?" asked a tech.

"I can't think of anything that would help us that is still there," replied Shawn. "Besides, the sub could always be in the area, and they may be watching the plateau through a periscope. The sub that took our aircrew didn't know about these buildings, or they would have searched them even if they thought they had the full aircrew. If they see us mulling about the plane, they may return and find the huts.

"Rob, I want you to take two of the techs and search thoroughly the three buildings nearer the plane. The other two techs and I will do the same with the remainder. We'll meet back here in an hour. Be careful so you won't be seen by sub personnel."

Shawn found no ski-doos, but he did find a very large hovercraft. It was hidden at the base of the cliff of the ice plateau, on the sea ice. He had gone over to the edge of the plateau, before searching the buildings, to relieve himself and to do a quick check to see if any foreign subs or military activity were on the ice.

The hovercraft was hidden under a tarp and buried in a great deal of snow. At first appearance, it looked like it was just another mound of snow about twenty-feet high, sixty-five feet long, and thirty-five feet wide. It was the hovercraft antenna that caught Phillips' eye. He just happened to notice the antenna of the UHF/VHF radio sticking out of the snowbank. He quickly lowered himself down the edge of the plateau and walked the short distance to the snow mound. He climbed the snow hill and started to remove the lightly compacted snow from around the antenna. Further digging uncovered the radar, and that was when he realized that he was standing on the roof of a large machine.

The techs joined Major Phillips and started to clear away more of the snow, revealing the windows, the windscreen, externally mounted searchlights, and the walkway that surrounded the deck. More digging uncovered the flexible rubber skirt of the vehicle. The skirt made him realize that it was an older air cushion vehicle that the survey crew probably used to transport men, supplies and equipment. The survey could transport up to twenty workers to and from their mainland base, which could be at Eureka or Alert. The hovercraft had been stored for the winter after the crew had been evacuated.

As Shawn cleared snow from the machine, a message appeared on the windscreen.

"Welcome to Rudolph, Santa's Reindeer. Have a Merry Christmas!" *At least someone has a sense of humor,* thought Shawn. He cleared the snow from around the hatch leading to the cockpit of the hovercraft. Two techs went off to the huts to see if they could find anything that would help start the flying arctic rover. Phillips stayed behind to check out the aircraft, so designated by the Ministry of Transportation since it flew above the ice.

He tugged on the hatch door until he broke the ice covering the hatch frame, opened it, and stepped into the cockpit area of the craft. There were many similarities between this cockpit and those on aircraft that he had flown in the past. There were many dials and gauges he recognized on the control console. He noticed the rudder pedals and controls, elevator levers, an instrument panel, propeller pitch and engine controls. The main difference between the two types of aircraft was that this one had a skirt control. The control console for the engines was located between two seats. These two seats were for the operators, with the main operator on the starboard side and the relief driver or radar operator at the port side. A full-width bench seat was located across the cab's back, with two doors that provided access to the cabin. Shawn squeezed himself around the chairs, stepped over the bench seat, and went through the doors into the cabin area. There he found more seats and a section of the cabin devoted to crew survival. It contained sleeping bags, emergency survival rations, a rifle, and ammunition, as well as the usual life raft and jackets. There were canvas tarpaulins, flashlights, ropes, blocks, tackles, shovels, picks, axes, tool kits, operator manuals, and spare parts for the craft in a wooden box. Closing the box, Shawn picked up the rifle and ammo and left the cabin and the craft through the same hatch that he entered. The tarp was pulled over the hovercraft's exposed area and held in position by a few boot loads of snow. He returned to the Mess Hall.

Shawn gathered his techs around the warmth of the stove.

"Rob, tell us what you found that might come in handy, especially if we have to confront the men from the sub."

"We didn't find anything of interest, just some rope and wood that we can use for marking poles. There were no weapons, except this knife, and we didn't see any snowshoes or skis."

"Let me see the knife and holster, please."

Mackenzie passed the knife, and Shawn looked at the weapon and smiled.

"What you have here is pure kitsch. The knife is really a camouflage comb. If no one claims it, I'll add it to my kitsch collection. Sgt. Petrie and M. Cpl. Aucoin," Shawn addressed the two SAR techs, "did you guys find anything of interest? Tell us what you found in the other buildings."

"Like WO Mackenzie, we didn't find anything of much use, replied Petrie. "There's a bit of food in the cookhouse that might come in handy, along with some gasoline and kerosene barrels and an auxiliary power unit in one of the buildings. Just like you guys, we didn't see any guns or sturdy knives."

"That reminds me," said Shawn, "I have too many weapons for myself. Rob, you can have this rifle and take some of the ammo that I found, and Sgt. Petrie, you can have the gun that belonged to Captain Winters. I still have the gun that was in the canister addressed to Brian Lowery. Besides the rifle, I know where there are sleeping bags, ropes, shovels, picks, flashlights, and much more. I found them in an old hovercraft, probably 1975, parked under a tarp at the base of the cliff. I don't know if we can get it started, but if we do, I'm pretty sure that I can operate it."

"A hovercraft... very interesting," said Mackenzie. "It's worth a try to get it going. We might need it to get to MIR and for us to get out of here, especially if the sub returns before we get any help. As a hobby, I tinker around with motors in my spare time. If it used to run, then I bet that I can get it going again. We have a hovercraft, but I regret to point out that it doesn't look like we have the tools to damage a submarine."

"We may not defeat them, but we may be able to screw up their plans. The hovercraft, if we can get it going, might come in handy for more things than visiting MIR and escaping." Shawn wondered aloud if ramming the sub's sail with the hovercraft would cause sufficient damage to prevent it from submerging.

# 22   CANADIAN + RUSSIAN LEADERS

28 December 1000 hrs local, Thule Air Base, Greenland

Shanahan walked to his office in the mini RCC at the Thule Airbase, sipping his hot coffee and occasionally staring at the computer monitor, willing it to display another message from Major Shawn Phillips. His Search Master was sitting in some cold shack along with four SAR techs, hundreds of miles away on an ice island in the Canadian Northern Territories. It would probably be a couple of hours before he would hear again from Phillips, but he kept hoping that a message would appear saying that the aircrew had now been located. He had briefed the main RCC in Halifax on all that was safe for them to release to the press, namely that the plane had been found, but the crew was still not located. The RCC was not notified that the pilot of the downed plane was resting in a room just down the hall from him. The question remained as to whether he should tell Vice Admiral Lowery about Winters. Lowery didn't need to know, and he wasn't interested anyway, even though all aircrew were his responsibility. The Admiral had never in the past shown concern over the health and welfare of the men and women who protected his fleet. The fact remained that someone from Vice Admiral Lowery's organization could have put the aircraft in harm's way.

A light was flashing on one of the phones in the Thule RCC, indicating and incoming call. It was answered by Captain Kendall, the pilot who had switched places with Captain Leech. Mari was now on route to the site of the downed plane while Kendall took over her place manning the RCC.

"Sir, it is for you, from NORAD."

"Shanahan here!"

"You are a hard man to track down. I certainly never thought that I would find you in Thule. It's Lieutenant Reilly at one of the NORAD desks. Just thought that you should be the first to know our satellites have spotted four Russian helicopters heading towards the place where MIR crashed."

"Thanks, Bob, I owe you a beer. I'll pass the word to Defense Headquarters and to Maritime Command HQ."

Shanahan searched for the phone number for Vice Admiral Lowery at his Frobisher Bay location. Maritime Command HQ, who provided the number, had not heard anything from Lowery since his infamous newscast from the capital city of Nunavut.

The Frobisher airport at Iqaluit answered the call. He asked for Vice Admiral Lowery.

"Lowery! Who is this?"

"It's Brig. Gen. Shanahan. I want to let you know what is happening regarding our missing plane. Is this phone safe?"

"Sure, what's new?"

"Our search crew has found the missing aircraft, but the strange thing is that there is no sign of our twelve-man crew anywhere near the crash site. Our Search Master was able to establish that the plane crashed because a wing was torn off by a guided missile, fired by a foreign submarine."

"What? Are you sure?"

"Absolutely. The Search Master saw the torn wing, and there is evidence that a submarine surfaced near the crash site."

"I knew those damn Russians were using our northern waters and landing on our shores. They will have to pay for this."

"Excuse me, Sir, but we are not sure that it was a Russian sub."

"Well, who else could it be?"

"We should keep an open mind since the Americans, the Brits, and the Germans are among others that use the polar sea route as well as the Russians."

"It couldn't be the Americans. I speak with their Naval staff every day, and they want to protect our northern border for their own benefit."

Shanahan didn't pursue the argument; instead he moved on with his debriefing.

"It's possible that the crew of the submarine have picked up our own crew and are returning them to us with some explanation. I would suggest that Defense Headquarters contact the Russian and U.S. governments to ask if they have seen our crew. What do you think?"

"It's a waste of bloody time asking the Americans."

Shanahan didn't comment on Admiral Lowery's non-answer, instead he reached for a related topic.

"By the way, the Aurora flight was not planned to be in that area of our Canadian Arctic. Our Search Master was told by an aircraft technician that the Aurora pilot had been ordered by a Maritime Command Officer to drop a package off at Eureka, not far from the point where the sub surfaced. If the Aurora had not been in the area, it probably would not have spotted the sub and would not have been shot down. Would you know anyone at your HQ who would have a reason to divert the Aurora's route to fly over Eureka?"

"Did your search crew find such a package? Did you say that all of Aurora's crew is missing, including the pilot, Capt. Winters?"

Shanahan couldn't recall telling Admiral Lowery that the pilot was Captain Winters.

"The package could have been lost in the wreck. Yes, Captain Winters is part of the missing crew. The technician was sure that it was a senior officer from Halifax that gave Winters the package. And you don't know anyone who would have a reason to have the Aurora fly over Eureka?"

"The technician must have been mistaken," Lowery paused. "I don't know anyone who would have a reason to drop a package at Eureka."

Again, Shanahan switched topics even though the Admiral had just lied about the package.

"You may have heard from the news that the Russians are having a problem keeping their MIR Space Station in orbit. NORAD has advised that it left its orbit and has crashed near our downed plane. They have also advised that there are four helicopters that left a Russian airbase and are now heading for the MIR crash site. Will you pass this information along to Defense Headquarters so that the PM can be alerted?"

"I'll talk with NDHQ, but briefing the PM is a waste of time. He won't do anything about the Russians invading our lands. The fact that the Russians are on their way in helicopters confirms to me that it was a Russian sub that did this deadly deed. They attacked our plane, and we should blast their helicopters out of the sky. Leave it to me. I will handle this with NDHQ and the PM. Anything else?"

"No, Sir, that is all."

The MAG Commander thought that Admiral Lowery might have jumped to conclusions that weren't supported by the evidence. He had concluded that there was a connection between the downing of the plane, the MIR crash, and the helicopters on route. He was not concerned that the Admiral might be misled about some of the information that he provided. He rationalized that he had not really lied to Vice Admiral Lowery. He just didn't tell him the whole truth. On the other hand, Lowery had definitely lied about the package for his brother.

Shanahan needed to talk with the Chief of the Defense Staff in Ottawa. It took an hour of playing long-distance phone tag, but the captain at the mini RCC desk was able to connect Shanahan with the top officer of the Canadian military.

"Office of the Chief of the Defense Staff," said a dainty female voice.

"Brigadier General Shanahan here. I need to talk to Major General Le Beau."

There was a momentary pause while the soft velvet voice conferred with someone.

"You can go ahead now, Brig. Gen. Shanahan."

"Good Day Sir, I'm calling from the Thule Airbase. You have probably been briefed by your Operations Center, but I need to add some info that you may not have."

"Dave, nice to hear from you, what's happening? I need to broadcast your conversation since I have other generals in the room with me."

"Did Vice Admiral Lowery talk to you in the past hour?"

"No, he didn't. Why? What's up?"

"Perhaps he had some communications difficulties getting through to you as I had. Well, Sir, we may have some problems heading our way. The MIR space station has crashed some five miles from the location where our Aurora was forced down. We can now confirm that our plane was brought down by a missile fired by a sub that surfaced in the area. Eleven members of the Aurora crew are missing, and we suspect that they have been brought aboard the sub by a landing crew. We don't know the nationality of the sub, but we have now heard that the Russians have sent four helicopters over the Pole towards the MIR landing site. The site is in the Canadian Arctic."

"I did know most of what you mentioned except the plane being brought down by a missile and the missing crew on a sub. Do you think it was a Russian sub?"

"Could be. Other countries also send subs through the polar sea."

"That's true. The Americans use the route all the time. The Russian government has already contacted the PM about the fact that they want to retrieve the wreckage of MIR. They didn't mention the sub, the missile, or that they are already on their way."

"I don't suppose that they mentioned rescuing our crew and perhaps explaining the downing as an accident?"

"No, they didn't, but as you say, it may not have been the Russians. I'll ask the PM to ask the Russian president."

"Our search crew are still on location. Should I try to get them out of there, or should they hunker down?"

"I'll have to find out from the PM. I know that he has no difficulties with the Russians picking up what is left of MIR. He wanted them to do it just in case there was some radioactive material on the craft, but he thought that the Russian cleanup would occur under the supervision of Canadian troops. The downing of our plane puts his agreement with the Russian president in a whole new light. I'll get back to you ASAP regarding your missing aircrew and the safety of your search crew."

"As you probably surmised, I have apprised the Commander of Maritime Command, Vice Admiral Lowery, about the situation, and he was going to contact you. I told him about the Russian helicopters on route to the Arctic crash site of MIR. I also mentioned to him about our shot down plane and missing crew. I think he may have jumped to some wrong conclusions and may do something drastic."

The line went silent for a few moments.

"I understand that you had to mention it to him since he is your boss, but I have to tell you in confidence that the PM and I are not too happy with him at the moment because of the little speech that he gave recently. I just hope that he doesn't use those Gulf War Apache gunships to go after the Russian helicopters and the sub. We could lose your aircrew if they are, in fact, aboard a Russian sub. I'll talk with the PM immediately and try to get hold of Vice Admiral Lowery. Do you know where I can contact him?"

Shanahan provided the information on how to contact Lowery along with his own phone number and email address.


**28 December 1100 hrs, National Defense Headquarters, Ottawa**

The Chief of the Defense Staff told his aide to request an immediate conference for him with the Minister of Defense. Five minutes later, the aide spoke.

188

"The Minister is now available for you in his Parliament Hill office. Your car is waiting for you."

General Le Beau took the elevator down from his tenth-floor office at 101 Colonel By Drive in Ottawa and walked out the front door to his car. The uniformed driver saluted and opened the door for the General, and he was whisked away to arrive at the Members Block on Parliament Hill. Five minutes later he walked down the hall to the Minister's office, where he was ushered in by an aide in a lieutenant's uniform.

"General Le Beau," said the Minister, "please have a seat and tell me about this need for an immediate conference."

General Le Beau relayed the gist of the conversation that he just had with Shanahan. The Minister was shocked to learn that a Canadian Forces plane had been shot out of the Arctic sky. The Minister was aware that military planes were sometimes 'lost' over foreign countries, especially during war times, but he never expected to hear of his own planes being destroyed in his own backyard.

"Do you think that it was Russians?" he asked.

"We have no evidence to that fact, but it is a coincidence that MIR landed nearby."

"But why would they land their space station in our territory if the landing was planned and the sub was nearby waiting for it? Why not land in their own country?"

"I must admit that I'm puzzled by that question, Sir, and I would have no answer unless its landing was predictable but beyond their control."

"I don't think so," said the Minister. "The fact that Vice Admiral Lowery is in the area, and he has a passionate dislike for the Russians, concerns me. Also, he has an arsenal. He has all that hardware and equipment at his disposal to deal with the Russian choppers. These facts are very disturbing to me. Have you talked to him?"

"No, Sir. I wanted to discuss the matter with you first."

"I'm glad you did. The PM and I discussed Lowery's speech and the assets last night over cocktails, and he was very disturbed. He has contacted several of his friends in different parts of Canada to get a feel of how Canadians think about the Lowery gift. The public seems to like the idea of providing more protection for our northern border but not at the expense of tax cuts. The public is definitely not in favor of the northern territories, or any other province for that matter, having their own military force separate from the Canadian Forces. What it boils down to is the fact that Vice Admiral Lowery must turn over these assets, especially the Apache helicopters, to the control of Maritime Air Group, under the command of Brig. Gen. Shanahan. The ships and men would formally become the responsibility of Maritime Command Headquarters.

"I have been tasked with handling the Lowery situation as I see fit. The PM does not want to talk with Lowery in case the press makes a bigger deal out of this situation. If Lowery doesn't agree with turning the military equipment over to the Canadian Forces and returning to Halifax, I will relieve him of his command. It's as simple as that! The PM doesn't want anyone in Canada with their own army, navy, or air force."

"That's what I thought. He would probably turn these assets over more readily if there was some commitment to station more of our Canadian Forces men and equipment in the north. He would also expect some plan to place listening devices on the sea bed entrances to the Northwest Passage."

"That is not about to happen, and I'll tell you why. You are always telling me how your forces are stretched to the limit. You know as well as I do that, at present, that we just don't have the manpower to put more forces in the north at this time. And we can't buy any new equipment because our defense budget has been drastically cut in the past six years while the PM and Finance Minister wrestled with the deficit problem. While there is a bit of a budget surplus at this time, Canadian people are now screaming for tax cuts. There is little likelihood that the Minister of Finance would give me more funds for a sub detection system for our north. It is just not on. Besides, the PM and the Cabinet doesn't see the Russian Government as a threat to our northern sovereignty. Perhaps in a few years, we can add men and equipment to the Arctic forces. Now, I better call Lowery before he does something drastic."

General Le Beau provided the Minister with the number to contact Lowery. The Minister told his secretary to make the call and put it on speakerphone. She placed the call and was able to locate Lowery in his office at Frobisher Bay. Within minutes, the call reached the Arctic Circle.

"Lowery here!" said the edgy sounding voice.

"Vice Admiral Lowery, this is the Minister of Defense. The Prime Minister and I want to thank you for obtaining, on behalf of the Government of Canada, the helicopters, weapons, ships, and men that you recently disclosed to the Canadian people through your press conference. I must say you caught us by surprise, but we are all grateful for these resources. They will be very helpful in defending the sovereignty of our country wherever we deploy them. We are looking forward to hearing more details on how they were obtained. Tell me, how soon can they be brought on inventory? I'm anxious to send a commander to Frobisher Bay to bring them on charge so that you can return to your command in Halifax."

There was a long pause before Lowery answered.

"Thank you for calling me, Minister. I was expecting to hear from you or the Prime Minister. The conditions upon which this equipment and men were given to me were that they would be used exclusively to defend Canada's north and the entrances to it. If these conditions are not met, then they cannot be given to Canada. You know that I have sent letters to you and to your predecessor to place more emphasis on defending our northern border, and I have sent numerous submissions requesting a detection system to keep foreign vessels out of our Canadian Arctic Ocean. Could you tell me of the status of that request?"

"Vice Admiral, you must know that the government is under tight financial strains, and our defense budget has been shrinking. We need to prioritize the use of our funds. Right now, we need every dollar just to pay the salaries of our forces and to modernize our fighting equipment."

"You are telling me that funds for the defense of the north are not in the cards."

"Well, not in the immediate future. We need most of our men for peacekeeping duties when they are not in training, and we don't have the money to acquire more manpower or equipment. But our intention is to place more emphasis on our sovereignty in the north as budget funds improve, and as the situation demands."

"The situation demands more men and equipment now!" Vice Admiral Lowery shot back in reply. "You may not know that Russian helicopters are on the way to land on our territory, and one of their subs just destroyed one of our planes and captured our crewmen."

"I am aware of this situation. We don't know for sure that it was a Russian sub, and the PM has already spoken with the Russian president regarding salvaging the wreckage of MIR. They have agreed that the Russian military can retrieve their own space station in case there is some radioactive material on board the craft. They will be out of our northern ice pack within a week."

Again Lowery spoke hastily without regard to the fact that he was critical of his boss.

"The downed space station is just a ruse that they used to invade our North. These four helicopters are just the start of many more to come, and we've got to stop them now," Lowery said emphatically.

The Minister of Defense was starting to get annoyed. He was trying to be sensitive to the Vice Admiral's feelings regarding the North's sovereignty, but Lowery was not cooperative. The Admiral was showing reluctance to follow the Minister's long-term plan, so the Minister decided that it was time to drive home the point more assertively.

"That is not your concern. I'm sending another general to work with the Russians to help them retrieve the MIR wreckage. The PM will talk to the Russian president and ask if he knows about our missing crew of the Aurora. You are to go back to Halifax today!"

There was a longer pause this time by Vice Admiral Lowery. For almost thirty years, he had followed the orders of his superiors religiously, even if he felt the orders were wrong at times. But there was a time to take a stand for what he believed. Besides, there was more at stake here than just a few Russians on Canadian ice and missing crew. He had to think of the vast resources of Nunavut that were available to him. He calculated that his lost pension paled in comparison to the wealth that could be his in this new land. Finally, he answered.

"I'm sorry, Minister. I will not comply with these orders. I owe it to the Inuit people to defend their culture, their way of life, and their resources. I'm staying here, and I'm using my resources to defend our land from these invaders."

"Then, I have no choice but to relieve you of your command. I am also ordering a court-martial hearing to consider your conduct, specifically your failure to obey orders of a senior government official. The court marshaling trial could result in the reduction of your rank and your dismissal from the Forces for disobeying an order. I am exercising my prerogative to relieve you of your authority. I will be sending Brig. Gen. Shanahan to take control of the Apaches, and you are forbidden to use them in the interim."

The mention of Shanahan enraged Vice Admiral Lowery. His years of hatred for the man, and for the military system that took away his navy planes, came boiling to the surface.

"If General Shanahan shows up anywhere in Nunavut, he will be arrested and imprisoned, maybe even shot. We don't need him here. Myself, my men, my equipment, and my friends will take care of the invaders." He hung up.

The Minister placed his receiver on its cradle. He looked at General Le Beau, the Chief of the Defense Staff.

"As you heard, that didn't go well! That is not the result that I wanted. Lowery sounded like the governor of an independent nation just before he hung up. We better go see the PM. The Russian government needs to be warned that we have an insubordinate general in command of some serious equipment. There are assets that could be dangerous to the Russian helicopters and their crews. We also need to get the PM to ask the Russian president about our missing aircrew. Maybe the PM will call a Cabinet meeting to devise a plan to get Lowery out of Frobisher Bay before he causes embarrassment to the government."

Together, the Minister and the Chief of the Defense Staff used the tunnel to walk from the Member Block to the House of Commons building. They climbed the stairs to the top floor to where the PM's office was located. The PM's secretary announced them, and they were admitted immediately to the spacious office.

"Prime Minister, you know our Chief of the Defense Staff, General Le Beau."

"Bonjour General!" The French-Canadian PM switched to English for the benefit of his defense minister. "Yes, certainly, we know one another. We met just after you appointed him Chief. Nice to see you again, General Le Beau."

"Bonjour Prime Minister Le Chance."

The Minister told the PM about the missing Aurora, how it was shot down by an unknown sub and how the crew was captured and taken aboard the sub. He mentioned that the event occurred in the same area where MIR crashed, but they didn't know if there was a connection. He said that they were not certain if the sub belonged to Russia or some other nation, or if there was some logical explanation for the kidnapping of their crew.

"You spoke to President Dmitri Gazenko about the landing of MIR. Did he mention a sub?" asked the Minister.

"I've known President Gazenko for the past six years, and I met him on several occasions. I believe that he is a straight forward individual. He called me earlier to tell me that their Space Station was out of control and was going to crash on the ice near the Magnetic North Pole. Dmitri said that the remnants of the station might contain items that are useful to the International Space Program, of which Canada is a partner. He assured me that there would be little radiation associated with the spacecraft, and he asked if his military could come on to our ice for about a week to clean up the debris. I saw no problem with that, so I said it was OK. He didn't mention anything about a submarine in the area."

"May I suggest that you call him straight away and ask him if any of his military forces have seen our crew? There is another reason to call, as well. NORAD has advised us that they now have several helicopters on route to the MIR crash site. Last night, you and I spoke about Vice Admiral Lowery and his gunship helicopters and ships in the eastern Arctic." The Minister paused and lowered the tone of his voice. "Well, I spoke to him just moments ago, and he refuses to turn over the assets to us, and he refused to return to his post, as we agreed. I had no alternative but to fire him. It sounded to me that he is considering using the gunships against the Russian salvage team. You may want to forewarn the Russian president of this possibility."

"I didn't know that the Russian military would be on their way so soon. I thought that his Space Program officials would contact ours so arrangements could be made to work together to recover all of MIR in the next week or so. I'll call him right now, but I won't mention Lowery's helicopters until he tells me about his country's role, if any, in the whereabouts of our crew."

The PM used the red emergency phone on his desk. He told the receptionist to get him the President of Russia. While awaiting the connection, the three men spoke about what to do with Vice Admiral Lowery.

After a ten-minute discussion, they agreed that Brig. Gen. Shanahan would be promoted to Major General, the same rank as Lowery. Further, the new Major General would be given the authority to court martial Lowery and return him to Ottawa. If Shanahan needed help in achieving that goal, he could use any of the Canadian Forces in the Arctic, including those at Alert and the Arctic Rangers, if need be. But it had to be done quickly and quietly. All of the assets that Lowery had assembled would be placed under Shanahan's control until further notice. The CDS promised to issue the orders as soon as he returned to his office.

The red phone rang, and the PM spoke gently into the receiver.

"President Gazenko, it is Rene Le Chance, from Ottawa. How's the weather in Moscow? Just a moment, I want to put you on speakerphone, if it is OK with you. I have my Minister of Defense and my Chief of the Defense Staff with me here. They can answer any questions you may have."

"Hello Rene. The weather is beautiful. It is unusual, but it is OK for me to be on speakerphone. If you were American, I would worry about being taped."

Renee thought about President Nixon and laughed.

"You are lucky about the weather. It is so cold in Ottawa that it would freeze the balls off a brass monkey. We have something that you need to know about, in regard to the safety of your military people, and I have some questions about the safety of my military people."

"Well, go ahead, enlighten me. We Russians have nothing to hide." Le Chance could tell that Gazenko was suppressing a laugh.

"Dmitri, you and I go back a half dozen years, and we have been through a lot together. Remember the Berlin Wall and the attempted coup in Moscow? We Canadians stood behind you as you struggled to bring democracy to your country and to the republics that once were part of the Soviet Union."

"You have been a good friend to my country."

"Yes, both you and I, and our countries have been good friends for a long while. But I heard today from my defense minister something that disturbs me. As a friend, I would appreciate an honest answer to a tough question that I have to ask you."

"I'm waiting, my dear friend. What can I do for you?"

"Alright, I believe that you will give me an honest answer just as I would give you the same. Here is the problem neither the world nor the Canadian people know yet, but one of our surveillance planes was brought down by a guided missile from a sub, and the fourteen-man crew was taken aboard the sub that brought her down. We don't know where our military aircrew is presently located. This terrorist act will inflame the people of Canada once it becomes known, and the people will demand retaliation. Myself, my defense minister, and my CDS alone know about this dangerous and deadly deed. We are all sickened by the act. We are extremely worried about our missing aircrew. The incident occurred close to the MIR crash site. I need to know, did one of your subs fire on our plane?"

The tough question was out in the open. He and the others waited for the answer. All three men in the room held their breath. There was a pause, then some rapid talk at the other end of the phone. The Russian president was obviously asking his minister a similar tough question. The much-anticipated answer came.

"We know nothing about your missing crew, and we certainly didn't shoot down any aircraft this week." Another chuckle by Gazenko, since Russia had been blamed in the past for such occurrences. "Do you know anything about the sabotage of MIR?"

"Thank you, Sir," said the PM. "I can honestly tell you that it wasn't the Canadian government that sabotaged the MIR Space Station and made it land on the Canadian Arctic ice pack. Canadians are not that sort of people." The PM almost said, "unlike Americans", but bit his tongue.

The mention of sabotage caused the three men to look inquisitively at one another.

"We have no interest in obtaining your space program material, nor did we have an opportunity to disrupt it. But I will check with our Canadian Security Intelligence Services to see if they heard of any nation or group that might want to sabotage your space station. I will let you know if we hear anything. Now, what is the answer to my question about a Russian sub in Canadian waters?"

There was more talking on the other end of the secure emergency phone.

"I've got to say no again. We have had no Russian subs in Canadian waters in ages. We didn't know that MIR was going to land near the Magnetic Pole. It was not us that brought down MIR prematurely. We had no reason to preposition a sub at the Pole. You had some information about the safety of my helicopter crews?"

"I do appreciate your honesty, and I believe you when you say that your government did not post a sub in Canadian waters and didn't destroy one of our planes. I realize that you want to double-check with your navy, and I know that all militaries, including yours and mine, have disgruntled officers that sometimes take actions that are not authorized by their governments. I would appreciate it if you get back to me as soon as possible after you've double-checked. We will continue to authorize you to retrieve MIR. I would appreciate it if you would have the commander of the helicopters that are currently on route to MIR site contact and work with our Search Master, who is in the area. Perhaps he can be of help to your men, and perhaps your troops can help him locate our missing airmen."

"I am waiting to hear about my people's safety. What do you know about my people that I don't already know? By the way, we may have to send a sub to retrieve the remnants of MIR."

"You probably don't know that we watch you all the time, especially the activities of your military. Dmitri, you know we watch you like a hawk. We saw your helicopters the moment they took off. We can even tell the color of the eyes of the pilots."

Gazenko laughed at that crack, and Le Chance spoke again.

"Since we are honest with one another, I need to tell you that we have a former member of the Canadian Navy who is presently in the eastern Arctic. He has acquired a number of Apache helicopters, troops, and a ship. He has threatened to take unauthorized military action against your helicopters and your troops. We have ordered this individual to stand down these assets, and we have relieved him of his command. However, we have not been able to get him to agree, nor have we been able to disarm him yet. He is a renegade who may just decide to take some missile shots at your helicopters since he thinks your forces brought down our plane, kidnapped the crew, and have intentions to invade our northern territory. I have sent officers to his last known location to detain him, but at the moment, he is still on the loose and must be considered dangerous. I suggest that you forewarn your pilots and have them contact our Search Master, Major Phillips."

Bystanders in the room could hear talking coming from the phone while the PM listened. After the talking stopped momentarily, the PM jumped in and spoke.

"OK, Demetri, I can hear your people in the background. As I understand it, you will call back within an hour if any of your forces know anything about my plane and about my missing crew, and I will contact you immediately if we hear anything about the sabotage of your Space Program. It is agreed that neither of our governments will issue any statements about sabotage and missiles. Have a good day." The PM hung up the red phone.

"There you have it, gentlemen. I tend to believe him."

"Should we contact the American president?" asked the Minister.

"I expect that he and I will be talking later today as the Russian forces enter our airspace. He will want to know what I intend to do about it. I'll let you know what he said after he has called.

"In the meantime, General Le Beau, you will have to contact General Shanahan about our agreement on how to handle Lowery, and also have him contact the Search Master to have him work with the Russians to recover MIR and find our missing crew."

"OK, Sir, I will contact Shanahan as soon as I return to work."

The General and the Minister left the PM's suite and returned to their respective offices.

# 23  SEA DEVIL QUESTIONS

27 December 1300 hrs local, Sea Devil, from under Arctic Ice

Commander Bill Hayes anxiously waited to contact Rear Admiral Heiserman and brief him about the accidental bringing down of the Canadian plane and rescuing the survivors. Over forty-eight hours had passed since the survivors were brought aboard the Sea Devil, and the crew had been able to keep their identity secret from the Canadians. The ship was on station waiting for a transmission from Heiserman telling them that their mission objective was at hand, but the sub had not received any signals from the Admiral. Hayes decided to return to the same lead that the sub previously used and to send off an urgent asking for further instructions.

"XO, bring her back to the lead that we used previously. We need to find out if MIR is still airborne or if it bit the dust."

"Aye, skipper, it will take us about twenty minutes."

Jack Murphy ordered the helmsman to bring the Sea Devil around to a new course zero-six-zero. The new course path was repeated back to him.

"All ahead one third," the XO said quietly.

Since there were twenty minutes of opportunity to refresh himself, Hayes visited his room, laid down on his bunk for ten minutes, then had a quick shower and changed into heavy clothes. He would need them once they surfaced and he climbed the sail to the bridge. Just before leaving the room, he sat at his desk and wrote out a message to Admiral Heiserman. Returning to the control room, he passed the written message to his communications officer to be encoded using the personal codes provided by the Admiral.

"Our small lake is just ahead, Captain," mentioned the XO.

"Bring her up slowly to periscope depth."

"Bringing her up to periscope depth," repeated the XO, just as a seaman eased back on the controls of the diving ship. The Sea Devil changed its angle from horizontal to a gradual incline and continued floating towards the surface.

The communications antenna broke the surface of the lead as the sub leveled out just below.

"Keep her steady," ordered Hayes.

The communications officer transmitted the scrambled message to Washington for the personal attention of Admiral Heiserman, Chief of Naval Operations. It read:

"Your missile operator Marsh inadvertently shot down a Canadian Forces Aurora near our assigned geographical location. The crew of eleven on board the plane survived, and they are now isolated in the Sea Devil. The identity of our ship is still secret. Advise soonest the status of the object of mission and the disposition of aircrew."

The message was beamed by the satellite to its recipient's address and automatically redirected to Heiserman's current location in Frobisher Bay.

"Maintain stability at sixty feet," Hayes ordered, as the sub hovered just below the surface of the lead. He kept it out of view from prying eyes of anyone who would be watching for his ship. The sub's radar had not detected any aircraft in the vicinity when its bridge array of antenna and radar broke the surface during the upward glide, or during the short period of time while it gradually settled to its current position. For the moment they were safe, but for how long no one knew.

The reply from Heiserman came within moments. Hayes took the message to his cabin, where he decoded it.

"I expected to hear from you sooner. The mission object is now on the ice near the Magnetic North Pole. It has been there for several hours. Proceed soonest to retrieve all the listed items AT ALL COSTS as per instructions in part 3 of orders. You are to destroy MIR after all the items are obtained!

"Continue to maintain secrecy from the Aurora aircrew. As for their disposition, the aircrew are to be discharged to a blackened out B7 hovercraft off Frobisher Bay in forty-eight hours. Call me at 902 271-9816 when you enter the area, for further instructions. Destroy these orders after reading." Heiserman's name didn't appear on the message.

Hayes opened the safe that was concealed in his cabin behind the small fridge that contained his refreshments. The third set of orders that were in a larger manila envelope contained detailed drawings of the items that were to be retrieved from the MIR Space Station. The list of the drawings included the computer's hard and floppy drives, computer memory, random access memory chips, tape recorders and tapes, video cameras and videos, and other items all related to the storage of data. Even the black box was listed. The drawings indicated exactly where the items were located in the MIR core. Commander Hayes stuffed the papers back into the envelope and tucked the envelope into his jacket, then returned to the bridge to speak to Murphy in private.

"You and your men will have to go back out onto the ice. According to the message from Admiral Heiserman, the MIR Space Station is now on the pack ice near the Magnetic Pole. I have a list of things that you will have to fetch from the wreckage. Heiserman's latest directive is that he wants us to destroy MIR after we've plundered it. That is my word, not Heiserman's. That is what he wants after we've gathered the equipment and treasures of MIR."

"But why?" A confused look appeared on the face of the Executive Officer. He received no clarification, just a questionable shrug of shoulders.

"You can use the same snowmobiles and the skis that you used for the last trip out. But before you go, let me see if we can get the ship closer to the actual landing site so you can avoid some of the pressure ridges and rubble ice that you ran into on your last foray. We may have to crash through ice again if there is no lead nearby."

The Magnetic North Pole was approximately ten kilometers from the present location of the submarine. Unfortunately, between it and the MIR crash site was the ice island plateau that contained the ruins of the Canadian plane. Hayes knew that he would have to submerge, make his way around the island, and surface again on the other side. He was hopeful that MIR landed in the near vicinity of the Pole and wasn't spread around it for miles. It was going to be tricky to surface near the spacecraft, not only due to the thickness of the pack ice. The compasses would be practically useless. He ordered the navigator to plot their track around the ice island to the Magnetic Pole.

The Magnetic Pole's new average position was on the southwestern coast of Ellef Ringnes Island. Officially it was currently located at 78.3 degrees N, 104 degrees W, which placed it 1,300 kilometers south of the North Geographic Pole. Sea Devil would have to find a polynya, a lead, or thin ice around 78 degrees' latitude and 104 degrees' longitude. Ice this thin was not easy to find being smack in the middle of the permanent ice pack.

The XO and navigator piloted the sub around the ice plateau while completely under the ice. There were some ice protrusions measuring twenty feet or more below the surface, but they were avoided by the use of the inverted fathometers and the diver's lights working in conjunction with the TV camera in the periscope. The inertial navigator system and additional compasses enabled them to bring the ship within meters of the Magnetic North Pole.

While the magnetic compass spun like a top, the gyrocompass and the inertial navigation set pointed the way. The thickness of the ice was five feet according to the trace of the ice detector. This ice was thicker than the ice that the sub last punched through, but it was still within the limits of her capabilities. For Commander Hayes, this was one time that he hoped that the shipyard manager was absolutely correct in his calculations. He didn't want to spend eternity under the Magnetic North Pole due to some fowl up in mathematics. The sail of the Sea Devil would once again be the battering ram that would get him to the surface. It contained hydraulically hoisted masts, antennas, periscopes, TV cameras, ventilation pipes, and other arrays that were critical to the safe operation of the ship under the ice. If the three and a half thousand-ton submarine hit the underside of extra-thick ice, these devices could splinter and endanger the ship.

The Commander intended to follow the same procedure that he previously used to bring the Sea Devil successfully through the ice. The first step involved bringing the ship lower in the waters under the thinnest part of the ice. The sub was just ten meters from the floor of the Arctic Ocean when he gave the order to bring it straight up at a steady pace.

The ballast tanks emptied, and the ship started to rise like an elevator; slowly at first, then faster at a steady pace. The extra depth and increased rate of ascension caused the sail to hit the pack ice with a driving punch. The submarine shook from the shock, and the crew members staggered and fell against walls and pipes. The hull followed the sail as it emerged through the ice and into the frigid Arctic night. They were through the ice cap.

"Stop the blowing of ballast and maintain trim," said Hayes to Murphy. The Commander reached for the periscope, slid it upwards from its base, and did a 360-degree check of the surface of the ice. He then did another complete rotation with the periscope tilted to check the sky for planes.

"We're clear. Nothing on the ice and nothing in the sky, as far as I can tell, but there's a lot of snow blowing around so it's hard to be sure. Get the hatch open, and we'll do a visual check from the bridge."

A member of the crew pulled hard on the hatch until it opened; he was rewarded with a pile of ice and snow that slid down the hatch onto his head. He pushed the heavy metal hatch until it was fully opened against its stop. The sailor climbed the ladder out onto the platform, but the second ladder to the bridge was blocked by some ice chunks. He offered a hand to Hayes and the XO as they emerged, and together they shoved the ice blocks to one side and climbed the ladder to the bridge. Once there, they used their night glasses to do a visual check of their surroundings.

Satisfied that they were alone in the coldness of the Arctic and just a couple hundred meters from the Magnetic Pole, they relaxed and looked along the hull to see if the ship would be able to submerge again. Their previous experience with the ice that crushed against the hull taught them a valuable lesson not to get in a similar position. Most of the loose chunks of ice had sunk below the water after the ship came to a standstill; the ship was completely free. There was about a foot of free ice water around the sides of the submarine, and it was resting against the side of an ice floe.

Hayes dismounted the ladder to the platform, slid down the side of Sea Devil, and stepped out onto the pack ice. He walked a hundred yards away from his vessel then turned to look at the long black hull. It sat like a log on a farmer's snowy field. He felt a sense of satisfaction knowing that he commanded the only sub that ever surfaced at the Magnetic North Pole. But he had no time for celebration. The MIR Space Station had to be found, and the items retrieved before the Canadians or Russians got them first. This was one race that he expected to win.

Hayes returned to the bridge and instructed Murphy to prepare his group for their over-ice trip to MIR. In the meantime, he sat with the radar operator to see if the space station could be picked up by radar.

The operator was picking up faint blips not more than five miles away. It had to be MIR. There was nothing else out there but ice and snow. The direction of the blip was determined, and Hayes handed the information, along with the detailed drawings of the MIR components, to Murphy when he reported that he was ready to depart.

"Have you got everything," asked Hayes, "lights, tools, flares, plastic explosives, radio transmitters, and automatic weapons?"

"I think so. I hope we won't have a problem finding our way back here. The location is driving our compasses crazy."

"Let me know when you are about to leave the site, and I will fire off a flare to give you a general direction back to the sub. I intend to stay on the surface, if possible. If we have to submerge for some reason, we'll leave you food, clothing, and tents to provide you with some protection until we return. If we're not back in twelve hours, you better start to head for land, and we'll try to find you. I know there's a weather station at Eureka, but it's about a hundred miles from here. Let's hope that it doesn't come to that."

The XO pulled the hood up over his head and signaled his group to get ready to leave.

"Well, we are off now. Hopefully, we can retrieve everything and be back here in four to five hours."

"Keep me posted on your progress by radio."

"Aye, skipper."

Hayes watched the convoy of snowmobiles snake away from the Sea Devil. They proceeded slowly since the lights on the ski-doos didn't cut very deep into the drifting snow. A sudden gust of raw wind accompanied by blinding snow caused the convoy to be lost, and it couldn't be seen even with night glasses. He returned to his cabin to await their safe return.

Hayes laid on his bunk and was soon in deep thought. He was beginning to question why Heiserman was going through such an elaborate hoax. He found it surprising that none of the orders had given a reason for the mission, nor had the message from Heiserman. At first glance, he thought that the secrecy was necessary because he and his crew were in Canadian waters without permission. He thought that the U.S. Navy was helping the Russians to retrieve a space station that was predicted to fall in this location. Maybe the Russians thought it was easier for a U.S. sub to get into Canadian waters to retrieve MIR than a Russian sub. But now that he had seen the list of items to be taken from MIR, and that it was to be destroyed after it was stripped, to conceal evidence of tampering, he was concerned. Hayes was beginning to think that perhaps they were on a spy mission. Were he and his crew industrial spies stealing Russian secrets? Was the mission for the good of the USA? Would it help their space program?

He didn't have answers to any of these questions, and he didn't like the idea of risking the lives of his crew, and possibly even a world war, just to obtain data that the U.S. government could certainly afford to buy.

Hayes strongly believed in following orders, but he was not absolutely dedicated to authority; he needed to be convinced that the mission was for the good of his country. So far, he wasn't convinced that this whole trip was even necessary. He was also suspicious of Admiral Heiserman. Not once had he ever been told by a superior that he was to destroy orders after reading them.

Why did he have to destroy these orders? Was there some reason that Heiserman didn't want to be tied to this operation? More puzzling was the phrase that Heiserman used in his last message. He wanted the items retrieved at all costs. Did that mean that Canadians and Russians would be killed, if necessary? Did Heiserman have the power to execute members of foreign military in a peacetime world?

Hayes wished that there was some way that he could double-check the legitimacy of the orders before he went any further. He may have drifted off to sleep, but suddenly, it was crystal clear what he had to do. Captain Hayes recalled that it was Rear Admiral Gunston, the Director of Submarine Warfare, that had handed him his orders at the Pentagon. He also remembered how put out the Admiral was about his lack of knowledge concerning the orders. Perhaps Hayes could use that annoyance to his advantage. He needed to send a properly worded message to Admiral Gunston, written in such a way as to obtain confirmation of his orders without giving the impression that he was being subordinate and questioning the validity of Heiserman's orders.

Every ounce of his intuition told him that he had to double-check the orders. There were times when it was prudent for military personnel to ask pertinent questions about orders. While it may be frowned upon, and could mean the end of a promising career, he couldn't in all consciousness risk the lives of his crew, or take the lives of Russians or Canadians in a peacetime environment.

"The hell with it," Hayes said aloud to himself. He rose from his bunk, sat down at his desk, and drafted a message to be sent to the Pentagon.

"To the Pentagon Defense Department: for the personal attention of Rear Admiral Gunston, Director of Submarine Warfare Division. Classification: Top Secret. From: Captain Hayes of the U.S.S. Sea Devil.

"Please confirm that Admiral Heiserman, Chief of Naval Operations, has the authority to order this submarine's crew to ransack the remnants of the MIR Space Station, to retrieve its data components AT

ALL COSTS (Admiral's emphasis), and to sink and destroy the remainder of the Russian spacecraft. Russian and Canadian Forces are expected to arrive on-site before our operation is complete. Warfare is anticipated."

Hayes needed to know the level of Heiserman's authority and wanted to emphasize that point, so he decided to add another paragraph to his message.

"A marine provided to this ship by Admiral Heiserman, Battery Commander Marsh, has a rocket launcher. He already shot down a Canadian Forces plane. Admiral Heiserman has ordered that the 11 survivors be held incommunicado on the Sea Devil until they can be deposited aboard a hovercraft near Frobisher Bay in three days. Please confirm ASAP Admiral Heiserman's authority to risk the lives of my crew and to hold these survivors as captives. Lieutenant Commander Hayes."

He left his room and walked to the Communications Officer's console.

"Send this message off immediately," he ordered.

The Communications Officer read the message and whistled.

"Boy, this will shake them up at the Pentagon, and put Sea Devil on the map." He started the transmission, and within minutes it was bounced by satellite to the Pentagon.

The Duty Officer at the Operations Centre at the Pentagon read the transmission from Captain Hayes as it came pouring out of the teletype machine. Before it stopped printing, he was dialing Rear Admiral Gunston's home phone number.

In the interim, Lt. Cmdr. Murphy and his convoy of ski-doos made their way slowly towards the spot that the radar had indicated as the location of MIR. They weaved and bobbed to avoid snowdrifts and chunks of ice. Murphy estimated that they had gone about four and a half miles when they came upon a debris field containing shiny metal parts of the spacecraft. Murphy ordered the men in the party to shine their lights around the debris and look for items belonging to the data storage system. The first stock of parts was found in an enormous crater in the middle of a field of deep snow on the ice surface. The snowdrift was about twelve feet deep and the size of half of a football field.

To Murphy, it looked like MIR had impacted in the field of snow. The snow had cushioned its fall and reduced the damage. Still, there were parts of the shielding, retro rockets, solar panels, and other pieces strewn about. The main core of MIR had bounced after its first impact and struck again some seventy-five feet away from the crater. There were more parts of the space station there. It had continued to roll another fifty feet before coming to a standstill against a huge pressure ridge approximately fifteen feet high.

The men were in awe as they approached the remains of the legendary station. For thirteen years, this craft had circled the earth thousands of times and was the home for nearly a hundred astronauts. Now, here it was, in the middle of the Arctic ice pack and severely damaged. It was hard to believe that this badly dented and torn craft was once the pride and joy of space voyagers. They approached with reverence, but they had a job to do.

"Find a hatchway and open this thing up like a tin can. Use the crowbars or explosives as a can opener if you have to," Murphy said to the Reactor Control Officer.

There were some men prying while others tugged; it didn't take long for the hatch to open, revealing the mass of instruments, gauges, wires, and hoses that once were the controls for thousands of experiments and observations that advanced man's journey into space. The XO and the RCO each took several pages of Part 3 of the orders and a team of men, and they set about removing the equipment detailed on the pages. The parts were removed one by one and brought to the snowmobiles to be covered in canvas for transportation back to the sub. At the rate of removal, Murphy estimated that all items on his checklist would be stored within two hours, and an hour after that they could be loaded aboard the submarine.

It was time to update Hayes on what they have achieved so far. He had the Communication Technician establish radio contact with the sub.

"Captain, I hope that you have some warm coffee ready for us very soon. We got most of the items, and they are in excellent condition with very little damage. The interior of the craft had very little damage compared to the exterior. We know where the remaining equipment is located, and it's just a matter of time until it's disassembled and on the snowmobiles. Have the chief cook prepare some hot meals to be ready in three hours. Murphy."

"Thanks for the update. We copy that you will be back in three hours. Out."

At the MIR site, the contact was cut and the radio packed back aboard one of the snowmobiles. It was time to remove the last of the data and information stored in MIR's computer memory banks.

Meanwhile, on board the Sea Devil, Commander Hayes thought he would have gotten some sort of a reply from Washington in regards to his message. He would have liked to tell Murphy to call off the mission, leave all the equipment where it was, and bring back the crew so they could submerge and proceed to the drop-off point for the Canadian aircrew at Frobisher Bay. But he knew that things grinded slowly at the Pentagon, and most likely his message would sit in someone's 'IN' basket until regular work hours, which was still six hours away. His concentration was broken by another incoming radio transmission, but it wasn't from the XO. It came from Frobisher Bay.

"Commander Hayes, this is Admiral Heiserman. What is the status of your orders in regard to the MIR equipment that is needed for the International Space Program? The Russians want to know if we got the equipment that they are donating to the program."

Hayes was stunned. Did the Russians really authorize the U.S. Navy to fetch the equipment? Did he screw up his career by questioning the Admiral's orders? He visualized his career and life going down the drain.

"Sir, Lt. Cmdr. Murphy, the Executive Officer, has just reported that the majority of the equipment is on the snowmobiles, and the remainder will be ready for transport in two hours. I expect him back on the ship in three hours."

"Excellent! There has been a slight change of plans. I will use a Navy V-22A Osprey, a vertical take-off and landing aircraft, to personally pick up all items. Since it cruises at around 272 knots, I should be in your area in three hours. Appoint someone to find and clear a site for the Osprey to land near the sub. With the possibility that you may have to submerge before I get there, I will have my pilot contact your XO to get the exact coordinates of the pickup point. Give me the frequency to contact your XO. Do you understand?"

"Yes, Sir. If I may, would it be possible for you to pick up the Canadian aircrew at the same time? I know that the Osprey is capable of carrying troops, equipment, and supplies. There would be plenty of room for the eleven survivors."

Admiral Heiserman hesitated for a few moments.

"That will not be possible on this trip. We'll stick with the original plan to deliver them to a hovercraft. But I will pick up the operator of the SAM launcher. Since I provided this man, Marsh, I will take care of his punishment. Out."

Heiserman was given the frequency of the XO's transmitter and ended the transmission. Hayes was still confused. He had now been given a partial explanation of why his crew and his ship were retrieving the equipment from the Russian space station, but the answer caused more questions in his mind. Why all the secrecy? Why hurry? Why obtain the data equipment AT ALL COSTS? Why did one of Heiserman's men shoot down a Canadian military plane? This mission was a giant puzzle to him. Did he do the right thing by questioning the Admiral's orders, or did he just kiss his career goodbye?

Hayes was more confused than ever. He recalled an old English saying, 'In for a penny, in for a pound.' He pressed the issue with Washington by drafting a new message to Rear Admiral Gunston, cross-referring his previous one.

"Request reply ASAP as the situation has changed. Admiral Heiserman has advised that he will personally pick up MIR's data equipment at sub's location in three hours. Captain of Sea Devil."

He transmitted the message and realized that the Sea Devil could be the last ship that he would ever command. He loved his ship, and he would do anything for his crew. If he had to give it up, he would be heartbroken.

# 24  THE GENERAL SPY

28 December 1300 hrs local, Thule Air Base, Greenland

Dave Shanahan watched the fax as it emerged from its resting place in the holding tray. It was a National Defense Headquarters press release issued to all major newsgroups and all Canadian Forces bases and headquarters. There were additions to the list of regular recipients of similar news releases. This one was also sent as information to the Thule Air Base, to the attention of Canadian Search Center, Brig. Gen. Shanahan, and to the Frobisher Bay Daily News. It was datelined Ottawa.

"The Minister of National Defense announced that effective today, Brigadier General Dave Shanahan has been promoted to the rank of Major General. He is currently Commander of Maritime Air Group and is now also the interim Commander of Maritime Command." The short statement was followed by a photo and a summary of his military career.

Shanahan was pleasantly surprised, but dismayed by the news since it meant that Vice Admiral Lowery was no longer head of Maritime Command. His moment of reflection was broken by a phone call from the Chief of the Defense Staff.

"Dave, you have probably seen the news release by now. Congratulations on your promotion!"

"Thank you, Sir. I'm sorry to hear that Vice Admiral Lowery is no longer Commander of Maritime Command."

"He brought it upon himself, Dave. Both the Minister and the PM wanted him to turn over the military assets that he obtained, and we wanted him to return to Halifax, but he refused. We had no choice but to remove his rank and to remove him from his position. The Prime Minister doesn't want any private or provincial armies in Canada, so we will have to take them over by force if necessary. That's where you come in. We don't want you to return to Halifax right away. We want you to go to Frobisher Bay, bring these assets on to our inventory, and distribute them as you see fit. That may not seem as simple as it sounds since Lowery is acting like he is the Governor of Nunavut and has vowed to arrest and maybe kill you on sight.

"You have been given authority to detain him and charge him with failure to obey a senior government official's order. You are also authorized to use whatever force necessary to bring him to a court-martial. You will have to play it cool until you get the lay of the land, see how much support he has, and see what forces you can muster on your side. We will, of course, support you one hundred percent, as will the RCMP. You need to be extremely careful while in Frobisher."

"Can I bring in some military police from Maritime command?"

"You can try. Speak with your people in Halifax, but you know that they are stretched pretty thin with all the peacekeeping duties that we have. I suggest that you go to Frobisher to see if it is necessary. Perhaps some or all of Lowery's military troops have no loyalty to him and will fall into your command, but somehow, I doubt it."

"OK, Sir. I'll spy on Lowery to see what he and his cohorts are up to and bring him back any way that I can?"

"Exactly, we need to know who he contacts and what the strength of his supporters is."

"Alright. Did you have any success finding our aircrew through the Russians or the Americans?"

"The PM spoke with the Russian president, and he swears that his government did not officially authorize the shooting down of our plane or the capture of our aircrew. The President couldn't say for certain if insubordinate troops were responsible, but he is fairly certain that it was not any of the Russians. On the other hand, he thought that we might be responsible for the sabotage of MIR." The CDS, General Le Beau, waited while Shanahan expressed surprise at the fact that MIR had been sabotaged and that the Russian President would even think that the Canadian government would be part of such a scheme.

"That's right! MIR didn't come down under Russian orders, and it just didn't fall out of the sky. Someone brought it down deliberately in our Northern Arctic. Of course, our PM assured him that we didn't have anything to do with it. In fact, the PM offered to help the Russians find and retrieve MIR.

"We are to cooperate fully with the Russians that are on route to the impact site. The Russian president has offered to help us find our aircrew in any way that he can. Would you contact our Search Master,

Major Phillips, and tell him to cooperate with the Russians? They, in turn, will assist him in finding our aircrew."

"Certainly. But what about the Americans?"

"The PM hasn't yet spoken to the U.S. president, but he was expecting a call from him as soon as the Russian helicopters crossed into Canadian territory. I'll let you know as soon as we hear from the U.S."

"Just how cooperative do I have to be with the Russians?"

"The PM told President Gazenko that he wants his commando troops to work with Major Phillips. Prime Minister Le Chance limited their retrieval actions to one week. He forewarned the president that Lowery has some Apache helicopters, and that they may be used against his forces. The Canadian government will not take any retribution measures against the Russians if they have to take defensive action to protect their interests. Does that answer your question?"

"Yes, I think so."

"OK, Dave. Again, congratulations, and be careful when you go to Frobisher, and keep me informed."

Shanahan now had some instructions and advice that he could pass on to Major Phillips that might help him find the missing aircrew. Sitting down at his laptop computer, he dispatched an email for Phillips.

"Four Russian helicopters are now on route over the Pole to retrieve MIR. The Canadian government has authorized us to cooperate fully with their efforts to recover MIR. In return, they will assist with the recovery of our aircrew in any way possible. They insist that the Russian government had no role in the downing of our plane and with the capture of our crew. We, in turn, assured President Gazenko that we played no part in the sabotage of MIR.

"Lowery's assets, including Apache helicopters, are not authorized to interfere with MIR's retrieval, and the Russian government is authorized to take whatever actions necessary to prevent such interference by Lowery's forces. Lowery has been relieved of his position and his rank. I will be moving to Frobisher Bay as soon as Captain Leech returns to command this RCC. My computer address will be forwarded to you ASAP. Major General Shanahan." He hit the send button, and the encrypted email went flashing through the ether.

\* \* \*

Six hundred kilometers away, Shawn Phillips sat drinking coffee with his rescue crew. They were making final preparations to leave their warm building and venture out to see if they could get the old hovercraft started. One of the techs saw the mail notification flash on the laptop computer screen.

"Major, your computer."

Shawn read the message, then he read it again, and a smile came on his face when he noticed Shanahan's rank. He pressed the button on the mouse and activated the save command then turned off the machine. Reaching for his parka and his mitts, he turned to face his men.

"We better get started since we'll have some company soon. There are four Russian helicopters on their way, and we have been ordered to help them retrieve MIR. We may need the old hovercraft, if we can get it started, to help the Russians and look for our crew. Apparently, the Russian president said they don't have our crew and had nothing to do with bringing down the Aurora. That leaves me wondering just who was manning that sub. The Russians have offered to help us find our men, but I don't see how the Russians can be of much help if they don't already have our people. Incidentally, we and the Russians were told by Ottawa not to let the ex-Vice Admiral Lowery's forces interfere with the retrieval of whatever is left of the space station."

Five of the men finished drinking their coffees. They placed their cups in the sink, threw on their parkas and gloves and left the building. The last tech stayed behind to man the radio transmitter.

Together, Major Phillips, W.O. Mackenzie and the techs made their way to the shack containing the APU. Mackenzie worked his magic to get the APU started by pouring some of the gasoline that was in the shack into the carburetor. A touch of the start button and a pull of the throttle control rope made the APU spring to life, much like starting a lawnmower after a long cold winter. Now that they knew it worked, the APU was switched off. Two of the men pulled the APU out of the building while the others carried tins of fuel. The group trekked warily towards the cliff edge of the ice plateau towing the APU behind them.

They used their high beam lights to see the path they had taken previously. Upon reaching the cliff edge, two of them descended the face of the snow-covered ice cliff. They worked as a team as those on top of the plateau lowered the APU and the fuel down the twenty-foot embankment to the two techs at the bottom who secured the machine and the fuel. They all carefully stepped out onto the pack ice towards the hovercraft.

Shawn directed the techs to remove the tarp and clean away the snow from the skirt, the intakes, the deck, and the windows.

Mackenzie climbed up onto the balcony, opened the hatch door, and entered into the craft. Looking around the interior, he was able to locate the box containing the battery, and they connected the auxiliary power unit to the terminals. The hatch door was opened, and one of the techs was asked to start it up. Soon after the APU was running, a charge started to show on the battery of the hovercraft. At the same time, Shawn sent the techs to a small door on the side of the cabin, behind which was the gas tank cover. They began to pour the tin containers of gasoline into the spout of the gas tank.

W.O. Mackenzie left the cockpit, walked the exterior deck bypassing the passenger module, and headed towards the propeller at the rear of the craft, where he turned the propeller to free the transmission. Returning to the battery box, he saw that the needle on the gauge indicated it was now sufficiently charged. The APU cables were disconnected and reattached to the internal master heater. In moments, heat started to pour into the cabin, and the four other members of the group entered the craft to thaw out.

Shawn sat in the pilot's seat and fired up the machine. At first, the engine only turned over and whined but did not catch. Rob reached down between the seats and pulled the choke to give the motor a bit more fuel. Shawn tried again to start it; it whined for a few tense seconds before coming to life. He switched on the windscreen deicers, radar, and internal heaters, then sat there for fifteen minutes while the craft warmed up. While waiting for the ship to reach its operating temperature, Shawn tried the radio and contacted the other tech sitting in the Mess Hall. The tech told Shawn that the Aurora #740 was now overhead and had picked up three sets of radar targets.

The sub was back on the surface of the polar waters and another set of targets indicated several small crafts surrounding a large blip which was probably MIR. The third target was the Russian helicopters which had just shown up on Aurora's radar screen. Shawn manually adjusted the directional radar finder and tried to pick up MIR on the hovercraft's radar without success. He switched on the searchlights and sent a tech to disconnect the external power. Once this was done, the APU was manhandled aboard the machine. The techs then found seats and strapped on their seat belts.

Shawn applied full power to achieve lift-off. There were crackling sounds as the skirt filled with air and broke loose from its contact with the ice. The craft hovered there with approximately six inches from the dress's edge to the surface. He manipulated the levers that caused the craft to move forward. At first, the craft moved all over as Shawn learned how to control its movement. Becoming familiar with the controls, he attempted to avoid the pressure ridges just in case the skirt was damaged. He adjusted the heading and speed, and the craft rushed forward, crossing the smaller ridges without any damage to the skirt. He took the craft around the ice island, looking for a smooth incline to the top of the plateau; it was reasonable that such an angle existed since the survey crew could not lug the APU and fuel to the cliff each time they made a journey.

Halfway around the island, he found the incline. It was just like a road with four-foot embankments of snow on both sides. He gunned the craft's engine, and the ancient piece of machinery chugged slowly up the inclined canyon from the embankment until the craft was at the top; it was then just a matter of finding their way back to the Mess Hall.

A surprised tech wondered what was going on and ran out the door when he heard the hovercraft approaching. Shawn turned off the engine, and the air deflated from the skirt. The craft settled down at the front door of their accommodation. They were now ready to welcome the Russians or take a run at the submarine, whatever was necessary to retrieve their aircrew.

# 25   THE CHINESE CONNECTION
28 December 1400 hrs local, Greenland to Frobisher


Dave Shanahan thought about how to get to Frobisher Bay quickly, while avoiding Lowery's forces, as he flipped through the yellow pages of the Greenland phone book. After dialing a local travel agency in the City of Thule, the agency informed the him that it could not provide a direct booking by commercial airlines from Thule to Frobisher. However, the young lady on the other end of the line mentioned that she had relatives in Frobisher who visited her for the holidays, and they were about to return home.

The relatives had used a First Air charter flight, billed as a weekend shopping trip, to Greenland. Many of the Inuit and Southerners used the occasional charter to leave Frobisher Bay's small town with its population of 4,500, a couple of hotels, The Bay store, and a few bars. They left to visit relatives and shop in the bustling city of Nuuk, with its population of 12,000, its paved streets, big stores, and smart shops. The agent informed Shanahan that Nuuk was the former city of Godthab, the Capital of Greenland, some fifteen hundred kilometers south of Thule. If he wished, she could make a reservation for him on the return flight to Frobisher Bay leaving tomorrow morning, but the connecting flights would not get him from Thule to Nuuk on time for the flight.

Shanahan agreed to the reservation from Nuuk to Frobisher but told the young lady that he would find his way to Nuuk. He would use the Canadian Forces Hercules that had brought over the dismantled helicopter to drop him off at Nuuk since it was returning to its home base in Edmonton. Shanahan reasoned that using a charter flight out of Nuuk would allow him to enter Frobisher without being detected by Lowery's friends and cohorts, mostly if he wore civilian clothes instead of his Navy uniform. The civic clothes would enable him to blend in with the other Southerners on the return flight.

Shanahan called Base Ops at Thule Air Base and asked for the Canadian pilot of the C-130.

"This is Major General Shanahan of Maritime Air Group. You will have an extra passenger on your departure today. I need to be dropped off at the Nuuk, Greenland airport in time to catch a flight tomorrow to Frobisher Bay."

"No problem, General, we can drop you off in Frobisher if you wish."

"No, Nuuk is fine. I have other business there."

"OK, General. You know that the Herc is not very comfortable, but we'll make a place for you in the cockpit. We leave in three hours."

"Great. I'll meet you at Base Ops."

Shanahan packed his suitcase and called for a staff car to take him to Thule's Officer's Mess for lunch. Before leaving his suite at the on-base accommodation center, he quickly called the mini RCC to check on any further information from Major Phillips. The Duty Officer advised that Phillips had not contacted the RCC. Shanahan told the DO to mention to Capt. Leech that she would be in charge of the RCC since he had to make a sudden trip to Frobisher Bay. There was time for another call before the car arrived. The latter call was to the second in command at Maritime Command Headquarters in Halifax. They exchanged pleasantries, after which the 2nd in command congratulated Shanahan on his promotion and his new position as interim Commander.

"That is why I called you. I have to do something for the Chief of Defense Staff in Frobisher Bay in Nunavut, but you mustn't tell anyone that I am going there. I'll be back in a few days. In the meantime, remember Lowery is no longer an Admiral, and he has no authority to authorize anything without my approval. Got that?"

"Yes, Sir."

"One more thing, I may need 20 or more military policemen in the next few days. Will you check around the command to see if they are available on short notice? I'll call if I need them."

"No problem, Sir."

"Good! As soon as I return, I'll recommend to the Chief that he appoint you as Commander since the Navy needs a Navy Officer to run Maritime Command, not a pilot. See you soon."

After lunch, the staff car took him to Base Ops, where he boarded the C-130.

The flight to Nuuk was smooth and effortless. The pilot flew south down the coast of Greenland, passing the cities of Aasiaat and Maniitsoq. As they flew south, there was less darkness. Even from the air, Shanahan could see a few icebergs in Davis Straight near the Greenland coast, mainly due to the Gulf Stream which kept the Greenland coast warmer than the coast of Baffin Island.

The Gulf Stream brought all-season ports on the Greenland side, along with green meadows and willow trees. At the same time, the coast of Baffin Island would be ice-covered even though Frobisher Bay was on the same latitude as Nuuk, just south of the Arctic Circle. Still, the one thousand miles that separated them made the difference in weather like the difference between day and night. The forecast for Frobisher meant that the tuque and overcoat purchased in the Thule PX would come in handy.

The Hercules flew over the ice-free deep-water harbor of Nuuk and started its landing pattern for the tiny airport. In the evening light, Shanahan could see that the town had the sea on three sides of it, and there were jagged snow-capped mountain peaks just beyond the city. Stone houses were spread throughout the old town, established in 1728. Many buildings seemed to be foundation-less in the town, while the hillsides were dotted with square peaked-roof cottages. There were several four or five-story apartment blocks that were several hundred meters long and probably used to house most of the city's population. The Herc pilot lowered the wheels and made a smooth and seamless landing at the airport.

An airport taxi brought the General to the comfortable Hotel Gronland. In a blazing red uniform, a hotel clerk registered him for a one night stay then led him to his room. Moments later, the same clerk wheeled in a cart containing a tray filled with reindeer meat and multi-colored vegetables. Following the delicious meal, Shanahan went into the streets to do a little business shopping. It was noticeable that the Inuit of Greenland and the blond Danish people were well dressed in western style clothing rather than the more traditional clothing that he knew most of the Inuit of Frobisher Bay to wear. Most of the Nuuk people would be classed as a middle class there compared to a lower class in Frobisher. The streets and stores were nearly filled with residents going about their evening shopping.

He wandered up and down streets looking for an open shop that would sell him the merchandise he needed. A brisk walk through the city deposited him in front of a gun shop just ten minutes from the hotel. He purchased a handgun and ammo that he hoped he would not have to use while in Frobisher. There was a chance that he might need such a weapon to defend himself against Lowery's more aggressive followers.

The flight next morning was on a First Air Hawker Siddeley 748 twin prop aircraft. The craft seemed loaded to capacity as most of the 44 seats were full of happy Inuit loaded down with packages of gifts and necessities that they had procured in the Nuuk business district. He sat among a group of white businessmen who could only be considered as Southerners. Most were originally from Ottawa or Montreal, were temporally employed in Frobisher, and had set out for an opportunity to enjoy the nightlife of the Capital of this Danish Island. Most of them looked hungover. The aircraft bounced up and down as it climbed out of the Nuuk airport into the turbulent skies. The faces of the Southerners turned green as they started to regret the indulgences of the previous evening. For Shanahan, the flight passed quickly, since he slept most of the way over the Davis Strait.

He could feel the temperature change in the cabin as the craft left Greenland's warmth behind and passed over the Gulf stream, continuing its trek towards the colder shores of Frobisher Bay. It sped along at 250 miles per hour.

Four hours later, the 2800-meter runway of Frobisher was in sight. The newly promoted General was thankful that this part of the Arctic was not covered in complete darkness, as was the area where Phillips and his rescue techs were. The evening sun was sitting on the horizon, allowing him to get the lay of the land as the craft approached the Capital of Nunavut. The Hawker Siddeley 748 flared its flaps, stretched its landing gear, and prepared to land. The land around Frobisher was low hills with no trees, only brown clay and snow surrounding the town. As the plane flew over the bay towards the landing strip, long low buildings emerged from the semi-darkness. Individual homes of one and two stories dotted the countryside with stretches of snow-covered fields between them. Out of the light glare trying to push back the night appeared at least a half dozen four-story buildings. They gave a jagged appearance to the skyline. Hundreds of wooden light poles stood like sentinels about the city, carrying its electric lifeblood to its residents.

The aircraft approached the runway a little too fast for Shanahan's taste, but the pilot made some hasty adjustments and brought the craft around into the glide path.

The U.S. Air Force originally built the runway during World War Two. The airport was equipped with a few old wooden hangars at one end and a newer hangar at the other end, which was used for the daily air connection to Montreal and Ottawa.

The pilot bounced the Hawker Siddeley twice before it was under control and taxiing to the airport building.

Shanahan merged with a number of Southern people as they left the plane and entered the Customs and Immigration office. The recently purchased gun made a bulge in his sock, but he had already decided that he would not declare the pistol since he was not sure who was on the Lowery payroll. While it was a felony not to report a gun at Canada's borders, Shanahan hoped that his military passport would gain him a speedy entrance.

He didn't have anything to worry about. The customs and immigration officers and customs agents discussed among themselves troop movements that they had seen earlier in the day in this small city on Frobisher Bay. None of the passengers were stopped or asked any questions, which made the Inuit and other passengers happy since they didn't have to pay any duty on their recently acquired treasures, and their bottles of booze were not confiscated.

Through the terminal windows, Shanahan saw that the Ottawa flight had just landed, and the passengers were lined up awaiting cars to make the short drive into the city. A well-dressed Asian man walked out of the terminal and proceeded to an awaiting limo with diplomatic plates on it.

Dave didn't want to hang around this small airport too long since part of it was the location of Lowery's new enterprise. Outside the terminal was a Mountie, ticketing cars for parking in a no stopping zone. Shanahan showed his military ID, containing his rank, to the Mountie and asked him for a ride into town. The Mountie gestured that he was just about finished with his tickets and clearing parked cars. Thankful for his good luck, Shanahan hitched a ride with the officer into town. The RCMP officer dropped him off at the Navigator Inn, used by Nordair and other air crew whenever they stayed overnight before returning to Montreal.

Shanahan cautiously approached the hotel desk and asked for a room facing the main street. He started to fill in the registration card using the name Mitchell. Then he saw, near the counter, a navy uniform approach with an outstretched hand. The uniform was covered with gold braid, which made Shanahan's nerves bristle. Fortunately, the uniform passed him and offered a hand to another man in a business suit. Dave could hear the Navy suit speak.

"Ambassador Lin, I'm rear Admiral Heiserman, from the U.S. Navy. Welcome to Frobisher Bay, and thank you for coming. Please join me for a drink in my suite."

The Asian man followed Heiserman to the elevator. It was at that point that Shanahan recalled meeting the same Chinese Ambassador to Canada at last year's New Year's Levee at the Air Force Officers Mess in Ottawa. What was he doing here in Frobisher Bay with the U.S. Navy Chief of Naval Operations? That was a question that made Shanahan wonder.

Once registered, he declined the bell hop's invitation to carry his bags; instead, he used the stairs to get to his third-floor room. Laying his suitcases on the bed of the room that looked out onto the main street of Frobisher, he used the window to establish his surroundings, looking for possible escape routes if an emergency exit was necessary. After unpacking his suitcase and hiding his pistol behind the tank of the toilet, he called a local rental car company to have them deliver him a run-of-the-mill vehicle.

Shanahan turned on the TV and sat on the edge of the bed. It must have been a boring program since he suddenly awoke from a light sleep to the ringing phone. It was the rental car company, and they were at the front desk. The driver was instructed to drive the car to the garage where he would be met. Shanahan took the elevator to the basement and walked to the garage entrance and signed for and accepted the car.

He drove it to a secluded parking spot in the garage and was about to exit the car when he heard the squealing of tires as another vehicle entered the garage. The suddenness of this black car approaching at high speed made him crouch down in the seat. Shanahan peeked through the window, watching as the black car skidded to a halt. Lowery emerged from the vehicle and entered the hotel elevator with two men. He was easy to recognize, even in the darkened garage, wearing his Navy uniform displaying three stars on the shoulder.

The doors had barely closed on his nemesis when Shanahan's heart slowly stopped racing and returned to an average pace.

*They found me already*, thought Shanahan. Racing for the stairs, he flew up the steps two at a time and trotted down the hall to his room. He ran for the bathroom to retrieve his pistol and crouched down beside the bed. He waited. There was no clamping of boots on the stairs and no pounding on his door. After ten minutes, he opened the door a crack, but could hear nothing. He tiptoed down the hall to the stairs;

there was no one in either area. It was now obvious that Lowery was just visiting someone in the hotel, perhaps Heiserman.

Thirty minutes later, from the window in his room, Shanahan watched the vehicle return. Lowery and his guards left the hotel and entered the car. Shanahan couldn't help but notice that Lowery's suit was now decorated with four stars, and the word, 'Canada', was missing from the epaulets.

*Would I have used the gun?* Shanahan's mind questioned. *Probably,* he thought, *I have a job to do for the Chief and the Prime Minister. I can't leave a half-baked ex-military man, who thinks he's a four-star Admiral, to interfere with that mission.*

Twenty minutes later, another staff car pulled up to the curb, and Heiserman entered into it wearing a pilot's flying suit. This vehicle also headed in the direction of the airport.

# 26   SURPLUS ASSETS

27 December 2300, hrs local, Washington, DC.

Rear Admiral Gunston was not accustomed to duty officers suggesting that he get out of bed and down to the Operations Command as quickly as possible. When he asked if it could wait until tomorrow, the DO said that they could be at war by that time. He quickly dressed, kissed his wife goodbye, jumped into his car, and drove himself to the Pentagon. This had better be a real emergency, thought the Admiral, or he'd have that duty officer's balls for bookends. Upon arrival, he entered the Operations Centre and marched over to the officer that called him.

"Well? What in hell's name is so important that you had to drag me out of bed?"

The officer held out Hayes' message, which Gunston tore out of his hand. He scanned it then read it again more slowly. His first thought was to court-martial this Commander Hayes to doubt his boss's orders, a four-star Admiral. But then he reread it, especially the part about one of his subs shooting a Canadian military plane out of the sky and capturing its crew. Then there was the part that indicated that a battle could occur at any moment with Russian Forces.

*My God!* thought Gunston. *What in the hell is going on?* The President would go crazy if he heard that one of his senior naval officers had antagonized his closest neighbor's forces. Not only that, but the U.S. Admiral was picking a fight with a nation that had nuclear capability by stealing its assets. The duty officer was right. This was a critical situation, and it had to be sorted out immediately. Perhaps the President had been involved in the Chief of Naval Operations' plans, but what if he wasn't? It was better to be safe than sorry. The only option available was to check out Admiral Heiserman's orders to see if the President was in the loop. This could have severe consequences for the safety of the nation as well as for the President's re-election bid.

After nearly thirty-two years of service, Rear Admiral Gunston was a bit reluctant to go over the head of his ultimate boss, the Chief of Naval Operations, Admiral Heiserman. But the possible consequences of something going exceedingly wrong with the mission were too horrible to consider. It drove him to question his supreme boss' orders.

The Chief, Admiral Heiserman, whose charges were being questioned, couldn't be approached even if he was the principal naval advisor to the President and the Secretary of the Navy. But the Chief had several ranking officers that were directly subordinate to him; there was the Vice Chief of Naval Operations and the Deputy Chief of Naval Operations. Usually, Gunston would hand the problem to his immediate boss, the Deputy Chief of Resources, Warfare Requirements and Assessments. Unfortunately, he was away on NATO business, and that made Gunston the Acting Deputy Chief. Since his immediate boss was out, he could broach the subject with the next person up the chain, who was the Vice Chief of Naval Operations. As Acting Deputy Chief, it was within his rights and responsibilities to talk directly to the Vice Chief. Still, he wasn't sure if it was politically correct to ask the Vice Chief of Naval Operations to investigate the Chief of Naval Operations. He would soon find out.

Rear Admiral Gunston used an emergency phone to call the Vice Chief, Admiral Johnson.

The gist of the Sea Devil message was delivered via phone to the Vice Chief. Admiral Gunston recalled that it was he who gave the sealed orders from Heiserman to Commander Hayes.

"They were for the 'Eyes Only of the Captain of the Sea Devil'. It was disappointing that I was not privileged to know the mission of one of my subs, but I never pressed the matter with Admiral Heiserman." Gunston wished that he had spoken out and demanded to be informed of the secret operation.

Admiral Johnson was not aware of any mission that was authorized in the Canadian Arctic pertaining to the Russian Space Station. He was briefed daily on all ongoing tasks, but he had to admit that this one was a new one for him. Both naval officers agreed that it was a grave matter, and that it required the Secretary of the Navy's attention. They both further agreed that the situation was near critical and could only be resolved at the political level if the President immediately contacted the leaders of Canada and Russia, assuming that he was not involved in the first place.

The Secretary of the Navy was reached by phone and reluctantly agreed that they come to his home. The Vice Chief called for his staff car, and they were inside the Secretary of the Navy's home within the hour. He offered them a brandy and took one himself even though it was now past midnight.

"Now that you got me out of bed, what is this all about?"

Gunston handed him the message from Captain Hayes. The Secretary was well known for the quickness of his intellectual prowess; once he read the message, he grasped the implications of it immediately and turned to the Vice Chief of Naval Operations.

"I didn't authorize such a mission. Did you know about it?'

"No, Sir, Secretary. I thought perhaps you or the President worked directly with Admiral Heiserman on this matter."

"Well, it certainly wasn't me, and I doubt if the President would be dumb enough to get involved in taking equipment from the Russians. And then endanger the lives of the servicemen of our good friends to the north. We are also concerned about our servicemen on that sub. I'll ask the President. He may have mistakenly taken the advice of the CIA.

"You two gentlemen sit here in the den and help yourselves to another brandy while I get the President on a secure line." He left the den for another part of his house. Fifteen minutes later, he reappeared, filled with anger and frustration.

"The President knew nothing about this operation, and he wants this, I quote, 'ridiculous nightmare' stopped immediately. You are to contact the skipper of the Sea Devil immediately, and his crew is to cease removing items from MIR. He is also to turn the Canadian aircrew over to the first and closest Canadian establishment to treat their injuries. The President also said that as it is daybreak, they will contact Canada's and Russia's leaders to issue a major apology and promise massive retribution costs. And he and I want Admiral Heiserman brought to us by the fastest means possible. That young commander of the Sea Devil should be commended for following his instincts and not just blindly obeying authority.

"The President took the opportunity to ream me out about another thing that has been bothering him for a few days. He wants to know where Admiral Lowery of the Canadian Forces got the helicopters, the ships, and the missiles, etc., that he recently donated to Nunavut, Canada's newest province. The President recalled that this Lowery fellow said that the Apache helicopters had been used in Panama and the Gulf War. I must admit that I missed that point. Since only our military had Apaches in the Gulf War and Panama, it would seem that they must be our helicopters. How did that happen? How in the hell did our military assets end up in the tundra of the Canadian Arctic? The President wants that information, and he wants it yesterday."

While it was getting to be early in the morning, both of the Admirals took the staff car to the Pentagon to see if they could sort out the immediate critical problem at the MIR crash site. Admiral Gunston undertook the responsibility to send off the necessary messages to the Sea Devil and contact the director in charge of the military police. He arranged for Admiral Heiserman to be escorted back to Washington. Concurrently, Admiral Johnson worked on determining the source of the equipment given to Admiral Lowery. In regards to the U.S. military equipment being in the possession of a Canadian Admiral, he felt that the best place to start was with the U.S. Federal Surplus Utilization Program.

As the clock reached eight a.m., Admiral Johnson reached a man by phone, who seemed to be the record keeper of the program. The conversation was recorded on speakerphone. The head clerk agreed that airplanes, helicopters, ships, and similar equipment were among the millions of items that the program received each year from all of the government agencies for disposal, and he would be happy to undertake a computer check to see if any Apache helicopters were disposed of recently.

"Yes, Sir, my records show that eight were recently declared surplus in November, and they were immediately claimed the same day."

"By whom?"

"They were signed for by an Admiral Heiserman."

"And just how much did he pay for these Apache helicopters?"

"My records show that they were not purchased but were claimed by an organization that is eligible to obtain excess property."

"Was the Canadian government eligible?"

"No Sir, just federal agencies, some government contractors, some judicial agencies, and the like. There's a long list, but the Canadian government is not one of them."

"What organization did Heiserman represent when he obtained the Apaches?"

"It says here that the Veteran Naval Association needed them."

"Did it ever don on anyone at the asset disposal project that the Veteran Naval Association is basically a Legion, where everyone goes to the bar to drink and get blotto, and they don't need attack helicopters?"

"I guess not. All I do is mark in the books what transpires, and I don't make the decisions."

"Sorry. I know it is not your fault. Could you check the computer to see what else Heiserman has signed for on behalf of this Naval Association?"

"No problem, it will just take a moment while I type in his name. Oh my gosh, he has a huge list of items, including a hovercraft, missiles, trucks, uniforms, rifles, ammunition, and some other things, including a bomb with a timer on it."

"Could you provide a copy of all that paperwork ASAP to me, U.S. Navy Vice Chief Admiral Johnson?"

"No problem. I'll do it right away."

"Just one more question, which government agency declared all of this equipment surplus, and who signed the surplus orders?"

"Just a moment. It was the U.S. Navy that said that all the assets were surplus, and it was Battery Commander Marsh, acting on the authority of Admiral Heiserman, who declared everything as excess."

Admiral Johnson slammed down the phone to face Rear Admiral Gunston, who was working on the message to the Sea Devil.

"It seems that our Admiral Heiserman has been a busy man. He has written off many Navy stores, claimed the same for an association that doesn't need them, and then gave them to his buddy, Admiral Lowery. Not only is he carrying out a mission without authorization, but he has stolen millions of dollars in equipment from the Government of the United States." The rage in the Secretary's face showed in red blotches on his forehead.

Gunston couldn't understand how it was possible, in this day and age of computers and checks and cross-checks on inventory items and items under disposal orders, how one man could rip off the government for millions of dollars of military assets. His anger showed as he spoke.

"I have asked the director of policy to find out exactly where Heiserman is, and I'll send a dozen or more armed policemen to drag his sorry ass back to Washington so that he can be court martialed."

"I concur with your sentiment. Now, what do we do about the Sea Devil message?" asked Johnson.

"I wanted to be one hundred percent certain that the message was not phony and to make sure that the Captain of the Sea Devil was not overreacting. It would be hell for us to pay if this Commander Hayes just had a grudge against Heiserman and was making up this story.

"I checked his records, and he is a very reliable young officer with an up-and-coming career. His submarine is indeed located in the Canadian ice pack, according to our ship positioning board. Our Operations Centre tells me that the Canadian Forces are in the midst of an air search for one of their planes missing in the Arctic.

"Upon confirming that Commander Hayes' messages are legitimate, I dispatched the President's orders to the Sea Devil. I only hope that the sub receives our reply."

"Ideally, we prefer that he gets the message before MIR is ransacked, and before the Russian troops arrive. All we can do in the meantime, Gunston, is pray that the Sea Devil surfaces soon and picks up our message."

"I checked to see what other orders Admiral Heiserman has issued recently. He had ordered, for this week, a Naval exercise with the Canadian Navy near the place where this Canadian Admiral Lowery has set up camp. I sent orders canceling the exercise and ordering all ships back to their home ports. I also issued a general order relieving Admiral Heiserman of his authority to initiate any functional exercises until our investigation is complete."

"I would say that about wraps it up. I just wonder why Heiserman and Marsh would need a time-activated bomb. I won't stop worrying about that until I know the answer."

"I suggest that you pass this information about the missing military equipment along to the Canadian government," added Gunston. "This Admiral Lowery may end up using these military assets for nefarious purposes, and we want to disassociate the U.S. military from his 'gift' to Nunavut. I'm sure that they would want to know that Admiral Heiserman, and not the U.S. government, is responsible for providing all the military equipment that Admiral Lowery is now using in the Canadian north. Better mention the time bomb just in case it somehow gets used."

"I think that's a good idea, but I'll clear it with the Secretary of Defense before I release the info to Canada."

# Part 2

## NUNAVUT IS BURNING

# 27 BUYING AND BURNING

28 December 1630 hrs local, Frobisher Bay, Nunavut

Buzz Lowery needed to see Admiral Heiserman, and he was told to wait. That made him grow more impatient. Soon after entering the Navigator Inn, he was told by an aide at the door of the Admiral's Suite that Heiserman was busy for the next ten minutes. That was fifteen minutes ago. Buzz was told by the aide to wait in a suite down the hall and help himself to the drinks. Lowery and his bodyguards reluctantly waited, pouring and drinking a large whiskey during the time-lapse. Buzz didn't like to be kept waiting even by someone that he admired, and who was helping him to achieve his goals.

Admiral Heiserman was in the midst of finishing his conversation and negotiations with Ambassador Lee, of the Republic of China.

"You just heard me confirm with my contact on the submarine that the various components of MIR's data storage system have been recently retrieved from the downed space station, and they are all in excellent condition. I will have them in my possession within a few hours. You know that the storage system contains thirteen years of data that would take your government twenty to twenty-five years to replicate even if you had the technology to do it. The data includes thousands of photos, videos, and recordings of the territories, militaries, and weapons of every country on earth. In addition, it holds the secrets to hundreds of technological advances as a result of the hundreds of experiments conducted on board.

"These experiments and observations will put your country light years ahead of any major powers on earth. The data will create thousands of jobs for your people and make your military superior to all other armies in the world. I'm sure that you have some people in your scientific community following MIR's exploits over the past decade. They will be able to confirm to you that everything I mentioned is true."

"I have had discussions with some of the brightest scientists in China, since you talked to me in Ottawa two weeks ago about the possibility that you could supply all of MIR's memory tracks," stated the Chinese

Diplomat. "They have assured me that obtaining all of the data that MIR possesses would be a goldmine for our country. But what is it going to cost? That is why I am here."

"As a matter of interest, I can tell you that my government, particularly the U.S. Defense Department, were paying the Soviets a couple of million dollars for a small fraction of the data contained on this equipment. The MIR computers contain a thousand times or more data than the pittance that the U.S. government procured." The Admiral stopped for a moment to let that bit of information sink in. "You can have it all for only one hundred million dollars."

"Sounds interesting," said the Ambassador. "I would, of course, have to talk with my government beforehand. Besides, we would have to see some of the data before we conclude such an agreement."

"No problem. Just tell me what sort of information you want, and I'll get someone to extract it for you."

"We have given it considerable thought and decided that we want some photos of the Russian border troops and their equipment in Mongolia. You know that Mongolia was under the domination of China from the sixteenth to the nineteenth century when it was lost in 1911 by the Chinese revolution. Since then, the Soviet Union has treated Mongolia as a satellite territory, although the Mongolia government prefers to consider its relationship with Russia as a fraternal alliance. We consider Mongolia as a lost territory, and we find it galling that Russian troops would be stationed in Mongolia and massed against my country. While some of the troops were reduced under Gorbachev, we think there are still enough of them to be considered a threat. We need to know just how many troops are still in Mongolia."

"That will be no problem. I'm sure that all of that information is contained on the files lodged in MIR's memory banks."

"You understand, Admiral Heiserman, that if we buy this equipment, we want the original equipment and data, and that there are to be no other copies retained by yourself or sold to anyone else. You also agree that my government is not to be connected in any way with your sabotage of MIR."

"Absolutely, on both counts. I will need about a week to find the photos that you want from the millions in the memory banks of MIR. You understand that I cannot let you have the Mongolian photos unless you buy the whole lot, and I hope you realize that I am prepared to offer this equipment to other governments or organizations if you are not interested."

"I understand, perhaps we can get together again in a week?"

"Agreed."

The Chinese Ambassador left the Admiral's suite, and Heiserman joined Lowery in the adjacent suite. The guards left, leaving the two alone.

"Buzz, nice to see you again. What's new?"

Lowery swirled the ice about his whiskey glass. He was still annoyed for being kept waiting.

"You were right. The foolish government in Ottawa is not prepared to do anything to defend our north and will do nothing to stop the goddamn Russians that are invading our Arctic."

"You talked to them?"

"You're bloody right, I did. I wanted to blast those bastards out of the sky for destroying one of our planes. Instead, you know what the defense minister did? He stripped me of my rank and position and told me that I couldn't use the helicopters and missiles you got for us. Those dumb-ass idiots! Then, they had the unmitigated gall to make Brig. Gen. Shanahan the acting Commander of Maritime Command and even published his promotion in the Frobisher Bay newspaper. That was just to annoy me!"

"Hold on a second, simmer down! I don't even know this Shanahan that you are talking about. You and I spent weeks in Washington planning to get the Russians to come to your northern territory so we could convince the press that Canada's north was being invaded. Once the Russians were there, we figured that we could pressure both of our governments for more equipment and have them install detection systems in the waters of the Northwest Passage. Are you telling me that our plan to crash MIR in the Arctic to draw in the Russians has worked so well that the Russians are already on their way? Have any of them landed yet?"

Heiserman thought that his grip on the MIR data might slip away from him if the Russians got to MIR before he did.

"No, not yet. The bastards weren't satisfied with destroying my plane with their sub, now they have a flock of helicopters on their way. They have to refuel along the route, but they could be on the ground in 10 to 12 hours. And what does my ass-licking government want me to do? They want me to 'cooperate,'" he said with air quotes.

"I told them that I wouldn't have anything to do with those bastards. That's when they took away my three-star rank and took out the only Navy job that I ever wanted."

Heiserman relaxed, knowing that he still had time to get to the MIR site before the Russians.

"You mentioned a destroyed plane. What about your plane? What happened to it?" He already knew the answer to his own questions but he needed to know if Lowery was aware that it was one of his subs that had shot down the plane.

"One of our Aurora's was in the area and must have spotted the Russian sub. The sub fired at the plane, bringing it down. Now my twelve-man crew is missing. The sub must still be there with my men on board." Lowery's anger was plainly visible.

"Perhaps the crew will still show up. What can we do now? We got the Russians to invade your country, following our plan. They even destroyed one of your planes, and your weak-kneed government still won't send more men, equipment, and ships to the Arctic. They won't even make any commitment to set up a listening system on your coasts. You and I can't just sit back and let that happen."

"We've got to do something, but what?"

"We have our own equipment, and we can use it. And my ships are on the way to your eastern coast for a naval exercise. We can call on them if we can't handle it ourselves. But it means defying your government and taking things into your own hands. You will have to become the Commander of the Armed Forces of this Northern Land!" Heiserman declared with a scheming smile.

The Admiral knew that he needed Lowery to control the levers of power in Nunavut if he was to get the government to agree to his scheme to put listening devices at the entrance way to the North. He needed to stoke the fire within Lowery to get him to do what was necessary.

"Your government, including the ass-licking cabinet, is just rolling over to Ottawa's directions. If the Nunavut government caves in again to Ottawa, soon the invaders will steal all the valuable land and the treasures that belong to the Inuit. Do you know what your people will get if Ottawa has its way? Nothing!

"Do you want foreigners to take our oil, gold, and other precious metals and walk away after destroying thousands of years of tradition and customs? Inuit children will have nothing to look forward to in the future. I say that we need to burn the current political process and all the structures associated with it. What is required is a strong-willed leader who hates corruption, and who has the nerve to tell Ottawa that we, we-the-Inuit, will control our own destiny. Buzz, you are that leader. You need to do something, now that you have all the resources, to make the changes happen. What do you have to say?"

Lowery listened with interest and was even nodding his head in agreement.

"You're right. The North never could depend on Ottawa's bleeding hearts. They never had the guts to stand up for this part of Canada. The hell with them, we'll do it on our own. I have already talked to the Premier about putting me in charge of all of the equipment and men that you so generously provided. Perhaps I should talk to him again about using the equipment on our own, to defend the North without begging Ottawa for help. I'll burn this city to the ground if that's what is necessary to eliminate this Nunavut government, and I'll stop the Ottawa greedy politicians from coming to our precious homeland."

Heiserman needed Lowery to go further than defying his central government. It would suit his plans if Lowery ran the government in Nunavut.

"You can talk to him if you think that it will do any good, but I think he is in league with the low lives in Ottawa. He already sold out his people by giving up the Inuit land claim, and he settled for only fifteen percent of the land that rightfully belongs to them. Besides, Ottawa put up big bucks to support his election, making him a puppet. You may have to go over his head to the Inuit people if he disagrees with your armed forces defending his country. We need action NOW."

Heiserman used a lot of words that he knew Lowery was itching to hear. He was playing Lowery like a fish on a fly line, and he needed Lowery to become the power broker in the North so that he would be the kingmaker and get the commitment to boot out the Russians and put in a detection system. If he played Lowery right, Admiral Heiserman could end up with most of the glory of getting the Russians to back down from their 'invasion of Canada', just like Kennedy did during the Cuban crisis. He knew that he could easily manipulate the press to show that he was the one that supported Lowery in the showdown with the Russians. That could make him an international hero. Perhaps this glory and the millions from the sale of MIR data could give him the steak-hold that he needed to become the next president of the United States.

"You're right. When I spoke with Premier Alaka earlier in the week, he didn't support my cause. It would be worthless to discuss the matter with him again. I told him when I left his office that his decision not to put me in charge of the Nunavut Forces could come back to haunt him. It looks like I have no choice but to lock him up along with his corrupt cabinet and do the job myself."

"Now you're talking. I have a present for you." Heiserman reached into his luggage and drew out his spare set of four-star epaulets.

"Put these on! You deserve them! Get rid of the three stars and the Canada shoulder flashes."

Lowery was thrilled. Slipping off the three-star epaulets and tearing off the Canadian emblems from his tunic empowered him. He slipped on the four-stars and stood in front of the mirror to admire himself.

Heiserman attempted to reinforce Lowery's decision to go it alone against the Russians, using the equipment and men already at his disposal.

"That looks one hundred percent better. Remember that our American benefactors have more money to pay your troops and to get you more ships and planes. You can always use the money to hire more mercenaries if you need them. The benefactors were the ones that provided the money I needed to get a programmer to make a diskette for MIR's computer, to override Moscow's commands and bring it to descend to earth exactly where we wanted it. They also provided the money that I needed to get the French astronaut to slip the diskette into MIR's computer drive. These benefactors are our friends, and they just want the United States to be safe from the Russians."

He didn't mention that his primary benefactor was the chairman of a global corporation. Several other corporate executives were also benefactors, and they counted on the windfalls that would follow, if he reached his goal of being president. He also didn't mention that they could be counted upon to donate millions more if he could find a way for them to have access to the mineral wealth of Nunavut. Before any of this, he depended on the MIR data sale for millions of dollars.

"I'm sure that my friends, my benefactors, would go the extra mile and provide the funds that you need to set up your government here in Nunavut."

"You're right again. This northern land deserves better than the government that they've got here and the socialist bastards in Ottawa. Those Ottawa politicians are just like those commies in Europe that want everything given to them and won't stand up for any ideals. I've always hated socialist governments. My father taught me that you have to work hard for what you want, not sit back and wait until someone gives it to you. The recent governments that we've had in Ottawa are getting more and more socialistic. It makes me sick to see the Prime Minister coddle the Russian president simply because the Ruskies can't make a go of it as a capitalistic regime. It pisses me off to see the Russian president crying to the West for more money. To hell with him, I say."

Lowery was not yet finished. It was clear to Heiserman he was just getting a full head of steam.

"I'm also not too impressed with the way the Premier of Nunavut allows his people to be screwed royally by Ottawa. I'm not going to put up with it anymore."

Lowery started to realize that the extra star gave him more confidence; he was convinced that he could take on Ottawa and the Premier of Nunavut. He also realized that the cards might fall in such a way to leave him in a position of power, and maybe, just maybe, some or most of the resources of this rich province could fall into his lap. He would have to give this scenario more thought.

Admiral Heiserman suggested that Lowery return to the legislative building to pay a little visit to the Premier. In the meantime, he would be leaving Frobisher shortly on Navy business, but would be back later in the day, and perhaps Lowery would join him for a late drink as the premier-in-waiting. That remark caused Lowery to smile.

"Where are you off to? The fun is just getting started in this town."

"I have a Navy V-22A Osprey VTOL picking me up at the Frobisher airport and taking me to one of our aircraft carriers. I have a routine inspection and an award ceremony to attend, so I'll be back this evening," he lied.

As Lowery left the suite, Admiral Heiserman called for his staff car and put on his flying suit to make his three-hour planned flight in comfort. He took the elevator to the ground floor and exited the building just as the staff car pulled up. He jumped in, and the driver closed the door behind him, walked around the car, and eased himself behind the wheel.

From his hotel room window, Shanahan saw Heiserman leave in the airport's direction and decided to follow. He pocketed the pistol and walked down the hall of the hotel to the elevator. Shanahan pressed the basement button, and the elevator took him to the underground floor, where a short walk brought him to his parked rental. He hoped that the car was inconspicuous, allowing him to use the few kilometers of road in Frobisher without being too noticeable.

The darkness was getting heavier, but he decided against using his lights. Shanahan kept the Ford several car lengths behind the military staff car. He let two cars ease in between his and the military vehicle just to be on the safe side, and it was evident to Shanahan that the driver of the staff car was not aware that he was being followed. He did not attempt the lose him as he made a beeline for the airport. The driver of the military car pulled up adjacent to a plane with its rotors already spinning.

Shanahan found a spot behind a building where he could park unnoticed and left the vehicle. He ran to an area behind some air-transportable crates and trained his binoculars on the staff car. His arrival at the spot coincided with Heiserman's exit, who climbed the stairs and entered the plane. Shanahan saw a tilt-rotor vertical takeoff plane when the propellers swung ninety degrees towards the perpendicular. The pilot applied power and the craft went straight up. The propellers then rotated back to their normal position, which turned the helicopter into a high speed, fuel-efficient turboprop airplane. The plane departed at full speed out over the pack ice that covered Frobisher Harbor.

By using a VTOL, it was clear to Shanahan that Heiserman was going somewhere that a plane could not land, and he wanted to be there faster than he could if he used the average helicopter. Heiserman was also using an aircraft that could carry much more equipment and supplies than any one of the AH-64 Apache helicopters.

The Apache all-weather attack helicopters that Lowery proudly displayed were parked on a side ramp near one of the hangars, yet Heiserman neglected to use any of them. It was a safe bet, Shanahan concluded, that Heiserman was heading to the downed Aurora and to the fallen MIR. He would use the VTOL to land like a helicopter on the ice pack in a matter of hours.

The Apache helicopters started to come to life as Shanahan watched the VTOL disappear over the horizon. Several technicians filled the 30 mm chain automatic gun cannons under the Apaches' fuselages, and others attached 16 hellfire missiles to each machine. The pilots and the gunners stood around a small table nearby looking at maps. They got into a small bus, and Shanahan thought they were probably headed for the operations building for a weather briefing.

Shanahan wondered just how much time he had to prevent a war from breaking out.

If these helicopters were heading for a showdown with the Russians, they would have to refuel at Alert or Eureka since they only had a two-hour endurance. He would have to alert Phillips to their ETA as soon as he got back to the hotel and set up his laptop.

Shanahan turned his glasses to the buildings near the Apache helicopters. He saw about fifty troops, fully armed, exit their sleeping quarters and form up in a squad near two camouflage trucks. Lowery emerged from his airport office and walked out in front of the men. They were brought to attention by someone dressed in an Army Captain uniform with Nunavut flag insignia. Lowery spoke for ten minutes, then all the troops entered the trucks. A black staff car approached with a small Nunavut flag with four stars mounted on each side of its front fenders. The Lowery car led the parade of vehicles back toward the downtown area.

Shanahan began to follow the convoy. Three vehicles belonging to Lowery drove into the city and stopped at the front door of the building housing the Nunavut Legislation. From his car, Shanahan saw Lowery and about ten of his troops rush the building.

There was a hidden driveway that Shanahan found near the legislative building, where he could park the Ford. He carefully made his way to an alley directly across the building and waited. Fifteen minutes passed when suddenly the quiet streets were disturbed by the exploding sounds of gunfire. The remainder of Lowery's troops ran from the trucks and into the building with their rifles in the combat position. There were a few more shots, then all was quiet. From his observation post, Shanahan could see the smoke billowing from the legislative building's upper floor.

He continued to watch. None of the residents ran into the city's main street, yet Shanahan could see some of them peeking from behind closed curtains. Lowery and a dozen or so soldiers left the building pushing the same number of men dressed in suits. The suited men were hustled into the back of one of the trucks, which drove off while the other truck and car remained. Several more troops took up positions around the building, blocking the entrances and exits. Unable to get into the building to see what transpired, Shanahan decided to follow the truck that was carrying the politicians.

The truck drove through the city, then turned north using the road that used to separate the United States airbase from the main village.

The area in between was now one extensive urban development. As the truck passed the airport, it was joined by a half dozen other camouflage trucks, also filled with Lowery's soldiers. They continued to roll out of town; the road ran parallel to the runway. It was now no longer a paved road but a snow-covered gravel road. Shanahan continued to remain well enough back so that his rental car could not be seen. The convoy continued for a few kilometers until the trucks turned onto a small path leading to an old building near the very end of the runway.

Realizing that the convoy was near its destination, Shanahan pulled his car to the side of the road and ran to a nearby hill overlooking the area. Using his glasses, he saw the trucks stop near a building with the letters 'USAF' painted on it. They were barely legible. The building was a long, corrugated metal shed that was likely home to U.S. Air Force equipment during the war.

Lowery and the soldiers emerged from the trucks and stood around talking. At the same time, another smaller group of men, who looked like the group leaders, were huddled in the middle of the road conversing among themselves. The conversation seemed to last for several minutes when Lowery and one of the leaders walked towards the troops. The leader selected ten of the troops and marched them down the road behind the building, out of sight of the other men. Shanahan's position on the hill was high enough to see the men as they marched behind the shed. The soldiers were placed in a line facing the shed's back and stood at attention with their rifles at their sides.

Lowery watched over the arrangement. He stood straight and tall with a pistol in his hand. Another officer left the group in the center of the road and pointed to two of the soldiers speaking to the men in business suits inside the back of one of the trucks. The business suits, who were politicians or legislative staff, were manhandled from the truck and marched by the two soldiers down behind the shed.

Shanahan counted ten men in business suits. He saw the line of troops lift their rifles as soon as the other two soldiers and their officer had left.

Lowery was the lone officer left on the scene. There appeared to be a spoken command by him, and the line of ten soldiers fired simultaneously. Small traces of smoke emerged from the rifles' business end. Lowery walked over to one individual who was still moving on the ground. He approached and turned him over with his boot. Lowery spoke to the politician, then he shot the individual in the head and casually walked away.

Shanahan was shocked by the actions of a senior Naval officer, who he had known for years. He was shocked that this educated, highly regarded sailor who was held in high esteem by many, was a killer! How could he display such contempt for human life? He just realized how cold hearted this man was. Shanahan had completely misinterpreted the Lowery's personality.

"You will pay for this act," Shanahan uttered quietly.

He continued to lay on the hillside, dismayed by the actions of Lowery and the line of troops. He had just witnessed an ex-senior officer of the Canadian Navy, and some men dressed in military clothing execute, in cold blood, ten of the bureaucrats belonging to the Nunavut government. There was no doubt in his mind that he would receive similar treatment if he got caught.

The remaining suited men, most likely politicians, were dragged from the truck and pushed and shoved towards the shed. One of them was shackled at the hands and feet. He had difficulty walking since he fell when he was pressed. A soldier struck him in the back and dragged him to his feet. Shanahan wondered if he was about to be executed.

The man was then pushed inside the shed, and the door slammed shut. All of the troops and officers climbed back into the trucks. One soldier, wearing an officer uniform, ordered several guards to be posted around the shed. The vehicles made a three hundred sixty degree turn and headed back down the pathway. Shanahan instinctively lowered his head while praying that he would not be seen. The trucks rumbled by, and five minutes passed before the he dared to raise his head. He ran down the hill and jumped into his car. His vehicle caught up to the convoy on the city's outskirts, where he followed the trucks as they reentered the town.

Shanahan watched as the trucks peeled off, going left and right at various intersections, and stopped at different buildings throughout the city.

The first truck stopped at the local TV station building, another at the French Inuit language radio station, while a third, full of troops, pulled up in front of the RCMP Detachment. The shooting was heard as the soldiers ran into the Detachment. Two of the remaining four trucks were dispatched to guard the local bank and the telephone exchange. The remaining trucks and troops split up, and one truck stood guard at the west entrance to the town while the other took up a position at the east end. The city was practically sealed off. Buildings started burning around the city, including some at the airport where most of Lowery's men were still located.

Shanahan parked his car away from the Navigator Inn, in case he needed it again. He carefully made his way back to his hotel and climbed the stairs towards his room. He didn't want to use the main lobby and elevator if Lowery's troops were looking for him. He realized that it was now too late to call in the military police to help him bring Lowery back to Halifax to face a court-martial.

# 28 INDEPENDENCE

2 28 December 1800 hrs local, Frobisher Bay, Nunavut

Dave Shanahan desperately needed to contact the Chief of the Defense Staff in Ottawa and Major Phillips on the ice cap. It was only a matter of time before Lowery's troops would lock down all means of communication with the outside world. Picking up the phone in his hotel room, Shanahan asked the operator to connect him with the private number of General Le Beau. He hoped that Lowery didn't have someone loyal to him working on the switchboard and listening to calls outgoing from Iqaluit. Otherwise, his presence in the province's capital would soon be known.

"General Le Beau," said the voice fifteen hundred kilometers to the south.

"This is Shanahan. I may be disconnected so I'll make this call brief. I believe that Buzz Lowery has initiated a coup and taken over the government of Nunavut." Shanahan spoke quickly so that he could get all the essential information out to the CDS. "I saw Lowery and his troops pull up to the legislative building here. Shortly thereafter, I heard shots fired. The troops escorted about a dozen men in suits into several large trucks. I followed these vehicles to the outskirts of the city. The trucks drove to a remote site known locally as Upper Base, which I believe is an old Pinetree radar site. I saw ten politicians or legislative staff executed by firing squad by Lowery's forces. I think the Premier in shackles was subsequently imprisoned in a shed near this old USAF site. Lowery's forces were then dispersed throughout the town at all of the strategic areas. They occupied the TV station, the French Inuit radio station, the bank, and telephone exchange. Fires are still burning throughout the city. I'm surprised that this phone line hasn't been cut yet, but it could be cut at any moment."

The Chief of the Defense Staff didn't speak at first due to the shock. He finally managed to utter a statement.

"This is unbelievable. I knew that Lowery desperately wanted the additional military equipment and forces in the Eastern Arctic. I never thought that he would go as far as to overthrow the elected government of Nunavut and take innocent lives just to accomplish his goals. There must be something else that is driving him. Otherwise, he would have waited until the Canadian government had a budget surplus and would have been more willing to provide the Defense Department with more money. I told him that I could get more funds for our northern sovereignty in a few years. He had only to be patient. I wish I knew what he really wanted. I'll have to tell the PM immediately about this radical turn of events. He'll probably call the cabinet to an urgent meeting. Our forces will have to deploy to avenge these actions. What else can you tell me about Lowery's strengths?"

"I saw four of his Apache helicopters armed with missiles and cannon ammunition take off and head out over the ice pack in the direction of our plane and the MIR crash site. I suspect he is out to attack the Russian helicopters. I also saw Admiral Heiserman of the U.S. Navy head in the same direction a few hours earlier."

"Admiral Heiserman! Chief of U.S. Naval Operations! That's interesting. I wonder what he is up to."

"He had a meeting with the Chinese Ambassador to Canada earlier in the day, but I have no idea what they were discussing. The Ambassador resided at the same hotel at the same time as Heiserman and Lowery. Lowery may have been at the meeting, but I can't confirm it."

"There's no doubt that the PM will talk to the Russian president and warn him that Lowery's helicopters may be after his troops. I'm sure he will also call the U.S. president and talk to him about Heiserman. Is there any way that you can get a message to the Russian helicopter pilots? Perhaps you can contact Major Phillips and have him contact the Russians?"

"I am going to send an email to Phillips as soon as we are done."

"Good. Give me your new email address in case I can't get you by phone. I'll contact our listening station at Alert to see if they can locate Lowery's helicopters." General Le beau took a deep breath and continued, "I'm going to see the PM and the Defense Minister right now. They will have to decide what we are going to do about Lowery. This coup and the execution-style death of our northern residents and elected officials will reverberate throughout Parliament and the media. Thanks for keeping me informed. I suggest that you lay low while Lowery's forces are running amok. Still, any additional information that you can get to us about the strength of his troops will be very useful."

Dave Shanahan provided his email address to the General, the hotel phone number, and the name, Mitchell, that he was registered under. Following the call, he opened his laptop and typed an email to Major Phillips.

"Admiral Lowery's forces have taken over the government of Nunavut. No doubt, he will close all Nunavut airports to prevent the Canadian Forces from striking back. He has troops in most Nunavut communities including Alert and Eureka. Establish contact with Thule for assistance. You are to treat all of Lowery's forces as hostile, including four fully armed Apache helicopters that are heading your way. This information needs to be passed to the Russian helicopters ASAP. Admiral Heiserman of the U.S. Navy was seen, earlier in the day, flying north. He may also be on route, by VTOL, to your location, but this info is not confirmed. Shanahan."

He pushed the send button and closed his laptop while turning to the window. The street was clear now. Just a few hours ago the sidewalks were full of local people shopping and strolling about the town checking out the store windows. What were the residents planning to do about the military takeover of their government? How many of them already knew about the coup? What would their reaction be when the they heard about it?

Shanahan tried to think of what he could do. He couldn't go anywhere outside the city. Lowery's troops controlled all the roads and the airport; the city was in lockdown. The local TV station was still broadcasting as nothing had happened. So was the local radio station.

Outwardly, the Frobisher Bay world appeared as if all was normal. *Did I imagine it all?* wondered the MAG Commander.

Fifteen minutes later, both the TV and radio stations went off the air briefly, then a voice on the blank TV screen said that an important message was to be broadcast from government house's steps. The news was to be delivered to the people of Nunavut in twenty minutes. A similar message blared from the radio.

There was a need to see this broadcast in person since it might answer some of the CDS' questions about Lowery's forces. Pulling his civilian parka, with its hood, out of his suitcase, he quickly zippered it up. The parka was over an old sweater that matched an equally old pair of jogging pants. With the hood up, he would be unrecognizable. To be on the safe side, he slipped the pistol into the pocket.

Upon leaving the Inn, Shanahan found a back street route to the new legislative building. It was still under construction and sat next door to the Parnaivik Building. That building housed, for the interim, the nineteen members of the assembly.

Walking inconspicuously, he used side streets that headed towards the downtown center of the area known as the Four Corners. This section was under development to accommodate the offices and legislative spaces of the newest Canadian province. Once he reached the construction site, he climbed the new building's construction fence to reach the premises. An unlocked door allowed him access to the new facility. He could easily see that it was completely vacant and at least another six months away from completion. Crossing the concrete floor, he climbed the steps to the third floor and moved silently to a window that overlooked the Parnaivik Building's steps. The window had a cranking mechanism that allowed him to open it enough to hear what was going on without letting in most of the minus 15-degree air.

From where he was perched, Shanahan could see that the present legislative building's steps were covered with red carpet, and there was a speaker's dais. Behind the platform were several huge flags of Nunavut, yet there were no Canadian flags. As he watched, ten of Lowery's troops took up their positions on the steps with five on each side of the dais. They were armed and wore a small flag of Nunavut on each shoulder. A small crowd had gathered at the foot of the steps, and the TV cameras were already set up and rolling.

The troops came to attention as two men emerged from the building and approached the dais. The man who adjusted the microphone was an Inuit, and the other was Lowery, wearing his four stars and the flag of Nunavut on his old navy uniform. The Inuit addressed the crowd.

"To those who don't recognize me, I am Willie Nageak. I ran in the last election to become your premier. Unfortunately, I supposedly ran 'second' place." He held up both hands and flashed two fingers on each hand as an air quote.

"Supposedly, the people chose a thirty-five-year-old lawyer, who has been running your government for the past year. I have just received evidence that the election was rigged. I will speak about that matter in a few moments.

"I regretfully announce that Russian troops have invaded the territory of Nunavut near Ellef Ringnes Island. They arrived by helicopters, but our intelligence has informed me that Russian submarines are also in the same area. We know that one of the Russian subs used a missile to destroy a Canadian Forces airplane, killing twelve crew members."

Shanahan was probably the only one present, besides Lowery, who knew that Willie Nageak was fast and loose with the truth. Willie was blurring the facts to fit his agenda.

"They also crash-landed one of their radioactive space stations on our lands to give them an excuse to come here. This information was provided to the government of Canada, but they refused to provide any assistance to our province to rid ourselves of these invaders. They refused to help. Instead, they were taken in by the Russian ruse to recover their spacecraft. The Canadian government ordered that we cooperate with them. The Canadian government cannot be depended on to protect our land and our people.

"You will recall that a few weeks ago, Friends of the North, a group of capable military officers and men, gifted Nunavut with several helicopters, planes, and ships, all to protect our province from these invaders. This gift was courtesy of Admiral Lowery." He turned and pointed to the man in the navy uniform.

"Today, I and Admiral Lowery approached the Premier of Nunavut and his cabinet and other members of the legislature. We recommended that this province declare a State of Emergency to take action to repel the Russians. We strongly suggested that we use this gifted equipment and men, so generously provided by our friends, to defend our homeland. I repeat, the Canadian government has neglected its duty to protect our territory. Admiral Lowery and I could not stand by and watch as these invaders take over our lands and seas. These properties have been ours to live on and to use for thousands of years. The members of the Nunavut assembly would sit on their hands while this communist army ravished our resources. We had no choice but to set aside these politicians while Admiral Lowery and our Nunavut forces dealt with this threat to our survival. As runner up for Premier's position in the last election, I took it upon myself to declare a State of Emergency.

"I have had the corrupt politicians held incommunicado for the near future. I have suspended their intention to govern this land for their Ottawa friends' benefit and hand it to the enemy. Instead, I have ordered Admiral Lowery, our new Commander of the Nunavut Forces, to use all of the assets given by him, to destroy this enemy that dared invade our homeland and attempt to ravish it of its wealth of resources.

"Admiral Lowery will call upon the U.S. Navy to provide him with additional support. Once we decimate these invaders, you can bet that the Russian communist state will not dare send any more military troops and risk the wrath of our forces and those of the United States."

Willie Nageak waited for preordained applause to die down from some of those at the foot of the stairs. These supporters were Lowery paid. Shanahan was beginning to understand the depth of Lowery's strength.

"I want to assure you that this is a temporary measure. We will have a new election shortly, to elect some local leaders, men and women with some backbone, to ensure that we rid ourselves of these and future communist forces. In the meantime, I will be operating the government with some of the other honorable politicians that were also defeated in the previous election. Together with the legislative staff, politicians who have backbone will give you the courageous government you deserve. I have asked Admiral Lowery to be Commander of the Nunavut Forces and help with the finance portfolio.

"I mentioned that I have evidence that the last election was rigged. I have learned that most of the nineteen politicians were bankrolled by Ottawa. The evidence indicates that all of the southern-born elected candidates accepted bribes. This evidence will be presented at their trial after we rid our land of the communist invaders. In the meantime, their bank accounts have been seized along with their bank files. These sources provide evidence that shows that these so-called elected officials, including the Premier, have received thousands of dollars of Ottawa money to help with their campaigns. They had an unfair advantage over the other honorable candidates in the election. Ottawa's donations to these politicians allowed them to buy the votes of thousands of residents, who were mostly trucked in from the south. And what did they have to give back to these Ottawa bureaucrats in return, you ask?" Willie Nageak was on a roll.

"Did you know that the agreement that they signed with Ottawa to establish Nunavut as a separate entity includes the fact we have given up eighty-five percent of our lands? This same real estate that we have claimed as our own for the past five hundred years! They have also allowed Ottawa to own all of the precious metals and oil and gas that make up mother earth.

"Ottawa will collect and keep royalty payments from developers. You will get nothing! Instead, the developers have been sharing these royalties with the corrupt politicians in our government. These politicians allowed for the export of OUR gas and minerals... And what did Ottawa give you? Only an entirely new way of life that conflicts with our culture and our traditional methods. They also gave us the highest unemployment rate in Canada. The Canadian bureaucrats and their corrupt friends gave us a suicide rate that is seven times higher than the Canadian average, and these same Canadian politicians fed alcohol and drugs to our young folk. We can't allow that to continue!

"Canada has no interest in protecting Nunavut. In the late eighties, Admiral Lowery and others proposed that the government build 12 nuclear-powered submarines capable of operating under the polar ice. Nothing was done. The lack of a Canadian military presence here in the north, except for a Nor Pat flight every three weeks, amounts to a confession that they have no interest. In northern sovereignty, they have no priorities in protecting or promoting this great land of ours. They have reneged on their responsibility to watch over us."

Willie raised his hand and gripped the flag. The yellow and white flag with the north star adventurist in red on it. The red figure, or stone man, was a traditional trail marker centered in the middle of the flag for leadership. The flags covered the stage giving the impression that the speech was very patriotic.

"We are now a new province, and we have the same rights as all other provinces. If Quebec can have referendums to become independent, then so can we! Since Canada has acted in bad faith by buying our politicians, by stealing our culture and our resources, by corrupting our children, by refusing to help us defeat the invaders, we, the new leaders of the Territory of Nunavut, as a result of this, make a unilateral declaration of Independence from Canada. I promise you that we will shortly have a referendum on the conditions under which Canada can trade with this tremendous new Inuit nation of Nunavut. In the meantime, I have seized all of the assets belonging to Canada. For example, eighty-three percent of the Nunavut residents live in subsidized housing. The homes that you now live in and for which you pay outrageous rents to Ottawa, are now legally yours to keep, for free.

"This is the first act of my new government. Furthermore, there will be more government jobs for Nunavut natives and fewer for immigrants from the south. We readily accept and welcome southerners who come here with a generous heart, that want to stay here and become part of this great new country, but we reject any southerners who come here to exploit us. Any southerners who come to take our resources then take their new wealth, which rightfully belongs to you, and return to the south are not welcome. We need to be careful that we don't become a minority in our land." Nageak continued with his promises.

"I warn the politicians of Ottawa not to try and destroy our newfound country. We know that the United Nations support us as Aboriginal people in establishing full self-government. When it comes, the referendum will ask the twenty-five thousand residents of Nunavut, including our young folk, if they wish to stay free. Do they want to continue with this self-government that my colleagues and I have established, or do they want to return to the old way of being slaves to the dictates of those from the south? At the moment, some southerners claim Nunavut citizenship, yet most have never set foot in the north.

"But there are Canada supporters who would steal from us, this opportunity to be rulers of our destiny. I ask the people of Frobisher and our other Nunavut communities to be on the lookout for any aliens seeking to take away what rightfully belongs to us. I know that there are spies among us who would help Ottawa to destroy this fragile flower we call independence."

Shanahan could see that many of Nageak's statements were hitting home and being favorably received among those at the foot of the steps. After a momentary pause, Willie continued again.

"I have ordered our protectors to remove all Ottawa people from our government establishments. As such, we have seized the facilities at Alert and Eureka. The RCMP will also no longer have any powers to arrest you and lock you away for following your traditional way of life." The crowd cheered right on cue, realized Shanahan.

"We will establish our schools and social services and teach the traditional Inuit way of life to our children. There is no reason why our new nation can't be as prosperous as the Inuit in Greenland. I know that many of you have visited the sites of Thule and Nuuk. You have seen how prosperous the Inuit residents of those cities are compared to us. But we will never become like them if we let Canadian politicians dominate. They and their puppets in Iqaluit, such as the former premier and his cabinet, robbed us of our birthright. Even the Western Arctic

Territory, under Dene leadership, is more economically healthy than Nunavut.

"It is not because the Dene are harder working or smarter than us. They just don't let Ottawa politicians run their lives as we did with our former premier and his colleagues. The same Ottawa politicians are also allowing their big fat corporate friends to ruin our ecosystem with their resource exploitation goals.

"Canadian politicians and our former Premier allowed huge tankers, full of oil, to cross through our clean seas. The same crowd OK'd these ships, knowing that there was always the danger that the ship could break up and spill oil everywhere. Crude oil will destroy the land, the sea, and wildlife for thousands of years, but they don't care. Well, we are not going to put up with it anymore."

He wrapped himself in the flag and yelled out to the crowd.

"Long live free Nunavut!"

There was more applause when he started to give the same speech in Inuktitut. Shanahan could recognize a few words of the native language and surmised that the address was being decorated with additional promises to benefit other Inuit. There were Inuit in the other 27 communities that made up Nunavut. Many of these original residents didn't speak or understand English, and Nageak wanted them to understand his message in their native tongue. He wanted them to support the actions that he took that day, and he would do what was necessary, even if it meant buying Inuit support with their mineral wealth.

For Shanahan, it was time to move on before the speech finished. He estimated that he had at least fifteen minutes to put some distance between himself and Lowery's troops. Again he would use the back roads to get away.

He stopped at the Grind and Brew Cafe for a warm coffee and to watch the residents. He selected a booth where he could see and hear the locals' reactions to the speech still being shown on the TV in the cafe. Some of the men and women nodded approval, but they were the minority. Most of the cafe's inhabitants lowered their heads and grieved. It was evident that most of the people in the cafe and on the street outside the cafe's window were supporters of Nunavut remaining in Canada. They disagreed with the direction that Willie Nageak and Lowery were taking them.

These were the people that Shanahan wanted to talk to, but who could he trust? Where could he start the counter-revolution?

Behind his booth, Shanahan heard several men referring to some strong Inuit leaders. They said these leaders would be outraged at the proposition of establishing the new nation of Nunavut. They mentioned that Simone Aokalik, President of the Frobisher Community Council, was probably the most influential and definitely pro Canada. It was he who initiated the Arctic Rangers Corps, known locally as the First Canadian Rangers Patrol Group. Its goal was the protection of Canadian sovereignty in the north.

As Willie's diatribe continued on TV in the Inuit language, it became clear what Shanahan had to do next. Instead of massive Canadian troops being deployed and the possibility of considerable casualties, an alternative strategy would be successful. The Rangers and their supporters had to be organized into a resistance movement. With some help from Ottawa, they could overthrow the coup leaders and re-establish the democratically elected government.

Near the igloo-shaped Anglican Cathedral of St. Jude's, Shanahan found a phone booth and phone book. Simone Aokalik was listed as living in Apex Hill, a small community eight kilometers south of the downtown area of Frobisher. Tomorrow, he would find a way to reach Apex Hill and talk with this Inuit leader.

# 29   THREE LEADERS

29 December, all hours, in Ottawa

While Shanahan was out and about, he overheard the local folks talking about Ottawa's reaction to the coup. Many were in favor that the Prime Minister should do something to rectify the situation in Frobisher Bay. Of course, some were not in favor of the Federal government because of their political philosophy. Some swore that the PM, Rene Le Chance, would not do anything to reverse the situation. Some considered Le Chance as weak-kneed and incapable of making tough decisions. Some backed up their reasoning by remembering how Le Chance became the PM. Some of these folks argued that Le Chance was not the right person for the job from the moment he decided to attend the Leadership Convention. These locals recalled the general opinion of the attendees at the time of the convention. That opinion was that Le Chance was not PM material.

Rene Le Chance was considered by many as too young to be Prime Minister of Canada. They said that he had no experience and could not make the hard decisions at the ripe old age of forty-four. A babe in arms in the political world of old boys who were used to Prime Ministers who had been around the party for thirty or more years before they obtained the highest pinnacle of power.

But Rene was different. He struck a chord with many young Canadians; he had charisma. He was a philosophy professor when the Liberal party was looking for a new leader to replace the PM, who passed away from a heart attack while making a speech in the House. Some Liberal movers and shakers saw Le Chance as a dynamic and inspiring leader with a photogenic young bride and a new child who could grace 66 Sussex Drive in Ottawa. But by and in large, he was not well known by the vast majority of delegates at the leadership convention. Rene preferred Montreal's beer houses and nightclubs rather than the private clubs on Ste Catherine Street.

The Liberal leadership convention, a dress-up affair, was being held in Edmonton, and many of the old boys wanted the job; they were cutting each other's throats to get it. There seemed to be not one of the old boy candidates who commanded enough respect to obtain a majority of the votes to make him the governing party leader.

Rene had attended the convention because he thought that it would be a great party. Instead, he saw no unity among the delegates and that the convention was dull and boring because of all the in-fighting and throat-cutting. When the rookie had a chance to voice his opinions into the microphone, he encouraged all of the young representatives to walk out and join him at the first available club. He called all of the candidates boring and without solutions to problems facing the nation at the end of the twentieth century.

As he spoke, the applause grew from a few hands clapping to a thunderous roar; it encouraged him to go on. This convention was a waste of time, in his judgment, since there wasn't a new idea in the bunch, and without new ideas young Canadians wouldn't vote for these old farts with their nineteenth-century attitudes. He said that it would be young Canadians who would drive Canada in the twenty-first century, and all candidates in the room better not forget it. More applause. Soon he was being pushed to the stage and encouraged to continue to speak his mind. Once at the podium, several of his ideas gushed out; ideas that he and his friends in a philosophy club were considering. While some of the candidates in the convention room had heard about this young good looking Liberal supporter, he reminded Canadians of the current young president of the United States. But most of the delegates didn't care about the looks or philosophy of their voters.

As Rene spoke, more and more of the representatives realized that he was voicing the same opinions they also had, not only about the present old boy Liberals network but also about the economy, education, and health care. Before Rene realized it, the crowd was on its feet and applauding, and he was nominated to be on the ballot for the party's leadership.

When the vote was finally taken, he had won the leadership on the first ballot. Everyone was pleasantly surprised and happy; even the old boys said that they would support his initiatives. He won his seat in Montreal riding by a landslide margin and was hailed as the new Prime Minister of Canada.

A year later, the PM had new, more urgent problems than those he faced in his first year. As Rene reflected on his first year as PM of Canada, he realized that it was a very responsible job, yet it was very fulfilling. In the past year, there had been some tough times, mostly making budget cuts, but overall, he knew that he had an eighty percent approval rating by Canadians. Not bad for a young man born and bred in the slums of old Montreal.

But would this approval rating continue? What he did in the next twenty-four hours would test his resolve and his mettle to make tough decisions. First, there was the problem of the Russians flying into Canada to retrieve a space station. It would be difficult to explain to the Canadian public that the old Russia with its drive for world domination was dead and the new Russia, he believed, was only concerned for its people and their economic well-being. It would take time, but he knew that he could convince Canadians that the Russians were not out to invade Canada's northland.

There was another more difficult problem. He had just heard from the defense minister that there had been a coup in Nunavut and that the new revolutionary government had just announced their independence from Canada. The PM knew that these situations had to be handled tactically, but his reign as prime minister could be a short one with a large show of strength against him. This was not a time to use the kid gloves approach. For this problem he may even need the advice of the old boy network.

While he considered his options, his aide announced that the Minister of Defense and the Chief of the Defense Staff had arrived at 66 Sussex Drive and waited for him in his Operations room.

"Welcome, Minister and General Le Beau. Tell me what you know about the situation in Frobisher Bay."

"Well, Prime Minister, we are fortunate to have one of our generals presently in Frobisher Bay. The man is undercover. Our general saw the killing of ten politicians by a firing squad, and he saw the takeover of the Legislative Assembly. I think that he may even have been nearby when Willie Nageak made his independence speech. The General sent us an info copy after the speech was made to several Lowery supporters who attended the press conference. You probably saw it by now, it's been in rerun for the past hour. Did you notice the former Admiral Lowery was in the background during the speech?"

"Yes, I did. I can't help but feel that he put Mr. Nageak up to this independence declaration. This Nageak person could just be a front for Lowery. He could then control parts of the government. I see that he made himself the Chief of Defense for Nunavut."

"Yes, and he also made himself Minister of Finance. What does he know about finance?" asked the Minister.

"It may be that he wants to control the hundreds of millions that we transferred to their Frobisher Bay bank account when the new province was created. Did your General in Frobisher tell you how many troops support Lowery? Troops that we may have to deal with in Nunavut?"

"Our General in Frobisher is General Shanahan," The Minister of Defense replied. "It was General Le Beau who spoke with General Shanahan."

"Sir, General Shanahan is in Frobisher undercover," stated CDS Le Beau. "Lowery is not a friend of Shanahan and has threatened his life. Shanahan saw approximately fifty troops and another fifty supporters at the press conference. Earlier, he saw four armed helicopters take off and fly in the North Pole's direction, to the location where the Russian space station landed. Several days ago, Lowery mentioned that he donated two hundred troops to go along with the eight helicopters and the hovercraft ship given to Nunavut. We don't know if he has received all of the equipment he mentioned in his press conference, equipment supposedly surplus to the U.S. Navy. As I understand it, his buddies have formed a new Nunavut force. They have already taken over Alert, Eureka, and all of the RCMP Detachments. Our operation specialists calculate that Lowery must have at least two hundred and fifty troops at this time since he has been able to capture all of our facilities. We were outgunned. We had only a hundred fifty men in total at these locations."

"I'm worried that this wrong-headed bunch may go after the Russians and destroy the fine working relations that I have been able to build up with Moscow," said the PM. "I'll have to call the Russian authorities immediately and brief them on the situation."

"Sir, did you notice that Nageak said that he had the support of the U.S. Navy? General Shanahan mentioned that Admiral Heiserman, Chief of the Naval Operations for the U.S. Navy, was in Frobisher at the same time as Lowery. He was seen by Shanahan flying out over the pack ice in a VTOL towards the site of our crashed plane and in the general direction of the Russian Space Station. With a VTOL, he could land on the pack ice just as easily as with a helicopter. May I suggest that you clarify with the U.S. President just what is his position on the independence declaration of the coup leaders in Nunavut, and whether or not his Navy will be supporting the Nunavut Forces?"

"Good idea. I was about to call him anyway about our downed plane and our missing aircrew. While I make the call, please think about what we can do. I know that the only way to liberate Frobisher and other sites is by plane. What do we do next?"

The PM told his aide to get him the president of the United States on the red phone. He was about to return to talk to his two guests when the red phone rang.

"Good evening, President Reese, how are you?" He waited and listened to the response, then added, "I should mention that I am sharing this call with my Minister of Defense and the Chief of the Defense Staff. They are both anxious to hear your opinions on this matter." There was a brief pause before Le Chance continued.

"It is indeed a coincidence that I'm calling you at the very moment that you were trying to get hold of me. No, you go first. I can wait." He listened intently as a vein throbbed on the left side of his temple.

"Is it possible that one of your subs may have shot down one of my military planes? How could that happen?"

"I have been told that the event did happen and it was an accident. The commander of a sub, the Sea Devil, has reported that a new crew member panicked and fired the missile without orders. That man is now in custody."

"With respect, Mr. President, I have to ask, do you believe this captain of the Sea Devil, that the incident was an accident? Am I to believe that someone panicked?"

He waited for the President to respond. The throbbing in his head increased a hundredfold, but continued despite the headache.

"Yes, I suppose it is possible, and I believe you intend to have a full investigation. You say there is some good news amidst this fiasco?"

"Yes, I believe that there is a bit of good news. We have your aircrew! They are safe aboard our sub, and their injuries are being treated. I speak on behalf of the entire U.S. nation in saying that we are incredibly sorry for this rare accident. We love Canada and are happy that you have been our friend and neighbor for over a hundred years. We sincerely regret the loss of your airplane, and we are looking after the aircrew to the very best of our abilities. You will be compensated for your plane and the injuries to your men, and I will personally apologize to Canadians."

"Well, all things considered, that is good news that eleven of our crew are safe aboard your sub and being taken care of. Tell me, why was your sub in our waters?" Again, the vein throbbed as he listened.

"As with most militaries, there are rogue sailors, airmen, and soldiers. I have such a rogue in my Navy, and unfortunately, he is a very senior officer. He took it upon himself to sabotage MIR and tried to steal all the secrets and equipment that it contained. We are attempting to court-martial him."

"You and I disagree about the Northwest Passage as an international sea route. And you are not sure, but you think that the sub was there because it may have something to do with the Russian MIR Space Station landing in the Canadian Arctic. Again, I know that you intend to investigate that possibility. Tell me, President Reese, do you know the whereabouts of Admiral Heiserman, your Chief of Naval Operations?" The PM held the receiver away from his ear as the President's volume increased.

"You know about Admiral Heiserman? He is the Admiral that we are trying to arrest. You would not believe what he has been doing to make himself rich and powerful. He deserves to be executed! He is a disgrace to our Navy and to my country. Excuse me, but this infuriates me."

"I can tell that you are not sure of Heiserman's whereabouts. I'll tell you what I know about Admiral Heiserman. He was in the vicinity of Frobisher Bay earlier today when a certain Willie Nageak and a former Canadian Forces Admiral killed ten members of the Nunavut government and declared themselves the government of an independent nation. Did your Admiral have anything to do with this slaughter of politicians and town folk? Did he supply arms and money to our rogue Admiral?"

"This is the first I've heard about his political activities, except for the fact that he wants to replace me as president. I didn't know about his involvement in Canadian politics."

"We were under the impression that your aides would keep you informed on neighborhood politics, especially those that fill the airwaves. The aides should have brought to your attention the evident U.S. Naval officer in an independent Nunavut supporter's movement. Heiserman indicated that this freedom movement has the support of the U.S. Navy. Did you hear that they had the help of the U.S. Navy? Is this true?"

"I think I mentioned that the Admiral is under arrest and will be court-martialed. Among the other crimes committed, he raided our surplus equipment department. He took advantage of some loopholes that are now being eliminated and gave the assets to your Admiral Lowery."

The President once again declared his full support for a united Canada and pleaded for the PM to believe that his government didn't supply arms to renegade armies. Le Chance spoke again into the receiver.

"While I believe that you fully support a united Canada, and the U.S. government did not officially provide any of the Nunavut forces resources, many Canadians may also want to know why part of your Navy is heading to our eastern Arctic?"

The President could be heard talking to someone else in his office.

Le Chance listened then laid aside the receiver. He waited for a few moments and put the receiver back to his ear, only to pull it away again. The Minister and the CDS assumed that he was waiting for the President to get back on the line after getting advice from others in the Oval Office when they heard Reese's voice.

"That military exercise has just been canceled. All ships have been ordered back to their ports. Now that Heiserman has been stripped of his rank, he can no longer arrange for any NATO exercises."

"Admiral Heiserman was involved in providing these military assets to our ex-admiral Lowery. Your Heiserman ordered your Navy to have an exercise in our territorial waters. You say these exercises are now canceled. This Admiral Heiserman sounds as dangerous and out of control as our Admiral Lowery."

"You are one hundred percent accurate. Most militaries have rogue men. This rogue man is particularly difficult since he is a senior officer, and their activities generally go unchecked."

"So, I have your word that your government did not supply any equipment officially to Admiral Lowery. Further, you will investigate how one of your Admirals could write off millions of valuable government military assets. You will find out how this Admiral managed to smuggle tons of assets into Canada. I'll take you at your word that your government is not backing this revolt in the Nunavut Legislature. Getting back to your announcement about downing our plane, I will expect to receive full compensation from your government, and for the pain and suffering that your sub caused my aircrew and their families."

"Absolutely. What are you going to do about this revolt in Nunavut?"

"To bring this independence matter to a close, my cabinet and I are discussing it at this time. I heard one of your crew who is with you ask about the whereabouts of Heiserman. As far as we know, he is on route out over the pack ice in the direction of our plane and MIR. You are also going to investigate the possibility that Heiserman had the sub waiting for MIR for some reason? By the way, President Gazenko suspects sabotage to MIR since his Space Agency did not deliberately crash land the spacecraft. In fact, they couldn't control it's decent. Would you know anything about that matter, or would you rather not tell me?" He listened for several minutes before speaking again.

"Will you be speaking with the Russian President? If so, please tell him that we had nothing to do with the sabotage of MIR, although it is possible that Admiral Heiserman, of your Navy, may have played a part in its disappearance."

"Yes, I plan to talk to Dmitri Gazenko in the next thirty minutes. I will do as you ask and tell him that your government had nothing officially to do with the descent of MIR, and that you will call him as soon as you learn more about Heiserman's past activities."

"Excuse me, Mr. President, but before I go, I need to know where and when my aircrew will be returned."

"I will find out from my people and have one of them call you later today. It has been nice talking to you under these unfortunate and difficult circumstances. You have a good day, Mr. Prime Minister."

The PM waited until the last moment to get in one more word.

"I will be speaking to the press later today. I can't cover up the situation to the media, nor would I. I plan to l tell them just how our plane crashed on the pack ice due to the missile attack by one of your subs on our Nor Pat Aurora plane. I plan to tell them that you came forward and apologized for the downing of the plane. I will mention that your people think that it may have been caused by an act of panic by a sailor on one of your subs. I will also mention that you are initiating an investigation, and anyone responsible will be severely punished. You are planning on reimbursement to our government and our families for some Navy members. Regarding the U.S. Navy near the eastern arctic, I will tell the public that your exercises are canceled immediately. And, one further point, I will assure the public that the renegades in Nunavut do not have the support of the U.S. Navy in their illegal overthrow of a democratically elected government."

The PM rose from his desk and approached his guests.

"You can probably guess what most of the talk was about. The good news, of course, is that we now know our aircrew whereabouts and that they are all OK. I'll give you the details of where to pick up our men before you leave. Now let's see what we can do about this coup in Nunavut. Minister, any ideas?"

"Prime Minister, it seems to me that this situation is dissimilar to the recent separatist activities in Quebec. If there had been a clear separation question put to the population of Nunavut and the separatists won, then I would say that we would have to negotiate such a separation. But in this case, there has been no referendum. This case is closer to the seventies' separatists' actions where some terrorists from Quebec kidnapped and killed one of our politicians. In that case, you will recall Prime Minister Trudeau invoked the War Measures Act to establish Martial Law, and he sent the troops into Quebec to capture the criminals. It worked in that situation, and it should work in this situation as well."

"General Le Beau, what do you think?"

"I agree with the Minister of Defense, Prime Minister. The act should be invoked, and our military forces should be sent in. The only problem would be on how we get the troops to Nunavut and how we support them. The subs that you mentioned are not feasible since they are located on our west coast, and it would take a couple of weeks to get them into position. They could be used only against Lowery's ships and to a lesser extent, against his helicopters. They would be of no use against his land forces. You also mentioned that we could use aircraft to abort this coup, but Lowery will probably seal the airports so that fixed-wing aircraft can't be used. That leaves us with helicopters and aircraft on skis if we could find places for them to land."

"What about your Navy ships and their Sea King helicopters?"

"It would take them several days to reach the edge of the pack ice. Once there, some missions could be flown, at least as far as Frobisher Bay, using the Sea King helicopters to carry landing troops. We did modify them during the Gulf War to bring landing parties, and we mounted a 5.56 mm light machine gun in the cabin door and installed an infrared hammer and chaff dispenser to give them a self-defense capability. We did it once before and we can do it again."

"In regards to freeing the captured facilities of Alert and Eureka, that might prove more difficult," stated the CDS. "I can probably round up a brigade of paratroopers and some Hercules planes and make an airdrop on at least one of these establishments. That would surprise the Nunavut forces holding the facilities."

"Could the local population that supports Nunavut staying in Canada be counted on to establish a resistance force?"

"General Shanahan and I agree that most of the older Inuit want to stay with Canada, as do most of those born in the south. But half of the Nunavut population is below the age of twenty. We just don't know where they stand until we talk with our General in Frobisher Bay. It would seem that a lot of the lies told by Nageak would be believed by the young Nunavut people that want adventure and jobs. These are the same generation that has emotions for independence, and they would want to own all of the Nunavut resources. Both you and I know that it would be challenging for Nunavut people to become economically viable without the help of Canadian tax dollars for the next ten years. But these young people won't think of the hardship that it will cause to the older Inuit and the children while they fight. Still, I think it is possible to start a resistance movement with the Arctic Rangers as a starting point. It won't surprise me if the General that we have undercover has already started such a movement."

"Sir, it may be presumptuous of me, but could we not ask the Russian President for his troops' help, especially since some of them are already on route to the Arctic? If the Russians help us, under the command of my officers, I think that it would give the people of Nunavut and the populace of Canada more confidence. The Russians' help would cause the locals to doubt Lowery's and Nageak's statements. Together, the Russians, the resistance movement, our paratroopers and Sea King landing troops could free the police and the army people held at either Alert or Eureka and later the RCMP Detachments. They, in turn, can help us free up the rest of the province."

"That might just work, Minister Le Beau. President Gazenko would welcome the opportunity to be a peacekeeper, and he would be sympathetic to our cause since he is against any of his republics using rebels to fight for independence. Of course, he may want Canada to support him in his fight to keep these republics under the influence of his government. I have to call him as soon as we are finished, and I'll broach the subject with him. Imagine Canadians and Russians fighting together! That would be a first and one for the record book."

"You could remind the Russian leader that we had nothing to do with the MIR space station, and we are willing to help him retrieve it. I suggest that you mention to him that it was a U.S. sub that brought down our plane and it may have been waiting for MIR," added Le Beau.

"That's true. Now, if you will excuse me, I need to make some quick calls to the President of Russia and the U.S. President, followed by an emergency cabinet meeting to discuss the options that we just spoke of. Defense Minister, I'll see you at the meeting in one hour or so at my office in the center block. Here are the details about the whereabouts of our aircrew. Make sure that the crew gets home quickly and safely."

As the Minister and CDS left the PM's home, Le Chance was already speaking to his aide about calling an immediate cabinet meeting. He also asked the aide to get the President of Russia on the phone, and later the leader of the free world. He ordered that his car be brought around to the front door.

It was a short time after that his aide announced that the Russian President's call was now available on the secure phone.

"Dmitri, it is Rene Le Chance again. There are a couple of things that I have to tell you. Then I have to ask you a big flavor before rushing off to an urgent cabinet meeting." He stopped, took a deep breath, then replied, "yes, we need to talk about the Arctic situation. My cabinet meeting is in regards to it. You've probably been briefed on the coup in Nunavut and about the speech by the self-proclaimed premier, named Willie Nageak. We know that he has lied, and that your troops are not invading our north. I need to convince Canadians, especially those in the north, of your good intentions, and I need to convince them that this Mr. Nageak is a liar. First, you need to know that the rogue Canadian admiral, that I told you about earlier, has already launched four fully armed Apache helicopters in the direction of your troops on route to MIR. Yes, I'll hold."

The PM could hear Gazenko bark out some orders to others in the room with him. He waited until it was silent and continued.

"OK, Dmitri, I also need to tell you that the president of the United States and I were talking, and he mentioned that one of his subs accidentally shot down our plane. Our crew was picked up by them and is safe aboard their sub." The PM paused upon interruption, then continued.

"Thank you for your concern over my aircrew. But it is essential to mention, and the U.S. President asked me to tell you, that the American sub may have been positioned by a malcontent admiral, waiting in the area for MIR to land. This admiral wants the data and equipment onboard MIR. President Reese is undertaking an immediate investigation to see if this same U.S. Navy Admiral may have been involved, without the backing of his government, in the sabotage of your space station. The President will call you as soon as he knows more about the Admiral's activities.

"You know that you have my support to find out what happened to MIR. I have agreed to your request to retrieve the remains and also help you with that objective. Now, I need to ask for your assistance. You know that I have this problem in our northern province with many rebels who have taken over the elected legislature and killed some of the politicians there. They have even declared a sort of independence. My Minister of Defense and Chief of the Defense Staff wondered if your troops who are on their way to the area could eradicate the rebels, after the MIR situation is finalized. This is not a formal request at this time. I just want to know if you can help, and if your troops are available to act under the orders of my officers."

"Will you help me out in the future if I have problems with rebellious residents?"

"Yes, Dmitri, I will support you should you have any rebels, as long as there is no bombing of innocent civilians. And I can assure you that we are not mistreating our aboriginal residents of the north. This rebellion results from a misguided former Canadian admiral that now wants to destroy your helicopters by acting on his own. I will speak to my cabinet about your offer to help and contact you shortly. I would appreciate it if you would mention to the commander of your MIR retrieval team that we may need his help, and that you have agreed to provide it. Thank you again. You can expect a call from the U.S. President regarding MIR."

# 30 RESISTANCE

28 December 0500 hrs local, Frobisher Bay, Nunavut

Dave Shanahan got out of bed early. He wanted to leave the Navigator Inn before it got busy with prowling waiters, sleepy guests, watchful troops, and other workers from the town. They often stopped at the hotel cafe for a coffee before reporting to work. By leaving early, he could avoid people that might be looking for him. He figured that he would have a better chance of getting out unhindered.

As he showered and shaved, he watched the local TV station, which was broadcasting again, the speech made by Nageak. It was followed by photos that were supposed to be examples confirming Nageak's statements. When Nageak's words referred to Canada's lack of concern about Nunavut's environment, photos were displayed of a Manhattan oil tanker traversing the Northwest Passage without Canadian authority. The photos were followed by a scene of men and women carrying placards.

"Free Nunavut! Long Live Nunavut!" shouted the placard holders.

A photo of Nageak and Lowery shaking hands appeared next, and Shanahan wondered if Willie was congratulating Lowery on his appointment as Commander of Defense Forces of Nunavut, or if Lowery was congratulating Nageak on becoming Premier. More likely, thought the General, that Lowery was praising Willie for correctly reading a speech written by the former admiral. The TV screen shifted to a scenario with Nageak's words about Inuit teenagers using alcohol and drugs, followed by images of Inuit teens under arrest by RCMP, and another shot of two teens from Pond Inlet who overdosed and died. The obvious message was that Canada caused this tragedy. It was the start of the propaganda war to sell the idea of independence to the residents of Nunavut.

As Shanahan was dressing, the phone rang, which was surprising since he thought that the line would be cut by this time. Only the CDS knew that he was at this number. He would have to be careful of what he said since the line was probably monitored.

"Hello, this is Mitchell."

"It's your Chief from the Canal Building. How is the weather up there? I have some news from our neighbors to the south. It seems that they were kind enough to pick up our flying friends after killing our lone bird. They have them in a can in the deep freeze near your man on the island. They are not involved with the pest movement in your area. Our other neighbors to the far north are willing to help locate the can and sort out the pests. Let our man in the deep freeze know about the help. Also, try and get local seal hunters and red caps to help you exterminate the unwelcome pests. You can count on the acts of the prime Montreal philosopher to help eradicate the pests. Understand?"

"One hundred percent."

Shanahan opened his laptop and prepared a coded email to Major Phillips. It indicated that the Americans had the aircrew on board an American sub somewhere in his vicinity. The written message also mentioned that the Americans were not officially involved in any way with the Frobisher coup. The Russians were prepared to help him find the American sub. They would help the Canadians defeat Lowery's military men and equipment at locations near him such as Eureka and Alert.

Shanahan waited for the computer to indicate that the message was sent. He then deleted the email from the memory chip along with all other messages that could betray his identity. He closed the laptop and placed it upside down under a blanket in the hotel room closet.

He finished dressing in worn coveralls that would give the impression he was a hard-working laborer. Leaving the room, he took the stairs to the basement and walked out to his car. Using only his parking lights, he headed south out of the town on a gravel road. It was rough driving, but at least the snow had been cleared. The plow had made one pass down the road, leaving both sides banked with snow ridges.

About a kilometer out of town, he rounded a curve, and a roadblock suddenly appeared ahead of him. There was nowhere to turn or to leave the road. He had no choice but to keep going towards it. Shanahan put his right hand into his pocket and gripped the gun as the car came to a stop.

"What is your name and where are you going?" asked the lone armed guard. He wore a uniform with the Nunavut flag on each shoulder.

"Mitchell, and I'm going to the suburb of Nunavut."

"Any identification? Why are you going to Apex Hill so early in the morning?"

"My elderly aunt needs her driveway cleared so she can go to church. I didn't want to lose my wallet while I was shoveling snow, so I left it at home."

"You know there is a curfew that closes this road from 7 PM to 7 AM."

"No, I didn't. Is it new? Do you want me to go back until seven o'clock?"

The guard became suspicious, raised the gun, and pointed it at Shanahan.

"Get out of the car! Right now! Get down on the ground, on your knees!"

The guard pointed the rifle through the lowered window and into the face of the General.

Shanahan reached for the door handle and gave a sharp, quick shove so that the door hit the rifleman in the midsection causing him to crunch to the road. He pulled out his pistol while quickly exiting the car. As he did, the guard fired his rifle. The bullet sped through the air and passed through Shanahan's coverall, splitting open the rear windshield.

Shanahan instantly fired a return shot, slaying the guard where he had fallen. He looked around and was alone in the break of day. Checking his clothing, he found no blood since the shot had passed through dress that was away from his body. He quickly dragged the dead guard into some trees that were twenty yards from the road and covered him with branches and snow, leaving his body to solidify in the minus twenty temperature. He then drove the guard's vehicle a kilometer down the road and abandoned it in the bushes.

Shanahan continued his drive to Apex and found the street where Simone Aokalik lived. He parked the away from his destination, near the old Hudson Bay Company building.

He walked slowly down the street, using a small flashlight to highlight the house numbers until he found the home belonging to the Inuit leader. Some dogs were howling in the neighborhood at a stranger in their midst. Fearing that they might wake the village residents, he decided that he better do something soon or return to the car. Throwing caution to the wind, he walked up to the door and rapped on it. For a while, there was no answer, and he thought there was no one home. His venture to Apex was not only a waste of time but nearly cost him his life. He tried one more time before he would leave. A light came on and someone approached the door.

"Yes, what do you want?"

"Are you Simone Aokalik?"

"Yes. Why?"

For Shanahan, it was time to take another risk. Was this man a friend of Canada, or would he betray him to Lowery?

"I believe that you have something to do with the Arctic Rangers. I'm Major General Shanahan of the Canadian Forces. I'm head of the Maritime Air Force and Acting Head of the East Coast Navy." He flashed his ID card. "I need your help in stopping the Nunavut independence movement."

The words that could cost him his life were now out in the open. He waited as the man at the door scrutinized him carefully. He held the ID card to his eyes and carefully looked at the General. For Simone, it was also a moment of truth. He could send the stranger away or accept him as the Major General. He didn't look like a general in his workman's clothes. Simone took a gamble and decided to risk his freedom. He looked up and down the street before replying.

"Come in, quickly please."

Shanahan entered the small home and followed the man to a back room. The Inuit lowered the blind and turned on a small lamp. He was a man in his fifties, but his face showed that the traditional ways of living in this cold land had been hard on him. His face was like leather, all wrinkled and dark. He held out his hand and a broad smile showed some missing teeth.

"Welcome to my home, General. How did you get here?"

"I came to Frobisher before the independence speech. The Chief of the Defense Staff sent me to arrest the former Admiral Lowery and bring him back to Ottawa to be court-martialed. Now I'm locked in Frobisher Bay, so I have been instructed by the CDS, General Le Beau, to try to start a resistance movement to see if this act of rebellion can be stopped."

"You can count on the Arctic Rangers. We are all loyal Canadians, as are most of the older Inuit people. The Inuit elders are slowly convincing the younger Inuit that if they want real freedom, they better vote to stay with Canada. But we are worried that the new government politicians and the new military leader will flood Nunavut with shiploads of people sympathetic to their agenda. These new residents would give Willie Nageak the result he wants in the referendum. I have talked with a number of the Rangers, and we want to do something, but we need more equipment and guns. We have only the Rangers' rifles. They won't be much good to us if the U.S. Navy gets involved."

"Ottawa is working on getting you more military equipment and help, but it may take a while. You don't have to worry about the U.S. Navy. Contrary to Mr. Nageak, it is not supporting their revolt. I have it from the PM. You have to let the residents of Frobisher know that the Russians did not invade Nunavut. They are simply after the contents of their spacecraft. It landed at Ellef Ringnes Island. Again, Nageak is spreading lies about the Russians invading your land. The Russians have offered to help put down the revolt, and we can call on them to help if needed. Have you got any ideas on how to bring this Lowery movement to an end?"

"We thought that if we could free our former politicians that they would convince other Inuit and the Southerners to attack these madmen."

"I saw the troops execute ten of your politicians and I know where they are holding the Premier."

"They killed them? They said that they are being held incommunicado."

"They don't want to upset the people. They are trying to buy their support and votes, and they are using propaganda to convince the people of Nunavut of their agenda."

"What do you suggest we do?"

"I have a man, along with some Air Force people, near Ellef Ringnes Island. As I mentioned, the Russians are also near there. I'm sure that my guy can get the Russians to help. At least together they can release the men at Eureka, followed by a raid on Station Alert. The two groups of Canadians and Russians can free up the military men held captive. Then, along with any RCMP officers in the areas, they can move on to smaller communities We can defeat Lowery's forces as we move through the province. We will need all of them, and troops from Ottawa, to free Iqaluit. I expect the Canadian Navy to get as close as they can into the pack ice, then use their Sea King helicopters to drop off more troops. Ottawa may even try an air assault using paratroopers on some outlying communities."

Shanahan had given considerable thought to how best to defeat Lowery. He mentioned some of his ideas to the Inuit leader.

"The former Admiral Lowery has at least a hundred troops here in Frobisher. We should forget about attacking his main force. Instead, we need to concentrate on smaller groups of his men. We can employ sniper fire at small troop gatherings. We also need to destroy his equipment, such as those helicopters and any ships that he has. Do you have any explosive substances?"

"Here in Frobisher Bay, there are about twenty companies using explosives to locate precious metals and our precious oil. I'm sure that we could liberate some of the stock from their warehouses."

"Then get what you can, and get some timers as well. Use them at the airport on the Apache helicopters. Can you get into the building where they store their armaments? Are there any roads where their trucks may pass? I know the Prime Minister will be invoking the War Measures Act, so blowing up of trucks and troops in defense of Canada will not be considered a crime. The road to Apex, among others, is blocked by Lowery's so-called forces. I was forced to kill an armed provocateur in self-defense just to get to you today. He will be reported as missing, and his troops may investigate this area, especially you! So be careful."

The Inuit leader looked at the man in workman's clothing and felt a greater confidence that they could make a difference together. The Major General didn't look like a killer, but Simone had a newfound respect for the fragile-looking white man from the south.

"You will have to use your snowmobiles," continued Shanahan, "to go cross country and get out on the ice. You will find Major Phillips with his search crew, the Russian crew, and a hovercraft. Use all of these assets to sink the hovercraft owned by the Lowery forces."

"I'll contact the other Rangers and some of my people that I know who can be trusted. We will start our activities later today."

"Be careful who you trust. If you need to contact me, I'm staying at the Navigator Inn, under the name of Mitchell. I'll make a point of having a coffee in their cafe twice a day. If you need me, come to the cafe, and I'll watch for you. We can meet at the back undetected. Now I better get going."

Simone opened the door and again checked the street for moseying neighbors. They might be tempted for a few lousy bucks to let Lowery know about the comings and goings at the home of Simone Aokalik. Shanahan slipped out and made his way back to the car.

The General was expecting trouble at the checkpoint, but was waved through by a guard, while two similarly dressed Nunavut soldiers were digging in the snow near some trees. The MAG Commander needed no further invitation. He increased his speed and drove quickly through the checkpoint. He was lucky this time. In twenty minutes, he was at the Inn and parking his car in its secluded spot.

After climbing the stairs to his room, he gave it the once over to see if anyone had been in it. There were no apparent clues that anyone had been there. He had taken precautions previously, such as leaving his Air Force uniform behind in Thule. It would have meant his imprisonment if it was found. He knew that he was extra careful, perhaps unnecessarily. Still, he didn't want to jeopardize the mission by overlooking something as simple as leaving his uniform sitting on a hanger in the closet. He had even taken all of his identification papers with him to Apex Hill and had hidden them in his car where they remained. He finally relaxed. There was no one here who knew who he was, so there was no reason for anyone to check on him. He did expect increased vigilance of the security forces now that they knew that one of their own had been slain.

He went to the closet to get his laptop to see if there were any emails. That's when he noticed that the laptop was under the blanket in an upright position. General Shanahan's room had been searched.

# 31  MIR DESTRUCTION

28 December 1600 hrs local, Ice Field Off Ellef Ringnes Island

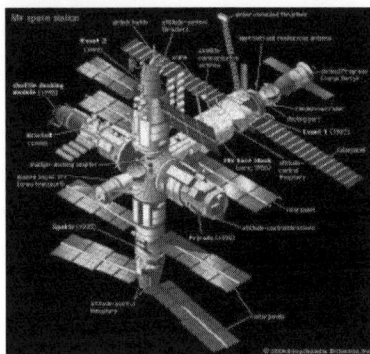

Lt. Cmdr. Murphy checked off the last of the computer's components as one of his men tied it securely on a sled that was travailing a snowmobile. He walked over to the remains of the MIR spacecraft and climbed up inside the core. There were loose wires everywhere. Some of the more sensitive MIR equipment had literally been ripped out of the sides of the craft, by his men, leaving gaping holes in wall panels and desks where consoles once resided.

The MIR craft now reminded him of some of the wrecked vehicles he used to see in his father's auto scrap yard business. Much like cars and trucks that had been cannibalized, the MIR was now just an empty hull. The lifeblood had been drained out of it, and the guts of the creature laid strewn on the ice. Any resemblance between it and a viable space vehicle was purely coincidental. If there was an auto crusher nearby, Murphy would have confined this shadow of a once-proud space vehicle to its death bed. MIR was now a candidate for the scrap heap since it was now no more than two tons of scrap metal. He no longer had any guilt about its destruction. In fact, it was more of a relief to Murphy to put MIR out of its misery since it was no longer a piece of wonderment. It was better that it didn't exist in this condition and that it not ever be seen again by other human eyes.

Before he commended the craft to oblivion, he looked around for a small souvenir for his emblem collection, to remind himself someday of his contact with this fabled outer space vehicle. On a small panel door, there was a crest resembling the coat of arms of the Russian Space Program. Some Russian astronauts had obviously glued the crest on the panel door while on a space mission. It was common practice in most militaries to leave a reminder of their visit in some part of the establishment that they visited. It told the regular inhabitants of the facility that it was visited by others from some competing squadron.

It seemed that the practice was also held among astronauts, thought Murphy. This particular crest was more than just a casual addition to his collection since the word MIR was part of the Russian inscription. With a quick twist of his wrist, he wrenched off the small panel door containing the crest and gently put it in the pocket of his white parka.

Removing crests from mirrors and other unusual places, like a panel door, was a technique that he learned from another sailor, who had a similar affliction for collecting mementos. Murphy couldn't wait to be back in his cabin to commence the work of lovingly removing the crest and mounting it on an oak panel with the 435-sqn coffee mug nearby. He could already see the crest holding a place of honor in his growing collection.

Murphy left the core module and ordered the attachment of explosive devices and timers to the outer shell. He instructed his men to attach the larger explosive devices to the part of the hull near the ice surface and in and around a three-foot trough that circled the craft. He visualized that the explosion would cause the four to five-foot thickness of ice to crack and swallow the remains of the sorry craft.

Once accomplished, Murphy moved his convoy of snowmobiles, men, and sleds a half-mile away from the space station. A thin wire led away from the derelict station to a plunger mounted on a black box at his feet. Like any true sailor about to witness the sinking of a ship, he said a small prayer and depressed the plunger.

The initial explosion caused the ice to shake beneath them, even though they were a half-mile away. It was followed by several other smaller blasts that made the ice buckle under his ski-doo.

At last, the explosive sounds receded and the light from the fiery remnants of MIR dimmed for the last time. He thought that he saw MIR stand upright like a proud soldier just before it sank into the ocean under the ice, but it may have been his imagination. Or it may have been his desire to give MIR one more bit of glory and hide it's damaged exterior before it became a part of the frozen north, permanently under the ice cap. MIR sank like a stone into the human-made ice hole and into the deep cold Arctic waters.

A depressed XO led his convoy back towards the ship. The landing crew of the Sea Devil had to be extra careful with its precious cargo to avoid any open leads or pass over crevasses. The booty on board the sleds had cost the crew days and days away from their families at this holiest time of year. Murphy didn't want to jeopardize the mission's success now that they were so close to being home free. The lights of the snowmobiles cut through the darkness like a razor through flesh. Murphy was in the lead ski-doo, and he kept a sharp lookout for the Sea Devil's outline. After forty-five minutes of traveling in the whirling snow, there was a brief period of clarity when he was startled to see an intense light in the distance. It was where he expected the Sea Devil to be located, but the profile was all wrong. Murphy continued to advance towards the light, but as he got closer, he realized that it was not the submarine. It was an airplane sitting on the ice, with its props rotating and its landing lights on. He could see that the aircraft pilot had used his retractable skis to land instead of using his wheels. The skis cushioned his landing and spread out the weight of the helicopter-like plane. Landing on the ice at any time, especially in near darkness, was an extremely hazardous operation. Murphy had read about a helicopter that had landed on a ridge. It immediately leaned on one side, causing the chopper to sway and eventually fall in the same direction until its rotors hit the ice and shattered in hundreds of pieces, killing everyone on board.

The only conclusion that the XO could reach was that the Vice-Admiral of Naval Operations had arrived early. Murphy had intended to get to the sub before Admiral Heiserman arrived. He had even made arrangements for some of the sub's crew to open and clear a landing pad for the Admiral's plane. It was no longer required since the VTOL had already landed on the ice. The question of where the Sea Devil was played on Murphy's mind.

As he drew closer, he could barely see through the snow that was thrown up by the props of the plane, a pile of supplies and accommodation equipment sitting on the ice. Standing next to it were two men in an animated conversation.

Murphy stopped all the snowmobiles with the wave of his arm. He got off the ski-doo and walked over to the men. One of them was the Admiral, and the other was Marsh, the operator of the SAM battery. The man with the missiles. Murphy wondered what other destructive weapons Marsh might have.

"Admiral Heiserman, I'm Lt. Cmdr. Murphy. We met when you made a surprise visit to the New Redford dockside the day before we left. I'm sorry that I wasn't here when you arrived."

"No problem. We arrived early. Battery Commander Marsh managed to set up some flares in an area that he thought would make a good landing spot. With the guidance of his lights, we were able to make a safe landing."

"But where is the Sea Devil?"

"No worry. Marsh told me that Captain Hayes was warned by his radar operator that there was another Canadian Aurora overhead searching the area. The operator also picked up the blips on his radar screen. It looks like helicopters are on the way, that he thinks belong to the Russians. If that wasn't enough of a problem, the sonar operator warned that there is a Russian sub in the vicinity as well. Commander Hayes thought it prudent that the submarine dive for a short period until it was safe, then come back to pick up you and your men. He left some supplies for you, including some tents to shelter you from the cold. He also left sufficient food for a couple of days, if they cannot return immediately. Could you tell your men to put the MIR items on board the Osprey? I would also like to get out of here as well before anyone else arrives."

"Of course, Admiral." Murphy told his men to load the items on board the plane.

"Should we stay here and wait for the sub or should we go with you?"

"No, No. You'll stay here. Hayes will be back, that I'm sure off. He needs you and your men to operate the sub on its return voyage under the ice. We should do what is good for the Sea Devil. If there is some reason that he can't make it, call me and I'll come running back for you with this plane. I told Commander Hayes that I would take Marsh back for discipline for firing that missile without permission."

Murphy had his men stow the MIR data system onboard the VTOL. He noticed that Heiserman talked very chummily with Marsh; it didn't look like disciplinary talk.

When the loading was complete, the Admiral and Marsh climbed on board the VTOL with its props still turning, causing snow and ice pellets to expand outward from the craft in all directions. Murphy handed the Admiral the checklist containing all the MIR items that were to be retrieved.

"All items on the list have been obtained and are now accounted for," said the XO. Admiral Heiserman asked Murphy to give his thanks to the men for a job well done.

"By the way, what happened to MIR after you finished with her?"

"The destruction is complete. We sunk the remainder of it."

"Good. Use your radio to contact the sub for pick up. Once we are gone, the Russian helicopters shouldn't find you, especially now that the Sea Devil has submerged. Now that MIR is no longer visible on their radar screens, neither you, nor MIR, nor the sub will be detected on or near the ice pack. Call me by radio in a few hours if the Sea Devil can't make it to the surface, and I'll send the plane."

Heiserman slammed the door of the aircraft. The props increased their velocity, and the VTOL craft shook off the friction holding it firmly to the ice. Ever so gradually it put an increasing distance between the ice surface and itself.

Murphy had to rush his men back to safeguard against the prop wash as the plane rose vertically, blowing snow in every direction. The men covered their faces with their balaclavas and with their hands to keep out the snow and the small pieces of ice that were being blown with force towards their faces.

The plane rose like a helicopter for two hundred feet. Then the props rotated to enable the VTOL to become a twin-turboprop. The Bell-Boeing aircraft started to accelerate forward, and at the same time it began to climb and turn towards the coast of Ellesmere Island. In moments it was lost in the darkness of the Arctic sky.

Lt. Cmdr. Murphy felt very alone with his men on the pack ice, several hundred kilometers from land and warm shelter. He had no alternative but to direct his men to construct the igloo-shaped tents so that they would have protection from the blowing winds while waiting for the return of the Sea Devil.

\* \* \*

Meanwhile, onboard the VTOL, Heiserman and Marsh grinned and started to laugh. The Admiral reached into a cooler that was near his seat and produced a bottle of wine. He pulled the cork and poured two full glasses.

"We pulled it off! This deserves a drink. Cheers." Battery Commander Marsh returned the toast of the Admiral.

"We've got it made now," said Heiserman. "In a couple of hours, we will have this equipment safe and sound in a hangar building that I set aside at Frobisher Airport. Once it's unloaded, I have a few specialists waiting to reconnect all of its parts and set it up in the mock MIR display built there. These technicians are true specialists. They are very proficient at this sort of thing. Once it's set up, just as it was in the original MIR, all of the equipment will operate just as it did aboard the spacecraft. I will have access to the millions of bites of invaluable information contained in its innards. We can run off all of the photos that the Chinese want.

"I didn't tell you earlier, but I have made a deal with the Chinese Ambassador to sell him all of the equipment and data for a hundred million dollars. Still, he wants proof beforehand of the type of data that is contained on those precious recorders."

The Admiral lovingly patted one of the recorders, followed by a wave to the video equipment sitting in the back of the plane.

"I promised him some photos of Russian troops in Mongolia. Once we show the photos to Ambassador Lee, we sit back and wait for the money to roll in. Another drink?" Again, the SAM Commander raised his glass in a toast as the Admiral continued.

"The best part of it is that very few people know that I had anything to do with the crash of MIR, and that I have MIR's instrumental guts of the storage system. The men on the ice know that I had something to do with MIR's destruction and so do the men on the Sea Devil. However, those men on the ice won't survive very long out there in the cold since I have no plans to pick them up. If they are lucky enough to get back aboard the Sea Devil again, then that explosive device that you stuck on board when you joined the crew should take care of all of them. I hope that you set it."

"Sure, I did. Don't worry about it. I've been setting detonators for twenty years; it's guaranteed to go off in forty-eight hours. I figure that they should be under the ice by that time and on their way to Frobisher with the Canadians. That tin can will sink to the bottom of the Arctic Ocean like a rock, and it will never be found."

"It was quick thinking on your part to take care of the Canadian airplane when it spotted the submarine. The missile did the trick. It has kept the world from knowing about our part in the forced crash of MIR. As a result, my image as a future presidential candidate is squeaky clean. But then again, that's why I put you on board the Sea Devil. You are going to be a big part of my campaign team as I take a shot at running for president."

# 32  THE RUSSIANS HAVE LANDED

27 December, 0505 hrs, Canada's Ice Island, Nunavut

Major Shawn Phillips saw the cursor on his laptop computer blinking with a message indicating he had mail. In a matter of seconds, the contents of the email spilled out onto the pure white computer screen.

It was from Shanahan in Frobisher Bay. And it was good news. The message said that his missing Canadian aircrew was now on board some American submarine. The email revealed that the same American sub was also responsible for the destruction of the plane in the first place. This whole mess didn't make much sense to Phillips. The message didn't provide any more info on the sub nor its whereabouts except that it could still be in the vicinity. Now it seemed that the team could even be considered to be a danger since American naval authorities had been unable to contact the sub. The email also said that he, as SAR Commander, could count on Russian cooperation to locate the sub and use their help with defeating Lowery's Nunavut Forces. These forces were causing havoc in their vicinity, and Eureka and Alert were indicated as being overtaken by Lowery supporters.

Shawn mentioned all of the good news to the other search and rescue technicians. Rob Mackenzie stopped pacing the mess hall floor long enough to state emphatically that he was now looking forward to the arrival of the Russians. Their landing would bring them one step closer to locating the American sub, and he was eagerly awaiting the return of his friends from Greenwood that were on board. His enthusiasm for the mission was returning.

The previous twelve hours had dragged by as Phillips and the SAR techs waited for the message from Shanahan. Nothing was happening, and they were bored. They had done all that they could do to find the missing crew. During their waiting period, the only incident of note occurred when Shawn and the techs heard a loud explosion followed by several smaller ones. The explosions shook the walls, and pots and pans rattled around the room.

"What in the hell was that?" wondered a tech, as he rushed to the door to determine the cause. The sounds appeared to be coming from the area over the horizon where they saw the fiery MIR zooming towards the ice. Once the loud noises ceased, shoulders were shrugged as they returned to the cozy boredom of the Mess Hall. They were unable and unwilling to travel to the area of the explosion when their primary goal was the recovery of their aircrew.

The techs were still monitoring the radio link with the Aurora circling overhead, piloted by Capt. Mari Leech. She reported to Shawn via the radio link that NORAD had informed her that the Russian planes had crossed over the North Pole and were technically now in Canadian airspace.

Phillips was restless, but could only sit and listen to the radio transmissions from the aircraft flying above. He had no way on his own of attacking an American submarine, should it surface again, other than ramming it with the hovercraft. But if this sub had the missing Canadian aircrew on board, it had to be protected until the missing crew was off the sub.

An hour later, Captain Leech made another transmission to the search crew. The static of the radio communication breaking the room's silence caused everyone present to turn towards the transmitter and listen intently. The transmission said that the Russians were now within Aurora's range for radio communication. Captain Leech inquired if the Search Master had any questions or information for the approaching Russians. Shawn took the microphone.

"Captain Leech, it's Shawn," these words were a bit informal, but after all, she was a potential girlfriend. "Please tell the Russians that they are welcome to use our spare buildings for living arrangements while they look for MIR. They can also use the hovercraft if needed. You might mention that during the past couple of hours we heard the sounds of explosions coming from the direction where MIR landed."

"Roger, Shawn," she also was a bit informal considering their individual military ranks. "I will pass on your offer. We didn't register any explosions on our equipment, but we may have been at the far end of our circle and too far away to detect them. By the way, we did see on our radar some of Admiral Lowery's helicopters during our flight to your location. They appeared to be heading for Eureka."

"Thanks for the information. If the Apache helicopters head our way, we would appreciate it if you notify us."

"Will do. Out."

Colonel Viktor Padalka, head of the Russian chopper fleet, was pleased that he was finally approaching his mission's target. The KA-32 Helix helicopters seemed to take forever to get to this point. While it had flown at 168 mph, its range of 248 nautical miles meant that he had to stop twice at remote Soviet Islands for additional fuel. At Dirksen, he had loaded each of the four helicopters with sixteen commandos, which he assured himself would be adequate to guard MIR and retrieve all of the important equipment. He was provided with a list of equipment by his commander, courtesy of Mission Control in Moscow.

Viktor was anticipating no trouble at all from the Canadian authorities since he had been told that they were cooperating with the Russian government. However, he had been forewarned just before departure that there was a rogue Canadian admiral with some fast, well-armed helicopters, who might cause him some problems.

The helicopters of this insubordinate officer had crossed over the North Pole and were now on the Arctic Circle's Canadian side. Their faster rate of speed should put them near the point of impact of MIR in twenty minutes. The rogue admiral's choppers were not looking for MIR but looking to destroy Russian choppers. Padalka's choppers. The pilot of the Colonel's helicopter motioned to him by hand signal to put on his headset. Through the earphones, Viktor heard the pilot of a Canadian patrol plane asking to speak to the commando unit leader. The pilot pointed out to the Colonel which buttons to push and where to speak into the mouthpiece if he was to be heard by the Canadian pilot.

"This is Colonel Padalka, head of the MIR retrieval team. What is it that you want?"

The question startled Mari. It almost sounded as if the Russians expected to enter Canadian airspace and not be challenged in any way. She decided to speak authoritatively, but to indicate that the Canadians were prepared to cooperate with the Russian soldiers.

"This is Captain Leech, Pilot of the Canadian Aurora. We picked you up on our radar screens as you entered Canadian airspace. You are authorized to proceed to the site of your mission. I know that you are here to retrieve MIR, and I know that our government is cooperating with yours. Is there anything that you need at this time?"

The Colonel was surprised to hear a woman's voice and was surprised at her authoritative tone, but was pleased with her offer of assistance. In Russia, there were very few female pilots, and he had never heard of one who became the captain of such a large surveillance aircraft. He tried not to let his surprise show in his voice.

"If you have the exact location where MIR impacted, it would be appreciated."

"I will provide the information to your pilot. Anything else?"

"I don't think so."

"We saw some Apache helicopters heading North, in the direction of a Canadian weather station at Eureka on Ellesmere Island. They are most likely the Apache helicopters that you have been forewarned about by your military authorities. My government's alerted your president about these helicopters.

"You should also be informed that there are Canadian military search and rescue technicians on an ice island near the MIR impact point. The Search Master is Major Phillips. They are there looking for the crew of another Aurora that crashed on the island very recently. The Search Master is offering you and your men accommodation on the island. If your troops find that it is too cold living on the ice, you could use several of the vacant prefabricated buildings on the island. Major Phillips also has an operational hovercraft that you can use to ferry your men to the MIR site if you so desire it."

"I heard about your Aurora being shot down by a submarine, and I can assure you that it was not a Russian sub. I'm sorry to hear about your missing aircrew. I don't think that I will take Major Phillips' offer at this time."

"Suit yourself. Major Phillips mentioned that he heard explosions coming from the MIR site several hours ago, and he thought that you should be forewarned in case there may be additional explosions. We will stand by in case you need us. Out."

Colonel Padalka's pilot received the specific longitude and latitude degrees for MIR before he terminated the conversation.

Fifteen minutes later, Padalka's pilot turned on the searchlights and put the helicopter into a slight dive to creep closer to the ice surface. The other helicopters followed. The pilot of the lead craft skimmed the area where MIR was supposed to have crashed, but he could not detect its presence from the air. That was odd since it was hard to overlook a two-ton space station over twenty feet tall. He circled the spot several times and still saw nothing.

"Colonel, this is the location that we were given, but there is nothing here. Could the location be wrong?"

"Possibly. Expand your circle and look again."

The pilot did as he was told but still had no success in locating MIR.

"Tell the other choppers to maintain their position, but I want you to set this one down near the spot where MIR is supposed to be according to the Canadian lady," instructed Padalka.

The pilot complied and gently brought the helicopter down using his searchlights. He was an experienced pilot, but he always hated landing a helicopter on the ice, especially in the Arctic darkness. He was well aware of the dangers of tipping to one side and about the possibility of one skid breaking through the ice while the other held. He was prepared to reverse direction if he felt the slightest straining of the craft or if he felt the ice give way. He prayed as he gently brought the craft down. He felt the skid touch the ice, and the body of the helicopter lowered itself ever so smoothly. They were down, and there was no danger of the plane tipping over or going through the ice. He kept the blades rotating as the Colonel slid open the door and stepped out on to the ice.

The cold wind and drifting snow from the wash of the blades flew into the cabin. One of the commandos quickly closed the door to keep out the chill. The soldiers and pilot watched as Colonel Padalka switched on his flashlight and stepped away from the plane. He walked off and was soon lost to the pilot in the dark. Ten minutes passed. Without warning, the door of the craft slid open, and the Colonel stepped inside the chopper and slammed the door shut.

"What is happening, Colonel?" asked a lieutenant in charge of one of the commando squads.

"MIR was here. Now she is gone. There is a lot of debris from the spacecraft spread over a wide area. The Canadian lady mentioned that the Search Master heard explosions. I think someone, maybe even the Canadians, blew up MIR. There is a large body of water with a thin sheet of ice where MIR must have sunk. There is evidence that there were a large number of people here with snowmobiles and sleds, so they must have removed some of the equipment from MIR before destroying it. We need to follow the sled tracks, but we can't do it from helicopters. We'll have to trust that the Canadians didn't destroy MIR, but tell your men to be on guard just in case. We'll take the Search Master up on his offer to use his hovercraft."

Padalka signaled the pilot to take off and contact the Canadian surveillance plane to get more directions to the encampment of Major Phillips.

The four Kamov 32 Helix helicopters turned in close formation and flew to the ice island. Captain Leech had passed the message to Shawn that the Russians were now prepared to accept his accommodation offer and were on route to the island. Instructions were given by Shawn to his men to prepare a landing site for the four Russian helicopters. The flares ignited by Major Phillips's techs lit up the sky. Padalka's pilot told the pilots of the other helicopters that they would land one at a time. Padalka's lead commando would direct them to land once the Colonel had spoken to the Search Master.

# 33 GLOBAL WARMING

28 December 2000 hours local, on route to Eureka

Heiserman had promised Admiral Lowery several weeks ago that he would visit his brother, Brian Lowery, at the Eureka Weather Station. It occurred to him that the VTOL would pass very near to Eureka on route back to Frobisher. The Admiral thought that this might be a good time to make a visit, especially since the MIR instruments were safely stored in the cargo area of the aircraft. It was not out of friendship alone that the Admiral decided to go out of his way to visit Lowery's brother. He had another motive. He was curious as to why Lowery would wreck his career over a dispute with Defense Headquarters regarding the extra equipment and extra personnel he wanted for Northern Canada's defense. Heiserman was acquainted with the fact, and he assumed that Lowery was as well, that the defense budget for Canada was expected to grow in the next few years. This was possible now that the Canadian government had slain the deficit dragon. The Canadian PM was expecting a budget surplus of over a hundred billion dollars in the next few years. Surely, thought Heiserman, that Admiral Lowery was smart enough to know that he would get the people and equipment that he wanted so desperately for the north if he only would wait for a few years. So why would Lowery blow his career at this time?

The question had been bugging him since Lowery had told the CDS and Minister of Defense to piss off. Heiserman was aware that his talk with Lowery probably was the catalyst that provoked him in staging the coup. But the question remained in Heiserman's mind.

Lowery was not a fool. Something new made him vulnerable to Heiserman's challenge to burn down the political process in Nunavut. He vowed to find the cause.

Heiserman already knew about the millions of dollars of funds that the Canadian government had deposited in a Frobisher Bay bank. This was founded to help the new government of Nunavut with its transition costs from a dependent territory to an independent province. Lowery could get his hands on that money, so that could be part of the reason for giving up his career. Lowery would have a hell of a time trying to spend that much money in the Arctic circle. He would be thrown in jail the moment he left Frobisher.

Heiserman also knew that Lowery now considered himself as a four-star admiral, but of what? A small force of men and equipment, when he used to be the chief, the commander of thousands of men and a hundred ships that were part of Maritime Command. This military force of his would not give him the honor that Lowery thought he deserved. Heiserman expected Lowery to be bored soon with his newfound command. He also knew that Lowery expected to run the new government of Nunavut using the new premier as a shield, a front man for him.

It was doubtful if the residents of Nunavut would tolerate that situation for very long. Lowery would have a civil war on his hands the moment some Inuit leader found out that a Southerner was running their government.

Heiserman was convinced that there was another major factor driving Lowery. There was something that he didn't know about his comrade in arms. Perhaps Lowery's brother would divulge some family secrets, especially if he could be plied with a few drinks. Heiserman was not a man to leave anything to chance. He wanted to know everything that he could about his old buddy, Buzz. He believed that it always paid to have an ace up his sleeve in case he needed it.

Admiral Heiserman ordered the pilot of the VTOL to divert to the Eureka Weather Station on Ellesmere Island.

The Eureka Weather Station was less than 250 kilometers from the Magnetic North Pole and just over an hour flying time. The VTOL had already been flying for forty-five minutes. Heiserman concluded that they would be there shortly.

In less than an hour, the pilot announced that they were approaching Eureka on the Fosheim Peninsula on Ellesmere Island's west coast.

Eureka was very near the 80th parallel. To be precise, the Eureka airfield was actually at 79 degrees, 59'41'N and 85 degrees 48'48'W and the 80th parallel actually bisected the runway. The pilot traced the landing strip on the map for Heiserman and indicated that they were now in the weather station's glide path. Heiserman just wanted the pilot to get the craft on the ground quickly. He hoped that the site had decent sleeping facilities since it had been a long day and he still had to work on Brian Lowery's ego.

The pilot passed over and followed Eureka Sound to the peninsula, where the main weather station was located. Heiserman looked out the plane's window to see if he could spot some of the five prefabricated weather station buildings first erected over fifty years ago by a joint Canadian and American team. There wasn't much to see, since it was the dark season, and there was very little moonlight. Once in a while, he would catch a glimpse of some of the dimly lit buildings on the site. As the plane passed over weather station buildings, he saw a number of radio dishes and radar towers.

As the aircraft continued its circle, he could see in the distance, on the peak of the Sawtooth Mountain Range, a newer building. It was at the 600-meter level, the unique world-class ASTRO observatory, built in the early nineties to study global warming and to measure ozone depletion as well as carry out a range of other scientific activities. The lights surrounding the ASTRO building that shone on the red structure made it stand out against the dark Arctic sky.

The pilot again approached the 5000-foot gravel runway from the north, while he flipped the switches to retract the skis and select the wheels down position. He called the station's call sign and soon received an answer.

"Eureka, this is a United States Navy turboprop requesting landing instructions," said the pilot.

"United States turboprop, the runway is temporarily closed. Snow blowing machines currently occupy the runway. Do not attempt to land."

"We can rotate the propellers and make a vertical landing away from the snow plows," suggested the pilot to Heiserman.

"They probably staged the vehicles on the runway to prevent any Canadian military planes from landing and capturing the mercenaries who overran the station when Lowery took over the government in Frobisher Bay. They may think that this is a Canadian Forces plane masquerading as a U.S. Navy craft. If we try to make a vertical landing without their permission, they may ram the plane with the plows. There has to be a better way. Let me talk to them. Maybe I can convince them that we are friendly." The pilot passed the headset and mike over to the senior officer.

"This is Admiral Heiserman, U.S. Navy, a friend of Admiral Lowery, the Commander of Nunavut Forces. I need to land and speak to his brother, Brian Lowery, the Chief Officer of the Eureka Weather Station."

Heiserman, Marsh and the pilot waited for a few minutes while the men on the ground conferred among themselves.

"Admiral Heiserman, the vehicles are being moved off the runway, and you can land in five minutes."

"I thought that might do the trick. Now get this plane on the ground so I can get out and use the bathroom and stretch my legs."

The pilot of the VTOL circled the airfield one more time then brought his aircraft in. It continued to roll after touch down and followed a yellow pickup truck that led the plane to a long metal building being used as a terminal. The pilot shut down the props, the door of the craft was opened, and Heiserman walked briskly from the plane to the building.

The building was connected to the others by a pathway where the snow reached the six-foot level on both sides. Anyone who spent time in the north knew that to stray from the guided path, especially during whiteout conditions, could mean certain death. One could easily become disoriented and lost just a few feet from well-lit buildings.

Heiserman continued along the well-worn path, passing the Post Office building. He couldn't help but notice that the Canadian flag lay on the snow, rolled up in a ball, while the Nunavut flag flew on the pole. He continued along the path, passing a number of men dressed in fatigues, with pistols on their hips and the Nunavut flag sewn onto the shoulders of their jackets.

The men were drunk and either didn't know about an admiral's presence in their midst or didn't care. They were too busy celebrating the overthrow of the provincial government and the independence of Nunavut.

Heiserman noticed that security was lax at the facility, something neither he nor Lowery would have tolerated in any establishment under their command. It was evident that Brian Lowery was not a military conscious man like his brother.

After some searching, Heiserman eventually found a duty officer, who also appeared to be half in the bag. The officer produced the room register, assigned Heiserman a room, and told him that the Chief Officer, Brian Lowery, was currently busy with weather station affairs. Heiserman could take a break and freshen up while waiting for Lowery, who would meet him at the bar shortly. The Admiral found his room in an adjoining complex.

Meanwhile, the pilot of the VTOL visited the Ops room, looking for anyone who would arrange to top up the fuel in his plane.

While the pilot was away, Brian Lowery went to the aircraft. He wanted to learn more about Admiral Heiserman and his visit. He didn't believe Heiserman was visiting the area and decided to visit the brother of an old friend.

While Brian was also celebrating the independence of Nunavut, he was still sober enough to think and walk straight. He climbed the VTOL stairs and entered the aircraft, walking down the length of the fuselage to the cargo storage area. He was looking for briefcases or luggage that he could rifle through for clues to provide information about Heiserman. His eyes widened as he glanced at the boxes of instruments and recorders piled high and labeled with Russian inscriptions. He could easily interpret the word, MIR, that was etched on several parts. The parts obviously belonged to some major data storage and processing system that had been a part of the MIR Space Station.

Brian picked up an instrument panel, labeled as the master control, and tucked it under his arm. He then made a hasty exit of the plane so as not to be seen by the pilot. He, too, believed in having an ace up his sleeve when dealing with enemies and friends. It upset him that he found no papers or documents to help him in his quest, but he was pleased with the MIR instrument that he pilfered from Heiserman's aircraft.

He stored the master control panel in his bedroom and walked towards the bar, passing several other rooms where his men stopped him long enough for a celebratory drink. He eventually arrived at the bar, where he waited for Heiserman.

In the meantime, Heiserman wondered about his room in the Weather Station quarters. He found the room to be somewhat lavish given that it was located near the Arctic Circle. The room even had a small fridge containing tiny bottles of whiskey and scotch. He immediately poured one of the bottles into a glass and mixed in some cola. The drink was Heiserman's method of celebrating his good fortune in having obtained the MIR equipment that would bring him a hundred million dollars.

On the dresser was a sample menu for the dining room. It indicated that beef, vegetables, salads, and five different pastries were available for the evening meal. Using the phone to connect him with the operator and kitchen, Heiserman requested that a meal be delivered later to his room, before he retired for the night. Satisfied that he could be comfortable in these surroundings, he left the room to meet Brian Lowery. He made a brief stop at the gift shop, which also served as a liquor outlet, to pick up a large bottle of rum. He believed in being prepared for all eventualities. He would break it open if Brian joined him in his room for a late meal and a drink.

At the bar, they greeted one another like old war buddies and ordered their drinks. They exchanged pleasantries and wished one another the best with the new country of Nunavut.

Brian wore a neatly pressed army fatigue uniform with the Nunavut flag sewn on to the shoulders. He reminded Heiserman of Fidel Castro in his youth. Heiserman couldn't help but compare Brian to his brother. Both were tall, well over six feet, both were muscular, and both had blonde hair, but Buzz's hair was beginning to bald. Brian had a sizeable blonde mustache that he kept neatly trimmed while his brother had no facial hair.

Heiserman could tell that both of the brothers were intelligent, although he knew that Buzz was shrewd as well as smart. Buzz was cold and calculating and even vicious at times. Heiserman didn't see the same features in Brian. The younger brother seemed to have a sense of humor that was missing in his sibling. Otherwise, they were almost identical twins. It was equally evident that Brian idolized Buzz.

At first, the conversation between Brian Lowery and Admiral Heiserman cantered on how and where the Admiral had first met Buzz. They spoke of different episodes in the relationships between the two Admirals since they first met, and the drinks continued to flow for more than two hours. Then it turned to more current matters.

"So, tell me, Admiral, what are you doing up in this neck of the woods?"

"Well, I promised your brother that I would contact you in December or early January and fill you in on events."

"I was expecting you in late December. Did Buzz give you a package for me?"

"I believe he told me that he was going to have it airdropped to you around Christmas, from an Aurora. You probably know that the plane crashed up near Ellef Ringnes Island. Was the package important?"

"Yes, it was. It contained a sum of money that I was to use to pay my men who helped me preserve this establishment as part of the new government of Nunavut. Most of these men are mercenaries, and they have no allegiance to any government. They will only stay loyal as long as there is money in it for them. I knew about the package being lost in the airplane crash since Buzz told me about it on the phone a couple of days ago. Still, he said he would try to get a second package for me and since you left Frobisher today, I thought that perhaps you brought a replacement package."

"No, he didn't give a package to me, but then again he didn't know that I was going to stop in Eureka."

"What's happening these days at Frobisher Bay? I haven't heard much since the overthrow of that traitorous government."

"Buzz and the new Premier seem to have everything under control. There are still some fires burning, but generally, everything is restful. So far, there's no indication that the Canadian government will attempt to return the previous government to power by bringing in troops. The federal government may decide to let the residents of Nunavut have their say in a referendum as they did in Quebec. Buzz is working on having the governments of other nations recognize his new government. So far, only Cuba has offered recognition."

"On the first day of the new year, in a new millennium... a fresh start if you will, he is having a huge party to celebrate the opening of the new government of Nunavut. He could have used that lost money to grease the skids in this area to get some of the locals to vote for independence in the referendum, and then throw a much bigger party than the one we are having at the moment. I hope that Buzz does replace it soon. Will the U.S. Navy help us out if the Canadian government does send in troops?

"Absolutely. The last thing I did before I left Washington was order the Navy to have war games near the coast of Baffin Island. That would put them nearby in case they are needed to prevent the Canadian forces from perverting the democratic will of the Nunavut people."

Heiserman believed in telling people what they wanted to hear since it generally made them more susceptible to his way of thinking in the long run.

"Just what do you do at this station, Brian, and why is it important to Buzz?"

"We do several scientific studies, but the most important one to us concerns the ozone hole and global warming. Buzz is very interested in the environment in the Arctic."

"Global warming is a lot of hogwash and media hype as far as I'm concerned."

"On the contrary. Global warming is the trend for this new millennium. Why just last week, one of your submarines provided evidence that the polar ice is 40 percent thinner than it used to be. And Norwegian scientists using satellite data have declared that the polar ice sheet is shrinking twice as fast as previously thought. You start to get a lot of these unusual things, and they begin to add up. Most of us here believe there has been a significant change in our climate, but just what's causing it is another question. Most of the scientists and electronic technicians at this station hold the view that Earth's atmosphere is slowly being warmed as man-made gases such as carbon dioxide absorb heat that would otherwise escape into outer space. This is the so-called greenhouse effect."

Heiserman could see that Brian Lowery was passionate about this subject, and he knew that it had something to do with Admiral Lowery's long-range plans and goals for Nunavut. Brian continued with his opinion on global warming while the Admiral ordered more drinks.

"An international panel of climate scientists has predicted that if the warming trend continues, temperatures could rise by 2 degrees or more over the next century, causing more extreme weather that would produce flooding in some areas, drought in others, and forests and agricultural zones would shift with the changing temperatures while the Great Lakes of North America would see their water levels drop. There is no doubt that there has been a shift towards warmer temperatures. In fact, over the past ten years or so, there's been a systematic shift in the weather patterns over the Arctic Ocean. The circulation pattern, known as the Arctic oscillation, normally moves back and forth across the ocean, but it has lost some of its variability during the past decade. The shift in that pattern in one direction has caused Siberia and Canada, in winter, to warm quite drastically.

"We have evidence, such as ice core samples and ocean sediment, that shows that the nineties were the warmest years of the past millennium."

Admiral Heiserman let Brian speak since the booze made him more relaxed and more confident in what he was saying.

"Did you know that the amount of sea ice in Arctic waters is shrinking by about 22,500 square kilometers every year as a result of global warming caused by greenhouse gases that are derived from human activity? That amounts to three percent of total sea ice per decade. One group of Norwegian and Russian scientists reported that multi-year ice shrank by fourteen percent in the last twenty years. Can you imagine what will happen to Nunavut if this trend continues as we expect, since countries are unwilling to cooperate to reduce greenhouse gases? Buzz and I were talking about the possibilities just a few months ago. This frozen north could easily become the fruit belt of North America while the current belt would die from lack of water. The ice covering the Arctic islands would disappear. Four of those islands are among the largest in the world. For example, this one, Ellesmere, at 77,000 square miles, is the tenth largest. It would become a tourist destination, much like Florida is today.

"Did you know that trees that presently grow in the Florida everglades once grew on Alex Heiberg Island just next door to this island?" Brian Lowery didn't mention that those trees grew forty-five million years ago.

"Think about the possibilities for resource development. Millions of liters of oil, for example, could easily be discovered since the land is no longer ice-covered and it would be no problem to ship these resources around the world, since the Northwest Passage would be no longer icebound. This land has a huge reserve of undiscovered mineral wealth that would open up when the ice is gone. Buzz and I want to own a very large part of this territory, and we want to be ready to capitalize on climate change."

*There it is!* thought Heiserman. Buzz wanted thousands and thousands of acres of the Nunavut landscape. That's what was driving him. At last, this was what Heiserman was waiting to hear. He now knew why Admiral Lowery was prepared to gamble with his career and break all his ties with Ottawa. He dreamed of being a land baron and being wealthy from the minerals in the Arctic land.

It was not the sort of dream that Admiral Heiserman had for himself. He would leave the Lowery brothers to have their dreams, but he doubted if the ice would ever melt in this God-forsaken north country. He couldn't wait a century for his dreams to be fulfilled. He needed the money now to bring them about. The Admiral needed to get back to Frobisher Bay and sell the MIR components' data to the Chinese. He needed to shed money on those that would help in his presidential bid.

Heiserman said good night to Brian Lowery without asking him to join him for a late drink and meal in his quarters. At seven the next morning, he returned to Frobisher Bay.

He presented the unopened bottle of rum to the VTOL pilot for keeping the plane and its cargo secure during the stopover in Eureka. Unknown to him, his pilot had thrown a monkey wrench into his plans by leaving his cargo load unguarded.

Admiral Heiserman noticed the four Apache helicopters belonging to Lowery's forces, parked on an apron next to the runway. They had arrived during the night after refueling in Grise Fiord, where they had to wait for weather conditions to improve before continuing their journey to confront the Russians.

Brian Lowery had contacted his brother after the Admiral Heiserman had gone off to bed. He called Buzz on the radio to congratulate him on becoming the leader of the newest country and to tell him about Heiserman's surprise visit. He joyfully told Admiral Lowery how Heiserman had tried to pry information out of him, and how his little brother had outsmarted Heiserman by stealing an essential piece of MIR from the boxes of instruments found stored in the plane. Before ending the conversation, he reminded Buzz that he still needed the package of money. Brian Lowery went to bed basking in the glow of praise from his beloved brother.

# 34    SHORE TEAM

29 December, 0700 hrs local, near Canada's Ice Island

Shawn Phillips could hear the twin rotors of the four Russian helicopters outside the mess hall. The drone of the chopper blades drowned out all conversations in the hut.

"Our Russian friends are here," he shouted out, which seemed obvious as soon as it left his mouth. WO Mackenzie used sign language to point out two of the techs who knew what they had to do. They left the building to select a landing spot and to set up flares. Mackenzie followed and held two directional flares, one in each hand, as he encouraged the pilot of Colonel Padalka's helicopter to bring her down.

There was no danger of breaking through the ice island or hitting a pressure ridge in the area. A landing too fast could cause severe damage to the underbelly of the craft if it suddenly hit the ice with a thump. Mackenzie continued to lower the lit flares towards the ice surface to indicate to the pilot just how many feet or inches he had left before the skis touched down. The lead helicopter gently kissed the ice and settled down on its haunches.

While the rotors were still spinning, Colonel Padalka slid out the door, ducked his head to avoid being hit by the rotors, and crouched away from the plane. He ran towards the man holding the flares. He had to yell to be heard.

"I'm Colonel Padalka. My men will direct the landing of the other helicopters. Where is Major Phillips?"

WO Mackenzie didn't try to answer him since it was hopeless that the Russian would be able to hear him. Instead, he waved his hand to indicate that the Colonel should follow him. Together they walked the short distance to the Mess Hall building.

"Welcome Colonel, I'm Major Shawn Phillips. I have been told that we will be cooperating to help you find your MIR spacecraft while you will help me find my missing aircrew."

"Thank you, Major. I'm Colonel Padalka, head of the Alfa Commando Unit."

He spoke in near-perfect English, as he should since he had been educated at one of the best universities in the United States before returning to the Soviet Union to complete his compulsory military training. That was fifteen years ago. He didn't know at the time that the military would become his chosen career.

"If possible, I could use someplace for my men to sleep and to stow their equipment. We also could use a place to plug in the APU. It will help start our helicopters when we need them."

Major Phillips directed WO Mackenzie to show the Colonel to the cookhouse where his men could be accommodated. Mackenzie showed him to the building where they stored the APU that was used to start the hovercraft and returned alone a short time later. Rob advised Shawn that the Colonel wanted to have the hovercraft ready in fifteen minutes to proceed to the MIR crash site. Sixteen of the sixty-four commandos would accompany them on the journey.

With the help of Mackenzie and the APU, Shawn was able to get the hovercraft started and left it running to warm it up for the Colonel's men. The turbo-powered fan forced air into the chamber beneath the craft and captured it under a four-foot flexible skirt. Once it was hovering, he flew it to a spot outside the cookhouse and waited. Mackenzie left the craft to return to the Mess Hall to pick up the equipment that they would need for the trip. He still couldn't get used to considering the hovercraft as a plane, but in Canada, it was the Ministry of Transport for Aviation that licensed the operation of the hovercraft.

Shawn's plan was to drive the craft down the snow ramp and out onto the pack ice. With luck, he could fly the craft at 30 MPH, if not faster, towards the MIR crash point. A lot would depend on how quickly the radar and searchlights would pick up the pressure ridges. Under average visibility conditions, the lights would pick up the ridges at 200-300 yards. Once he saw a steep pressure ridge, he would then make the necessary heading and speed adjustment to cross the ridge at the lowest point and at the correct angle. But this was not average visibility since it was pitch dark and there was blowing snow. It was unlikely that he could maintain a 30 MPH speed for the whole journey. He hoped that he would hit a stretch of ice that was smoother and more stable so that he could increase the speed of the hovercraft.

Colonel Padalka arrived with his men. They carried rifles while their leader had a pistol tucked in a holster strapped around his waist by a thick black belt. One of the commandos carried a radio transmitter, presumably to contact Moscow for any changes in orders.

Mackenzie returned to the hovercraft with their backpacks and with the guns belonging to himself and Major Phillips. He attached a ladder to the side of the hovercraft so that the Russian soldiers could climb up onto the deck and stow their gear in the cabin. Shawn directed the commandos to the rear of the passenger cabin while the Colonel, WO Mackenzie, and two of his techs sat in the cockpit area.

"Colonel Padalka, did your men find their accommodation satisfactory?"

"It will do fine. They were prepared to sleep on the ice if they had to."

"Before we go, I have to tell you that we heard several explosions coming from the direction where your space station landed. We don't know what caused it, but you may be disappointed in what you will find once we get there."

"Your lady pilot already mentioned the explosions to me, and I have already flown there. MIR is gone. There was some evidence that a number of men on snowmobiles visited MIR and perhaps removed some of its parts. I want to go back to see if we can pick up the trail of whoever caused the spacecraft to disappear. We needed your hovercraft since we couldn't follow the trail from a helicopter.

"I can't emphasize enough to you how important the MIR Space Station is to my country. MIR represents thirteen years of experiments and data. That project took countless hours and cost my government millions of rubles that could have been used to relieve the misery of some of my people. We were counting on the data generated by MIR to improve the living conditions of our people with high technology jobs and with an advanced technological society. We could have, if we wanted to, even sold a fraction of the data to the United States for several million dollars. Now it looks like some country or some organization is trying to rob us of our opportunity to improve the lives of the Russian nation. You can see that it is essential that Russia finds MIR and retrieves all of its equipment."

That came as a surprise to Shawn.

"I had no idea just how crucial it was to your country to locate MIR. Otherwise, we could have used the hovercraft to approach MIR once we found this flying machine. We saw where it crash-landed, but we were occupied with the location of our missing aircrew. We better get moving. Rob, you'll be the navigator, keep an eye on our direction, we don't want to get lost."

Shawn released the power, and the craft moved off like a huge beast stalking its prey. It moved slowly at first since the skirt was not fully extended, so it sat lower like a cat on its haunches.

As it descended the ramp and entered the pack ice, it picked up speed as the skirt fully deployed. The hovercraft rode higher, and the beast was in its element. There was occasionally the need to detour around massive pressure ridges and to reduce speed periodically to cross ridges three to four feet high. They were able to reach the site where MIR impacted in less than an hour. Shawn brought the hovercraft to a standstill while Mackenzie opened the cockpit door and lowered a ladder.

Colonel Padalka descended to the ice surface and walked around the debris of MIR that was visible on the ice in the glare of the hovercraft's lights. Shawn maneuvered the craft so that Padalka was constantly in the beam of the searchlights. The Colonel raised an arm and pointed in a northern direction. Shawn rotated the craft to shine the lights there. He could barely see newly formed ice; it was covering a large area that was open water a half a day ago. He guessed that MIR had found its permanent resting place hundreds of meters beneath the ice cap. The Colonel pointed in a northeast direction. The tracks of the snowmobiles were barely visible to Shawn from the cabin window.

Padalka reentered the ACV and noticed that Shawn was squinting to see the tracks left by the snowmobiles. Padalka had one of his men sit outside on the deck at the front of the craft to indicate to Major Phillips which way the tracks ran. Shawn moved the craft slowly off in the direction indicated by the Colonel. The pace was slower than previously, but the searchlights and the spotter enabled them to remain on the trail. After thirty minutes, the Colonel changed spotters since it was nearly minus twenty-five degrees at the front of the craft.

The game of following the mouse lasted over an hour, and at last, the Colonel directed Shawn to slow down. The trail looked fresher in this area, and there appeared to be a glow on the ice ahead. The hovercraft moved at a snail's pace. Finally, the Colonel asked Shawn to stop the craft.

Shawn had one of the techs take his seat and told him to keep the motor ticking over very slowly so there was minimal noise. He didn't want to have to use the APU to restart the craft.

Colonel Padalka ordered his men to jump from the deck out onto the ice. They would walk the rest of the way from here. Major Phillips and WO Mackenzie joined him.

"This is our concern, Major Phillips. You don't have to come. There may be shooting," said Padalka.

"We want to come along. Whoever caused the glow ahead may have taken our aircrew. We would like to ask them where our Canadians are being held."

The Colonel set up the transmitter and sent off a brief message to advise Moscow that they were about to approach the suspected saboteurs of MIR. The radio was once again packed away. Colonel Padalka and Major Phillips started to advance forward. Everyone was wearing white Arctic gear except the Canadians who still wore their insulated orange rescue clothing. Together they approached a pressure ridge that shot ten feet into the air. The Colonel raised his arm, and his Commandos halted. He indicated to Major Phillips that both of them should climb to the top of the ridge. As they reached the top, they stretched out onto the frozen snow and ice and brought their night goggles to their eyes.

Shawn could make out about half a dozen igloo-shaped tents, and there were at least ten snowmobiles parked in the vicinity. Beyond the tents was some freshly opened broken ice; the small lake was the size of a football field. The area was definitely large enough to accommodate a submarine. There was a faint glow of light inside each of the tents, and Shawn thought they were likely using a primus stove for heat. There were two armed guards posted at each end of the camp. Padalka and Phillips crept back down the side of the pressure ridge to the waiting men below. They briefed the group on what lay ahead.

Colonel Padalka split his men into two groups and spoke to them in Russian. They set their watches so that they would attack in unison. One group trudged off in a westerly direction while the other went east. The Colonel and the two Canadians crept slowly straight up the middle. The posted guards were one hundred yards away. Padalka and Phillips stopped short of the encampment and once again used their night glasses to review the situation.

"I told my men to take out the guards without killing them if it is possible, just in case the men on the ice are an innocent hunting party. But I don't think they are. I believe that they stole secret parts from our spacecraft before they sank it. We will do whatever is necessary to get the items back. If the guards can be taken out quietly, we will surround the tents and ask the men inside to surrender."

Shawn thought it seemed like a reasonable plan.

Just before the appointed time for the attack, one of the posted guards must have heard something. Shawn saw him remove his rifle from around his arm and start to bring it to a firing position. He went crashing to the ice before the rifle reached his shoulder. A white shrouded figure bent over the guard and removed a lariat from the guard's throat. The second guard was dead in the same fashion within seconds. The sounds of the running commandos must have been heard since the glowing lights in the tents were all blown out like birthday candles. Shawn could see men creeping on their bellies, out of the tents, towards mounds of ice that would give them some protection. They were dragging their rifles behind them.

The Russian Commandos all wore night glasses, so they were able to pick off the men on the ice like fish in a barrel. The air was filled with English yelling as more and more shots were fired. Shawn also saw that several of Colonel Padalka's men fell in the melee. The shooting continued, but it seemed like a stalemate. Russians and the men on the ice were using the mounds of ice and snow as cover. Every once in a while, a single shot would ring out, and occasionally you could hear someone cry in pain.

Suddenly the dark, icy, watery patch behind the men started to churn. Like some mythical beast, a large black metallic object started to emerge from the water two hundred yards behind them. As it continued to rise from its watery hole and fill the night skyline, the profile told Shawn that it was a nuclear submarine. As it emerged from the depths of its natural element, men emerged from the hatches and ran out onto the deck and set up a machine gun and a cannon.

There was a shout from the men who came from the tents, and they all left their hiding places and ran for the sub. The Russians continued to fire at them, and Shawn could see some of the icemen drop while others reached down to help them up. They seemed confused.

The men on the deck of the sub also started to fire, but not in the direction of Padalka's commandos. They fired at the men rushing towards the sub from the tents. All hell broke loose when the rushing men realized that this sub was not their sub. It had the Russian flag painted on its sail. In mass confusion and with the utter realization that they were caught in the open between two groups firing at them, the men from the tents quickly dropped their guns and raised their arms.

Shawn now recognized the profile of the sub as a Russian Sierra-II nuclear sub. He looked questioningly at Padalka.

"It is the Soku. It's a 1993 sub with a titanium hull. It has four torpedo tubes and the Sampson cruise missiles. It's capable of 33.6 knots, and it carries a crew of 61," said Padalka, who knew his nuclear subs. Padalka and the two Canadians rose from their observation position and advanced towards the commandos, who had surrounded the remaining icemen.

There was one tent individual who ran towards the snowmobiles. He started one of them up and gunned the machine in circles before heading towards Padalka. The tent man had his hand extended with a pistol in his grasp. Shots were whizzing around the Colonel 's head while he ducked behind another dead tent man.

The Colonel attempted to return fire, but his gun jammed. Shawn was several feet in front of the Colonel and off to one side. The snowmobile had to pass near him before it could reach the Commander of the Alfa Unit. As the snowmobile passed near Shawn, he made an Olympic style leap that dislodged the driver. His pistol fired wildly in the air. The empty snowmobile changed direction and went roaring off towards the sub and sank into the icy water. Phillips sprang upon the fallen driver and threw him to the snowy surface, kicking wildly at the gun until it was dislodged from the driver's hand, then drew out his own pistol and bashed the snowmobile driver several times on the back of the head.

The frustration of the past several days of finding Aurora shot down by a missile with two casualties, then finding Captain Winters deep in a hypothermic state, and the final frustration and emotion of not locating his aircrew merged into one gigantic rage in Phillips. He continued to let go with everything he had within his body. He pounded the poor sailor nearly silly when Padalka stepped into the brawl.

Phillips continued to pound on the hooded head of the snowmobile driver until Padalka finally stopped him. Otherwise, he may have driven the tent man into the ice. As it was, the driver lay motionless and exhausted.

Colonel Padalka helped Shawn to his feet.

"Better not kill him. We may need him later but thank you for saving my life. He might have shot me or run me over with his damned snow machine if you hadn't throttled him."

Together they removed the parka hood from the unconscious man, followed by the removal of all of the Arctic gear that the driver was wearing. Beneath the parka was a white naval uniform of the United States Navy with the rank of Lieutenant Commander. The man was still unconscious but was slowly reviving.

"Where did that sub come from?' asked Phillips.

"Just a little insurance that I asked Moscow to send."

"How come you know so much about subs?"

"I volunteered to spend six months aboard one earlier in my career. I knew that I might have to work with a sub crew someday, so I spent time onboard to get a feel for conditions on a submarine." This Colonel Padalka was becoming more and more interesting to Shawn.

The Commandos rounded up all of the mobile icemen and marched them towards the Russian sub. The white Arctic gear was stripped from each prisoner, revealing their U.S. Navy uniforms. Their rifles and pistols were collected, and the prisoners were hoarded onto the sub. Six American icemen and two Russian bodies were stretched out on the surface near the side of it. Russian submarine personnel surrounded the Americans as they boarded the sub and held them at gunpoint as the Russian commandos searched the tents and the snowmobiles for anything connected with the MIR space station. Nothing was found.

One of the Americans protested that they had done nothing wrong. He proclaimed that the men were a part of an American sub that was engaged in winter survival training, and they only returned fire to protect themselves from unknown predators. Colonel Padalka was starting to doubt his own actions. What if these navy personnel had nothing to do with the destruction of MIR? Here he had six dead Americans with another five wounded. What if they were not involved? He would have a major international screw up on his hands that would earn him years in the stockade.

The frustration that Shawn Phillips had earlier arose again as he looked over the man dressed in the commander uniform. Phillips pushed him to one side while poking him hard with his pistol.

"Who are you, and what are you doing here on the Canadian Arctic sea ice?"

The American man recognized Phillips for what he was; a very tired and frustrated Canadian Major who almost knocked him senseless. He didn't plan on getting hit again.

"I'm Lt. Cmdr. Murphy, First Officer of the Sea Devil. That is all that I need to tell you."

That didn't please Phillips. He dragged him towards the side of the sub and pushed him face-first up against its sides. The American stood with his hands above his head, and Shawn pushed the gun harder into the spine of the submariner. He felt something inside the uniform and searched the pockets of the officer, producing the souvenirs that the seaman collected.

First, Shawn found the 415 Sqn crest coffee mug that was on the plane. Then he found the crest from MIR. He tightened his grip on the throat of the U.S. Naval Officer and tossed the MIR crest to Padalka.

The Colonel smiled. His hunch had been correct. The Americans indeed had something to do with the destruction of MIR. Now the question remained, did they remove any parts before its destruction, and if they did, what did they do with them? He directed the commandos to move the icemen and take them to the sub.

Shawn Phillips, with anger in his voice, spoke harshly to the XO of the Sea Devil.

"I want to know what in hell you did with my aircrew after you bastards blew it out of the sky."

"I don't know what you're talking about."

"Like hell, you don't. This mug belongs to an Aurora aircraft that was shot down just several miles from here a few days ago. The Captain of the Aurora survived the crash, and you didn't find him to take him aboard your submarine. He told us about the missile that you fired, causing him to crash. The Commander of Maritime Air Group told me that our HQ has been in touch with the Pentagon. They have exchanged information, and we now know that your sub, the Sea Devil, has our crew on board. That information came directly from Washington via Ottawa to us. This crest on the cup tells me that you and your men were wandering around the crash of a 415 Squadron plane. That leads me to believe that the Sea Devil is nearby with my men on board, and I want to know where the hell she is located. You better come clean and get that sub to bring my men to me. Otherwise, I'll hand you over to my Russian friend so you can spend the rest of your life in prison in Siberia. Do you understand?"

The Lieutenant held his tongue. Then Colonel Padalka stuck his gun into the Lieutenant's mouth.

"I'm the Commander of this Russian Commando Unit, and it is my job to find out what happened to the MIR space station. I have been authorized to kill, if necessary, to get that information. I can also lock you away in prison in Siberia, if I want, for the rest of your natural life. And this crest tells me that the crew of the Sea Devil sabotaged our MIR Space Station and sank it. It is my belief that you stole secret and valuable components from it. This MIR crest proves that you have something to do with that vicious act of sabotage.

"The destruction of MIR and the theft of secret data is enough for me to kill you on the spot. I am deeply saddened by the death of two of my men during the firefight with your crew. That gives me another reason to blow your fucking head off. I can do it now, or I can decide that you will spend the rest of your life in Siberia. I might just spare your life if you can tell me what components you took from MIR and what you did with them."

Murphy continued to profess his team's innocence. He was not yet willing to disobey the orders of his superior officer, Admiral Heiserman. He kept insisting that his team was only out of the sub on a training mission.

"Since we are on Canadian soil, it is up to me to decide," replied Shawn. He gave the naval officer a final ultimatum.

"You can be given over to Colonel Padalka and the Russian government to punish you for sabotaging and possibly looting MIR, or I can determine that you spend the next twenty-five years in a Canadian prison for deliberately downing a Canadian military plane. You will also be charged with being illegally in Canadian waters and kidnapping the plane's crew. What will it be? Do you want to tell us everything and take your chances with the Canadian justice system, or do you want to waste the rest of your life, as well as the lives of your men, locked up in a Siberian prison? I can decide to take you with me or turn you over to this Russian commander right now. He might just decide to shoot you, and it would make no difference to me.

"Remember that your Naval commanders are now cooperating with the Canadian government. As a result, you can't depend on the U.S. government to get your ass out of this mess or out of a cold jail in the Russian far north."

Murphy saw the writing on the wall. It was no longer a difficult choice. If the U.S. Navy was cooperating with the Canadian authorities, that meant that Admiral Heiserman's orders did not have the support of higher authorities.

The Canadian justice system worked much like the American system. He was reasonably sure that he could convince a judge and jury that he and his crew were only doing what they had been trained to do, namely to follow the orders of a senior officer. He was told what to do by his CO and by other senior officers, and he was just a pawn in a major game involving sabotage and secrecy.

He didn't know if the Russian system was as civilized, and he doubted if he would ever get his day in court. He would likely just be locked up and never heard from again. The decision was an easy one, and he decided to tell Phillips everything he knew.

Lieutenant Commander Murphy explained how Admiral Heiserman, Head of U.S. Naval Operations, had given his boss secret orders. The orders directed the sub to be positioned near Ellef Ringnes Island. Somehow Heiserman knew that MIR was about to land at that location.

"How in the hell did he know that it was going to land here unless he arranged it?" asked Padalka.

"I don't know how he did it!" said a frustrated Murphy. "The Admiral told Captain Hayes that secrecy was to be preserved at all costs."

Murphy described how Heiserman had provided the ship with a Battery Commander named Marsh. He explained how Marsh had rushed to the deck of the sub just as the Canadian Aurora was circling above the surfaced Sea Devil. He said that Marsh panicked and fired the missile at the Aurora, but he didn't sound persuasive. According to Murphy, it was Heiserman who ordered that the surviving aircrew be brought aboard the Sea Devil. Heiserman's directive was in order to keep the secret that it was a U.S. Navy submarine that destroyed the aircraft. The aircrew was safe aboard the submarine, and they were to be dropped off shortly in Frobisher Bay to a B4 hovercraft. When questioned about the B4 hovercraft ownership, he was unable to supply the information. Murphy also didn't know where his sub was at the moment. He and his men were waiting for the ship to return and pick them up.

Padalka began to question Murphy about the destruction of MIR. Murphy confessed that it was Admiral Heiserman who ordered its destruction after it was plundered for its data processing system.

The Colonel jumped on the admission that parts were taken from the craft, and he insisted on more information, especially about their whereabouts. Murphy confessed that Heiserman provided a complete list of all the items he wanted from MIR. He insisted that it was Admiral Heiserman who authorized the sinking of the remainder of MIR after all the data recorders were recovered from the wreck. All of these items were delivered to Heiserman, who was waiting with his VTOL plane in this spot.

Murphy mentioned that he was surprised to find that Admiral Heiserman had arrived at the Sea Devil location by a VTOL. It came before he and his men arrived at the place where his sub, the Sea Devil, was last located. By the time he and his plundering crew arrived, the Sea Devil had already left with the Canadians on board. He told Padalka how his men had loaded all of the MIR instruments and recorders onto the VTOL and how Heiserman departed for Frobisher Bay along with Battery Commander Marsh.

Both Phillips and Padalka listened with astonishment as the story unfolded. They were amazed at the length that this Admiral Heiserman would go to, to take the data processing equipment from MIR. The Colonel was very concerned that Heiserman might use the information to the detriment of the Russian people. He admitted to Phillips that data in the equipment must not fall into enemy hands, especially information about military sites and facilities around the globe that MIR recorded. Such information would be invaluable to a country like China or America that might one day attack his motherland or other countries that were photographed by MIR.

They talked over what they should do next. Colonel Padalka wanted to go immediately after the MIR space components in Frobisher Bay. Phillips reminded Padalka about the coup and how the Frobisher runway was most likely closed to all traffic. The Russian choppers might be shot out of the air in Frobisher. Shawn wanted to wait in the area to see if the Sea Devil showed up with his aircrew. They were undecided on what to do next. In the end, they decided to find the American submarine to arrange a prisoner swap.

Phillips, who was fluent in Russian tongue, spoke to the commander of the Okun, the Russian submarine. The sub commander had detected the presence of another submarine under the polar ice at the same time as he was heading to the MIR crash location. But he had no idea where it was at this time.

Major Phillips suggested to the commander that he not take any action against the American sub in any way. The lives of the Canadian aircrew depended on the American sub reaching the surface and exchanging prisoners for the captive Americans.

They decided that the American prisoners would be kept locked up in the Russian sub until an exchange could be made for the Canadian aircrew and the MIR parts. However, Murphy would accompany them back to the ice island in case he was needed. His voice would be necessary to convince the Sea Devil Commander that part of his crew was now under detention in a Russian submarine.

The American prisoners were secured in the brig on board the Okun, which was still on the surface. The bodies of the deceased Americans were stored in a refrigerated room. Shawn ensured that the sub commander and Colonel Padalka had each other's radio frequency in case they needed to contact one another. If a prisoner exchange was to take place, the Russian sub would have to submerge to make room for the U.S. sub in the tiny opening in the ice. That plan depended on the captain of the Sea Devil agreeing on a swap.

The hatches were closed, and the Russian sub disappeared into the same dark ocean waters from where it appeared. The Sea Devil's shore team was now terminated. It might be a long time before they returned.

The Russian commandos loaded all of the American tents, supplies, and guns into the hovercraft; even the snowmobiles were taken and tied all around the outer deck. They might come in handy at a later date. The Sea Devil's radio transmitter that had accompanied Murphy on his run to MIR was loaded into the cockpit. Shawn wanted it nearby since he planned to use it to contact the American sub at the first opportunity. Murphy was bound and gagged and loaded at the back of the cabin in the hovercraft.

The commandos also took great care to carry the bodies of their dead comrades on board. It was traditional that the bodies of all brave soldiers who lost their lives in defense of the motherland be returned to Russia for a ceremonial burial. The bodies of the two commandos would be flown to Moscow on one of the helicopters after the mission was completed.

Phillips, Mackenzie, the techs, and all of the Russians climbed aboard the hovercraft and shivered together in the cold during their one hour and thirty-minute trip back to the Mess Hall on Canada's Ice Island.

# 35 SEA DEVIL LOSES

29 December 1000 hrs local, Under the Pack Ice Near Ellef Ringnes Island

Faith had left Commander Hayes with no choice but to leave his shore team on the ice when the Sea Devil had to dive. The radar operator had forewarned him that another Canadian Aurora was in the area. There was a possibility that the sub would be under attack, as it was when it was lodged previously in the ice. He couldn't afford to take that chance. The shore crew members, who were led by his XO, had not yet returned from their trek to MIR to recover the data storage instruments. Once the radar operator had warned Hayes of the approaching Aurora, he had only one option. He only had time to throw the prepositioned supplies and tents from the deck onto the ice before he submerged to wait below the ice opening. There was just enough time for him to order Battery Commander Marsh off the sub and onto the ice to wait for Admiral Heiserman's arrival.

The Admiral was expected to rendezvous with the Sea Devil at that precise location. It was left to Battery Commander Marsh to explain to the Admiral and to Murphy's party why the ship had to dive in such a hurry before their arrival. When the ship dove for cover, Hayes intended to have the Sea Devil return to the same spot after an hour to retrieve his men.

That plan had to be scrapped shortly after the crash-dive, when the sonar operator called him to the Attack Centre. The operator wanted Hayes to be aware that there was another sub under the ice with them. It was a Russian sub. The sonar operator identified the sub as a Sierra-II class nuclear-powered attack submarine. The Russian sub also knew that the Sea Devil was in the area and began to follow the Sea Devil around.

The two subs played cat and mouse with one another for the better part of an hour, with the Russian sub being the more aggressive of the two. The Russian sub forced the Sea Devil to give way on several occasions.

When the Sea Devil moved several nautical miles from beneath the small open lead that it created in the pack ice when it submerged, the Russian sub gave up its pursuit of the Sea Devil and immediately took up station directly under the opening in the ice and hovered there, awaiting further orders. The two subs eyed each other from a distance for nearly thirty minutes before Hayes decided to move further away from the Russian sub to a safer location.

As the Sea Devil left, the sonar operator spoke.

"The Russian sub appears to be surfacing. There are hull popping noises, and the ship is blowing her tanks."

"OK, Sonar," Hayes told the navigator, "we are not going very far. Keep an eye on her and let me know what she is up to. We want to use that hole again as soon as she is gone." He wondered what was happening on the ice surface that would cause the Sierra Class sub to act so aggressively.

The Captain and the Sea Devil crew were not aware of the pitched battle that had taken place directly above them between Colonel Padalka's men and Lt. Cmdr. Murphy's men. Hayes needed to know what had happened to his men that he had left on the ice surface, and he was about to find out.

Hayes became lost in thought, and the Diving Operator broke his concentration by telling him that the sub was receiving a radio transmission from Washington.

"I'll go and decode the messages."

He left the bridge, retrieved the messages, and took them to his stateroom where began decoding.

*"To: Captain of Sea Devil. Do not, and repeat, do not remove any equipment from MIR. Remove your ship and men from the vicinity immediately. The Pentagon does not approve Admiral Heiserman's orders. Canadian aircrew are to be immediately turned over to any Canadian authorities in the area. Battery Commander Marsh is to be placed in detention, and Admiral Heiserman is to be detained upon his arrival. Signed, Rear Admiral Gunston."*

"Bloody well too late," is what Commander Hayes said to himself. Admiral Heiserman had flown the coop with the parts along with Marsh, and now God only knew where his own men were located. His question was answered by the next message that needed no decoding. It was not from Washington, but from a location nearby.

The second message was from the Canadian Search Master who was looking for the crew of his crashed Aurora.

*To: The Captain of the Sea Devil*
*From: Major S. Phillips, Canadian Forces Search Master*
*"The Commander of the Russian Alpha Commando Unit and I have taken prisoner your entire shore team. They are being held for the downing of the CF Aurora reconnaissance aircraft and for the sabotage and looting of the Russian Space Station, MIR. The President of the United States is working with the Prime Minister of Canada and the President of Russia to resolve the debacle caused by the Sea Devil and Admiral Heiserman. If you wish to see your shore crew again, it is strongly suggested that you surface at the same location as previously and deposit the Canadian aircrew on the ice at 6 PM local time today. You personally are to remain on the ice with the Canadians while your sub departs to make room for the Russian sub containing your missing shore team. Do not take any action against the Russian sub or against those that will contact you on the pack ice, or you will risk losing your shore crew and possibly your ship. Plans have been made to arrange for the return of your shore crew in exchange for the Canadians and the return of the MIR components from Admiral Heiserman. You will be watched by myself and Colonel Padalka's commandos as you surface. We will join you after your ship has departed. Any deviation from this procedure will see your shore crew facing charges in Canadian and Russian Courts. Your XO, Lt. Cmdr. "Crusher" Murphy, is being held separately. Signed, Major Phillips and Colonel Padalka."*

Commander Hayes had no doubt that the message was authentic since he was the only one who called the XO by the nickname of Crusher. It was a name he tagged to Murphy in University, based on his football and romantic and sexual exploits. He returned to the bridge on the Sea Devil's sail and showed both messages to his diving officer.

"What are we going to do now, Skipper?"

"We are going to follow the directions given to us by the Canadian. The deadline gives us some time to send off a message to Rear Admiral Gunston, telling him what we plan to do. Then we will get the Canadian aircrew ready with warm clothing, and we will set them up on the ice in warm tents. I only hope that we get all of our crew back alive."

Both of the officers returned to the Attack Centre. The DO began to make preparations for the departure of the Canadians while Hayes prepared a message to be sent to Gunston in Washington.

*"Your message just received, and it arrived too late. Admiral Heiserman is now believed to be flying to Frobisher Bay with all the MIR data storage instruments along with Battery Commander Marsh. Arrangements will be made within the hour to transfer the Canadian aircrew to a Canadian Forces Search Master near Ellef Ringnes Island, hopefully in exchange for all of the Sea Devil shore crew who were captured by the Canadians and Russian Commandos. Signed, Commander Hayes."*

It was unfortunate for his career that Washington had to be told about his shore crew's loss. He was sure that the failure would be blamed on him even though he had no choice but to dive to protect the sub from a Canadian aircraft.

The despairing dive stranded some of his crew, who were on a mission ordered by Admiral Heiserman. He hoped that he would have the opportunity to explain to Admiral Gunston just how it happened. He would explain that he did later return for his crew members, but it was delayed by the actions of an opposing Russian sub that decided to play tag with the Sea Devil. However, he had no choice but to include the status of the lost crew in the message just in case the exchange was not consummated. Hayes coded the message and had it sent off as a flash message. It was on Admiral Gunston's desk within fifteen minutes.

The DO had several tents with sleeping bags set up on the ice near the ship, and the primus stove lit in each one of them to provide some warmth. The glow reflected from each tent onto the surrounding pack ice. As the deadline approached, the Canadian aircrew was directed along the corridors of the sub, up the hatches, and out onto the ice. The crew of the Sea Devil helped those that were unable to make the short journey on their own and no longer concealed their identity from the aircrew, but they refused to answer any questions. The second pilot of the Aurora, who had the broken legs, was carried from the lockup to the tent. He was told that a Canadian official would be with them very shortly. They all were told to wait in the tents for the arrival of their rescuers.

"As next in command, you will have to take the controls and take the Sea Devil several nautical miles away from this place," Hayes told the Diving Officer, then continued with further instructions.

"Move off and make way for the Russian sub. After the Russians depart, return to this lead. Hopefully, you will find myself, the XO, and the rest of our shore crew waiting for you in the tents. One of us will relieve you of command as soon as you pick us up."

"That will be no problem, Captain. Is there any possibility of a double-cross? Will they return all our men?"

"I don't know. They never promised a straight exchange. They also want the MIR components as part of the exchange, and we have no way of providing those components to the Russian commandos. Besides, they hold all the cards. We have no bargaining chips. They even have the President on their side, and they know that it was someone aboard the Sea Devil who brought down the Canadian plane. And, I don't imagine that the commander of the Russian unit is all too happy with the fact that our men stripped his spacecraft and sank it. We then let the conniving Admiral disappear with the parts. If necessary, I'm prepared to offer myself as a replacement for the release of our men until they get the MIR parts. In that way, the two victimized countries will have some bargaining power to dicker with our government in order to get restitution."

Commander Hayes gathered up Heiserman's orders from his safe. He brought along the decoded messages that he had exchanged with Washington. He took one last long look at his stateroom and the control centre and wondered if he would ever get to see either one again. He walked out onto the ice and watched as the Sea Devil once again submerged to make space for the Russian sub.

The Canadian airmen huddled as one near the warm glowing tents. Hayes looked around the ice pack, wondering if the Canadians and Russians were watching him. He entered one of the tents and laid down to await their arrival. Alone, he wondered how in God's name the exploits of Heiserman had to be at his expense. After all, he was a church going Christian. He cried for his men who were just following orders of a deranged senior officer.

Major Phillips and Colonel Padalka were watching Hayes after the departure of the Sea Devil. They were together high up the top of a twenty-foot ice ridge. They had arrived by hovercraft with the snowmobiles and sleds tied along the deck. WO Mackenzie and a dozen commandos filled the small cabin at the rear of the cockpit. The ensemble had left the Mess Hall moments after the message was sent.

When they arrived, the Sea Devil was already on the surface. The hovercraft containing the snowmobiles, sleds, and commandos were tucked behind a huge pressure ridge two miles from the sub. It had taken Phillips and Padalka thirty minutes to walk to another pressure ridge and climb its slippery slope to spy on the Sea Devil.

Before they left the Mess Hall building, Shawn and the Colonel discussed what they would do with Murphy. The Colonel still wanted to fly immediately to Frobisher Bay and remove all of the MIR components. He was sure that the choppers could set down some distance from the airport and sneak into the facility housing the MIR equipment. It would be dangerous, but he knew that his commandos could accomplish the mission. The question was, what would it cost him and his men? Would Heiserman destroy the MIR equipment if he knew that the Russians had come to take it back?

Shawn again had to convince Padalka that it was not the best move at that time. Radars at Frobisher Bay would be watching all incoming planes and helicopters, and they would be prepared to repel any attack that the commandos could muster. Besides, they were not even sure if Heiserman had, in fact, gone to Frobisher; he could have gone to Eureka, Alert, or several other communities. He may have even left the country.

Colonel Padalka was convinced to give up his invasion plan when Shawn mentioned that he had a contact, a spy in fact, in Frobisher Bay, who could tell them precisely if Heiserman had arrived with the parts and where they were stored. Padalka agreed to wait for word from the spy before attacking the community. After all, his primary objective was to retrieve the MIR parts, not to fight a revolt against some renegade military men and mercenaries.

Together, the Canadian and the Russian Commander agreed that they would try to lure the American sub back to the area by sending them a message with their transmitter, hinting of an exchange of prisoners. It was Colonel Padalka's idea that they include some personal detail about Murphy that would prove to the captain that they did hold the Sea Devil shore team as captives. The two officers drafted the message, and 'Crusher' Murphy was forced at gunpoint to send the message using his radio transmitter that Phillips had confiscated.

Shawn also sent a message to Major General Shanahan just prior to leaving to meet the American sub and its captain. The message that was sent to Shanahan asked him to be on the lookout for a plane arriving containing Admiral Heiserman and Battery Commander Marsh. The message stated that the two might have with them almost a ton of secret MIR equipment that must be returned to Russia or be destroyed as a last resort. If the aircraft was spotted with its passengers and its contents, a return message would be appreciated ASAP.

Just before leaving, Colonel Padalka had agreed that two of his own helicopters could be used to airlift the Canadian aircrew to the Thule Air Base should the two leaders be fortunate enough to secure their release.

Padalka and Phillips could feel the biting wind tear at their exposed skin at their observation post atop the pressure ridge. While they wore thick white parkas and heavily padded trousers along with seal fur-lined boots, the minus thirty degree Arctic air still managed to seep through the insulation. The coldness seeped into every bone in their bodies. Still, they stayed in position. They used their night glasses to watch the aircrew deposit onto the ice and as they entered the tents. They also watched the captain leave the ship and stand on the ice as his vessel sank beneath the surface of the ice cap. Once they saw the Sea Devil submerged, they descended the ice pressure ridge and returned to the hovercraft and the commandos. The snowmobiles were unloaded along with the sleds, and the commandos boarded the waiting machines.

The Colonel waved his arm in a forward motion, and all the other commandos started their machines, towing sleds, and followed the lead vehicle. The lights of the ski-doos cut through the night and the drifting snow; it was an eerie sight to see all of these machines advancing on to the group of tents. They drove their machines up to the tents and formed a circle around them. The lights from the machines provided the perfect stage for the act of the exchange of prisoners that was about to transpire.

Shawn dismounted his machine and walked to the tent where he saw the copilot carried. The Russian colonel advanced on the tent containing the Captain of the Sea Devil.

To the copilot and others in the tent, Shawn flashed a smile.

"Don't be alarmed, folks, it's just your friendly Canadian Search Master and a few of his Russian army buddies here to take you to the Canadian ice island, where you will be wined and dined. Just kidding, you will be kept warm until some Russian helicopters on the island can be used to ferry you to Thule for medical treatment.

"You are in safe hands now. In a few moments, we will make you warm and comfortable on the sleds, and we should be back in our Search and Rescue building within an hour. Shortly after that, you will be on your way home via Thule Air Base on Russian helicopters. Is everyone OK? Does anyone need immediate treatment?"

In unison, they answered no and said that the Americans had looked after them very well, although they didn't know that they were Americans until a few minutes ago.

In the meantime, Colonel Padalka opened the door to Commander Hayes' tent. He had his pistol in his gloved hand and waved it at the Commander, ordering him out of the tent. The Colonel searched Hayes but found no weapons.

"My name is Colonel Padalka. I am the head of the Alfa Commando Unit that is responsible for locating those who sabotaged the Russian spacecraft. On behalf of the Government of Russia, I charge you and your crew with the sabotage of the MIR Space Station and the destruction of it along with the looting of its equipment." He spoke in flawless English to the stunned captain.

Commander Hayes protested his innocence and that of his crew. He did not deny what the Colonel had said were actions done by the Sea Devil crew, except the part about the sabotage of the space station. He and his crew had no role in bringing the MIR station crashing out of the skies. For the other activities, he insisted that he was acting under the orders of a senior officer. Hayes insisted that his sailors be released. The Colonel placed Hayes under guard and walked over to the snowmobiles, where Shawn was directing the loading of the Canadian aircrew onto the sleds.

"Congratulations, you got your aircrew back. Now we need to concentrate on my mission of getting the MIR equipment back. The Captain of the Sea Devil wants me to release the members of his sub crew. You know that I'm opposed to giving up any assets until I get back the MIR parts, and until Russia gets fully reimbursed for the loss of its space station."

"Let me talk to him. You know that I don't think it's necessary for you to hold all of the Americans captive to get what you want. Perhaps we can reach a compromise, which is the normal way Canadians resolve a conflict."

Hayes was spread eagle on the ice with a gun at his back, held by one of the commandos.

Shawn waved away the Russian guard and helped Hayes to his feet. They were joined by WO Mackenzie. He offered Phillips and Hayes a cigarette and lit them both. Everyone relaxed for a few moments.

"You got my message. I'm Major Phillips, Search Master for the Canadian Forces Aurora plane. We have your XO. He has confessed to shooting down our plane and the taking of our aircrew to your sub under armed guards. He has also admitted to looting the MIR Space Station of its secret data processing equipment. He says that you were acting under the orders of an Admiral Heiserman."

Hayes was more relaxed now that he was dealing with a friendly nation.

"That's the truth, and I have the written orders to prove it. They were given to me by Admiral Heiserman. I also have a message here from Washington, that Heiserman had no authority to make such orders. Washington sent it after I questioned the Admiral's authority to give my crew such charges." He showed the various messages to Phillips.

Shawn was impressed by the fact that this young officer would put his career on the line by questioning the authority of a senior officer.

"You probably know that Colonel Padalka doesn't want to give up your crew members. They offer him some assurance that he will get the MIR instruments back and that his government will get reimbursement for the loss of their spacecraft."

"I understand what he needs. I don't have the MIR parts, but we will cooperate fully to help you and the Russians get them back if you can locate them. I'm willing to give you and him these orders if it makes it easier to get retribution. I am also willing to take the place of my crew members if the Colonel settles for me as a captive."

Phillips was again impressed by the commander's willingness to cooperate and his courage to offer himself as a captive, who could perhaps spend the rest of his life in a Russian prison.

"I will speak to the Colonel. As Canada's representative, I will agree that Canada will keep your XO in our custody until everything is resolved. I will also keep a certified copy, signed by you, of these orders, and I will try to convince the Colonel to accept your help in recovering the MIR parts. We think that they are on route to Frobisher Bay, which is still under siege by a number of disgruntled ex-military Canadians fighting, so they say, for the independence of the north. I could use your ship's help to free the Canadian people of Frobisher from terrorists and return democracy to the area.

"I hope that Colonel Padalka will settle for your volunteer confinement, the original copy of the orders, and the messages, as well as your agreement to help us with the firepower of your ship."

Hayes said that such an agreement would be welcomed by himself if Shawn could clear it with the Colonel.

Phillips sent Mackenzie and the commandos back to the Mess Hall building with the Canadian aircrew on the sleds pulled by the snowmobiles. Before they left, Shawn had a conversation with Rob.

"You know that the Russians have agreed to use their choppers to fly our boys to Thule, so you will probably be gone by the time I get back to the Mess Hall. I want to thank you and your boys now for sticking with me until we got our crew back. I knew I could count on you from the very beginning. When we all get back to Greenwood, the drinks will be on me, and you know that I will write a very favorable report on the performance of you and your men."

"I'm sure that I speak for all of the techs when I say that it has been a pleasure working with you again, Major. We knew that if any search master would find our guys, it would be you."

Shawn told Mackenzie to contact Thule mini RCC and indicate that the rescued aircrew would be leaving immediately on board two Russian helicopters. The RCC was to be advised that one Canadian aircraft was to be prepared for take-off upon arrival of the choppers. The plan was to return the Aurora crew and the two fatalities ASAP. Phillips knew that the airmen needed their families just as the families needed their men.

He was to hustle Murphy from the chopper to the aircraft and bring him back to face charges, without the Americans' knowledge, at Thule. To comfort the Canadian aircrew on route to Thule, Mackenzie was to take the two techs with him. They would be responsible for the Canadians' welfare until they arrived. Shawn also trusted Rob to bring the package containing the fifty thousand dollars back and turn it over to the legal officers since he was unable to turn it over to Shanahan.

The Canadian aircrew was secured with sleeping bags to the sleds. WO Mackenzie lined up the snowmobiles, and with a wave of his arm the convoy departed across the ice in the direction of the ice island.

Now there were just the three of them on the pack ice in the cold Arctic night. Phillips kept guard of Hayes, and the Colonel contacted his Russian sub by radio transmitter. The three of them waited, without talking, in the warmth of an igloo tent.

Soon, they could hear the Russian sub rising to the surface and breaking through the thin ice that had formed over the hole. All three left the tent and stood to watch as the sub fully emerged onto the surface. The sub's searchlight was turned on, and the hatch was opened. The Russian captain appeared to speak with Colonel Padalka. He explained the agreement. The Americans were to disembark from the sub. Captain Hayes would be taken aboard and confined and eventually returned to Russia. Colonel Padalka told the Russian captain to unload the American prisoners. After that, he was to submerge and immediately sail under the ice to Frobisher Bay, the MIR parts' most likely location. He was to wait in the area until Padalka contacted him.

Padalka returned to Shawn and Hayes. They waited while the prisoners were offloaded from the Russian submarine.

The Americans were led out of the sub carrying the bodies of their dead companions. Hayes grieved as he saw the bodies since he hadn't been told that there were American casualties.

The weakness of the captain was evident. He wailed when each casualty was deposited near his feet. He privately cursed Heiserman for causing the death of his men. They were only following his orders. They didn't know that the Admiral was corrupt and greedy and had no authority to issue such orders. Hayes swore that he would get even with Heiserman. He only wished that he had questioned the Admiral's authority earlier in the mission. He swore that he would kill Heiserman if he could ever get his hands on him.

Now that the XO was being held in another location by the Canadians and Hayes was to be held aboard the Russian sub, someone had to be left in charge of the Sea Devil. He told the RCO to instruct the DO, who was currently the acting CO aboard the Sea Devil, that he now had full command of the sub. The DO needed to send a message to Rear Admiral Gunston as soon as the ship departed to apprise him of the situation. Hayes mentioned to the RCO that the Sea Devil crew would be returning to the Sea Devil in the next hour, as soon as the Russian sub departed and the American sub arrived to take its place.

Hayes continued to instruct the RCO on what he and the DO must do to obtain the Sea Devil crew and help the Canadians and Russians with their objectives. He informed the RCO that he volunteered to stay on board the Russian sub all the way to Moscow as a replacement captive in lieu of the shore crew. The Russians would hold him until the Heiserman fiasco was settled.

The DO was to bring the Sea Devil to the Frobisher Bay harbor and await the Canadian authorities' instructions, or those of the XO.

Hayes was not aware that Phillips had already set in motion the transfer of Murphy directly and quickly to Canada via Thule. Hayes emphasized to the RCO that the DO and ship would be needed in cooperation with the Russian sub to put down a revolution by some former Canadian military men who had staged a coup in the capital of Nunavut. The ship may also be needed to help with the retrieval of MIR parts stolen by Admiral Heiserman.

Hayes returned to where Phillips and Padalka were standing. They were told that the Sea Devil would shortly resurface in the same spot after the Russian sub departed. Hayes walked aboard the Russian sub, the hatch was slammed shut, and the sub quickly disappeared.

Phillips and Padalka kept their distance from the Americans. Both still had their pistols while the Americans were unarmed. There was always the possibility that one of the sailors would take it in his head to attack for the loss of his skipper and their companions' deaths. But as a group, the Americans were disillusioned by the fact that one of their own senior officers had led them into this mess.

The Sea Devil surfaced, lights were turned on, and the Americans clambered onto the sub. The hatches were opened, and the remainder of the shore crew, headed by the RCO, quickly disappeared down the hatchway. Several of the crew, currently on the vessel and not wearing Arctic clothing, rushed out and fetched the dead Americans' bodies from the ice surface. Once the bodies were carried on board, the hatch was secured, and the sub departed.

Shawn and Padalka were alone on the ice pack. It was suddenly very quiet and lonesome. They walked silently side by side towards the hovercraft. Together they climbed up onto the deck and entered the cockpit. Phillips engaged the gears to inflate the skirt, turned the craft towards the ice island, and headed for home.

# 36 APACHE ATTACK

30 December 1000 hrs local, Canada Ice Island, Nunavut

Colonel Viktor Padalka spent time with his men discussing ways and means to recover the MIR equipment. Shawn busied himself about the Mess Hall on the ice island. He was writing his report on the successful search for the Aurora aircrew. All of them would be leaving the search area soon now that the missing Aurora airmen had been found and flown, more than twelve hours ago, to the medical facilities in Thule and onwards to home. As the lone Canadian on the island, since WO Mackenzie and the other rescue technicians had accompanied the aircrew to Thule, Shawn played host to the Russians and tried to accommodate their needs.

Upon checking his laptop, he saw he had unread email awaiting his attention. It was an email from Major General Shanahan in reply to the shaded email sent earlier by Phillips. The email indicated that a VTOL had recently landed at Frobisher Bay with U.S. Admiral Heiserman and Battery Commander Marsh on board. The email reported that his Arctic Rangers, his resistance movement, had reported that some equipment was unloaded from a VTOL into a building at the airport. The Rangers would try to find out more details about the equipment in the coming hours and forward the information. The email indicated that Shanahan suspected the unloaded items were the missing instruments from MIR. The email was an advance notice that the MAG Commander would have to change locations since his room had been searched.

Shawn sent off a reply as soon as he finished reading the incoming message. In a creative fashion, his response to Shanahan revealed that the Canadian aircrew had been located and was now on their way to the Thule Air Base. The rescue was mainly due to the invaluable aid of the Russian Commando Unit.

His email also mentioned that a firefight had broken out during the rescue. The battle was between the American sailors who had caused the destruction of MIR and the Russian commandos that had been sent to retrieve it. As a result of the firefight, several American sailors were killed in the engagement, and two Russian commandos lost their lives.

His email continued with the news that the Russians had captured some American sailors who were later exchanged for the Canadian aircrew. He also advised Shanahan that they now had positive proof that it was the Americans, acting under Admiral Heiserman's orders, who shot down the Canadian Aurora. The message also contained facts about who forced MIR to crash down on to the Arctic ice. Once on the ice, the American sailors had looted MIR's contents and then sank the station deep into the Arctic Ocean. Phillips ended his reply by attaching the documents that he got from Commander Hayes. They contained the U.S. government orders for the detention of Admiral Heiserman and Battery Commander Marsh. Phillips sent off the email, then reported to Colonel Padalka that the MIR items were indeed at Frobisher Bay.

On the other end of the exchange of emails, Shanahan was sending messages from his room in Frobisher Bay. His latest message thanked Shawn and his team, and the Russians, for freeing and rescuing the Canadian aircrew. He regretted the loss of lives of their Russian allies. The latest email asked the commando unit to please help the Canadian government free Nunavut from the mercenaries' clutches. In return, his Arctic Rangers would do whatever they could to protect the MIR equipment stored at the Frobisher Airport. The message to Phillips ended by stating that he would contact him as soon as he found a safe house. If, for some reason, Phillips was unable to contact the MAG Commander, then he was to contact, in person, Simone Aokalik of the Arctic Rangers in Frobisher Bay.

When Colonel Padalka joined Major Phillips for a cup of coffee, Shawn showed the Colonel the messages from Major General Shanahan. Padalka was delighted to read those parts of his beloved space station had been located.

"At least we know now the present location of the MIR instruments and data. We also know the location of the two vile men responsible for the destruction of our valuable space station, Heiserman and Marsh. We need to make plans now on how we are going to get to Frobisher Bay and what we are going to do once we reach that destination."

Shawn had left his radio transmitter in the on position; their conversation was interrupted by some static noises followed by a clear transmission.

"Calling Major Phillips, Search Master."

It was Capt. Mari Leech in her Aurora, circling the ice island. It was apparent that her plane had returned to Thule for fuel, then immediately headed back to the ice cap to watch over the lone Canadian and the Russian task force. Phillips wondered if Mari had been catching some much-needed rest.

"This is Phillips. Go ahead."

"We just picked up four Apache helicopters heading your way. They will be in your area in fifteen minutes. They came from the direction of Eureka and Alert."

"Thanks, Mari, for the advance notice. It will give us time to prepare some offensive action of our own. By the way, what are you doing here? I thought that you were back in your Thule bedroom getting much-deserved sleep!"

"Someone had to keep a watch over you, flyboy, and your Russian buddies, and it may as well be me. Besides, I already lost a previous partner, and I don't want to lose another, even if we haven't had a date yet!" Mari was seizing the moment and being slightly aggressive in advancing their relationship.

Shawn read into her transmission that she cared for his well-being, which made him smile. He also cared for her safety.

"Please don't attempt to engage Lowery's helicopters in any way. Instead remain at your altitude and keep us posted on the Apache movements."

"Will do. I couldn't just lie in bed in Thule knowing how much fun you are having."

Shawn had to laugh at her sense of humor.

"It is sure nice to have you back."

"Congratulations are in order. I heard in Thule that you were successful in rescuing the aircrew. All of my crew are thankful for your perseverance in returning our fellow airmen. Now we will truly have to have that celebratory drink or two in the Thule Air Base Officers Mess."

"I think you need to give most of that thanks to Colonel Padalka and his commandos for helping out. Now, we must get ready for the Apaches."

"My crew says thanks to your Russian friends. Out."

Colonel Padalka ran from the Mess Hall building to the cookhouse and ordered the pilots of the two remaining Helix helicopters to get their birds started immediately. The commandos' leader appointed several of his men to quickly fetch the APU from the shed and get the choppers started. It was preferable that his choppers fight the Apaches from the air than be destroyed on the island.

Padalka told the rest of the unit to spread out and shoot at any Apache helicopters that they saw. He was determined that Admiral Lowery's choppers would regret tangling with his commandos.

It seemed to take forever for the two Helix helicopters to get up and running. Colonel Padalka and Shawn agonizingly watched the rotors as they struggled to rotate. It actually took less than ten minutes before the rotors were spinning at maximum revolutions. Padalka directed that several of his commandos, equipped with rifles and missile launchers, join him in the lead helicopter. The remaining commandos were to be distributed to the other Helix helicopters. Padalka suggested that Phillips fly in the second chopper. All ran to the helicopters to take up their assigned positions while ducking the gyrating rotors.

Padalka's helicopter was the first to leave its parking spot. It rose gently into the dark skies, followed by the rest of the fleet. The crafts had just reached five hundred feet and were less than a mile away from the island when Lowery's Apache helicopters made their first strike.

The Apaches came screaming across the island at less than fifty feet. A missile was fired by the lead Apache helicopter at a group of buildings. The rocket scored a direct hit on the cookhouse, and fragments of the building went flying in all directions through the air. A fire erupted in the front half of the building. It looked like several of the Russians left on the island were in the lee of the building and were hit by the shrapnel. It was quite obvious to Shawn that Lowery's pilots from Eureka had used the services of his other mercenaries at the Alert Listening Station to know the precise location of the Russian helicopters. That was the only way that the Apache pilots could have armed their weapons and had them ready for firing as they approached the only ice island in this million square kilometers of pack ice.

Padalka directed the pilot of his KA-32 Helix helicopter to maneuver for a lethal shot. He was sitting next to the pilot and handling the helicopter's missile controls. When the pilot got his craft directly behind an Apache, Padalka pressed the button. The missile left it's pod and sped towards the Apache. Within seconds there was a very loud explosion as the rocket found its target.

The Apache exploded in flames, and debris fell outward and upward before the out-of-control chopper fell to the pack ice. Padalka's helicopter was shaken by the destruction of the Apache, however, it sailed through the fireball left by the missile's impact.

Shawn watched as Lowery's helicopters made another pass at the ice island huts and shacks. His face tightened as he saw another missile strike another of the survey buildings; it disintegrated before his eyes. Fortunately, his hovercraft was parked at the bottom of the snow ramp and out of sight. It would probably survive without damage.

The pilot of Shawn's helicopter made a sudden turn to the left while making an emergency dive to two hundred feet in a very quick order. A missile from an Apache sped past the diving Helix and out onto the ice pack, where it exploded. The heat from the exploding rocket could be felt through the open door of the Helix as it passed over the missile debris.

The commandos in both helicopters and on the ground were rapidly firing rifles at the remaining Apaches with little effect. It was evident that more powerful weapons were needed if they were to stop the attack.

An unused Air to Air missile launcher lay at Shawn's feet next to his seat. Without a second thought, he picked up the weapon and positioned it on his shoulder. He yelled to one of the commandos to feed the launcher while another made sure that the helicopter's door remained wide open. One of Lowery's Apaches made the mistake of flying in a parallel track at about two hundred yards distance from the Russian Helix. The pilot was only expecting the odd rifle shot from the Russian helicopter. He was not expecting a missile.

Major Phillips made some adjustments to the launcher mechanisms and pulled the trigger. The force of the firing nearly knocked him out of the chopper, but the missile flew straight as an arrow. It caught the Apache near the cockpit as the pilot attempted to elude it. The helicopter ruptured in a ball of flames that soon engulfed the craft's full length, reaching to the fuel tanks. An explosion sent it into a death spiral from which it didn't recover. It landed a few hundred yards from the camouflaged hovercraft. The blast sent slivers of cockpit glass and metal shreds flying through the air. One small chunk of metal flew through the open door of the Helix, ripping some flesh from Shawn's hand.

He and other commandos dove for cover from the fire of the remaining helicopters, and a commando used the emergency aid box to bandage the Canadian's hand.

The Apaches were not yet finished. Another missile was launched, followed by another explosion on the island at the rear of the Mess Hall.

*That's where I stored the radio transmitter,* thought Shawn, as he flew over the remainder of the building. The rapid-fire from the guns on Padalka's helicopter punctured the fuselage of the same Apache with a row of bullet holes. The pilot hastily called it quits, and the Apache pulled up and flew south, at over one hundred mph, towards its home base. As the one remaining Apache started to follow, the pilot loosed a string of fire from the craft's 30 mm automatic Boeing M230 chain gun towards the Russian chopper.

Shawn's helicopter was hit, and its pilot fell mortally wounded into his seat. Instantly, the Helix helicopter started to spin out of control. It was twisting and gyrating in circles as it dove towards the ice. Shawn struggled to reach the cockpit from his cabin seat. He used the legs of the seats to pull himself along the floor of the spiraling chopper until he could grab hold of the pilot's seat and ease the dead pilot out. He slid into the seat as the altimeter read just 200 feet to the surface. He had flown many types of aircraft during his military career but never a Russian chopper. His hand throbbed from the metal fragment embedded in it, but he pulled at the joystick, praying that the craft would straighten out. He pushed and pulled at different control levers in an experiment to see which ones were needed to pull the craft out of its death spin. By playing with the controls and floor pedals, he found the right combination and stabilized the craft. While pulling on his seat belt, he managed to execute a turn and head the chopper back towards the island. Now it was just a matter of landing the bird.

One of the commandos in the helicopter grabbed the radio and spoke to Padalka, and told him that the pilot was severely wounded and that the Canadian was flying it. Padalka's pilot passed instructions to Padalka, to pass to the Canadian, regarding what controls he had to handle in order to land. Padalka's pilot forcefully suggested through the Colonel's transmission that Shawn try to land first, before his own chopper, so that he would have plenty of room to maneuver. In the meantime, Padalka could tell him of any corrective actions that he needed to take in order to put the helicopter safely down. It seemed like a reasonable plan at the time.

Finding the landing site on the island was no problem as flames from the damaged buildings lit up the night sky. Shawn managed to get the helicopter over the landing site and struggled to get it to hover. Padalka continued to provide precise instructions on how to hover and how to bring it down gently. Everything was going fine until the craft was within three feet of the ice. The rotors suddenly stopped doing their business, and the craft dropped down the last few feet to the ice. It stayed down and in an upright position.

Padalka's helicopter landed next to Shawn's, touching down as lightly as a feather. The Commander was the first to rush to the other chopper to see if everyone on board was all right. A quick inspection showed that only the pilot and Phillips had any injuries. The commandos carried the pilot to what remained of the Mess Hall. Padalka fired a quick thanks towards Phillips while Shawn tried to extradite himself from the pilot's seat. He managed to get to the remains of the Mess Hall with only a few bruises to show.

Once the pilot was taken care of, Colonel Padalka walked around the camp to see how many of his commandos who had remained behind on the island were wounded or killed. The toll was six dead and three with severe wounds. A medic treated his wounded commandos and later re-bandaged the hand of the Canadian. The medic could reduce the pain of all the wounded and make them more comfortable.

After the wounded were treated, Major Phillips and Colonel Padalka toured the Mess Hall to see the extent of the damage. Fortunately, the generator was still working, so they were able to establish electricity to the building. The stove was still working, so the room was relatively warm. There was a hole in the rear of the building, and the radio had been badly damaged. Both combatants could see that it was beyond repair. The roof was filled with huge bits and pieces of the building. The hole in the corrugated building could easily be covered to keep out the cold air. On the other hand, the cookhouse was a write-off, and the commandos soon found accommodation in the remaining buildings.

After the inspection of the buildings, both the Russian and the Canadian walked to the edge of the island and down the snow ramp. They removed the tarp that covered the hovercraft and climbed into the cockpit. Major Phillips turned on the radio transmitter and tuned it to the frequency of the Aurora overhead.

"This is the Search Master calling Canadian Aurora."

"Thank goodness, you are alright."

Shawn could detect a sound of relief in Mari's voice. Padalka obviously caught the same concern of the female pilot since a smirk appeared on his face. Phillips thought that the romantic feeling that he had for Mari might just be matched for one that she had for him.

"We saw the missiles hit the buildings and thought you might have also been hit."

"I'm OK, but the Russian unit has several casualties. We lost the radio on the island, but I still have the one in the hovercraft. What happened to the two remaining Apaches that Lowery sent?"

"We watched them limp back to Eureka."

"I doubt that they will make another attempt to destroy us, so I'm releasing you and the Aurora to Thule to wrap up our mini RCC. I'll be staying behind with our Russian allies since Major General Shanahan wants their help in clearing Lowery's mercenaries out of Nunavut, especially out of Eureka and Alert. We will shortly be making plans for a counter-attack."

"Roger, Shawn. Take care of yourself. Hopefully, I'll see you soon at the Mess in Thule. Drinks are on me! Out."

"You know that lady pilot has some feelings for you," said Padalka as they left the hovercraft. They turned on their flashlights and walked the short distance to see the remains of the burning Apache helicopter. They saw the pilot sprawled on the ice a few hundred feet from the craft. Padalka used his boot to turn over the body, only to see parts of the stomach and chest had been ripped open and were already frozen solid. The pilot wore an army color fatigue uniform with Nunavut flags as epaulets. They returned to the Mess Hall.

"Those bastards have killed six of my men and wounded three others. I'm not going to put up with that crap. No one screws with my unit and gets away with it. I want to go after them ASAP."

"I'm with you. Let's give more thought to just what we can do to avenge our losses."

Lowery's helicopters had done the Canadians a favor. Before the attack, Shawn had no firm commitment from Colonel Padalka to get involved in this independence revolt among Canadians. He only wanted to get the MIR instruments and capture those that were responsible for its destruction. Essentially he was only interested in Heiserman and Marsh. Now he was fired up to take on Lowery's crew as well.

They spent the next two hours talking about how they would get revenge against Lowery's helicopters. They agreed that Colonel Padalka would wait on the island for the return of his other two helicopters from Thule. The choppers had been used to bring the downed Aurora's rescued aircrew to the medical facilities there.

In the interim, Shawn would set out towards Eureka with a hovercraft load of commandos. The plan was that they would meet on New Year's Eve for a revenge attack on Eureka. The helicopters would find a way to land near the Eureka station while the hovercraft commandos would attack from the Eureka Sound waters. It would take almost a full day for the hovercraft to reach Eureka by traveling over the permanent pack ice and across Ala Heisenberg Island. By setting out bright and early on the morning of 31 December, they would be in position when all four of the helicopters were on route to Eureka.

Colonel Padalka explained the plan to his men and pointed out all of the program's dangers and pitfalls. He then asked for twenty volunteers to make the long, arduous journey by hovercraft to the weather station. As a group, all stepped forward to volunteer for the ride.

# 37  ATTACK ON EUREKA

31 December, 0800 hrs local, On Route to Eureka, Nunavut

Bright and early on New Year's Eve, several of the commandos went with Shawn to fire up the hovercraft. They filled it with fuel, blankets, tents, weapons and ammunition, and anything else that they might need should they have a problem while out on the pack ice. The fully loaded craft floated up to the front of the Mess Hall building to await its passengers. Shawn left the cockpit and spoke to the Colonel while the commandos scrambled on board using the craft's several ladders.

"What are the chances of making it?" asked Padalka.

"The ice between here and Eureka should be the same as the ice we already encountered when we went after the submarine. Although there may be more jagged ice boulders and treacherous lanes of open water as we approach landfall, the hovercraft must have made the journey at least once in the past. This machine could only get here originally if someone brought it across the multi-year pack ice from some community. I think that we have better than an eighty percent chance of making it. Just in case anything happens and we have to abandon the machine, I have the frequency of the radios on your helicopters. If we don't make it, your troops may have to come and pull us off the ice cap." They shook hands and promised to see one another in Eureka.

The hovercraft, with Phillips at the controls, departed, and Colonel Padalka watched as it descended the snow ramp and headed out onto the ice. The lights of the hovercraft could be seen for miles in the Arctic darkness. When Shawn was five hundred meters away from his departure point, he spun the hovercraft in a full circle to catch a last glimpse of the ice island that was his home for the past week. The lights of the Mess Hall were barely visible atop the twenty-foot-high plateau.

His plan was to stay on the permanent pack ice all the way to Axel Heiberg Island.

Shawn hoped to find his way across the island from the west coast, near Strand Fiord, to the east coast. Crossing the island was the quickest way to Eureka. He would use the middle of the island, which would give him a hundred kilometer stretch over land and snow-covered hills. He would use the rivers in the western part whenever possible to avoid the higher hills and to help him cross. He would exit the island in the northeast, near the ancient fossil forest just across Nansen Sound from Eureka. The hovercraft had a global positioning system that would enable him to know where they were at all times. Once the craft hit the east coast of the island, Shawn would follow Nansen and Eureka Sound to Ellesmere Island and to the Eureka Weather Station.

Back on Canada's Ice Island, Colonel Padalka waited for the return of his two helicopters. He had his men clean their weapons, and they reviewed how they would attack the various buildings at Eureka. He said that anyone wearing an army uniform with a Nunavut flag, which he described, was to be shot if they didn't surrender the moment they were told to do so.

Four hours later, the helicopters arrived. They filled up from the barrels of fuel that they found stored in a shed and loaded the choppers with all of their remaining supplies. The bodies of the dead comrades would not be taken with them; instead, Padalka used his radio transmitter to contact Diksen airport on the Taymyr Peninsula in Siberia, to send another helicopter to the island to recover the bodies and return them to the motherland. The four Helix helicopters departed for Eureka to render justice for the death of their comrades.

The two hundred fifty-kilometer journey meant that Shawn was almost the whole day behind the controls of the hovercraft. The trip across the frozen sea to the tip of Axel Heiberg Island was filled with eerie sounds. Over the roar of the hovercraft engine, the occupants could hear and feel the ice groaning beneath the ship. It reminded Shawn of freight trains bumping together, hitching and unhitching. He had posted a lookout on the front of the hovercraft. This time the guard was equipped with night glasses and was watching for leads of open water and pressure ridges. Periodically the guard was changed as frostbite took its toll on the lookout. After two hours of travel, the ice boulders seemed to thin out, and patches of flat ice appeared as a welcome oasis to Shawn. He poured on additional velocity.

There were times when he wished that WO Mackenzie was with him. He could have used Rob as an additional spotter to watch for other hazards, such as Lowery's Apache helicopters. As it was, they were spared the chance encounter with this enemy.

The journey was tedious at times; Shawn and the lookouts had to constantly watch for open water, large pressure ridges and crevasses. The hovercraft operated without a problem across the frozen stretch separating the ice island from Axel Heiberg Island. Soon the craft navigated around the last pressure ridge and rode up on the land. Near the edge of the western side of the island, there was an abandoned runway where Shawn brought the craft to a halt. He stopped for a break on the makeshift runway near Strand Fiord. There the commandos and Shawn had an opportunity to stretch their legs and have a sandwich before getting back on board the hovercraft.

On the island, he had to skirt piecemeal domes and the Two Craters at Cape Southwest. The trip from west to east, over ice-covered frozen tundra, was spectacular as seen in the moonlight and in the headlights of the ACV. They stopped again for a pee break where the forty-five-million-year-old fossil forest was entombed. Maneuvering the hovercraft around the exposed petrified tree stumps was painful on Shawn's hand. He reached the flat beach area on the east coast and plowed out onto Nansen Sound, where the craft was occasionally again blocked by pressure ridges and ice. At that point he felt confident enough to radio Colonel Padalka. Fortunately, there appeared to be little atmospheric interference, and he kept the message short in case it was picked up by the Alert Listening Station and passed to Lowery's men at Eureka.

"Canadian craft nearing target. T minus ninety minutes."

"Roger, Canadian craft. T minus ninety."

They had an hour and a half left to cross Nansen Sound and up Eureka Sound to start pounding on the doors of the Eureka Buildings. One hour and forty-five minutes from now, Padalka's Helix choppers would begin looking for landing spots.

Phillips and Padalka both believed that a first attack from the seaward side of Eureka would catch Lowery's soldiers completely off guard, allowing the helicopters time to land safely. As the helicopters approached the base from the east, at that precise moment, Shawn's hovercraft would travel up the beach towards the first of the five original buildings built by Canadian and U.S. Air Forces in 1947. They were sure that Lowery's men would be surprised by the attack from the sea on New Year's Eve.

At T minus five minutes, Shawn had the hovercraft just a half mile offshore. He stopped the craft and opened the cockpit door. Using his glasses, he viewed the terrain known as the Eureka Weather station. All seemed to be quiet on the camp. There was no visible activity, and there appeared to be no guards posted. He spotted the route clear of jumbled ice that he would have to take to land on the Eureka Station beach. He returned to his seat in the cockpit, and the commandos donned their balaclavas and loaded their weapons, preparing for the assault. It was now or never.

Shawn shifted the levers and controls that provided full lift to the hovercraft. It was now riding at its highest level. He gunned the engine and headed for the first lit building onshore. The ACV sprayed snow and bits of ice in a ten-meter radius as it hit the edge of the ice and rode up on the beach. It sped towards the first building at forty miles an hour and slid to a stop, spewing commandos in all directions.

Fifteen minutes later, Padalka directed that one of his helicopters land at the ASTRO observatory site, fifteen kilometers from the main camp. With his chopper in the lead, the remaining three Helix helicopters headed for the tiny Eureka landing strip. The gravel runway was blocked by plows and snow blowers parked in strategic positions to prevent a fixed-wing craft from landing. The blockage wasn't a problem for his helicopters; they would have no such impediments.

After confirming that the helicopters on the tarmac were those that attacked him and his commandos, at T minus zero, Colonel Padalka fired a missile from his helicopter, writing off a large part of Admiral Lowery's naval air force. Padalka's missiles caught three of the helicopters on the ground, the two that had returned from the ice island battle plus one that was designated to stay at Eureka. In moments they were nothing more than tons of scrap iron.

While they were burning, Padalka brought his Helix helicopters into a safe landing without a single shot being fired at them. Lowery's men were too distracted by the attack of the commandos. They appeared so sudden from the hovercraft that they seemed to come out of nowhere. The commandos from both the helicopters and the hovercraft spread out so that they covered the buildings from the west, east, and north. The hovercraft was left running on the south side as Shawn went looking for Admiral Lowery's brother, the owner of the stash of money and pistol that he found on the broken Aurora. He removed the same pistol from his parka as he entered the building.

The Russian commandos advanced on the buildings using all entrances. They kicked open doors and ran down hallways. Shots were fired, and men were running in all directions. Shawn saw several dead Nunavut soldiers as he advanced down the hall of the first building that he entered behind the commandos. There was no doubt that the so-called Nunavut forces were caught completely off guard. They had not expected a return raid so quickly after their attack. Some of the soldiers looked like they had been celebrating the kicking of Russian butt. They would have little to celebrate as they laid curled up on the floor with their lifeblood draining from their bodies.

With the pistol firmly in his grip, Shawn cautiously rounded a corner in one of the buildings that seemed to be living quarters. He saw a tall blond-haired soldier running down the hallway. The figure was not wearing a balaclava, which indicated that he was not a Russian commando. The soldier turned and fired at Shawn, but the shot hit the wall behind him.

Phillips gave chase. The uniform ran down the hall and into a room, slamming the door shut. Shawn followed, yelling at him to stop and drop his weapon. Reaching the entrance, Shawn kicked the door in, revealing the man pulling an object out from under the bed. The blond soldier turned his pistol and fired towards the Canadian fighter. The bullet hit Phillips in his arm, causing him to drop his gun, and he quickly picked it up with his opposite hand. The blond man fired again. Shawn fired simultaneously, and the pistol jumped in his undamaged left hand as the bullet sped towards its target.

The bullet from the gun of the blond-haired combatant crashed off the ceiling while Shawn's bullet plunged into the body of the shooter. It found a home within inches of the man's heart. *Not bad for a left-handed shot,* thought Shawn.

The dead Nunavut renegade fell back against the dresser and slid down to the floor. Shawn's pain was uncomfortable, but he would be able to continue to root out other Nunavut radicals. He turned the body with his foot, and realized that he might have just killed the CO of Eureka, the brother of Admiral Lowery.

Shawn approached the man dressed in fatigues with the Nunavut flags on his uniform. A quick search of the body revealed a brown leather wallet. When Shawn opened it, he saw many photos and several pieces of identity cards verifying that the man he shot and killed was indeed Brian Lowery. The wallet contained several photos of his brother.

Shawn rolled the man away from the bed with his other foot and reached down and pulled out an object from under it. This was the object for which the Nunavut soldier had been reaching. It looked like some piece of electronic equipment, and it written on it was: MIR Master Control.

The sounds in the building and around the camp indicated that shooting was dying down. There was less screaming and yelling.

Shawn carried the object down the hall and walked into the cafeteria where Padalka's men held the Eureka residents against the walls. On one side of the room were civilians who worked at the weather station before Lowery's men took it over. On the other side of the room were two of Lowery's men, the only ones that remained alive. Shawn approached Colonel Padalka and threw the object on the table in front of him.

"I believe this is what you came for?" He pointed to the panel, and the Colonel picked up and examined the object.

"Where did you find it?"

"Down the hall, in the bedroom of the Chief Officer. There may be more pieces there or elsewhere on site."

Padalka sent half of his force to search for additional MIR parts. He contacted his helicopter men at the ASTRO Observatory to learn that the situation was under control at that location. There had been little resistance, and now there were only two of Lowery's soldiers who were slightly wounded. Padalka told the commando leader to search the ASTRO building for MIR parts and join him in the cafeteria.

All of the Eureka buildings were thoroughly searched with no other MIR parts being found. The bodies of Lowery's troops numbered twenty. They were placed in a shed where the cold temperature would preserve them. The same building also contained the bodies of eight loyal Eureka residents. They had apparently been killed by Lowery's forces when they took over the station.

The medic for the commandos again dressed Shawn's latest wound. It was getting to be a habit, thought Shawn. Fortunately, the bullet had made a clean exit, and no vital veins or organs were hit.

Padalka took control of the Eureka station. He directed that the snowplows and other vehicles be left on the runways should Lowery's forces attempt a counterattack. He also ordered guards to watch the dark Arctic sky and the shoreline for incoming aircraft or ships. The civilians, casual workers, and the scientists cleaned up the mess and provided the Russian commandos with a hearty meal. The residents included bottles of vodka that they were saving for a special occasion. The Russians had the good fortune not to have lost any of their comrades in the attack, although several were wounded. Life was returning to normal. The only question for Shawn Phillips and Colonel Padalka was what to do next.

# 38   THE CAPTURE

I January 1000 hrs local, Frobisher Bay, Nunavut

Major General Dave Shanahan was concerned that his room had been searched. He needed to find another place to stay while he continued to investigate and to watch the former Admiral. He decided that contacting Simone Aokalik of the Arctic Rangers would be his safest bet.

Since it was near to ten in the morning, he left his room to check out the Navigator Inn Cafe to see if the rangers' leader was in the vicinity trying to contact him. He sat at a window-side booth drinking his black coffee, no sugar, and watched as Simone crossed the road and entered the cafe. Shanahan checked the cafe for Lowery supporters and saw several men dressed in army fatigues with Nunavut flags on their shoulders having their breakfasts. They didn't appear to be interested in either him or Simone.

The Ranger and the Major General made eye contact, and there was a slight nod of the head by each man. The Ranger bought a pack of cigarettes and left the room, walking across the street into one of the many alleys in Frobisher Bay. The alleys sat between the small homes that lined the main street of Iqaluit. Like a shadow, within moments, Simone was swallowed by the darkness of the alleyway.

After finishing his coffee, Shanahan returned to his room, fetched his wallet, pistol, and laptop computer and put on his parka. He wandered down the main street in Iqaluit until he reached a shop that advertised snowmobile clothing in its showroom window. Entering the establishment, he purchased an outfit that was as near to snow color as possible. The store owner suggested that he only needed a snow machine to experience the thrill of the great outdoors. As it happened, the owner had an older ski-doo machine that he could rent if the customer wanted to feel the accelerating rush of flying over the snow at sixty mph. Shanahan took him up on the offer.

Wearing the snowmobile outfit and with the parka and computer secured tightly, the MAG commander mounted the creature and directed it out of town.

It was not the first time that he rode a snowmobile. As a youngster, he spent many a night zipping over the fields near his boyhood home in Baddeck, N.S. But on this very long Arctic night, caution was required. He was careful to stay on the roadway until he was out of the sight of Iqaluit residents. He turned the snowmobile into the surrounding snow-covered fields to give a wide detour to any roadblocks that might be set up on the roads leading out of town. The light of the snowmobile danced about the field as his body jumped and swayed on the beast to avoid hitting holes and fence posts. Once, he had to reduce his speed and turn off the headlight as he approached a section of roadway that ran across a body of open running water. There was no way to the other side except by use of the road. He left the headlight off for about ten minutes after making the detour. He only hoped that he would spot any fences before plowing into them. It was a known fact that people had been decapitated on snowmobiles that struck the top wires of fences while running at full throttle. After the wide detour, he steered the machine back on to a field running parallel to the road leading to Apex.

Shanahan parked the machine outside of the home of Simone Aokalik and noticed there were a number of other similar devices parked in the same area. He tapped lightly on the door, it opened a crack and Shanahan slipped inside. The room contained a dozen Arctic Rangers, all wearing their red hats and sweaters and cradling their rifles in their arms. Simone introduced Shanahan to his Ranger team while each reported on their activities.

One Ranger mentioned that he and his two sons had found a mother lode of dynamite at a developer's winter storage site. They managed to borrow most of it. The dynamite was subsequently distributed to all other Rangers who would put it to good use. On account of the explosives, Lowery now had fewer radars and airport storage facilities than he had the week earlier. Another Ranger mentioned that he used his explosives to destroy several of the Nunavut forces' trucks as they passed over a bridge in his village. All of Lowery's men on the trucks were killed.

A third Ranger, taller than the others, mentioned that the new Premier would not broadcast his propaganda messages to Nunavut residents by radio or TV any longer. The Ranger had blown the towers used to transmit the broadcasts, and the buildings were now beyond repair. Other Rangers reported their destruction of satellite dishes.

When the subject of plans came up, a younger Inuit ranger living near the coast mentioned that he and his friends had latched together two snowmobiles and packed them with dynamite. The machines would be directed towards the B4 Hovercraft that Lowery had proudly displayed during his 'gift' broadcast. The attack could take place at any time, whenever Shanahan wanted to coordinate it with another event.

The discussion continued among the group for more than an hour. Two more of Lowery's helicopters had been destroyed in outlying communities. However, they could not penetrate the veil of security at the Frobisher airport, so no action had been taken against the remaining Apaches. They were now well guarded. Several rangers also noticed that one of the buildings near a petrol refueling area was heavily guarded since boxes of parts were seen being offloaded from a VTOL and transported to the facility. None of the rangers had been able to approach the building due to the increased security.

Shanahan said that it was essential to direct their activities towards the local bank containing the hundreds of millions of dollars sent by Ottawa. The money was to help defray Nunavut's costs of transferring from being part of the North West Territories to being a separate province. He suggested that they prepare a truck bomb to blow up the bank and have it ready when it was needed. The money was insured, so Canada's government could easily replace the money without any loss, once Nunavut was back in Canadian hands. Destroying the bank and the money would keep Lowery from fleeing with it as his forces were eliminated.

Another main priority for the group was the rescue of former Nunavut politicians that were being held captive. Shanahan described the site where he saw the former premier being imprisoned. They were also asked to keep an eye open for Battery Commander Marsh, who was in the area. He described March's appearance. If possible, he would prefer that Marsh be captured alive since he was the one that fired the missile that brought down the Canadian Forces Aurora. The Canadian Defense Department wanted him tried for this act of terrorism.

With plans in place, the meeting broke up and the rangers left as quietly as they came.

Shanahan stayed behind for further talks with Simone. He asked if he knew of a place where he could bed down and store his computer as his room had been searched. Simone made a phone call that produced a room for the General on the outskirts of Iqaluit near the airport.

Shanahan suggested that his computer remain with the Inuit leader, in case it was needed to contact Phillips or Ottawa. The General showed the bearded fighter how to transmit messages by email using the computer to send a signal to a polar-orbiting satellite, which would relay the message to a ground station in Ottawa. After being assured by Simone that the computer would be safe with him, Shanahan checked his emails one final time. There were two messages.

The first message was from Major Shawn Phillips.

"Eureka Weather Station successfully recaptured from Nunavut Forces. Twenty of Lowery's forces were killed and the other two captured. There were no losses among the Russian or Canadian combatants. Eight of the previous residents of Eureka were found dead on-site, due to Lowery's men capturing the station. Three Apache helicopters were destroyed. A MIR master control panel was found in the possession of Brian Lowery. He did not survive the attack. Friendly forces, including a Russian sub, are now prepared to proceed to Frobisher Bay. Contact will be made shortly with yourself or Mr. Aokalik regarding a coordinated attack. Advise specific location of MIR parts at FB airport. Signed, Phillips." The email message was also read by Simone.

The second message was from General Le Beau at National Defense Headquarters, and it was classified as Top Secret.

"Be advised that there will be a coordinated attack at the Alert Listening Station and the town of Frobisher Bay on I January at 2000 hrs, in T minus ten hours. The Alert station will be attacked by Canadian Forces paratroopers while the attack on FB will come from Sea King helicopters on board Canadian Navy ships that have sailed as far north as possible given the ice conditions. The U.S. government now advises that Admiral Heiserman and Battery Commander Marsh are fugitives from justice. They are responsible for the destruction of Aurora, as well as for the crash and looting of MIR. These men are expendable since they provided all military equipment and supplies, including a time bomb, to ex admiral Lowery and his forces. Our heartfelt thanks go out to the rangers. You will be contacted. Signed, Le Beau."

Shanahan typed a reply to the Chief of the Defense Staff. He mentioned that Eureka had been recaptured and that at least six of Lowery's helicopters had been destroyed. Further, with the Arctic Rangers' help, several trucks, radar, and broadcast towers had also been eliminated. The B4 hovercraft and the bank containing the transition funds were expected to be destroyed before the target deadline. The message ended with the statement that Russian Forces, including a submarine and a commando unit, were also on the way to Frobisher Bay to assist with the liberation of the provincial capital.

Shanahan showed the Inuit leader the email from NDHQ as well as the reply. Simone smiled at the reference to the good work of the Arctic Rangers. The Major General then sent a response to his Search Master, indicating that the MIR components were most likely in a heavily guarded building adjacent to the petrol pumps at the Frobisher Bay airport. He would attempt to confirm this information ASAP. He suggested that the Russian Forces arrive on 1 January at 2000 hrs local to be part of a coordinated attack with Ottawa forces.

Shanahan announced to his Inuit friend that he would return to the airport and his hotel to retrieve his other belongings. Before he left, he borrowed a pair of wire cutters and night glasses.

After his Frobisher visitor left, Simone contacted the other Rangers to inform them of the top-secret coordinated attack on Frobisher Bay in less than ten hours. The detonation of bombs on the hovercraft and bank were to take place one hour before the attack. Unbeknownst to the General, Simone had appointed one of the Rangers to keep an eye on Shanahan. The General possessed all the knowledge about the attack. If something happened to him, and if it was ever forced out of the General, then the lives of his Rangers would be severely compromised.

Shanahan used the snowmobile to get back to town and to the airport. He made the same wide route around the roadblocks that he had used previously. When he reached the airport perimeter, he reduced the machine's speed to deaden the engine's noise. He found a tree near the airport fence where he could survey the expanse of the airfield.

As he looked through the night glasses, he saw a U.S. Navy helicopter hovering over the main tarmac, waiting for permission to land. Permission was evidently granted since it touched down shortly thereafter, and the engine turned off. A half dozen armed men wearing navy uniforms and white police labeled helmets emerged from the helicopter and walked the short distance to the nearest building. He watched as they commandeered a van, at gunpoint, then drove it in the direction of the town.

Shanahan returned to his machine and followed a track that traveled along the wire fence until he was near the petrol pumps and the building supposedly containing the MIR computer parts. He could see that there were lights on in the facility, and several guards were circling the building.

He used the wire cutters to snip through the fence. Fortunately, it was not electrified or tied to any alarm system. He crawled on his belly towards the building. The near-white snowmobile suit offered him warmth as well as protection since it camouflaged his movements. He was approximately twenty meters from the building, working his way around it and staying alert for guards. He was looking for a place where he could get up onto the roof of the building and see what was going on inside. At the moment, the guards were gathered together at the front of the place, having a smoke.

Near one corner of the building, an attached shed seemed to provide a way to reach the roof; he spotted a skylight from which the interior light poured out. He propped an oil barrel next to the shed and climbed up onto its roof. The guards were still busy chatting and finishing their cigarettes as he scrambled to the roof of the main building and laid down next to the skylight. Slowly lifting his head, he could see the inside of the building. For the moment he was safe.

Inside the building, a huge wall was covered with instruments and panels from the MIR Space Station. There were recorders, videos, and other storage devices that appeared to be connected. It must have taken the scientists many hours to set up the display, and considerable work given the fact that the components had arrived less than thirty-six hours ago.

Several men stood in front of the display while pouring over blueprints. Shanahan recognized one of the observers as Admiral Heiserman from their near meeting at the hotel reception area. The uniformed U.S. naval officer was escorting the Chinese ambassador to his suite at the time. Now he stood next to another U.S. Navy uniform, presumably belonging to none other than Battery Commander Marsh. One of the technicians, in a white coat, gave the thumbs up and pushed a red button, which was apparently to start up the MIR data storage system. Nothing happened. There was no clicking of printers, no video monitors lit up, and no voices seemed to come from the recorders.

The first reaction was that of Heiserman, who became very annoyed and started to yell at the technician as Marsh went about pounding the tops of equipment, hoping to start the flow of data. Heiserman yelled at him to stop. The technician carefully checked all the wires, and there appeared to be no faults with the connections. Heiserman must have suggested that they double-check all the instruments listed on the blueprints and confirm that they were all attached to the wall array. The technician walked around and pointed out each item as Heiserman called its name from the blueprints. He called one item, and the technician was unable to find it. Shanahan guessed that it had to be the master control panel, now safely in the hands of Major Phillips and the Commander of the Commando Unit.

Heiserman reached into his pocket and retrieved another list; the missing item had been apparently checked off on this list as well. He wandered around the display, scratching his head and trying to figure out how an essential piece of the MIR data processing puzzle was missing. It was there when the items were put aboard the VTOL since it was obviously checked off as having been included in the shipment. Shanahan could see that Heiserman was furious.

He watched as Heiserman spoke to the technician. From the hand movements and drawings being made by Heiserman, they seemed to be discussing the possibility of manufacturing their own control panel. The technician shook his head. The arguments continued for another ten minutes until Heiserman sent Marsh for his coat.

Shanahan could see both Heiserman and Marsh leaving the building through a door on the far side. He heard a van start-up, and there was a call to the guards. Shanahan watched them run to the vehicle and enter it before it drove away. The lights of the van indicated that it was leaving the airport vicinity. The technician started to shut down the lights inside, and Shanahan knew it was time to leave.

He wiggled his way off the shed and along the ground to the hole in the fence. He had been lucky that Heiserman had called off the security men from guarding the useless array of computer equipment. He patched up the hole in the fence as best as he could so that the break-in would not be discovered for several hours. After driving the snowmobile back to the shop from where he leased it, he walked to the hotel parking lot to store the night glasses, wire cutters and snowsuit in the trunk of his rental car. He put his parka back on and pulled up his hood.

The Commander of Maritime Air Group used the hotel stairs to reach reception at the Navigator Inn. He mentioned that he, Mitchell, would be checking out and would like to pay his hotel costs at this time.

As the clerk prepared his statement, a dozen U.S. navy policemen entered the hotel. They demanded that the clerk tell them the rooms belonging to Admiral Heiserman and Battery Commander Marsh. The clerk tried to indicate that he was presently dealing with Mr. Mitchell, but the lead policeman would not have any delay; he wanted an answer immediately. The clerk provided the room numbers but mentioned that neither of the gentlemen were in the hotel at this time since they both went to the airport. The policemen conferred among themselves, deciding if they should break up, with one party staying at the hotel while the other went to the airport, or travel together. In the end, they all left the hotel and jumped into the van that they had left parked and running in front of the doors of the hotel.

Mitchell paid his hotel bill and returned to his room. As he opened the door, he knew immediately that there was something different about the room. He didn't have time to react before two men dressed in Nunavut uniforms grabbed him and wrestled him to the floor.

His hands were wrenched behind his back, and a pair of handcuffs were placed on his wrists. He was dragged to a standing position.

"What in hell are you doing?" asked Shanahan.

"Are you Mitchell? We are interviewing anyone who has a computer. We will arrest anyone who can receive and send messages out of our country without our permission," said one of the guards.

Shanahan protested his innocence, emphatically shouting that as a reporter, he was entitled to record his news reports and send them to his editor. He threatened to call his boss in Ottawa, saying that his editor knew several Canadian politicians who would create a stink with the Nunavut army over his treatment.

He was taken upstairs to a lavish suite that could only belong to ex admiral Lowery. One guard made a tap on an adjoining door and then stood next to the Major General. The door opened, and Lowery stepped out into the living area of the suite. Shanahan's parka hood was still up over his head, so Lowery had not yet recognized him.

"So, you are Mr. Mitchell. I am curious about your business in Nunavut. Unwrap him boys, let's see what he looks like."

Admiral Lowery was startled, and he immediately became extremely red in the face.

"You, of all the goddamn people to see in Frobisher Bay! I should have expected you to show up."

The ex-admiral was still agitated but started to calm down when he saw that the situation was completely under his control.

"This boy," he said, pointing to the partially clad figure, "is none other than Brigadier General Shanahan of the Canadian Forces."

Dave Shanahan knew it was not a good time to remind Lowery of his recent promotion to Major General.

"This is one dangerous little bastard. Did you frisk him?"

They looked at one another and shrugged their shoulders. Lowery ran a hand over both of Shanahan's legs, finding the pistol in his sock.

"Why am I always stuck with incompetent people?" asked Lowery rhetorically, referring to the fact that the guards had forgotten to check the parka clad hotel guest for a weapon.

"I should have known that you were nearby. I bet you had something to do with one of my guards being killed at a road block. No doubt, you are most likely responsible for all the resistance that I'm getting from some local people. Did you have anything to do with all the damage to my equipment and supplies? I bet you did, and I should kill you right now, but you may be of value to me yet. Did you know that I told the defense minister, who probably told General Le Beau, that I would have you shot if you showed up here? Now tell me, what in hell's name is your purpose of coming here? I want an answer, or I may just change my mind and shoot you on the spot."

"I'm here to bring you back to be court-martialed for crimes against the Government of Canada."

"Well, that is just bloody dandy. Did you happen to notice that I control everything around this stinking town, including that dumb ass Inuit Premier?"

When the General didn't answer, Lowery told the guards that he was going to his war room to discuss strategy, and that they were to beat the crap out of this man until he told them why he was in Frobisher Bay.

# 39 ARCTIC STORM

1 January 1000 hrs local, NDHQ, Ottawa

The Chief of the Defense Staff walked around his operations center, which he had constructed by improvising changes to his conference room. With his own private Ops Center, he was able to look at and think out operational problems on a moment's notice. It had saved him time in decision making by avoiding the main Operations Center. It was a hardened shelter in the basement of the NDHQ building on Colby Drive.

Le Beau looked out the thirteenth-floor window of the building at all the Ottawa citizens on their way to work. Some were going to the University of Ottawa that sat opposite NDHQ, on the other side of the Rideau Canal. He enjoyed watching the skaters on the frozen canal, and he envied those that found the time and effort to do their daily jogging along the channel, even in the midst of winter. He sure didn't expect to be at work on this first day of a new year in a new century, but this coup in Nunavut had to be dealt with quickly. He was under pressure by the PM to resolve this issue.

In the room with him were the chiefs of the Army, Navy, and Air Force. His train of thought returned to the matter at hand, an attack on the Alert Station targets with a simultaneous attack on the city of Frobisher Bay. The conference table contained detailed maps and relief models of both areas. The room walls were lined with weather maps, the status of forces, reports, and location charts of deployed forces and equipment. It seemed like a thousand other details were plastered on screens and every available square inch of wall. The targets for the attack were already established, and they needed to work on the methodology. The CDS wanted to go over everything one more time. The plans that they would be using were open for scrutiny. If there were any flaws in the process, there was still time to divert or to make substitute arrangements.

This was one of a number of meetings that the General had called in the past couple of days.

The Prime Minister and the Minister of Defense had been receiving a lot of pressure from the public and the media to do something about the revolt in the new province of Nunavut. The PM had declared the War Measures Act and instituted Martial Law in the area, but the Canadian Government and Canadian Forces appeared to be doing nothing to reverse this revolution. A revolt by a province that didn't even have the decency to have a referendum before declaring itself independent of Canada.

A recent bill introduced in the House, and passed by the House and the Senate, allowed any of the provinces to legally separate from Canada if the government of the province asked the residents of the province, in a straightforward referendum question, if they wished to leave Canada. If they received a yes vote by a majority of the residents, it would then be possible for the province's government to negotiate with the federal government to separate. The terms of separation must be negotiable; without such a settlement, most Canadians would not stand for the breakup of their country. The new Premier promised a referendum after declaring independence. This was a coup. People were being killed in parts of Nunavut.

Le Beau knew that the PM could not tell the public what was being done behind the scenes, in secret, such as the work of his two military officers in Nunavut, Shanahan and Phillips. The Canadians knew nothing about the help and negotiated assistance of the Russian troops in the Nunavut matter. Discussing these activities in public would put the lives of all of his military personnel in danger. However, the PM did want something done, that he could reveal to Canada, to show that he had the situation under control. He felt that it was time that the military got involved in a substantial way. Le Beau tapped the table to call the meeting to order.

"This will be the final meeting before Operation Arctic Storm is implemented. Let's summarize what we know so far. The communication that we got from Major General Shanahan told us that our forces have taken Eureka. The enemy lost several helicopters, and there were sufficient casualties among the enemy that his force must be considered degraded.

We also know that the resistance in Nunavut, particularly in Frobisher Bay, has further eroded the capability of the enemy, namely the troops known as Nunavut Forces, under the leadership of ex admiral Lowery.

"The resistance has eliminated a number of trucks, some helicopters, and a number of TV and radar towers. They also have plans to cause additional damage between now and the time of our attack. They will blow up the hovercraft and the bank containing the transitional fund, before our Forces land. We also know that our combatants in Eureka consist mainly of Russian commandos working under Major Phillips's supervision. They are also on their way to Frobisher Bay, along with a Russian sub. As I understand it, they will be on hand in time for our invasion. We know that there is an American sub on its way to Frobisher, and we might be able to make use of it.

"In regards to our own plan, our Sea King helicopters, containing troops from CFB Gagetown, are about to be launched from several Canadian Navy ships off the coast of Frobisher Bay, at the edge of the ice pack. They will land here at the Frobisher Airport," stated General Le Beau, as he used the pointer to locate the airport on the model, "and here at the harbor, and here at the stadium near the center of the city." He used the pointer to point out each spot.

"Chief of the Navy, jump in please to correct me if I am wrong. The attack will be coordinated with other friendly forces, like the RCMP, by prearranged communication channels. Did I leave anything out, Chief?" The CDS was looking at the Chief of Naval Forces.

"No, Sir."

"At the same time, the Air Force Chief has two Hercs, filled with paratroopers, on route to Alert. The Chief of the Army has pre-positioned the Jump Companies in the light battalion of the Royal Canadian Regiment, Princess Patricia's Canadian Light Infantry and the 22nd Regiment at CFB Edmonton. The flights will leave Edmonton by 1600 hrs. As you know, the previous defense minister had disbanded the Canadian Airborne Regiment in 1995, so we had to scramble to find enough jumpers to attack the Alert Listening Post. Chief of the Army, do you think that we have enough paratroopers to take Alert?"

"I think so, Sir. We have seventy men split between two aircraft. As far as we know, there are only fifty of Lowery's men at Alert."

"Do they and the men from Gagetown have all the supplies and equipment that they need to do the job?"

"Yes, Sir. Every man has been issued with the latest automatic rifles, Arctic gear, infrared night goggles, and new chutes. Additional equipment including missile launchers and communication equipment are either located on the Sea Kings or on the Hercs, to be dropped after the troops jump."

"Show me where you plan to disburse the men at Alert."

"The main body of twenty will head for the gray sided operations building, the one topped with a dozen high frequency radio antennae on the west end of the main complex. Here," he pointed with the pointer to a metal-clad building, then continued, "as soon as they land, they will gather up their parachutes and assemble at a nearby site and begin to sneak their way towards this building. They have been ordered to shoot to kill anyone who will not surrender at a moment's notice. Another group of twenty will head for the station's gymnasium, here, where we believe the 80 Canadian Forces military personnel are being held. Most are radio technicians that generally inhabit the Station."

He tapped a slab-sided model building.

"The remaining men will venture from door to door in the three burgundy and blue-striped two-story, metal-clad, accommodation buildings. They resemble a set of mammoth Lego blocks linked with a one-story corridor. We estimate that the whole of the Listening Station will be in our hands one hour after we land."

"What are the chances that all of our sensitive listening equipment will still be in working order after the attack? We want to be able to monitor the airwaves for Russian radio traffic as soon as possible. We have not been able to do any electronic eavesdrop since Lowery's men took over the station. We may be missing some vital intelligence."

"Sir, my men, are not using explosives, so the equipment should be fine, unless the Nunavut Forces have already destroyed some of the electronic gear. As I said previously, I have instructed them to shoot to kill at the least sign of resistance."

"Chief of the Air Force, how are the Hercs performing?"

"No problems, everything is operational at this point," the Chief replied, hastily adding, "Sir," afterwards.

"Well, that covers the logistics of the attack. According to the Frobisher Bay newspaper, the government plans to celebrate the first day of their new government by having a firework display today at 2000 hrs. We have timed our attack to coincide with the exhibition. We hope that we will catch them off guard, and that there will be some confusion between their fireworks and our bullets and bombs. Unless there are some other points that I have overlooked, I would say that about wraps it up as far as I am concerned. When we meet again, this time tomorrow, I expect nothing but good news. I want to hear from you that Nunavut is back under the control of Canada. Now let us each say a silent prayer for the safety of our troops and the residents of Alert and Frobisher Bay before we leave the room."

The meeting broke up after the prayer, and each staff officer returned to his headquarters to take control of his part of Operation Arctic Storm.

# 40  TWO ADMIRALS, ONE GENERAL

1 January, 1600 hrs local, Frobisher Bay, Nunavut

Buzz Lowery returned to the living room of his suite after a one-hour nap. In the middle of the room was Major General Dave Shanahan, tied with his arms behind his back to a chair and badly bruised around the eyes and with swollen lips. He must have also been beaten with a club in the rib cage and stomach area since he was crouched over and moaning in pain. Lowery turned to his two henchmen that had done the beating for him.

"Did he tell you why he came here? Who is he working with?"

"He didn't say anything. He is one tough little bastard."

"I know this prick well. If he hasn't said anything by now, he probably won't say anything, ever. Perhaps if we put him on ice for a few days in the shed at the airport with the ex-Premier, he might talk if he freezes and starves for a few days."

At that moment, the door opened and in walked Admiral Heiserman. He was still wearing his U.S. Navy blue uniform, which contrasted with Lowery's army fatigues decorated with the Nunavut flags and four gold stars. Lowery certainly didn't dress like a Navy admiral. He was beginning to look more like Castro every day, thought Shanahan.

Heiserman looked at the man slumped in the chair and severely bruised. The tied-up man looked like a bum off the street in his soiled trousers and parka. Heiserman behaved as if he saw beaten prisoners every day of his life. He was red in the face and frustrated from some previous problem, and his finger pointed to Shanahan as he spoke to Lowery.

"Who in hell is that bum, and why did you nearly beat the living hell out of him?"

"Not that it is any business of yours, but I'm sure that this bastard is a spy who has come here to stop this revolution. That is Brig. Gen. Shanahan, of the Maritime Air Group formerly under my Command. This prick, along with the Resistance, is responsible for destroying my planes and my trucks. I have lost a number of my best troops to this clown, and now he is going to pay for it. What the hell is your problem?"

"I've had a little difficulty out at the airport with something that I have been working on during the past thirty-six hours. My planned project should have put me in a good position to continue my struggle to run for president, however, a setback is screwing up my whole project. I wish I knew how the hell it happened!"

"This bastard has been screwing up our work throughout this province. It wouldn't surprise me if this asshole caused your setback," said Lowery, pointing to Shanahan.

"I doubt it. I think one of my submariners screwed me up, but I'll get my revenge in about two hours." He paused to look at his watch, then continued, "I still might be able to get the project to work, but it's going to take longer than I thought."

Shanahan was in a severely weakened state, but he managed to regain clarity. A plan was formulating in his devious mind. He thought that he might be able to get the two admirals fighting with one another, and they might break ranks or might even leak some critical information that he could use in the coming battle, assuming that he survived this ordeal.

"It wasn't one of your Sea Devil crew, but I know who screwed you up," said the heavily bruised Commander of Maritime Air Group.

Heiserman did a one hundred twenty-degree turn and looked at Shanahan. How was this possible? He was surprised that this man knew about the Sea Devil and possibly about his source of frustration.

"What in hell are you talking about?"

Shanahan sat up as straight as his body would allow. He wanted to be able to see the expressions on the faces of Lowery and Heiserman as he played his cards and set them against one another.

"You are pissed off because you rigged all of the MIR data storage parts together but they won't work when you pull the switch."

Heiserman rushed to Shanahan and madly gripped him by the lapels of his parka, practically pulling him out of the chair.

"Jesus Christ, you are right! How in hell did you know that?"

"The Captain of the Sea Devil told your bosses in Washington that you stripped MIR of its recorders, videos, and hard drive memory in its computer. They are not too happy with you right about now. I know that you're missing an essential part to make the whole system work, and I know what happened to it."

Still holding the lapels, Heiserman physically lifted Shanahan out of the chair. Heiserman had no problem since he was a big man with enormous strength. He stood at well over six feet and weighed about 240 pounds.

"What about the missing part?" he demanded.

"Why don't you ask your buddy here, wearing your four stars? It was his brother, Brian Lowery, that stole the piece from your helicopter while you were in Eureka."

Heiserman dropped Shanahan's jacket and the General slumped again in his chair with another moan.

"Why would Brian steal a part out of my helicopter?" he asked Lowery, as he walked towards the ex-admiral.

"He did it on his own. He didn't ask me. I was going to give it back to you as soon as I could pick it up from him. I didn't know it was so goddamn important to you. And while we are on the subject of Eureka, why were you pumping him for information about me?" Lowery thought that going on the offensive would lessen Heiserman's anger.

Heiserman calmed down but just a little, now that he knew what happened to the missing part. He was alarmed that his devious questioning of the brother had been detected. He thought that Brian was near high drunk during the whole questioning period.

"I just wanted to know what you were up to with this revolution of yours. It seemed strange that you would give up a promising career just because you didn't get a string of listening devices on your Arctic sea bed to hear the Russian subs. I know now what you are really after. It's the millions in the bank, and you hope to steal thousands of acres of Inuit land in the strange hope that it will be worth millions someday, after global warming turns it into another Florida beachfront. I want the piece of MIR," he said loudly into Lowery's face. "Everything else seems to work. I want it back now!"

Lowery was perturbed that Brian had told so much to Heiserman about his dreams since he couldn't trust this man, Heiserman, with anything. He was also annoyed that Heiserman had spoken out in front of Shanahan. Some small part of him still wanted Shanahan to respect him for taking a stand against Ottawa and for the people of Nunavut. It bothered him for a short moment, but he shook it off since he planned to have Shanahan killed just for showing up in Frobisher Bay. After all, he had warned the CDS what would happen to Shanahan if he came to his newly independent country. It would then be Ottawa's fault for the death of Shanahan. But he had to counter the argument of Heiserman, first. He couldn't let him be one up on him.

"You'll get your goddamn MIR part when I get the help that you promised from the U.S. Navy, to help me with my takeover of this province. Your chances of becoming president will be very slim if the American public knows how you stripped the Russian space station."

No one spoke. They just looked at one another. Shanahan decided to up the ante.

"The U.S. Navy exercise has been called off. There will be no help, and Heiserman is going to be arrested. The U.S. Navy police are already in Frobisher."

The two admirals looked at one another. It was Heiserman who spoke.

"Is this true? Are there Navy police in Iqaluit?"

"A Navy plane did land today at the airport. I got the report. I thought that you had arranged for some troops."

Heiserman walked to the window of the hotel and looked out as if he was expecting to see the Navy police parked in front of the Navigator Inn. That's when Shanahan decided to raise the stakes even higher.

"You can also forget about getting the MIR part. The Russians got it when they attacked Eureka yesterday."

Lowery turned to his henchman, asking if they knew about Eureka. They looked puzzled. He walked to the coffee table and lifted the phone, asked the same question into it, and listened to the answer before putting down the receiver.

"The Canadians, with the help of some Russians, took Eureka. We just found out about it from our people at Station Alert. Apparently, Eureka was able to contact them just before they were overrun." He turned to Shanahan. "What about my brother?"

Shanahan just shrugged his shoulders. It was not a good time to tell him that Brian was slain in the firefight.

Heiserman knew that the end was near. His dream of selling the MIR storage system to the Chinese for a hundred million dollars was at a near end, now that the Russians had the central control piece. It would take him years to locate or manufacture a replacement part. He could try to bluff the Chinese that all the essential parts were in the crates, but he knew that the Chinese would not pay until they saw the system running. Now even the police were after him, which meant that they would drag him back to Washington, and his career would be in tatters, as would his chances of being president.

"This is all your fault, with your stupid idea of drawing Ottawa into a conflict with Moscow, supposedly just to get your additional protection for the North. That is a load of hogwash, and I fell for it," said Heiserman, showing his frustration.

Lowery couldn't take all the blame for Heiserman's fiasco. After all it was Heiserman that went after MIR for its storage system.

"It was your idea to plunder MIR. It was your idea to preposition a submarine in the Arctic and to pay the French astronaut to program the MIR to crash there." Heiserman countered with criticism of his own.

"Oh yeah, you were happy that I made the MIR crash, since you knew that the Russians would rush to retrieve it. You thought that the presence of a submarine and the Russians might lead the Canadian government to overreact, and that they might send troops, including Americans. You hoped that the Canadian government would finally agree with you and set up a Nunavut-Canadian force, with you in charge."

Back and forth went the arguments about who was responsible for the fiasco.

Once again, the room grew silent, so Shanahan pushed the poker into the fire a little more. He looked at Lowery.

"Heiserman knew our Nor Pat schedule, and he probably got it from you. He knew that we would have an Aurora aircraft in the Ellesmere Island area shortly after Christmas. Did you know that he arranged to have Battery Commander Marsh and a rocket launcher put on the Sea Devil? It was his man that brought down the Aurora, one of your planes. How do you think the Canadian public will react when they find out that you provided Admiral Heiserman with the Nor Pat schedule, then arranged for the Aurora to be near the site of the submarine supposedly just to drop off a package to your brother at Eureka?"

"How did you know about the detour to Eureka? What happened to the package? There was fifty thousand dollars in that package, and I wanted it back," shrieked Lowery.

"All of the crew of the Aurora are now safe and sound in our medical facilities in Canada. That includes Captain Winters. He told us that it was you who diverted the plane to Eureka. You blackmailed him with his career intentions. The detour resulted in the Aurora detecting the sub. It was only natural that the radar operator on board the Aurora would detect the sub that Admiral Heiserman prepositioned in the Arctic. It was also only natural that Winters would divert from Eureka to go and look for the sub. Canadians won't forget your role in the loss of the Aurora and the deaths of several crew members."

"You told me that Winters was part of the missing crew. I checked with Admiral Heiserman, and he told me that there was no Captain Winters on board the sub. I presumed that he was lost in the crash. He was the only person who knew that I wanted the plane to go to Eureka"

"He is very much alive. My Search Master found him, and we arranged for his transport to a medical facility without your knowledge," said Shanahan.

Lowery and Heiserman were at a loss for words over the amount of secret information held by Shanahan. The worst of it was that other authorities probably also knew the same information by now. Shanahan's strategy of revealing the crosses, and double-crossing to pit one admiral against the other, was paying off. He had already picked up several more pieces of the puzzle. He continued playing devil's advocate as he looked at the former naval commander.

"The Canadian government thinks that you are a traitor. Tell me what part did you to play in the plot to sell Russian MIR data to the Chinese? I saw the Chinese Ambassador to Canada talking to Admiral Heiserman at this hotel, in which you were both staying. Do you know that your buddy here stole all the U.S. Navy helicopters, trucks, and missiles, and turned them over to your revolutionary guard? What Canadian secrets did you promise to throw into the deal to entice the Chinese to buy Heiserman's MIR jigsaw puzzle?"

Lowery was infuriated when he turned to face Heiserman.

"You would sell secrets to those communist bastards? I hate the Chinese. Even more than I hate the Ruskies. I can't see how you would stoop so low to sell secrets to the Commies. I could never stoop that low."

"Now you think you are high and mighty," spewed Heiserman. "Just a few days ago, you shot a half a dozen elected politicians because they wouldn't go along with your ridiculous idea to declare independence! You shot these people because they wouldn't believe that Nunavut could become a new Florida. That's crazy! How were you planning on speeding up global warming? And, it doesn't bother you or your conscience that you planned to bring hundreds of former navy personnel into Nunavut and buy their votes in order to get a yes vote in the succession referendum? Yes, I know about that little plan. I also keep my eyes and ears open. It wasn't hard to figure out what you were doing with all that cash I was giving you from my corporate friends. How much land were you planning to steal from the Inuit people?"

Lowery didn't like being called crazy, and he certainly didn't like the fact that Heiserman considered his ideas ridiculous. Lowery wanted, it seemed, the respect of Heiserman and Shanahan for his ideas on global warming.

Shanahan decided that this might be a good time to show all of his aces and wrap up the game. He spoke to Lowery again.

"I suggest that you release me, and I will take you to the Canadian authorities, who will go easy on you for giving yourselves up. I'm sure that Commander Hayes of the Sea Devil will testify, and Admiral Heiserman should get off with a few years in Leavenworth, while you will probably have to spend time in a federal pen."

"Captain Hayes will not be around to testify against anyone, shortly," Heiserman said as he looked at his watch for a second time.

"What do you mean by that?" asked Shanahan. Then like a lightning bolt, it struck him. "Of course, you put the time bomb on the Sea Devil."

"You know about the time bomb? Christ, is there anything that you don't know?"

"I don't believe that you are so goddamn evil that you would blow up your own men on your submarine," replied Lowery with a pained look. Perhaps there was a bit of decency in him after all, though Shanahan.

"And I told you before that I'm sick and tired of your righteous crap. Don't give me that shit about blowing up my own boats when you deliberately put your aircraft in danger when you sent an Aurora to an area where my sub was waiting."

Heiserman was turning red with anger and he was trying hard to restrain himself from striking out at Lowery.

"You didn't have to blow the plane out of the sky. It was only doing its duty!"

"What was I supposed to do? I needed to protect the United States."

He was lying, just trying to protect his own identity, thought Shanahan. Heiserman went on.

"Besides, I was sure that it would cause the Canadian government to blame the Russians and send in the Canadian and American Forces to annihilate the goddamn Russians that were coming to get MIR. Who knew that your goddamn PM was so chicken-livered that he wouldn't fight? Instead, he preferred to negotiate with Moscow."

"I'm offering both of you some protection against the Russians," offered Shanahan. "They think that both of you are involved with the sabotage of MIR. Give yourselves up for your own protection. The Russians have a long memory. Neither you nor your children and their children will ever be safe. What do you say?"

"Don't be ridiculous," they both replied simultaneously. Just then, there was an explosion that shook the windows of the Navigator Inn.

"What in hell was that?"

A second explosion followed it. They looked out the windows, then at Shanahan for answers.

"That was your millions of dollars going up in flames at the Royal Bank. And that second explosion was the end of your hovercraft."

It was Heiserman who again rushed to look out the window of the hotel, only to see that the bank was on fire on the main street in Frobisher Bay. In the meantime, Lowery, who had also rushed to the window, could see flames erupting from the hulk at the harbor that once was his hovercraft.

"I knew that this bastard was working with the Resistance. Where is my gun, I'm going to shoot the prick."

"No, no, we may need him later," Heiserman interrupted. "Don't worry about the Navy policemen. They don't have any jurisdiction in this place."

"You seem to forget that he is my prisoner, and this man has been my antagonist for the past three years at Maritime Headquarters. They took away my Navy planes and gave him responsibility for them. You should know that it is humiliating. Your Navy still has Navy planes. Well, you don't have any planes or ships for that matter. Now that Washington is after your ass, you won't have anything if the President will send you to Leavenworth. Forget about using Shanahan as a shield, I'm having him shot."

Shanahan knew about the impending attack on the town, but wasn't about to give that information to either of these fools. Heiserman could see the handwriting on the wall.

"I bet that those explosions are just a softening up blow that precedes a real attack. I know that the U.S. Army and Navy used the same tactic in Vietnam. Your so-called country is going down the drain. I bet that the Canadians and Russians are already on their way to kick your ass right out of this new Florida."

Heiserman grabbed his coat, poked his nose out the door, then turned to Lowery.

"I'm not waiting around for the end of your revolution. I'm heading for the airport. I'll be leaving the country soon and heading for my nest egg in the Bahamas. If you want to join me, check your righteous attitude, smarten up, and meet me at the airport. I'll probably be on my way in a few hours."

Lowery opened the door behind him and called in his henchman.

"I would prefer to shoot this bastard myself right here and now, but I have a reputation here in Nunavut as Chief of Defense. There would be too many witnesses and it might cause me a problem later. But you can take him out to the airport and hold him with the ex-Premier. I'll be out later to fry them both just after I check to see if there's any truth in Heiserman's belief that the explosions are a forecast of what is to come."

Shanahan was manhandled out of the room and out of the hotel, but not before he was seen leaving the town by a red-hatted Arctic Ranger.

# 41   THE BEGINNING OF THE END

1 January, 1940 hrs local, Frobisher Bay, Nunavut

Shawn Phillips flew in the lead KA-32 Helix helicopter with Colonel Viktor Padalka on route to Frobisher Bay. The Colonel had just contacted his headquarters to let them know that he had found the MIR Master Control panel. He advised headquarters that the balance of the MIR data storage system should be in his hands by the end of the day. With luck they would be on-site and within reach of the MIR parts within one hour.

There were four Russian helicopters in the attacking party. Two had returned from transporting aircrew patients to the Thule medical facilities, and they joined the two that Padalka used to attack Eureka.

Phillips reluctantly parked his hovercraft at the Eureka Weather station, stored it under a tarpaulin, and left it in the hands of the new Chief of Station. It had served him and his passengers faithfully during the past five days. He would ensure that the survey crew would be reimbursed for its use and suggest that the machine be given a thorough overhaul and paint job at the expense of the Canadian government.

The helicopters flew directly from Eureka to Grise Fiord, where they planned to refuel. While in Grise Fiord, Phillips learned that the half dozen men positioned there by Lowery had fled the village on snowmobiles as soon as they caught sight of these four foreign helicopters hovering about the village and positioning for a touchdown. While the refueling was taking place, Shawn drove into town using a vehicle he borrowed from the weather forecast office. He drove to the RCMP office to find the constables locked in their jail. He released them and provided the mayor of the town with guns and ammunition that the townsfolk would defend themselves with, should the Nunavut Forces return.

Once refueled, the helicopters continued across Lancaster Sound and over Baffin Island. They flew low and around Pond Inlet so that Lowery's men in the community, as well as those in front of the radars at Alert, would not see them and forewarn Frobisher Bay of their approach. They hugged the snow-covered surface, and the pilots relied on their night vision glasses and the moonlight to guide them safely around the mountain tops.

The plan was to approach Frobisher Bay from the North and then head straight for the airport. If they had to, they would use their helicopter missiles to knock out any infantry or anti-aircraft guns set up to protect the airport. Any Apache helicopters still at the airport would be their primary targets, before landing to secure the building containing the MIR data storage system. Shawn looked at his watch. T minus twenty to the target.

The Canadian Sea King helicopters would be lifting off from their ships right about this time to head for the same target area.

Just as Shawn forecasted, the six Sea King helicopters containing sixty army troops left the decks of the tribal class destroyer, Athabaskan, and the operational support ship, HMCS Protector. A Restigouche class frigate, the HMCS Terra Nova was also in the task force, but it was not equipped to carry helicopters. The Terra Nova was along on the mission to provide advance notice to the other ships. The Terra Nova was also needed to forewarn the Sea King pilots if they were being targeted by incoming missiles or attack planes. All three ships had forced their way, in the track of a Coast Guard icebreaker, along Davis Straight, to the body of water called Frobisher Bay, which was covered with pack ice. The ships were able to penetrate five miles into the ice and twenty miles from their target before they had to call it quits. At that point, all hands were engaged in preparing the Sea Kings for their missions.

The antisubmarine C.H. 124A Sea King helicopters were hastily modified to make room for troops, which the Navy preferred to call boarding parties. All of the equipment that it normally used to detect subs or attacks had to be left behind on the ships to make room for the troops. The Sea King's only defense weapon was the 5.56 C-9 light machine gun that fitters installed in each cabin door, to be operated by one of the two pilots. Even the tactical coordinator and airborne sensor operator, normally part of the crew, remained on the ship's bridge to make way for two more of the boarding party.

The pilots made their way along Koojesse Inlet, which had a very long stretch of exposed area, until they approached the harbor. They headed for their pre designated sites, the airport, the port, and the stadium, that had been so carefully marked out on the Chief of Defense staff conference room table model.

On another front, the U.S. Navy Sea Devil was carefully following the Russian sub's path as they traveled under the ice pack from the Magnetic North Pole to Frobisher Bay. The Devil trailed the Russian boat by two miles. The route that the Russian sub seemed to be following went south from Ellef Ringnes Island towards Bratwurst Island into Parry Channel, which would give them more breathing room but still ice-covered at that time of the year. The two subs turned east along Devon Island into Baffin Bay and traveled south along the full length of Baffin Island. As they approached Hudson straight, they made a sharp swing north again towards Frobisher Bay. They passed under the hulls of the three Canadian ships carrying the Sea Kings. The Canadian ships' crews knew that Russian and American submarines were passing under their hulls since the planned attack was well-coordinated among all of the combatants. The Captains of the Canadian ships just ignored the pinging of the sonar. The crews had no need to protect themselves and continued their struggle to fight the ice into Frobisher Bay Inlet.

While the Canadian Navy ships had major problems plowing through the pack ice, the two subs had no problems under the ice since they both had the necessary equipment to detect large pressure ridges that protruded deep into the depths of the Bay.

The Sea Devil's Diving Officer was the acting Commanding Officer of the ship since the Captain, Commander Hayes was now aboard the Russian sub, while the XO was on his way to Thule and to some military court in Canada for shooting down the Aurora reconnaissance plane. The Diving Officer was aware that the Captain, the XO and all of the crew had been victims of Admiral Heiserman's plot to use the ship and crew to steal sensitive Russian equipment on MIR. The officers of the Sea Devil were aware that they had been duped by the Admiral for his own selfish motives and that the polar mission had not been authorized by his superiors in Washington. They would be painted in a shameful way when they returned to their home port.

The Commanding Officer was going to do his best in this war between the Canadian Forces and the rebel army in the capital city of Nunavut. It was a feeble attempt to save face and perhaps regain some of the prestige that the Sea Devil had, before it was fooled into taking part in the dreadful mission. By fighting for the Canadians, the Sea Devil was offering some measure of retribution for their part in the downing of the Canadian aircraft.

The Commander had his men draw the necessary Arctic gear and the guns that they would need for any fighting that they might engage while on the surface of Frobisher Bay. He hoped that the Sea Devil would be allowed to surface next to the Russian sub so that his crew could rush into the planned attack against the rebels and mercenaries. The plan was for the Russian sub to surface in T minus fifteen minutes, followed by the Sea Devil thirty minutes later. Both ships were approaching their designated positions.

Earlier in the day, Simone Aokalik rehearsed his Arctic Rangers' planned attack on Frobisher. As the target hour approached, he placed his twenty Arctic Rangers along both sides of the road leading to the airport. He suspected that Lowery's men would run like scared rats towards the airport as soon as they were attacked and the fighting started. He had a portable phone with him so that he could contact Shanahan or Phillips.

It was time for the Inuit Rangers to recover the land and freedom that they had before the advent of Admiral Lowery and his puppet Premier. But just as his men took up their positions, he learned from one of his fighters that Shanahan had been badly beaten and taken in a military truck to the airport. Fighting would start in T minus five minutes. Simone left the leadership of his Rangers in the capable hands of his deputy while he left for the airport to hopefully recover Major General Shanahan from his abductors.

\* \* \*

In the skies over the Alert Listening Station, the two Hercules' side doors opened, and seventy men jumped into the cold Arctic air and started their free fall and parachute jump to the Alert community, 817 kilometers from the North Pole.

Some of these men would be hurt in the jump, and some would be wounded or killed during the coming battle. All were convinced that the jump and fight were necessary if Nunavut was to be freed from the mercenaries holding hostage the freedom of the Inuit people. Alert was one more piece of the puzzle that had to be taken before cleanup of outlying communities could commence, since Alert was the second-largest community in Nunavut outside Frobisher Bay. By taking back these communities, the province would be well on its way to restoring its rightful place in the Confederation of Canada.

It was T minus 20 minutes until the attack. In the next twenty minutes, former admiral Lowery would be faced with the beginning of the end as his new empire came crumbling down around his ears.

# 42 ATTACK FOR FREEDOM

1 January, 2000hrs local, Frobisher Bay, Nunavut

The Russian Commando helicopters were the first on the scene and fired the first salvo of Operation Arctic Storm.

Colonel Padalka fired the first missile just as Lowery lit some fireworks for his first Independence Day celebration. The fireworks flared into the Arctic sky as the missile struck one of Lowery's remaining Apache helicopters. The rocket explosion caused fire and more explosions as the gasoline caught fire in the choppers. Lowery's Apaches never got off the ground. Within minutes, they were nothing but balls of fire.

Padalka's Helix helicopters buzzed the airport looking for gun placements, but there were none to be found. Lowery was a navy man and had no clue about how to defend a land site. The lack of armor and gun emplacements around the airport and other strategic targets indicated his poor tactical skills. A more capable leader would not bunch all his helicopters in one location to be picked off and destroyed.

The Russian helicopters took turns firing shots at the snow removal trucks that had blocked the runway as they went scurrying into the night with their headlights turned off. Finding no other targets and encountering no return fire, the four helicopters landed near their targeted building at the airport, next to the refueling tanks.

Padalka led the way out of the lead helicopter and headed for the front door of the building containing the MIR data system. He sent other commandos around the back. Men inside the facility were scurrying like rats out windows and doors. He kicked down the doors as shots were fired around the building, killing the guards that Heiserman had returned to the building just an hour earlier. He had sent them to the building to dismantle the MIR computer array and pack it in crates so that it could be moved to a safer location. He had not given up on the idea of getting the data processing system to work.

The building's front door was shattered by a kick from Padalka's heavy black boot, and several commandos rushed in. He could hear glass breaking in other parts of the building as doors and windows were busted by other commandos entering the facility. There were dozens of shots fired, then all went quiet. On the floor, the specialist technician in a white lab coat, who had first assembled the MIR parts on the wall, lay dead. It looked like he was trying to reach some detonating device when Padalka gunned him down. The building would have been enveloped in flames had Padalka not seen the white-coated figure reach for the trigger of the device.

Padalka ordered several commandos to check the other adjacent buildings while he and his unit checked the rest of this one. No Nunavut forces were found in the building containing the MIR parts or in the surrounding buildings. They had either run with the firing of the first missile or they were fighting elsewhere.

A commando turned the lights on, and there before Colonel Padalka's eyes stood most of the data storage system of MIR. It stretched up the wall for six feet. There were wooden boxes on the floor next to the computer array containing the MIR equipment's balance. Mission accomplished!

Now he needed it to be safely returned to Moscow. Padalka used his cell phone to check on the progress of his troops on the other gunships. One commando leader reported that his chopper had landed next to a group of Canadian troops that had arrived minutes earlier by a Canadian Navy helicopter. The Canadians had set up a machine gun nest and a missile launcher at the far end of the airport to guard against any retaliation. The Canadians also had troops patrolling the perimeter of the airfield.

Another of Padalka's commando leaders reported that his patrol had located a building containing rockets and missiles belonging to the Nunavut Forces. This info was relayed to a Canadian army captain, who ordered the Russians to detonate the building to prevent the missiles and rockets from falling into the wrong hands. The Russians used a missile from one of their choppers to destroy the building. The explosion caused bits of roof, windows and siding to shatter through the area.

Since both ends of the airport were secure, the Russian commandos and Canadian troops advanced toward the airport and the operations building. The hangars also had to be searched. Shawn borrowed Padalka's phone to dial Shanahan's number. There was no answer. He let it ring for several minutes before he hung up and tried the emergency number of Simone Aokalik. Simone had left his rangers guarding the airport road, while he drove toward the main gate to the airport. He had been keeping in touch with his men by radio as he moved toward the terminal. His rangers had destroyed several military trucks that left Frobisher as soon as the Sea Kings landed at the harbor and at the stadium. The road now looked like something out of a Gulf War news story, with trucks littering both sides of the highway. As he drove, Simone saw the Russian and Canadian helicopters land at each end of the airport, and he was waiting for an expected call.

"Mr. Aokalik, this is Major Shawn Phillips."

"Welcome, Major Phillips, to Frobisher. I wish our meeting could have been under more cordial circumstances."

"Yes, thank you, and please call me Shawn, all my friends do. I have been trying to contact the Major General Shanahan. Have you seen him?"

"Call me Simone. I regret to report that Lowery's forces have taken the General prisoner. My men tell me that he was badly beaten, and he was last seen being taken toward the airport. I think I know where they are headed, and I am heading that way myself to see if I can help him. The General told me where they were holding Premier Alaka and other politicians. I think that's where they took him. I'm at the airport's front gate. Could you meet me here, and we will go there together to release our Premier and perhaps find your General?"

"OK, I'm on my way as soon as I can get a set of wheels."

Shawn hung up and jumped into the Follow-Me pickup truck. He reached under the dash and crossed some wires. The engine caught, and he sped towards the front gate to meet the Inuit leader.

In town, the Canadian troops from Gagetown, New Brunswick, landed at the harbor and the stadium, and slowly made their way toward the legislative building. They received sniper fire along their journey and had to stop occasionally to return fire and flush out the snipers. The approach to the building had cost them two casualties and four wounded. Six snipers had been taken down.

By the time the troops reached the building's stairs, their adrenaline was flowing. They were full of anger from the loss of their fellow regimental members, and they were not to be denied their goal. They shot and killed, without hesitation, any Nunavut flagged guards that were protecting the entranceway. Rushing inside, they crept along the halls and up the stairs, where they found the new premier, Willie Nageak, cowering under his desk. He was immediately placed under arrest by the Canadian captain leading the ground force. The troops continued their search for the rest of Lowery's men, but most of them had fled. They went from house to house and from business to business, looking for Nunavut soldiers. They wanted most of all to locate ex admiral Lowery, Admiral Heiserman and his compatriot, Battery Commander Marsh.

Other Canadian troops learned from the reception clerk that both admirals were no longer registered at the Navigator Inn. While there, they did find twelve surprised U.S. Navy policemen that had slept through the invasion. The policemen insisted that they were not on the side of Heiserman and his Nunavut cronies. They had come to the Frobisher Bay capital to arrest Heiserman and his cohorts and drag them back to the States to stand trial for high treason, theft of military supplies and aiding the Chinese government in obtaining military secrets.

Outside the hotel, the Canadian troops threatened severe punishment to any of the Nunavut forces that were caught up in the sweep of the buildings, unless they disclosed the whereabouts of either of the admirals. Several of Lowery's mercenaries volunteered information, saying that the ex-admiral, wearing a camouflage uniform, was seen entering a camouflage truck and speeding towards the airport. The whereabouts of Heiserman and Marsh were unknown to anyone.

With the arrival of the first Sea King helicopters, and with the landing of their own Helix helicopters, the Russian sub captain gave the order to surface at entrance of Frobisher Bay. The submarine broke through the ice and sat as a vast black silhouette in the twilight. It waited with its machine gun and cannon on the deck. They were at the ready for any of the Nunavut forces that would be foolish enough to try to avoid capture by venturing out onto the ice pack. Other Russian sailors stood by with surface-to-air missiles, should any of Lowery's aircraft get airborne. The Russian captain was also waiting for the U.S. Sea Devil to make its appearance, and to make its firepower known.

The Sea Devil surfaced a hundred yards away, breaking the ice and popping up like a cork on the end of a fishing line. The Americans emerged from the hatch and set up their armament facing the town. The profile of the subs shone in the moonlight, sitting next to one another. The submarines of two of the most significant countries in the world would fight side by side for a familiar friend.

With the action quickly wrapping up, it was evident that Lowery and his men were caught completely off guard. They had no idea that a force of this magnitude, consisting of Russian commandos, American sailors, Inuit rangers, and Canadian army troops, could cooperate so fully to capture the town in less than an hour. It took Lowery's forces a full twenty minutes to comprehend that the explosions and shots that they were hearing were coming from invasion forces rather than from their fireworks celebration.

As a first priority, the Canadians, backed up by the Russian commandos, cleared the radio and TV stations and released the captive RCMP. Soon after the invasion had started, the Mayor of Nunavut and the townsfolk began to venture out into the streets, something that they hadn't done even for the celebratory fireworks. The townsfolk welcomed the freedom fighters and offered the Russians, the Americans and the Canadians bunches of flowers and wine bottles. For the Russians, being hailed as conquering heroes was something new for them.

Shawn Phillips met Simone Aokalik at the front gate of the airport. They greeted one another warmly, like old beer-drinking army buddies. They discussed the whereabouts of Shanahan, Heiserman and Lowery. Simone mentioned that at least two trucks had driven through their hail of bullets and made their way into the airport. Those vehicles could have been carrying and concealing Lowery and some of his rogue fighters.

The Rangers had a pretty good idea where the trucks were headed. Besides finding Shanahan, Phillips desperately wanted Heiserman and Marsh. They could be hiding in any number of searched buildings. He knew that the hangars, as well as a few other buildings on the airport complex, had not yet been fully checked. They would eventually be covered by the Canadian soldiers, but he didn't have anyone to spare to help. There was no point in asking the help of Colonel Padalka; he was way too busy guarding and dismantling the MIR data system, which was his primary goal.

Further searching of airport buildings would await the arrival of more of the Canadian forces from town. Shawn reluctantly gave up finding the two American villains and concentrated his efforts on locating his boss.

Shawn and Simone decided to check out the shed at the old U.S. Air Force site to see if the Premier was still being held there. Six Arctic Rangers jumped into the back of the pickup that the SAR leader had commandeered. Both men sat in the cab. They drove the short distance on the road running adjacent to the airport. Shawn cut the lights when Simone mentioned that the old shed was just a kilometer ahead.

Simone proposed that Shawn wait near the truck while he and his rangers check out the site. As they left the truck, they moved as effortlessly as water. They slipped into the bushes and into the darkness. Shawn heard two shots, and still, he waited. It wasn't long before Simone returned. He mentioned that there were three guards at the shed. Two were killed by gunshot while the other had his throat slit open. They drove the truck up to the hut and shone the lights on to the building. The door of the shed was busted open and the Rangers slipped inside.

Moments later, three Rangers emerged carrying three very emancipated men. They were clinging to life and looked like they had not been fed for days. Simone pointed out to Shawn the one man who was Premier Alaka and the other two who were cabinet members. The group also found the bodies of the executed politicians at the rear of the building. Shanahan was not there.

Shawn drove the Rangers and their starving political survivors back to the starting area. The politicians were gently placed in the rear of the

Rangers' cars and were taken to the hospital for treatment. The bodies of the other politicians could wait for another few hours. They weren't going anywhere soon.

Major Phillips and a few of the red-capped freedom fighters continued to search the airport in the hope of finding Shanahan. What they did find were Canadian troops surrounding one of the hangars. The captain in charge told Shawn that they had just started searching the building when they spotted, in the back of the building, two armed admirals and a third man who was holding a Canadian general hostage. In return for the hostage, they wanted their VTOL fully fueled and running.

The captain provided the Shawn with additional information on the weapons held by the captors. The two ex-admirals were armed with pistols and automatic rifles while the third man was guarding Shanahan with a gun to his head. He also had a rocket launcher. It had to be Battery Commander Marsh, who was fond of rocket launchers, thought Shawn.

The men requested to speak with someone in authority that could agree with their demands. Shawn indicated that he had such authority since the CDS appointed him to find the missing aircrew, retrieve the MIR space components, and to assist in the liberation of Nunavut.

Shawn would talk to these former admirals. He reasoned that Commander Hayes of the Sea Devil should be brought from the Russian sub to this hangar, and that there was a possibility that Hayes could talk Heiserman out of this hostage-taking situation. Perhaps Heiserman could be urged to give himself up to another U.S. Navy officer.

In order to get Hayes off the Russian sub, Shawn had to call Colonel Padalka, explain the situation to him and ask for Hayes' release. The Colonel reluctantly agreed to the request. He would contact the Russian sub and personally bring Commander Hayes to the airport. Padalka usually would call Moscow to get Hayes released temporarily, but he greatly appreciated the help that Phillips had provided him during the MIR hunt. He hoped that the hostage situation would soon be solved, and he would send Hayes back to his guardhouse aboard the Russian sub.

Shawn and Simone waited until Hayes arrived in a car driven by Colonel Padalka and guarded by a Russian commando.

Shawn explained the situation in greater detail to Padalka and Hayes, who was only too willing to help. Hayes wanted to do whatever he could to erase the shame brought on his Sea Devil by Admiral Heiserman. He was walked to the door of the hangar and given a bullhorn to get his message across to the former U.S. admiral.

"Admiral Heiserman, this is Commander Hayes. This hostage idea of yours is not a good plan. I suggest that you give yourself up and return with me to the United States. I'm sure that the Secretary of Defense will be lenient with you."

The reply was in the form of several shots fired from an automatic rifle that struck the shed door at the heart level of Commander Hayes.

"I don't want to talk to you. Send me someone who can release the VTOL plane." Another shot struck the building behind Hayes, a foot away from his head.

"I don't think that he wants to talk to me. I think he was trying to kill me."

"'Give it another try," said Phillips.

"Admiral Heiserman, please reconsider. Surely you could make the case to the Secretary that you were only thinking of what is best for the United States."

"Screw off, Hayes. I've burnt my bridges as far as the U.S. Navy is concerned. Now I have to think of my own welfare." This short chat was followed by more shots from an automatic rifle.

"That's it for me! He would never give himself up on my behalf," said Hayes. "He wants to kill me so I can't testify against him."

Shawn decided that his only recourse was to go and talk to Heiserman and Lowery. Simone and the Canadian captain thought it was not a good idea, and that it was far too dangerous. Phillips might just become another hostage. But Shawn insisted, saying that he had to try to save Shanahan.

Shawn opened the door and entered. It was dark and cold inside the hangar, but he could see a small Piper Cub plane off to the left, and the VTOL that took up most of the center of the building. Beneath the wing stood two men. One turned on a flashlight, and Shawn could make out Heiserman and Lowery. Both held pistols in their hands. Then he saw the beaten and bruised body of Shanahan. At first, he thought that he was dead.

Shanahan laid on the hangar floor. He was guarded by Marsh, who had an automatic rifle at his feet and a pistol in his right hand, held to Shanahan's head. A rocket launcher dangled from his left.

"What is it that you want?" asked Shawn.

"We want to leave together. We'll trade you this bastard," came Lowery's voice. "I would prefer to kill him, but my friend here convinced me that we could get our plane if we gave you Shanahan. Is it a deal?"

"I have the authority to release the plane, but why don't you give yourselves up? You know that we will catch you someday. If you give yourself up, we can get you less of a sentence for your actions."

"No deal. The only choice you have is to drag this goddamn plane out onto the tarmac, fuel it up, and put Heiserman's pilot on board. Once we are on board, then we will release Shanahan."

Shanahan raised his head and tried to talk, but only whispers came gurgling out of his swollen lips. He managed to utter some words.

"Don't do it, Shawn. Forget about me. Heiserman has put a time bomb on board the Sea Devil that is about to go off. You have to get the crew to abandon the ship." For his trouble, Shanahan received another kick in the ribs from Marsh. He started to cough up more blood.

"How do I know that you won't kill General Shanahan after you are on board?"

"You will have to trust us on that."

"Like you said, no deal! Your word is not good enough around here. I want you to hold General Shanahan under guard by Marsh, on the tarmac, while you two board the plane. Once you are on board with the engines running, Marsh can then leave General Shanahan on the tarmac and board the plane. I give you my word that I will allow Marsh to board the plane, and I will allow you to take off."

The three of them discussed the idea and agreed to the plan. They discussed the various possibilities of killing Shanahan and still making a getaway. They felt that Shawn's word was as good a guarantee as they would get under the circumstances. They also knew the building was surrounded by enough firepower to kill an army as well as to take them all down. They figured that most Canadian army generals didn't give a hoot about one Air Force general's life. With any other general or person of authority, they would not be able to make their escape. As they saw it, Phillips' plan could work for them.

"OK, it's a deal."

Shawn left the building to arrange the fuel, the towing of the aircraft, and the pilot. He first spoke to Commander Hayes.

"Is there a way to contact your crew on board the Sea Devil? Heiserman has placed a bomb on board the ship, and it is due to go off very soon. The sub needs to be abandoned immediately."

"Holy Christ, that's horrible! A time bomb aboard the Sea Devil! It is tied at the dock next to a Russian sub. A bomb could sink both of them! Normally, to reach the crew, I would have to contact Washington and have them pass the message either directly to her or through another U.S. sub to her."

"Can the Russian sub contact the Sea Devil?"

"I'm not a hundred percent certain. They have different frequencies, but it's worth a try."

Shawn spoke to Colonel Padalka while the VTOL craft was being refueled. He reported a bomb on board the Sea Devil that was timed to go off soon, but they needed the Russian sub to communicate with the Sea Devil crew to evacuate the sub. He reminded the Colonel that his own sub was next to the Sea Devil, and the Okun was also in danger. Colonel Padalka tried immediately to contact his sub to see if they could communicate with the U.S. sub.

Shawn left Padalka on the phone while watching the aircraft towing tractor positioning the VTOL on the take-off runway. An Ops vehicle brought the pilot. He boarded and started up the plane.

Phillips watched from under the VTOL's collapsed wings. The pilot would use vertical lift before engaging forward propulsion. He watched as Heiserman and Lowery walked to the plane and climbed up the stairs. Both still had their pistols, and they were trained on Phillips. Marsh was slightly behind, dragging Shanahan with one hand while keeping his pistol, in his other hand, to the General's head. The rocket launcher was over his shoulder.

If looks could kill, then Heiserman would be dead now due the hate in the eyes of young Commander Hayes. Once the ex-admirals were safely aboard the craft, Marsh stood about a hundred feet from the aircraft. Shanahan's beaten body was sprawled at his feet. The VTOL pilot rotated the propellers and to Marsh, it looked like the plane was about to lift off. Marsh was afraid of being left behind and started to run for the boarding stairs just as they were being pulled into the aircraft by Lowery.

Lowery stood at the doorway near the stairs, with his arm extended and fired a shot at Shanahan, hitting him in the abdomen. Marsh thought that Lowery was firing at him, so he fired back at Lowery and ran faster as the propellers increased their velocity. Suddenly there was a large explosion that seemed to be coming from the ice pack near the harbor. Black smoke was rising from the area where the Sea Devil has berthed. The explosion was followed by several others, and one could almost see the ice rising in the place where the bay met the airport runway. Both Shawn and Hayes knew that their efforts to contact the Sea Devil had been too late.

Shawn ran to Shanahan's side as Lowery began to fire intermittently, first at Shanahan, then at Marsh and later at Phillips. The Search Master tried to protect Shanahan with his own body. Most of the bullets were hitting the ground around Shawn until one pierced his midsection. Admiral Lowery switched targets, and he was now was firing fully at Marsh, who thought that if he also fired at the Canadians, Lowery would help him board the VTOL. Marsh fired a few shots at Phillips and Shanahan. He dropped the rocket launcher to concentrate on running.

The General was in in deep pain, with blood flowing from his mouth. He began to spit chunks of black blood and barely uttered that Phillips should shoot and kill the man that killed his Aurora. Shawn fired one shot at Marsh, who fell to the ground from the stairs. He was dead by the time his body hit the tarmac.

It was most appropriate that the man who brought down the Aurora aircraft by rocket fire was slain by the very man sent to find the plane and the aircrew.

The Canadians thought that Lowery was a prick. What sort of person would treat them one day as a best friend, then try to kill them the next day? You couldn't trust him or Heiserman. Did Heiserman know that Lowery was again double-crossing him? Lowery was trying to kill the best friend of Heiserman, his best rocket-launching buddy. Lowery was doing his best to kill the man that brought down the Aurora. Was this an act of contrition on Lowery's behalf? Shawn doubted it. The VTOL roared as it began its liftoff. The wheels started to leave the ground as the craft fought to gain altitude.

Shawn covered Shanahan's body as best as he could to keep debris from the rotating props from hitting him. Phillips could only watch as he saw Commander Hayes streak for the rocket launcher. Their eyes met, but only for a moment. Shawn cradled Shanahan in his arms and was in no position to stop Hayes.

The Commander's eyes showed only the need for revenge. His much-loved ship and crew had been taken from him by those on board the

VTOL. The young Lieutenant was no longer behaving rationally. His emotional hatred had taken control of his body and his mind. He reached the loaded rocket launcher and positioned it firmly on his shoulder. The VTOL was now about three hundred feet in the air. Lowery had closed the door and was about to take his seat next to Heiserman when Hayes pulled the trigger.

Both Shawn and Hayes watched as the rocket left the launcher and went streaking towards the rising aircraft. It was probably just a few seconds before they could see the flames spread like red flowers blossoming. They spread until they hit the gas tanks. Suddenly, the plane was a ball of hurling hot flames as the craft plunged towards the pack ice and blew up again as it struck. Hayes' body seemed to relax. He finally felt at peace with himself.

# EPILOGUE

The next two days were like heaven for Shawn. Captain Mari Leech brought the Aurora into Frobisher Bay after closing down the mini RCC, and met Shawn at the bar at the Navigator Inn for their much discussed first drink.

They had dinner and talked a lot more about flying days. Their love for one another was blooming. Mari was delighted to find that Shawn had decided to let his beard grow after six days of not shaving while on the hunt for the Gray Ghost. After years and years of discussions, the military authorities had decided that beards were now legal in the Canadian military. Mari thought that the Major's gray beard made him look distinctive, mature and intelligent. He was even more handsome than she remembered. They spent many more nights together both in Frobisher and in Shawn's apartment in Dartmouth.

Maritime Command Headquarters had previously decided that the crew of the downed plane should be treated in the Canadian hospital facilities at Frobisher Bay instead of the American hospital in Thule. Major General Shanahan' s health was improving, and he was well on his way to a full recovery, as was Frank Winters.

As the General recovered, he recorded all the knowledge that he had about the Iqaluit Revolt as it became known in the history books. Such a document would be needed during the investigation of all the events, by a legislation committee, in the coming weeks. The aim of the investigation was to ensure that such events did not occur again.

Major Phillips' wounds were medically treated, and there was no visible damage except the bandages on his hands. He had survived several near-death experiences, but thanks to his good health he was making a swift recovery. He was released from emergency care within a few days following the Frobisher battle. Shawn was promoted to Lieutenant Colonel. He would become the new Commanding Officer of the 415 squadron in Summerside, previously commanded by Digger Holloway, who was retiring. His squadron was the sister to the 406 squadron that Mari Leech called home.

Warrant Officer Mackenzie accepted a promotion to the rank of Captain and would be attending training classes in a few weeks. Afterwards, he would be posted to the RCC in Halifax, which Phillips commanded.

The Chief of the Defense Staff telephoned Shanahan to congratulate him on the excellent work that he had done as a spy. The coordinated Arctic Storm attack worked so well because Shanahan and his Rangers, along with Phillips and the Russians, worked as a team. They were all a vital part of the counter revolt. The CDS told Shanahan that the raid on the Alert Listening Station was also enormously successful with the loss of only two Canadian paratroopers. He said that a large number of Lowery's men had been captured throughout the province, and the remainder were crushed by the Canadian Armed Forces. The CDS spoke about the mop-up operations in the rest of Nunavut, which was still ongoing. The paratroopers were still making their way from village to village using helicopters, ski-doos and dog sleds, to snuff out any rebel fighters and to give confidence to the residents of Nunavut that Canada cared for their well-being.

The town of Frobisher was getting back to normal. The townsfolk showered the remaining Russians with gifts of all sorts. The Okun, the Russian sub, was not damaged when the Sea devil exploded. For several days it was all decked out in Canadian, Nunavut and Russian flags at dockside.

Colonel Padalka was promoted, and in charge of and inventorying the MIR parts. The parts were being loaded on a Russian cargo plane as soon as they arrived at the airport. The Russian Colonel was in a good mood, especially since the U.S. government had agreed to reimburse Russia for fifty million dollars for the loss of their space station, and they would buy two million dollars of MIR data. The Russians agreed that Commander Hayes would return to the U.S. to face disciplinary charges, although they would most likely be delayed indefinitely due to his mental condition. The U.S. would probably end up giving him a medal for stopping Heiserman's activities. As it was, Hayes was in a world of his own and would be incapable of facing charges for a considerable amount of time.

Colonel Padalka, would formally thank Lieutenant Colonel Phillips at a dinner hosted by Soviet government staff.

The French cosmonaut would be executed by the Russians for spy related activities.

The U.S. government also agreed to give Canada twenty million dollars for the loss of the Aurora plane and for the pain and suffering of its aircrew. The next of kin of the two casualties would each receive three million U.S. dollars.

The Canadian government was not willing to release Lieutenant Murphy to the Americans until there was a full investigation of all activities surrounding the downing of the Aurora.

The twelve U.S. Navy policemen would bring the body of Battery Commander Marsh back to the U.S. for burial. Heiserman and Lowery's bodies were likely burnt beyond recognition, in the crashing and sinking of the VTOL, and would remain at the bottom of Frobisher Bay along with the plane. The authorities said that the wreckage of the Sea Devil would never be recovered. It would become a monument, much like the ships in Pearl Harbor. The Sea Devil would draw tourists to the Bay to hear the whole story about its revolt and rediscovery of democracy. Tourist would flock to Frobisher, especially around Remembrance Day.

The Prime Minister spoke to Premier Alaka and assured him that Nunavut could legally leave Canada if they ever wanted to separate. The Premier assured the PM that it was not likely to ever happen. As for the protection of the north, the PM promised that the next budget would include enough funds to replace the aging Sea King helicopters. They would be permanently assigned with ships to a new Arctic Command based in Frobisher Bay. The ships, along with subs, were expected to protect the sovereignty of the Northwest Passage.

As for Ranger Simone, he became the Commander of all Arctic Rangers in the Arctic, including Nunavut. It was published that he would be awarded the Medal of Honour for his bravery. His Rangers would receive an increase in salary as well as new automatic rifles. There would be special mention for each Ranger, in what was named Mention in Dispatches in the books at the House of Commons.

# About the Author

*Major (ret) Joe Fougere in recent days*

*The author as a young Captain in the 1970's*

BIO Major (ret) J.J. Fougere; C.D.; MMSc

Joe Fougere was born in 1942. He joined the RCAF at age 18 while at University for a Bachelor's Degree. He enrolled in a military program as a cadet in which the RCAF paid his tuition in return for service upon graduation. In 1964 he became a Flying Officer and was posted to the isolated Goose Bay Station in northern Labrador. The base mainly served as host to USAF bomber squadrons. Officers of both forces interchanged at officers' clubs and exchanged stories. In 1966, as a Captain, Joe was transferred to the base in Trenton On. This base flew large transport planes like the Yukon and the Hercules. It also had helicopters for its Search and Rescue Centre. From Trenton, he was sent to 3 Fighter Wing in Zweibrucken, Germany. He sadly remembers the occasion when a fighter jet and pilot did not return from its mission. Just 2 years later he moved to the HQ of the Wings at Lahr for his remaining time in a routine 4 -year stint in Europe.

In 1970, he returned to Canada and joined the staff at NDHQ in a transport division, followed by two years in finance. He used his free time to do research in the NDHQ library on this book. He was selected by NDHQ to attend the University of Ottawa on a full-time, and on a fully paid, Master's Degree in Management Science (now called an MBA). His new family, his studies, his new corporation and his return to duty kept him away from his book for several years. Funding for the book was short since publishing houses only paid expenses to established authors on non-fiction subjects.

In 1976, Joe was promoted to Major and posted to Summerside, P.E.I. This base flew anti-submarine missions with its Argus fleet of aircraft. Unfortunately, one of them crashed on the runway while he was there. He easily recalls having a brew with some of the officers on that plane while they were recovering and still in bandages.

In 1979, NDHQ and Foreign Affairs needed post-grad officers to be representative Canadian officers at a new NATO establishment called NAPMA. Joe was selected as one of six Canadian officers to be working with officers from 11 other nations. NAPMA was located in Brunssum, N.L.; it was co-located with AFCENT HQ.

NAPMA's mission was to purchase a fleet of 17 Boeing 707s and convert them to E3As for strategic surveillance missions. It also built bases in Turkey, Italy, Norway and Geilenkirchen, Germany. Joe often enjoyed spending time at the Canadian unit on that base.

In 1982, Joe Fougere retired from the military after 20 some years of service during which he earned a Canadian Decoration with clasp and a NATO medal. He was immediately offered this same job as a NATO civilian by NAPMA authorities. He accepted, and eventually he retired from NATO and returned to Canada in 1990 with ten years of service. There is no doubt that his twenty plus years of service with the military and with NATO made him qualified to write this mystery.

During retirement, he continued to work on this book. Recently, a monetary windfall provided enough funds to publish. This techno thriller is now ready for you, the reader.

Joe has always been interested in the activities in the Canadian North. He is especially concerned with Canadian sovereignty; this book deals with the subject.

The author hopes that you have as much joy reading this novel as he had in writing and publishing it. It is his belief that this book, "High Arctic Odyssey" with "Mystery on Ice" subtitle, will keep you thrilled for hours.